LOCAL HEAVENS

"Glitzy and brimming with intrigue, *Local Heavens* is the queer cyberpunk Gatsby remix I didn't know I needed. Fajardo has built a dazzlingly unique world that is still as close to the Roaring Twenties as it is to our own times, and she has breathed new life into this classic tale about ambition and the American dream."

—Victor Manibo, author of *The Sleepless* and *Escape Velocity*

"A dazzling, propulsive take on a beloved classic, *Local Heavens* turns anew the timeless considerations of ambition, dreams, desire, and consequence in an astutely imagined and richly inventive cyberpunk reality. Full of gorgeous prose and narrative depth, this book was an absolute delight to read."

—Christina Li, author of *The Manor of Dreams*

"*Local Heavens* is the heady, sultry cyberpunk retelling of *The Great Gatsby* you didn't know you needed. Fajardo's writing is deliciously decadent and aching, both true to the spirit of the original and offering a fresh, startling spin on the carelessness of immense wealth and the people who get chewed up and spit out along the way. This is a gorgeous book. Keep your eye on this debut!"

—Yume Kitasei, author of *The Deep Sky* and *Saltcrop*

"Comprising a tech thriller, a speculative capitalist nightmare, and a cat-and-mouse noir against the backdrop of 2075-era New York City, K. M. Fajardo's cyberpunk remix of Fitzgerald's *The Great Gatsby* is effortlessly greater than the sum of its parts. A pillar of American literature becomes electrified and transmuted in this sensational debut."

—Jinwoo Chong, author of *Flux*

"*Local Heavens* is deeply true to Fitzgerald's themes and texture, transmuting the classic into a sultry, haunting exploration of the American dream through the lens of one of the most common and underrepresented Americans—the diaspora Filipino.

—Maya Gittelman, Ignyte-nominated writer and critic

K. M. FAJARDO is a second-generation Filipino Canadian writer born and raised in the Toronto suburbs. She graduated from the University of Waterloo with a degree in Global Business and Digital Arts before working in the tech industry. A speculative-fiction writer, she enjoys stories that straddle genres and characters that find home in a strange world. After a childhood spent roaming bookstores, she now lives and writes in Toronto with her rescue cat, Clementine, and can occasionally be found haunting the nearest café. *Local Heavens* is her debut novel.

kmfajardo.com

📷 @krismfajardo

𝕏 @km_fajardo

♪ @krismfajardo

▶ @KrisMF

LOCAL HEAVENS

K.M. FAJARDO

ZAFFRE

First published in the US by Inky Phoenix Press, an imprint of Bindery Books,
Inc, San Francisco, in 2025

First published in the UK in 2025 by
ZAFFRE
An imprint of Bonnier Books UK
5th Floor, HYLO, 105 Bunhill Row,
London, EC1Y 8LZ

A CIP catalogue record for this book is
available from the British Library.

Hardback ISBN: 978-1-78512-843-1
Trade paperback ISBN: 978-1-78512-844-8
Also available as an ebook and an audiobook

1 3 5 7 9 10 8 6 4 2

Typeset by IDSUK (Data Connection) Ltd
Printed and bound in Great Britain by Clays Ltd, Elcograf S.p.A.

MIX
Paper | Supporting
responsible forestry
FSC
www.fsc.org   FSC® C018072

The authorised representative in the EEA is
Bonnier Books UK (Ireland) Limited.
Registered office address: Floor 3, Block 3, Miesian Plaza,
Dublin 2, D02 Y754, Ireland
compliance@bonnierbooks.ie
www.bonnierbooks.co.uk

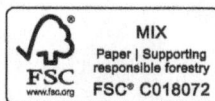

To Kuya. Thank you for everything.

In this country—the most favored beneath the bending skies—we have ... material resources in inexhaustible abundance—and if there are still vast numbers of our people ... whose lives are an unceasing struggle all the way from youth to old age, until at last death comes to their rescue and lulls these hapless victims to dreamless sleep, it is not the fault of the Almighty: it cannot be charged to nature, but it is due entirely to the outgrown social system in which we live.

—Eugene V. Debs, *Statement to the Court upon Being Convicted of Violating the Sedition Act* (1918)

Prologue
Wild, Unknown Men

IT WAS ONE OF THOSE heavy afternoons in late April, the sun a fierce pit in the Manila sky, stewing the city in record heat waves, when the events that would lead to that treacherous summer were set into motion.

I'd returned exhausted from my lunchtime stroll through overpriced BGC patios to my desk on the fiftieth floor of Trimalchio's Makati office, where I discovered an unwelcome surprise.

"Carraway." Bunsen Bustillo, occupying my chair, had kicked his legs up into the holo-screens, forming craters through my spreadsheets. "Fun name. Glad you're still using it." He jumped to his feet with a wide grin. "How's front court treating you?"

Across the floor of the security department, a dozen eyes flitted over their cubicle dividers. Bunsen was a loud, affable man with a princely disposition. That was to say, one could surmise instantly that he worked on the opposite side of the building.

"Quite well." I returned his handshake but only a fraction of his smile. "Never better, actually."

He hooked his arm around me, steering us to the elevators, laughing about something from our Yale days that I was sure never happened. Once we were alone, he smacked the emergency button with his fist. The sterile lights overhead snapped out, along with his joviality.

"Back court's huddling. It's urgent," he said. "Hate to do this to you, Nick, but you know how it is."

He didn't hate to do it. This was his job: strong-arming you into dirty work while convincing you no one was sorrier about it than him.

The air-conditioning whipped the sweat on my neck. "I'm not—"

"Yes, yes. You're squeaky clean and all that." His fingers drummed a sequence across the floor buttons. "How about we call it a favor?"

When the elevator shuddered awake again, it lurched us backward.

◇——◇——◇

Bunsen had provided my referral to the Manila branch of Trimalchio Global Solutions with the hope that I'd one day come around to joining his department. Once my college upperclassman, he'd made himself into a top account director, so I'd been grateful for his good word, despite my reservations about working at a full-service consultancy, which was the euphemistic way of saying only half their departments were public knowledge.

While the "front court" drew up marketing campaigns, cost-efficiency plans, and growth strategies, it was the "back court" that made any of it possible, for no major business decision in the world could be finalized without poking around in the right skirts, siphoning the right intel, and selling it to whoever was buying.

Trimalchio was far from the only firm of its kind, but it was one of the largest, was rather distinguished, and kept its two sides well separated. This was the reason I'd accepted the position—to grant my mother's wish that I take a break from the Americas and spend time with her, and because I was assured that I would not see the dishonest work cross my desk.

Bunsen had kept his word. My involvement until then remained in the margins. Sometimes his team was swamped, and he required a small file or two decrypted, deleted, fabricated. Nothing that couldn't be accomplished in half a lunch break.

Never before had he hauled me across the building.

The conference room was muggy and windowless. "This is him?" came the harried greeting from Benny Marcelo, a short and surly VP sweating at the head of the long table. I'd only seen him before through a holo-screen during company town halls.

He was joined by four heavily modded netdivers, their necks identically gold-plated and eyes replaced by solid white ocular-mods. Across from them sat eight frenetic project managers, holo-screens hovering inches from their faces. Strangest of all, a sophisticated android, deactivated, lay slumped in the corner of the room, wearing a striped robin's-egg blue uniform over its silver skin.

Bunsen motioned me into an empty chair, then stood behind me, hands on my shoulders as if he were my devout sponsor at Holy Confirmation. "Nick Carraway, sir. One of our front-court contractors. Oversees some VINE development down in the gallows."

I sat there, a bewildered mannequin, as the room stared back in grating silence.

"Gallows?" said the diver seated closest to Marcelo. "He's a diver?" VINE work—building and maintaining the foundation of security systems in deep cyberspace—wasn't quite an entry-level role, nor was it safe without robust cybernetic enhancements. My mods were more concealed than hers, and she looked me up and down, baffled, as if she couldn't tell me apart from an accountant.

"Ex-military, in fact, with a strong portfolio of counterintel contracts across the New East," Bunsen relayed. "Degree in cybernetics. Top scores."

"Amerikano," Marcelo muttered as one might announce a forecast of rain.

"A boon, in this case," Bunsen argued.

"Any diver can get into a locked room." Marcelo continued as if I weren't there. "We need someone important enough, they won't get kicked *out* of one."

"In my own field experience, if there's one thing about corpos, it's that they're too distrustful of their own kind." Bunsen clapped my back in a fraternal way. "Besides, Nick's no stranger to this crowd. He's a Yale man. Like me."

We were not alike at all. Bunsen was a nephew to a Trimalchio executive for the entire Southeast Asia division. I was the son of a hover-car mechanic and a lucky tax write-off for whichever company had funded my scholarship.

3

It was more accurate to say that I survived Yale. My acceptance came as a result of that fortuitous diversity grant, my parents' savings, and some of my grandfather's life insurance. I'd developed a knack for keeping a straight face when nepotism products spoke about their real estate on private islands, or feigning sympathy when they sobbed in my lap at parties, distraught over canceled vacations to lunar resorts.

I'd never once been confused as a peer among conglomerate heirs and future senators, though apparently Bunsen viewed this as an advantage.

He crossed the room, gripped the motionless android by the back of its neck, and dragged it up onto the conference table. I now recognized it as a service model called Klipspringer, an American brand stationed most often on airlines and in department stores. "These are owned by the same company that owns Gen Wealth. You've heard of them, I'm sure," he said.

I had. Gen Wealth was a burgeoning finance empire in the New East.

"They don't hire often." Bunsen flipped the Klipspringer onto its back, revealing a thick piece of grained cream stationery folded evenly between its polished fingers. "But this one showed up in our lobby this morning. Hand-delivering a job offer." He pulled the paper loose and held it out. "For you, Mr. Carraway."

I stared in disbelief—at my name, which was indeed embossed in a wide, straight font. There was no explanation for it except that, at best, this was a ridiculously elaborate joke, and at worst, these were the actions of a lunatic.

"The android had a direct line to Gen Wealth's head of talent. They confirmed this was sent from their offices. The offer is real. They wouldn't say more. We still scanned the thing for taps, cams, bombs." Bunsen knocked on its skull. "Everything's clean."

Marcelo dabbed the sweat from his face with a handkerchief, in a triangular pattern that was, unconsciously or not, reminiscent of the sign of the cross. "I won't have your friend from nowhere"—he waved at me—"running point on one of our biggest accounts. No matter that he's being sent for. We ought to treat this like a trap."

4

"Trap or not, it's our first and only chance at progress in two years. If we waste it, we risk losing the account entirely," replied Bunsen. "I wouldn't go along with it if I didn't think Mr. Carraway could handle it."

He looked at me encouragingly. It reminded me of the way he'd once said that I'd make a good politician. It was a joke at the time, but it had bothered me ever since to be considered even a bit deceptive by someone whose whole career was rooted in lying.

"In any case, it can only be Nick." Bunsen sat beside me. "As it happens, Gen Wealth isn't the only one to request him by name. Our client has as well—and isn't the client always right? Nick has a family relation there."

Shocked murmurs cascaded down the table. My skin prickled.

"Fay Medica. That's your account?" I asked, though it couldn't have been anything else. Bunsen nodded. My connection to the Fays was a thin branch on my paternal side. My father had kept it thin on purpose. Medica had no shortage of scandals and family drama. "Who requested me?"

"Your cousin. She liaises with us, through an intermediary, but she did want you to know it was her." Judging from the room's startled reactions, I didn't need to clarify which cousin. "This is the situation," Bunsen explained. "Gen Wealth's parent company has been attempting to initiate talks of an acquisition for over a year now. Problem is, they're too tight-lipped, and no one on their side will share whatever reason they have for making this move. Medica's made up of old-money traditionalists. They can't do business with a president who won't even take a phone call, let alone show his face anywhere. There's a lot at risk for Medica. You know Buchanan Group has a tight hold on them. This is just part of their due diligence."

The android's black eyes stared up at me, mouth parted like a cadaver. I shifted restlessly. Two corps playing tug-of-war—and somehow I was the one dragged out between them.

I read the paper again. *To Mr. N. Carraway*, it gleamed, between adornments of gold foil. At the end, it was impersonally signed: *Sincerely, Talent Team at Generational Wealth Inc.* There was no mention of which portal they'd dredged up my résumé from, or even how I'd merited the opportunity. Just an offer for a well-paying contract along with an address for a Long Island apartment.

Bunsen squeezed my shoulder until it ached. "Your cousin needs someone she can trust."

He was still smiling, but I saw in the cold edges of his lips that he was not awaiting my opinion, only my agreement, for I had not actually been posed any questions in this room.

"I see," I said. "How long is the assignment?"

"All we're after is a sliver of information on this president; then you're benched. You have my word."

One of the divers across from me requested my wrist. I hesitated.

"Don't worry. Standard precautions," said Bunsen. "Just need to sync your neural comm to our system. If you find yourself in a hard spot, we can knock you out cold in five minutes, all the way from here. It can be self-activated too."

"By piercing the skin over the comm-sensor?" I asked. I was familiar with these security measures. A similar one was implemented into soldiers' comms during my military service—remote incapacitation in the event of any "compromised" position, the definition of which was broad and extended most frequently to include whatever could be justified as insubordination.

"Yes, like that. But use is very rare," Bunsen rushed on. "A formality, really."

I laid my arm on the table, palm up. My hand trembled, but only for a moment. I forced myself still. The netdiver's eye sockets flashed in a burst of red light as her oc-mods scanned my comm. The muscles in my arm constricted; then a chill shot through my bones.

I drew my hand back, closing my fists under the table. I knew better than to let anyone see.

"This president," I said, steadying my voice. "Do we have a name?"

Part I

Large Parties

One

THE FIRST TIME I LEFT the insular suburban biodomes of Minnesota, my thoughts had drifted to my late father, who'd always carried the steadfast belief that every generation ought to live through some piece of grand history at least once.

"Ego is the soul killer," he'd told me. "Humanity should know its smallness."

My father had been shaped by this thought after a serendipitous night in his adolescence, when he'd switched on the television and seen a news report broadcasting the launch of a probe into deep space. The initiative had brought together about a hundred countries to curate a capsule of humanity's finest accomplishments.

Later, in my own youth, I'd studied the event in school, but it was my father's account that stuck with me most. This probe, holding the collected heart of an entire civilization, had disappeared like a speck of dust into the vast sky. To have witnessed it in real time could never truly be expressed in a history lesson, he'd insisted, and he'd come away from the experience with a solemn, cosmic hope for the future.

He'd lived long enough into the fifties to hear the latest update of the probe's leaving the Milky Way, but a few years later, we lost its signal. Soon after, my father passed too.

The sixties, the decade that followed, was defined by division and decay. Buildings grew taller, slums grew wider, bodies younger and souls colder, and at the end of it all, we had moved far from the society we'd been when the probe first launched, its romance diminished with each generation under the growing cynicism of our declining nations. When people spoke of the cosmos now, it was no longer with the sweet sentimentality of the rose-tinted twenties, but with apprehension and urgency. With militaries, budgets, and defense plans.

On the afternoon I arrived in New York from Manila, I found the airport crowds had churned to a standstill. Everyone around me, and perhaps everyone in the world, had halted before the nearest screen to watch the live news feed of an unidentified object glinting in our sky and crashing into the Indian Ocean.

It was on this day that humanity learned our long-forgotten probe, launched fifty years prior, had in fact mysteriously come back to Earth all on its own, at a propulsion rate far beyond the capabilities of modern human science. And inside the capsule—emptied of its original contents—was an encrypted message of inhuman origin.

As I listened to the news report, I thought again of my father, a product of a better time, who, with awestruck humility, had watched the probe leave the planet. In our current generation, however, the probe returned to us like a reanimated corpse, for we didn't yet know what was contained within that message, and we wouldn't know for months. Impending invasion, divine intervention, declarations of inter-galactic war. All of it simmered up into a shapeless unease we could not see the edges of, but which held all nine billion of us hostage to the possibilities.

Though in this disquiet summer, a summer that pushed us forward into hedonistic apathy, Gatsby was the singular exception, flying over the dust and toils of our world on fire. Beyond that famous, corrupted name, he clung to a vestige of that old cosmic hope I'd readily believed did not exist anymore, his indestructible sincerity blossoming like an act of defiance in the face of all our immeasurable dread.

If humanity ought to know its own smallness, then his ignorance of it was arresting—a gorgeous, comet-tail burn I witnessed so intim-ately, I was sure it should have killed me.

◇——◇——◇

I had been shipped to a nocturnal Long Island neighborhood called West Egg. It contained a plethora of bio-ink tattoo parlors nestled between pumping music clubs, illegal body-mod clinics, and nameless speakeasies, all run informally by the East's largest gangs. The broad opinion out here was that biodome folks were a gullible, sheltered sort, and I stuck out in that Midwestern way as I made the short walk from the train station to the address of my apartment, paid for by my new employer.

The living room window faced the polluted waters of Long Island Sound. Even less picturesque was the bedroom view, blocked entirely by a cylindrical hundred-story tower with marbly windows that, under the high sun, created the illusion of an impossible icicle sprouting out of the concrete, forever unmelted. The clouds were low that day, and I remember the very top of the tower was obscured, so that one could imagine the floors extended into the sky unendingly.

I spent the better part of the afternoon disassembling and reassembling the apartment's cleaning bots, turning over furniture for wiretaps, and climbing onto the counters to scan for cameras. There was nothing of the sort, and soon after, I prepared myself for the biggest hurdle of the day.

It had been ingrained in me by my parents that greeting the nearest relatives in a new city was of utmost priority. As most of my family was bunched up in various Midwest suburbs—save for my mother's side in Manila—the only relative I had in New York was my second cousin Daisy, who was married to a Buchanan, and so, my luggage still unpacked, I accepted their dinner invitation.

Over the comm, Daisy had whispered to me that she was elated I'd "agreed" to work on the Medica account, as if her summoning me hadn't eliminated any say I might have had in the matter. Bunsen had ordered me not to share details with the client while the assignment was ongoing, not that I had intended to. Sensitive business couldn't be treated like family gossip, and I didn't trust that Daisy cared about the distinction.

I ordered a hover-taxi in the early evening. From street-level, that monster of a tower blocked out the sun itself, and there was no sign of activity there except for a small commotion outside. An unruly group of four loitered before the doors, each of them unsubtly modded, as was the fashion in this neighborhood.

I'd been standing on the curb less than a minute when one of them—a woman, cloaked in shredded denim, with ice-white hair shorn unevenly to her chin—noticed me. Her limbs were dotted with amber-toned bioluminescent ink that cast her bronze skin in a reptilian pattern popular with a younger crowd.

But it was her eyes, or rather what bulged in place of them, that was most noteworthy of all.

Ocular-mods. Round as saucers and entirely too large, throwing off the proportions of her small frame. The size and color of the irises—deep black, outlined by a yellow light—could only be described as vaguely owlish.

It seemed she and her companions were locked in an argument. She muttered something harshly at them, then crossed the street. In my direction.

I stiffened. Stopping before me, she demanded to know if I had a shred of insight into who owned the tower. I informed her I wasn't from here.

"Yes, that's obvious enough," she said impatiently. "It's *why* I'm asking." According to her, the tower was newly built, construction having finished a month prior. None of the locals knew who operated the place. "You're a corpo. What business would you have in West Egg anyway?"

I hadn't told her I worked corp-side, but she must have had her own internal formula that brought her to an uncomfortably accurate calculation. I explained I was here on a short netdiving contract. These lodgings weren't my choice. That latter part went unsaid, though certainly she picked up on it.

"Diver, huh?" She seemed rather convinced I was lying. Then she tugged back the collar of her denim jacket, revealing the slots on the nape of her neck. "You and me both. But I suppose we're in two very different, ah, *industries.*"

Her line of interest in the tower was probably enough to warrant a tip to the nearest police station, but I'd been warned that West Egg's criminal underbelly was a rabbit hole that wasn't worth a glance. You'd find yourself buried three feet underground without any recollection as to how.

"Different indeed," I replied.

She was a foot shorter than me, but she looked me up and down in a wordlessly critical way. I recognized the look well enough. Netdiving was an ecosystem, and corpos were an invasive species. To her type, at least. Likely, she saw some treason in me, a sellout overly willing to betray the anarchic origins of the field.

The odd group in front of the tower interrupted us, calling her back. It was early enough that the bars and mod shops hadn't opened for the night. Voices slid easily across the hot, unpopulated street, and I overheard scraps of their rekindled argument.

"A suit?" one of them grumbled at her. "The hell'd you say?"

"Nothing! Sue me for asking around. The rest of you are lazy as shit," said the woman. "Penguin, Parrot—pop into the mod shops. Docs have a whisper network. Ask 'em questions, sly as you can."

"And what'll *you* be doing?"

"Pigeon and I ought to find a floor plan. I'm starting to doubt the place is corp owned. Big new bootlegger, most likely—"

My taxi landed just then, and I stepped inside. Through the window, the woman's bulging glass eyes found mine once more, staring at me until the car was up and off the ground.

◇——◇——◇

An evening with the Buchanans, and the detached pleasantries that came with it, was more a thing to endure than enjoy.

I happened to know Daisy's husband, Tom, from our time at Yale. They lived across the bay in East Egg village, the most exclusive residential area in the country. It was notable, of course, for the density of its billionaires, though I found this less exciting than the fact that the grounds of East Egg were well preserved despite the deteriorating climate conditions.

The vicious pendulum swing between scorching summers and frozen winters, smoggy autumns and wet springs, had pushed most suburbs into biodomes and left few spots of real nature intact across the world. East Egg's retractable dome was installed in the last decade, the first of its kind, and went up within minutes during weather emergencies.

Presently, however, the dome wasn't erected, so I got a sweeping view of the entire village as I rode the taxi over the Sound. Its gates were shrouded in great oaks, drooping willows, and other greenery that had survived a hundred years or more.

Before I was even out of the taxi, Tom offered his hand in greeting, shaking it powerfully and lurching me from the vehicle, before taking me up the wide steps of an immense redbrick mansion. It was a drastic change from their industrial Chicago penthouse.

A pair of bay windows jutted out from the brick, framing the front door, with four bright ivory columns holding up a wide, square balcony—a very symmetrical, very Georgian home, Tom boasted, though it seemed rather like a shiny re-creation of one, with the plastic look of a life-sized diorama, without any scuffs to suggest a history of character.

Tom was, relative to other Buchanans, not a terribly important one. He sat on a few of his family's less scintillating executive boards. In college, he'd been a varsity football star with a passion to go professional until he made a whole show of deciding not to undergo the body-mod surgeries required to be competitive. I believe, ever since, he'd sealed his fate as a bitter man, though he buried that bitterness beneath a thick crust of stalwart American values.

"It's actually for the better," he'd said to me back then. "Mods like that, they're irreversible. And football's not forever. After retirement, I'd just—what? Go around looking like a fool, *that's* what!"

Despite his startling mediocrity, being a Buchanan remained Tom's greatest accomplishment. He would have never pursued a sports career in exchange for the inevitable scorn of stepping out of his rarefied circle into what the old crowd considered a garish one. Buchanan Group owned much of the New East Americas, and so Tom kept a white-knuckled grip on his exalted name. In return, it afforded him a very large house, the beach just behind it, and a famous wife.

At the base of the elegant porch, Tom steered me around by the shoulders, pointing out all the renovations he'd ordered in the last month. This included new trim, the finest grass this side of the East, and real, freshly planted rose beds imported from the famed nature conservatories in the West.

He brought me through his high-ceilinged foyer, crowned in the center by a double staircase and accented with bronze railings. To the

14

right of the foyer, he shuffled me down an embellished corridor, where we suddenly walked a bit slower. He'd adorned the walls with his college football accolades. I moved my head this way and that as he maneuvered me around, like an audience member plucked onto the stage at a magic show, and recounted the highlights of each of his victories. ("Yes, I do remember that game," I interjected at the appropriate times.)

I hadn't yet seen a trace of Daisy in the enormous house, not even one or two of her Happy Sleep awards tucked between Tom's trophies.

We turned into a sitting room at the end of the hallway. It was gusty, all the curtains untied, and the French doors thrown open to let in the breeze. A pair of voices and giddy laughter flapped alongside the wind, which pushed me farther inside, more so than Tom's hand on my back.

A woman I didn't know was stretched out on a plush love seat. She was so extensively modded, I'm embarrassed to say I did a double take at the sight of her in the Buchanan home. Her steel leg propped up onto a leather ottoman, knee plate unscrewed, she was adjusting the joint-bars with a small drill. The skirt of her satin gown, a deep mahogany shade that rather blended into her skin, was bunched up at her thigh, and the dress gleamed just so as the evening sun fanned into the room through the open doors.

Head lowered in concentration, her face was hidden behind a thick veil of black curls. She spared me a glance—fleeting, as if I'd disrupted her peripheral view of the billowing curtains—and I opened my mouth to introduce myself before I was swiftly interrupted.

"Is that Nicky?"

The top of Daisy's short cinnamon hair emerged from behind a chaise lounge. It was her eyes that I latched onto first, always the eyes. The whites of them held an extra shine, jellylike and just as sweet, so that when the light hit her face at the right angle, it felt as though there were a million stars within them and she could cry at the sight of you. People liked to speculate that she had some subtle custom oc-mod, but it wasn't true; even as a girl, she'd had this enchanted affection about her.

She rose from the chaise, her white dress pluming around her, and threw her arms around my neck. Pushing herself up onto her tiptoes, she whispered in my ear, "I'm paralyzed with happiness to see you."

15

That couldn't be true—we hardly knew one another, after all—but I laughed and decided to believe her anyway. We sat together on the chaise. I mentioned that I'd passed through Chicago for a few days on the way here.

"Do they *miss me*?" she gasped.

I remember being surprised to hear that she and Tom had uprooted themselves so suddenly. My understanding was she'd adored Tom's native Chicago—or rather, the social circle that revolved around her there, filled with ex–Happy Sleep stars like herself and similarly bored socialites. East Egg was far more isolated. I suspected she and Tom were the youngest couple in the village.

I smiled. "About a dozen people send their love."

"How gorgeous. Do you hear that, Tom?" She didn't wait for Tom to reply. "You ought to see the baby," she added a bit robotically.

"I'd like to," I said.

"She's three—"

Tom, who'd been breathing audibly behind me, clapped my shoulder then. "I hear you were at one of the big consulting places, Nick."

"Just for a year. I've taken up a new contract."

"Who with?"

"Gen Wealth."

"Never heard of them."

I expected that. Tom was proud to be unfamiliar with anything established less than twenty years ago, as if that made the venture less important.

Beside me, Daisy sighed and stared at the parquet floors. Tom's eyes darted around before he leaned forward, clutching the back of the chaise tightly with both hands. "I could get you any good contract you like, you know. Just say the word."

Of course, that wasn't true, but I nodded, thanking him. Then from the love seat across the room, the woman I didn't know exclaimed, unprompted, "Absolutely!" She stood up with a yawn. At her full height, she was about as tall as me. "I'm stiff."

"Don't look at *me*. I told you to have a drink before tinkering around for hours." Daisy grinned. "Fix one for Nick too."

16

Now I realized it wasn't a coincidence she had a friend around this evening. If the gossip was to be believed, then Daisy fancied herself a puppeteer of sorts who could write her way into the narrative of future wedding speeches. I'd unknowingly become her next victim.

On the far side of the room, the woman surveyed the drink cart. She seemed the exact sort of person Tom would have scowled at when we were in college. But here she was, in his sitting room, and a bright curiosity about her sprouted within me.

"No thanks." The woman turned her back on the drinks. "I'm in training."

"It's still the off-season!" protested Daisy.

"For one more day," said the woman, then looked my way again. There was contempt in the set of her shoulders, an overt examination of me that she made no effort to hide. I felt as though I'd encountered her somewhere else before but couldn't imagine how.

She was an athlete, evident by her mods alone. I eyed the plating in her elbows, her hands, and each individual finger; the swirls of bio-ink adorning her forearms, lines of glowing yellow and blue that shone prettily against her dark skin.

Daisy got to her feet and stood between us like a pastor. "The heat's made me forget all my manners. Nick, this is Jordan Baker. Jordan, this is my favorite cousin, Nick—" She stopped, turning to me. "Oh, you're something else now, aren't you?"

"Carraway," I supplied.

"Carraway! A funny little name, isn't it?" said Daisy.

"Very," said Miss Baker. "You live in West Egg? I know somebody there."

"Do you?" Daisy strung their arms together. "Who—"

Another gust of wind washed in from the bay, rinsing the room clean of the entire conversation as a bell tinkled lightly from down the hall.

It was time for dinner.

Two

T HE BUCHANANS KEPT A HANDFUL of maids and butlers and two chauffeurs in their service alongside a standard set of housekeeping bots. The human staff was a new addition. I'd stayed with them in Chicago once, during one of my military breaks, and while they'd never been anything less than nauseatingly rich, they'd only had two androids back then, a chef and a cleaner.

The house help here seemed closer to display than practicality—not unlike Tom's curated fine art collection or the driveway lined with unreleased hover-car models—for there were butlers stationed inexplicably in every room, and the only thing that separated them from the paintings and the stone busts was that they bowed each time you walked by.

A table had been set on the wide veranda that fronted the beach, and a few bots whirred about four feet above us, blowing cool air. Tom spoke at length about next season's Super Bowl predictions; Daisy picked at her synth-steak, blinking slowly until anyone addressed her; and Miss Baker, who generally seemed happier not to be addressed at all, took sips from her black wine as if it were ceremonial tea.

A few glasses into Tom's good claret, I asked, "Do you ever miss the performance life, Daisy?" The real question I had was why there wasn't even a glimmer of her era-defining career on the walls.

"If I missed it, I wouldn't have married!" said Daisy, smiling distantly.

Miss Baker cleared her throat. "Are you excited about Gen Wealth, Mr. Carraway?"

It was the first time she had spoken to me directly the whole dinner. I was startled into sitting straighter. "I think the work will be interesting enough."

"What's wrong with the family business?" asked Tom.

There was nothing "wrong" with it, but Tom always liked to assume the worst. "It's fine," I said. "I wanted to see New York. I was stationed all over during the war but never here."

"Nick served until '69. On the front lines," Daisy informed Miss Baker. "He's very intelligent."

There hadn't been any literal "front lines." On both sides, battles had been quiet things that were resolved in quiet rooms. In the end, the conflict amounted to nothing—no sweeping tragedies, but equally no valiance. Just a few tense, wasted years until everyone went home exhausted and older. Daisy didn't seem to care for the details, though.

"It's just practice," I replied.

"Of course." She nodded. "But you still have to be *intelligent*—"

Tom's hand came down onto the table, rattling his cutlery. "We got through one war just six years ago, and another one might be dropping on us soon from God-knows-where. We all saw that wretched news about the probe."

Daisy swirled her wine. "That's all right. You paid your way out of serving in the last one, and if there's another, you won't be anywhere near it either."

The claret had made me a little foggy, but not foggy enough that I didn't see the dangerous flash in Tom's hooded eyes.

"We don't know that it'll be a war, of course," I said quickly.

Tom scowled. "I say it's a waste of time to sit here, twiddling our thumbs, waiting for anyone to decode anything. What's there to decode? There's something out there, and it's headed our way. Why else would that thing get sent back to us if not to threaten us into a panic?" He pointed his cigar to the sky. "It's time to funnel everything into our militaries as we speak. That's what we oughta do."

"Mm-hmm. That's what we oughta do," Daisy repeated solemnly.

"Nick, have you read 'The Rise of the Global South' by this man Goddard?" demanded Tom.

Across from me, Miss Baker whipped her head up like something had jerked her by the collar. She looked right at me then, as if there were nothing in the world she wanted more than to see my reaction. Daisy slumped in her chair with a yawn.

"Why, no." I leaned forward, looking at Tom as I spoke, but flicked my eyes to Miss Baker, and I was pleased to find that apparently I had said the right thing. She smiled at me behind her wineglass.

"Well, it's a fine essay, and everyone ought to read it," continued Tom. "The idea is that America's in the midst of a horrible *brain drain* that'll only worsen the longer we let our best and brightest get swayed by third-world Asia and its floating cities."

"Brain drain?" I asked—not because I didn't know where this would lead, but as an irrelevant statement to prompt him to go on.

"Yes. You know all the angry activist types, whining about this country's cavernous 'wealth gap' and wanting to burn any and all conglomerates to the ground for 'causing' it?"

"Indeed," I said.

"Well, the media has it wrong. They say our slums are growing, while the opposite's happening in Asia's south, and they cite any reason under the sun for why that is—except for the truth!" Tom said, and I nodded quicker to show him I was eager to hear this truth as soon as possible. "Which is that a lot of those places—they fancy themselves tech hubs now, but people forget it's not even been, I don't know, fifteen years since their hover-cities were established? Those places were filled with trash heaps and jungles not long ago—in our very lifetime." He took an enlightened pause. "What's more, well, people aren't educated the same way we are out here, and still, everyone's flocking over there like it's the new center of civilization. We've got to beat them down."

Daisy winked at me. "Beat them down," she echoed sagely.

"Yes." Miss Baker sighed. "God forbid they've saved themselves from these climate swings, but I do suppose they're still—what was it? 'Third world'?"

Tom shook his head in a pitying manner. "The media's all too happy to devalue the Americas these days, Jordan. It's a trendy narrative, if you don't think about it critically. We need to preserve the Western World, and all we've done throughout history. Anyway, it's all covered in the essay. Scientific stuff."

"Tom's getting very profound," said Daisy glumly. "He reads long articles with big words—"

"Nick understands me," interrupted Tom with spectacular confidence. "All I'm saying is we can't let ourselves fall behind them."

It always intrigued me the way he wielded *them* in that other-ing manner, as if *them* couldn't possibly encompass me or his own wife.

I did understand him, though. In his eyes, I was one of the good ones—a third-generation immigrant raised in Minnesota with the same Yale breeding. I was a remnant of some faded concept that had once propped America up onto the world stage as the primary beacon of success to poorer, darker nations. I think he was very glad to raise his glass at me across his golden dinner table and pretend circumstance was simply a mindset all the other third-world Asians could escape too if only they weren't so lazy about it.

Just as I was trying to find the right words to say nothing of consequence in reply, a lilting melody floated from the house and onto the veranda. About half a minute passed where no one spoke, and I looked up from my plate, wondering if we'd been dropped into a funeral.

One of the butlers murmured to Tom, "Call on the holo-bar for you, sir."

Tom wiped his mouth on a napkin and followed the butler inside. The veranda doors closed behind him, and Daisy sucked in a gulp of air, leaning into me. "Nick, you mustn't turn into a West Egg man," she said, her voice pitched high in her whimsical throat. "The longer you're there, the more you'll be—you'll be tempted into that lifestyle, but it just *wouldn't* suit you. You understand?"

I was surprised she'd say something like that in front of Miss Baker, who was maybe a part of "that lifestyle," but Miss Baker didn't appear slighted. "Ease up, Daisy. Maybe he's one of those funny purists."

Of course, I wasn't a purist, but the military netdiving enhancements weren't cosmetic. She could not see the trail of slots down my spine or my imperceptible ocular-mods.

Tom's voice rose up from inside, cutting me off from any reply. Daisy clutched my hand. "You remind me of a rose, Nick. An absolute rose." She looked with desperation at Miss Baker. "Doesn't he?"

Neither Miss Baker nor I had a chance to disagree because Daisy rose from the table immediately and ran inside.

Alone with Miss Baker, I sipped my water. "You mentioned you knew someone in West—"

She shushed me. "I want to hear what happens."

"Is something happening?" I replied carefully.

Miss Baker leaned all the way back in her chair. "My, you're good at that."

"I'm sorry?"

She crossed her arms, a dash of laughter in her voice. "We both know Tom's only confident about Goddard when he thinks he's the strongest person in the room. Of course, what he doesn't understand is that a weaker man wouldn't have kept his fist as still as you did."

I wasn't sure that it was strength that kept me in Tom's orbit; rather, I was quite used to the regular intake of his moldy opinions, and perhaps she was too. Nonetheless, she held my gaze approvingly as she emptied her glass.

Through the thin curtains, we could see into the living room where the shadows of Tom and Daisy moved restlessly. He was a massive silhouette, looming tall and wide over her as they traded shrieking profanities.

"She might have the decency not to call him at dinnertime," said Miss Baker.

"Who?"

"You mean you don't know?"

I'd heard traces of rumors here and there, but it seemed impolite to say it at Tom's own table.

"Tom's got some woman—" started Miss Baker as Daisy's shadow grew larger against the curtains before bursting forth from the doors.

"It couldn't be helped!" Daisy waved her hands about, out of breath again. "I just *had* to go see it! I looked over, and the ad-drones on the other side were changing their signs for the new hour, and all the lights looked so romantic. ..." Color flooded her cheeks, and she stared at us expectantly. "Isn't it? So romantic?"

"Very romantic," said Miss Baker and I in unison.

◇——◇——◇

Dessert was served, but no one had an appetite anymore. A brief, unreadable look passed between the women before Miss Baker announced she wanted to take a stroll along the beach. Tom offered to join her, probably because he couldn't tolerate Daisy right then.

"I've seen pictures of Pammy," I said, standing with Daisy on the veranda. "She looks just like you."

"You don't know me very well, Nick." She gazed absently at the streaks of setting sun over the water. "Would you like some wisdom from me?" She spoke as if she were beckoning this wisdom from an unreachable dimension, though she was only a year older. "You have to learn how to be a good judge of character to make it through this life."

She and I belonged to very different lives, but I humored her anyway. "Are you?" I asked. "A good judge?"

"I wasn't always. If I were, then I wouldn't have married Tom. Don't you think?" She didn't say this lightly. The edges of her lips tensed, notched and drawn tight like a readied arrow, and her sad eyes followed Tom's lumbering figure on the beach as he dragged his feet alongside Miss Baker. "I know you're curious why I asked for you."

I did want to know, for it had puzzled me thoroughly. "Fay Medica is a very important account, and this seems a very important assignment. I'm flattered by your trust, but I'm not—" Perhaps she'd gotten things mixed up about my background. "What I'm trained for is *cyber* intelligence, Daisy. Out here, this is different."

Fay Medica was owned by Buchanan Group, and abandoning that organization would be a sort of betrayal on her part. It made me feel somewhat sympathetic toward her plight. She was keeping a big secret from her husband—that the family was entertaining such a departure.

"You know, Nick. Being a spy—" She paused. That word sounded juvenile and unscrupulous in a way that unnerved me. "Working in intelligence, I mean, and being an entertainer—oh, they're not so different from each other. You have to get to know a person, figure out what matters and what doesn't. Assets, offshore accounts. That's the easy stuff." She wrung her delicate hands together. "But ... what wine a person likes, where they vacation, their most tender memories, or private proclivities," she murmured. "Their weaknesses."

23

It was said by many that during the peak of her career, Daisy Fay's appeal came from this unearthly ability to balance both joy and sorrow in her face at the same time. But I had learned over the years, in the sporadic interactions we'd shared at family functions, that if you saw her in person and stared long enough, there came a point where this quality unsettled more than it captivated.

"People think it's all about sweet talk, but really, that won't get you far." Under the brutal half-lit sun, her voice assumed a quality I'd never heard before. It didn't sit so high in her throat. It didn't rise and fall like the effortless compulsion of a siren song. "It's not about how well you can speak, but how well you can listen. That's why you came to mind."

Drifting against the horizon, Tom and Miss Baker seemed to be engaged in small talk, their exchanges short, with extended pauses between. She glanced up at us from the beach, our eyes locking. I remembered the flippant way she'd said "some woman" at the dinner table, and despite all this hassle, I couldn't help but feel sorry for Daisy.

"Nicky," she implored, "I haven't anyone else to turn to." A spark of her flowery brilliance shone through, like a valve twisted in incremental calculation. "And—and aren't we family?"

Looking back, I realize Daisy really was a good judge of character. Whether I knew it or not, her practiced tenderness unlocked me that evening. *Family.* In the end, I was my parents' son, raised on that sacred pillar, and it didn't matter that this cousin was more distant than a friend.

"We are," I said.

She hugged me, and when we drew apart, her gleaming shield rebuilt itself.

"Everything's terrible anyhow!" she exclaimed, voice airy and melodic once more. "Tom has very hard opinions about that probe. He's been on edge all day. Do you suppose we're all going to die very, very soon?" She hiccuped into a laugh. "Personally, I think I should just fly up there with the ad-drones. Even higher! I could greet the aliens with a tray of homemade biscuits. Wouldn't *that* be lovely?"

I found it wasn't very hard at all to picture Daisy flying amidst the quilt of shifting holograms, cycling their lights and slogans and logos

24

beneath the clouds. We talked for another short while—asking cordially about each other's mothers—and as the sun fell and the sky darkened, the patchwork of holo-ads grew ever brighter.

Tom and Miss Baker looped around into the gardens, disappearing from view. Soon Daisy decided she'd had enough of the hot evening too. I took her hand to help her up the veranda steps, but as soon as my thumb curled over her knuckles, she winced.

"Are you all right?" Concerned, I looked down to check she wasn't hurt, but her skin was smooth and unblemished.

She touched my cheek with her other hand. "Just perfect," she said, her smile wavering like a candle flame.

◇——◇——◇

In the dusky warmth of the sitting room, Miss Baker lay on the chaise lounge, reading news headlines aloud from the holo-bar while Tom, armed once again with his cigar, stared at nothing in particular.

At the sight of us, Miss Baker swung her legs to the ground, tapped the holo-screen off, then stretched her arms and announced she was off to bed.

"Jordan has a game tomorrow," Daisy informed me. "Start of the season."

Now I recalled where I'd seen Miss Baker before. She was the face of modern bullet-golf and the only person ever to receive *Forward Sport* magazine's Athlete of the Year twice in a row, a feat that hadn't come without controversy, even outside of sports circles. I remembered, at the time, reading accusations about her "poor sporting attitude" and budget-cap breaches on her mod procedures.

"Oh—you're *that* Jordan Baker," I said, feeling very stupid.

She grinned, as if I'd finally won some secret game between us. "Good night, Mr. Carraway." She offered her hand, and I shook it. "I should hope to see you again soon."

Daisy clapped. "Of course you will. In fact, I think I'll arrange a marriage."

Miss Baker smiled once more enigmatically, then made her exit.

"Come over often, Nick," suggested Daisy. "Jordan will be staying with us for the entirety of her New York season."

"She's a nice girl," said Tom in a low, suspicious tone, as if he were still trying to convince himself of this. "You'll take a liking to her, I think."

I didn't believe Miss Baker was nice at all, but it was true I had taken a liking to her.

"She needs a good influence. Someone solid," Tom continued. "She hasn't had anyone like that her whole life."

"He means to say a *man*," muttered Daisy.

"The only solid thing in her life has been golf, and when she retires—"

"Shush, Tom."

"When she *retires*, which we all know won't be very far off—"

Daisy appeared to be getting quite annoyed, so I asked, "Is Miss Baker from New York?"

"Yes, but brought up in Louisville! Is that surprising?" Daisy grinned at me, then at Tom. "We shared a very *all-American* girlhood together."

It wasn't surprising. It answered the question I'd had all night—how someone like Miss Baker seemed so intimate with a pair of staunch, old-money Buchanans. I hadn't missed the way Tom eyed Miss Baker's modded body, in snatches, with equal displeasure and fascination.

Of course, the paradox of the old-money world wasn't that they modded any less than the crowds they scoffed at. The only difference was that while the new wave of body-mod culture basked in a trend of defiant self-expression, East Egg types like Tom and Daisy paid extra to show less. To them, it wasn't so much fashionable as it was expected of their vast richness that their mods faded imperceptibly into the skin.

Tom possessed a hulking build and angry vigor, sustained by a set of cosmetic enhancements. He appeared a shade or two younger than his actual age and returned regularly to his private mod-doc to reinforce the procedures. It kept the fine lines away from his sharp eyes, the sunspots out of his wide cheeks, and many other subtleties to ensure he could remain thirty as long as possible.

He frowned. "What were you and Nick whispering about on the veranda?"

"Oh, I believe we spoke about the Philippines," Daisy teased. "Yes, the—the brain drain, and those awful hover-cities that are taking away all the proper Americans from our workforce."

26

I smiled. Tom glanced distrustfully between us. "Don't speak on what you don't know," he said to her.

"Oh, you're very right. It's *far* too complex to be understood by either me or Nicky. It's not as if we have half our families over there, or that Nick isn't very well acquainted with the 'workforce' himself. Not from articles, mind you, but actual experience."

Tom started up with quotes from his beloved think-piece again. They bickered on until they weren't debating Goddard anymore, and when their voices became fast and shrill, I interrupted and said I'd call for a taxi.

Tom insisted he pay for it, and for a few minutes, we did the whole song and dance about that, which he'd always been very good at. Tom liked me enough. I think if he liked anyone enough, then he enjoyed spending money on insignificant things and calling it kindness. So I let him win the argument, and he promised he'd take me into the city at the nearest chance.

I shook his hand. My car came, and I was at the edge of their long driveway when Daisy suddenly yelled from the porch steps, *"Wait!"* and I stopped. She cupped her hands around her mouth. "We heard you were engaged to a girl recently! Is it *true?*"

I think she was referring to the last inconsequential flame who'd followed me around Manila for a few weeks before I left, but the whole thing hadn't been close to an engagement, let alone close to a girl.

I shook my head. "Libel," I joked. "I'm too poor."

"But we heard it. We heard it from three people, so it must be true," said Daisy sullenly, and as Tom pulled her back into the house, the stars in her eyes snuffed out.

⋄——◇——⋄

The lights in my West Egg apartment hadn't yet been synced to my comm, and so I trudged along through the dark, fumbling for the manual switches on the walls. I managed to illuminate the foyer, enough to stagger into the bedroom, where I fell onto the mattress.

As I floated somewhere between wakefulness and slumber, an odd sight caught my eye—the tiniest hint of movement in one of the wide windows of the neighboring tower.

At first it was nothing more than a shadow, the back of a dark figure cut in a white suit. I lay there, in unmoored stillness, watching the figure through lidded eyes, wondering if I'd stepped halfway inside a dream. After a moment, or several, the man took a step forward. His figure flattened into a silhouette against a sudden and warm light, bright as an emerald. It came from somewhere I couldn't see, somewhere just in front of him. . . .

The light pulsed—a slow heartbeat in the vast darkness—and the man raised his arm as if to try to hold it in his hand.

Reaching, reaching . . . his fingers grazing the edges of that fresh halo.

[LOADING]

.

.

.

[PLAY]

"I'd like to open a café."

"How wonderful. Have an area in mind?"

"Why, in the valley, of course. That's my neighborhood."

"I'm sorry?"

"The valley. The old smart town."

"Yes, I know. Surely, there are lovelier places. With lovelier people. Or rather, with *any* people."

"A place is lovely when there're people. And there're only people if there's a thing to do around. That's why someone has to start a café, or else how's the valley going to get a chance to be lovely too?"

"I ... see. Well, Mr. Michaelis, there'll be a high risk on your loan. We'll have to include an extra negotiation fee. You understand."

"Actually, I don't! Am I supposed to serve customers with no place to sit but next to the GPUs with fifty fans pumping in the corner? Coffee'll go cold the second it's poured."

"This is a good thing you're looking to do, Mr. Michaelis. It really is. At Gen Wealth, we're in this business to help *anyone* achieve their dream—"

"And what about this negotiation fee?"

"Let me explain it simply. Ninety-eight percent of the properties in the valley are owned by corpos. Ninety percent of those corpos use the properties as GPU farms. Now, as you are aware, most of these folks are generous—"

"Utter saints."

"They forfeit some of their space to renters at significantly cheaper prices. But to ask them to clear out the entire first floor of their farms? It'll be a hard sell. Where will the GPUs go? The lost profit from the downtime? They'll be stubborn. You may attempt to negotiate yourself, but to be plain, sir, they won't give you the time of day."

"So what am I looking at?"

"We can pin you somewhere at $18,500 per month. Before utilities."

"Would you like to take a kidney as well?"

"Of course not. Though if you submit to us your DNA kit, complete the attached questionnaire on your medical—"

"Oh, I gave that 'questionnaire' a thorough read. You could clone a man with the data you're demanding."

"I assure you, it's to your benefit. We can calculate a more precise prediction of your family tree for the next four generations. Then provide a recommendation, looking at your current income, take a big percent off that monthly fee, pass it one generation down. Our clients, on average, have their payments reduced by thirty percent or more."

"Christ on high. Let's ... get on with it, then."

"Wonderful! We'll figure out a payment schedule for you to transfer over the first installment."

"Which amounts to what exactly?"

"This counsel is on the house. We'll just need the negotiation fee, along with the first four months up front, and that is ... $89,234. How's that for a deal?"

[STOP]

.

[ERROR—]

.

[ERROR: ACCOUNT NOT FOUND]

Three

A WIDE STRETCH OF INORGANIC LAND separated West Egg from the city, where stacks of decrepit mid-rises clustered together under a sea of ad-drones and chipper holograms that smiled down on the valley's barren street corners. The nav-holos had been set up every few blocks as friendly AIs that guided people all over the neighborhood. But as there were no people to guide in this deserted strip, all hundred or so of the holograms had nothing to do but flicker uselessly with their wide, pixelated grins.

Before all of the mid-rises, they had once called the place a "valley of ashes," as it had been New York's industrial dumping ground for most of the twentieth century. When a keen Buchanan Group development company had popped up in the 2040s, they had pitched a blueprint for a neighborhood like no other.

A pilot project for the East's first smart town.

In the glitzy commercials of the early sixties, there were overblown promises for a state-of-the-art community—a residential paradise where the buildings would know you by name. The nav-holos on every street would offer personalized recommendations from restaurants to spas, and your apartment would calibrate seamlessly to your needs, so acutely that the kitchen-bot could have whatever you were craving laid out on the table before you even realized you were hungry.

As with most lofty endeavors, the novelty was short-lived. The East's hungriest rental corporations wasted no time buying up all the units and pricing out wishful tenants. Within the first year of the town's construction, the renting war was swiftly won by a swath of new-money crypto moguls, AI companies, and anyone else looking to house their vast and ever-growing farms. They filled the apartments with floor-to-ceiling racks of heat-pumping GPUs, and in no time at all, every building in the town had completely sold out, without a single living resident occupying any of them.

But as the state mandated a minimum human population be maintained in order for the neighborhood to be deemed "residential," landlords and aspiring tenants had arrived at a mutually beneficial arrangement—one where tenants got rent at half the price, and landlords turned a profit by exploiting a very curious loophole.

I saw this loophole with my own eyes, a few days after dinner at the Buchanans', when I found myself trapped next to Tom on a commuter train that dropped us right into this valley's unbeating heart.

It was Bunsen who had forced me into the outing, after I'd mentioned during a status call that Tom had requested my company. "Go along with him, then," he'd said.

Selfishly, I hadn't wanted to spend a whole day with Tom. "Why?"

"Because you never know what you'll learn," Bunsen had replied, as if this were obvious. "Nick, your personal connection to the client and her family is a special advantage. Do you know how much harder other point guards have to work to get this sort of casual access?"

They had graduated in the same year at Yale, so I thought Bunsen would agree with me that Tom was objectively uninteresting, one of the least influential Buchanans in his family, but this argument hadn't been convincing enough.

It was a blistering Sunday. The train made a short maintenance stop in the valley, and Tom grabbed me by the elbow. "We're getting off here," he said, his insistence more aggressive than usual. We'd departed from West Egg's station that morning, and I had been confused by his suggestion of taking the train until he added, "I want you to meet my girl."

An attendant tutted disapprovingly as we hopped onto the platform, though he made no effort to stop us. Tom was a brawny man who strained the seams of his tailored suit and walked like someone who knew exactly where he was going, even in a place with nowhere to go.

Our footsteps echoed in the empty station. It had been built to be a bustling commuter hub, but as the smart town had never come into fruition, it stood cold and abandoned like all things in the valley. We exited onto street-level, and when I pushed open the doors, I heard what sounded like a rush of muffled air from all directions—though there wasn't even a breeze.

Tom put on his sunglasses. "You'll get used to it."

"What is it?" It felt like we had tumbled into the depths of some metal-bellied monster digesting its food.

"Just the fans." He waved his hand around, gesturing at the boxy mid-rises that surrounded us on all sides. "For the farms. To keep them cool."

There was a nav-holo just outside the station gate. It was shaped like a woman, in a dark pencil skirt and collared blouse. At the sight of us, she exclaimed, *"Welcome! Where can I lead you today?"* Then she smiled unblinkingly in anticipation.

Tom ignored it, and I followed him warily through the empty streets. At each corner, the bluish-green nav-holos continued their disjointed chorus of *"Welcome! Where can I lead you today?"* as we passed. The farther we drew away from the station, the more I found other nav-holos hadn't stood the test of time, their terminals toppled over or unlit, crumbling into the cracked pavement. Some were still functioning, just barely, with the screens jammed up so that the woman's grin twitched endlessly, while her audio stuttered, *"Welcome—welcome— welcome—"*

More than a few nav-holos appeared to have been graffitied as well—in boredom, amusement, or protest. Their displays had been hacked with all manner of middle fingers, or screeching profanities, or a clever mix of both. A dozen or so had simply replaced the nav-holo woman altogether and now depicted blocks of text, gleaming, FEED BUCHANAN TO THE FARMS!

And yet of all the curiosities the sterile valley had to offer, the most striking one loomed about fifty feet above our heads. Amidst the colorful marketing drones, shifting through the usual cycle of advertisements, one in particular was triple the size of them all.

It took no less than a hundred drones to illuminate it—two colossal, disembodied eyes leering behind a pair of gold-rimmed spectacles. Above its gaze, in twirling lights, flashed the name "Dr. T. J. Eckleburg," likely an ocular-mod doc who perhaps, many years ago, had far different hopes for the valley's clientele. The other drones that completed the elaborate advertisement were broken, I presumed, as the rest of the face was missing entirely.

The roving eyes blinked every half minute or so, as though they were awfully bored by the sight of the empty valley below.

Tom squinted at Dr. T. J. Eckleburg. "Terrible place, isn't it."

It was, but he seemed unfazed by the part his clan had played in that. Buchanan Group had abandoned its smart town venture to the highest bidders, hadn't cared whether the apartments turned into homes or glorified warehouses, and more or less had left it to rot.

"A shame so much space's gone to waste," I said.

Tom looked at me sharply. "Come," he muttered. "We're nearly there."

I was surprised there wasn't even a pedestrian in sight. I had expected it would be optimal grounds for a large encampment. When I voiced this, Tom explained there were many attempts at this in the past. "But thankfully, they have androids that walk around and patrol the place. To keep those unseemly sorts out," he said.

"Patrol?"

"You know, to deter people—or subdue them, if they resist," he replied, as if this were a perk built into the neighborhood, same as the nav-holos. "People know better now than to take their chances." *Subdue.* The thought rather sickened me, and I was afraid to ask for the details.

We spotted one of these androids marching past us as we continued along. It was an older model—alabaster white, faceless, and bare, like an old-fashioned department store mannequin. I waited for it to give us some trouble, for we were "nonresidents" too, but the android barely glanced our way.

"We look put-together, you and I," explained Tom. "But if you try to sleep on the streets, it'll drag you off."

Then it was clear why we were the only things moving and breathing out here—that was, until we rounded a corner and I saw up ahead that the ground floor of one of the apartment buildings was in fact a shop. The sign flickering in front of the open door read *Repairs. GEORGE B. WILSON. Mods Bought and Sold.*

Beside the sign was another graffitied nav-holo display, this one hacked more intricately than the others. Instead of standing upright, the holo-woman lay flat on her back, dressed in tattered shorts and a see-through mesh top. She balanced a cigarette between her thin fingers, and her hair hung about her face like greasy sea moss.

When she noticed my staring, she snapped her head up. *"Ha!"* The echoey greeting was half scream, half cough. *"Tha fu'kyou looking at!"*

The grating noises that had followed us through the vacant streets hit us at full force as we entered the shop. I saw the fans first. Perhaps a hundred of them dangled from the ceiling, and another dozen massive ones were plugged around the perimeter, blasting cool air toward the shelves of GPUs.

But my attention snagged, most of all, on the signs of life nestled in the slivers of what little empty space remained between the GPU racks. A plastic foldout table, with two chipped coffee mugs. A small, shabby couch. A vintage television that sat meekly on the floor, set to a dead channel.

We walked through the humming GPUs and spotted a steel body-length table beneath a row of sizzling light bulbs. Piles of secondhand mods—all of varying legality—stretched high as the ceiling, along with arm-blade extensions in different lengths and sizes, and hundreds of jars filled with cold eyeballs that I realized were ocular-mods, stored away like jam.

The last remarkable detail was a sallow, thin-haired man tucked in the far corner, reclining at an obtuse angle on a worn leather office chair. A metal-legged rig crowned his head with two rusted lenses that hung down over his eyes. The whole contraption resembled a robotic spider, which after a moment, I recognized as a cheap Happy Sleep headset.

The man's breaths moved at an unstable tempo.

"Bet he's been under all night," muttered Tom, then, to my deep horror, he tore the headset free without so much as a warning.

I cringed. "You can't just—pull him out like that. It'll hurt—"

"Ah, this one's a junkie. He'll be fine."

The man shot upright. A long, desperate gasp escaped his throat. For a second, he thrashed viciously in the chair as if he were drowning.

"Wilson." Tom smacked the man's back. "How's business?"

Wilson tensed, stumbled to his feet, then glanced around in a daze, like a cat dragged from a nice spot of sun. "Can't ... complain," he groaned.

He was a stocky and skittish man, with one pale blue eye and the other hidden behind a patch of dark cloth. Both his arms and legs were sheathed haphazardly in grubby metal plates.

"When're you going to sell me that oc-mod?" he asked Tom.

"Soon. I got my doc working on it now."

"Works pretty slow, don't he?" Wilson snatched a jar off one of the shelves, emptying the oc-mods onto the steel table. He rounded them up clumsily in his arms before they could roll away. "I'm—I'm looking for new parts. Customers want the new stuff, you see, and I'm short on stock," he said, adjusting his sweat-stained eye patch.

"My man works just fine." Tom folded his sunglasses away. "But if you feel that way about it, maybe I'd better find a different buyer."

Wilson trembled. "I just meant—"

Footsteps rushed urgently from the stairwell, and the door flew open to reveal a tall, full-figured woman dressed in a silver gown. Her waist-length red hair flamed against the dim light behind her. When she tipped her chin at a certain sharp angle, I thought her eyes looked so dark, they could have been two black gemstones.

But then she blinked, stepped closer, and they were instead an odd shade of glow-in-the-dark green, and I wondered if I'd imagined it.

Her gown seemed cartoonishly formal in the shop and bounced harsh light in every direction as she sashayed toward us—or rather, toward Tom, as she made no indication that she'd noticed anyone or anything else. As I'd soon learn, this was Mrs. Myrtle Wilson.

"Get some chairs, why don't you, so somebody can sit down," she said in a soft rasp, as if she had a cold and couldn't be convinced to clear her throat.

"Oh, sure." Her husband floundered and disappeared into a storage closet.

"I want to see you," murmured Tom in her ear. "Get on the next train."

Color ascended into Mrs. Wilson's powdery, wan face. I coughed loudly, so as to be heard over the gargling GPUs, and feigned checking the messages on my comm.

Tom pinned me with a hard stare. "Myrtle'll be hurt if you don't join, Nick. Won't you, Myrtle?"

"Deeply." Mrs. Wilson wet her lips. "I'll call my sister, Catherine, to join us!"

By the time Wilson emerged with two stools tucked beneath each arm, Tom and I were already out the door. We rounded the corner past the rumpled AI woman who once again spared no hurled insult. Tom reaffixed his sunglasses as Dr. T. J. Eckleburg's eyes passed over us, the sunshine blazing behind his enormous pupils.

Tom called for a hover-taxi, and as we soared up and toward the city, I watched the valley shrink beneath us like a lifeless body, with wires for veins and the whir of ten thousand fans holding it together.

◇—◇—◇

Manhattan. The dense tinsel of the New East.

There was the noise and the stench, and the ad-drones galloping above, the holograms more detailed and opaque than any I'd seen before. They made a colorful ceiling of advertisements that shone brighter than the afternoon sun. There were the androids, too, demanding patronage in front of stores and fuming food stalls, police hover-cruisers floating above us like beasts of prey, and tired beggars nestled into the shadows, ducking out of sight with every passing cruiser.

It was clamorous, oppressively hot, and I felt as exhausted as I was impressed by the tumult of the perpetual people and their perpetual activities.

From the valley, Tom and I were dropped off somewhere in Queens and then forced to take the train farther in to meet Mrs. Wilson. Hover-traffic was limited during rush hour, and so when we joined her, Tom had to hail a ground taxi to take us to yet another destination. It was all so convoluted until it occurred to me that he was determined not to be seen with Mrs. Wilson. He didn't state this outright, but I understood it to be true, given his insistence on our separate arrivals. Even now, Tom was several feet away from us, poised at the street curb, watching the oncoming traffic with a scowl.

I stood with Mrs. Wilson for several agonizing minutes. In the short hour since I'd last seen her, she had swapped her silver dress for a lime jumpsuit—a strapless, form-fitting thing made of gleaming rubber that cut a V-shaped path from her bosom and stopped above her navel. Paired with her cherry hair, I rather thought she could have been a mascot for some candy ad.

She hid herself away from the harsh sun with a yellow parasol, twirling it lazily over her shoulder. "Are you a nervous fellow, Mr. Carraway? My sister, Catherine, is said to be very beautiful by people who ought to know."

I wasn't nervous about any sister, beautiful or otherwise, but as Tom had made clear, my opinion on this didn't matter much. My eyes went to her hair again.

"Oh, Tom adores the red." She stroked her curls. "What about you? You strike me as secretly adventurous. Ah! Blondes, I bet?"

Not a moment after the words left her mouth, the wash of red leaked out of her hair—root to tip—and her curls fell straight into a platinum-blond sheet. I stared. She smiled at my shock. Earlier at the garage, when I'd thought her eyes had swirled from black to green, I'd convinced myself I'd imagined it. I was wrong.

What Mrs. Wilson had was a very curious mod, one that cycled instantaneously through her features. Beauty-changing mods weren't unheard of, but the seamlessness, intricacy, and speed of hers verged on superhuman.

"How delightful," I offered.

"Tell the bumbling husband that. He designed the damn thing," she muttered from under the scalloped shadow of her parasol. "Fancied himself a *visionary* once upon a time—and where did all that vision take him? Why, nowhere! Spends all his useless nights double-stimmed in low-grade Sleeps."

She flicked her eyes up at me, and I watched her make the wordless assumption that perhaps I didn't know what double-stimulation was. "See, what I mean, Mr. Carraway, is that he wastes all his next-to-nothing money on whatever putrid liquor he can scrounge up, gets himself utterly shit-faced, then dives ass-first into one of those acid-trip Happy Sleeps, so he can be *doubly* shit-faced. He once told me

38

if he could get this mod to scale, we'd fly out of that despicable place in no time. Guess when that was? Years ago!" She laughed shrilly, and the red returned to her hair. She tousled her rejuvenated curls. "Well, anyway, if blond wasn't doing it for you, you must like"—her lips twitched—"short hair?"

From the curb, Tom glanced back at us, as though sensing something was amiss. Mrs. Wilson sighed. "Well, I'd show you that trick, too, but . . ." Her voice plummeted to a whisper I could hardly hear over the station bustle. "Short hair is *off-limits*, I'm afraid."

She raised a finger to her pink lips, and it would be a few more hours before I'd learn she hadn't shared this with me as a joke, but as a solemn vow.

One she would soon break.

Four

THE CULMINATION OF THAT AFTERNOON led us to Morningside Heights, where Tom kept a penthouse for Myrtle. It was encased in black marble, from living room to kitchen, and was bursting with incongruous furniture. In the center of the room stood a cluster of old divans, and by the kitchen island, three curved transparent structures that perhaps were bar stools. A heart-shaped love seat, artfully stained in spots, was also positioned alarmingly close to a cavernous fireplace, which sprang to life as soon as the elevator slid shut behind us.

The walls were adorned with a mixture of floral-themed oil paintings, hung without frames and spaced much too closely together so that if you were drunk enough, it could have appeared as though the paintings formed one singular, catastrophic garden. Atop the length of the fireplace, a long holo-bar flickered in a row of vibrant photos, the subjects of which were eclectically dressed women against the harsh lights of the city. It took me about a minute to notice these women were, in fact, the same person—Myrtle—photographed in various outfits and hairstyles.

Tom marched in the direction of the drink cart. Myrtle pranced into the living room as a small bot hovered from around the corner to stop at her side. She drummed her fingers across its screen, and the apartment rearranged itself. From above, an array of colored lights reflected across the marble floors like fish scales, and the tall glass windows lightened to reveal a broad view of the Hudson and the West Harlem skyline.

Just as Myrtle began surfing through up-tempo music, the elevator doors dinged open again, and three more bodies poured into the apartment. Myrtle squealed, taking the hand of a lanky pink-haired woman I could only assume was the supposedly beautiful sister, Catherine. It wasn't that they looked alike, but they shared a distinctly earsplitting laugh, and greeted one another in rapid, tumbling shouts.

Catherine was followed closely by a couple called Lucille and Chester Matsuki, who I'd later learn were the downstairs neighbors. Mrs. Matsuki was a mousy woman with dark blond hair that fell to her waist like rope. She wore a blue chiffon dress, the same color as her husband's abundant bio-ink that curled in thin tendrils up his exposed arms and neck. The tattoos—I observed through his white shirt—decorated his entire chest and back, and glowed with a faint firefly dimness. Quite politely, he shook hands with Tom on his way in. Amidst all the excitement, I stood near the elevator, feeling rather displaced.

"Something wrong, Nick?" asked Tom, replenished by his drink.

Many things, I wanted to say. His shamelessness, most of all.

I contemplated storming off from this disconcerting scene, but then he leaned in close, our foreheads nearly touching. "I promised I'd show you a grand time in the city, and that's what I'm going to do. Now, why don't you try *enjoying* yourself?" His grip whitened around his whiskey glass, and I decided I didn't want to poke those rumors about his anger, much less cause Daisy any trouble. Slowly, I followed him into the living room.

Catherine had stretched herself out on the love seat, her head perched in the lap of Mrs. Matsuki. The women passed a stim-stick between themselves, blowing out rings of chalky blue smoke that were swallowed up again as they shared a kiss.

"You won't hurt anyone's feelings if Catherine's not your type," said Tom.

I bristled. "Catherine is fine."

Tom seemed to detect this lie, along with my prickling discomfort, and he interpreted it another way, for his jaw snapped shut as though he'd been startled into an epiphany.

His gaze darted off to the far side of the living room. "Chester!" He waved at Mr. Matsuki, who was occupied at the drink cart, pouring himself a tall glass of something bubbly and green. He strutted over to us calmly.

"Chester, this is Nick—ah, *Carraway*," said Tom. "He's family of mine."

I resented this introduction but shook Matsuki's hand when he extended it. His fingers were cold from his glass.

Tom snaked a heavy arm around Matsuki's shoulders. He was about half Tom's size in muscle mass, but just as tall. "Take good care of him, won't you?" said Tom. "Show him the Sleeps. Maybe give him something spec. That'll be a nice unwinding." Then Myrtle floated toward us and spirited Tom away.

Matsuki watched me over a sip of his bubbling drink. "Have you ever been double-stimmed, Mr. Carraway?"

"Yes," I said.

He smiled like he didn't quite believe me.

◇——◇——◇

Matsuki brought me farther into the living room, placed one of his long-fingered hands on my back, and waved at two luxury Happy Sleep terminals pressed up against the windows. "You can have first pick," he said.

The terminals appeared commercial grade, similar to the ones in a professional lounge. Cube-shaped and wrapped in frosted glass, each terminal stood about waist high, with a blinking holo-screen above it, waiting to be connected. Hooked onto the side of the terminals was a tray filled with those spidery headsets, lighter and slimmer than the outdated one George Wilson had. True to Matsuki's word, no one had taken one yet.

At the drink cart, he asked what I liked, and I told him, "Whatever you're having," which seemed to please him. He filled another tall glass of his concoction, and I sipped it cautiously. It went down like fire.

Within minutes, the apartment grew hot. I stepped out of my suit jacket and ripped off my tie. Matsuki said, "You look rather nice without all that armor."

"Chester has an eye for these sorts of things," his wife added glee-fully. "Just look at his Myrtle series."

42

She waved her hand in the direction of the holo-bar, where the string of different Myrtles grinned back at us. "You're a photographer?" I asked Matsuki.

He nodded once—a gallant dip of his chin, as if he were on the verge of a bow. "And you?"

"Contractor."

"How suitable."

I was getting loose-tongued now. "How would you know what suits me?"

"There's an air about you corpos." He didn't elaborate. "What sort of contracting?"

"Netdiving."

"Oh my," he said in an impressed tone. "Knew a fellow like that once. Left him paralyzed first day on the job."

That wasn't uncommon, but it didn't seem like good party conversation to say as much. I'd known far too many aspirants who assumed the rush and high of connecting the conscience to cyberspace was as fun as these drunken Happy Sleeps. Most learned the hard way that a Happy Sleep was an inflatable pool and true cyberspace was the deep sea—a delicate fabric of virtual environments, woven layers upon layers of data, trillions of motes of human dust. Braving those waters unprepared meant risking more than paralysis.

"It isn't for everyone," I said.

"You must have mods, then. To hook your body onto those rigs."

"I do."

"Don't see them on you." He smiled. "Where are they hiding?"

I hadn't lost myself far enough to entertain that question. His charm was forgettably amusing, skin deep and glimmering only in proportion to my conscious effort at noticing it. I smiled back, distantly, and his eyes lit up with a sort of resolve.

At this point, Mrs. Matsuki and Catherine had climbed atop the round coffee table, dancing in a thick cloud of their own stim-stick smoke. Later, once I was properly dizzy, Matsuki took me by the arm and guided me back to the Happy Sleep terminals.

Despite his doubtfulness, I really had been double-stimmed before. Just once in my second year at Yale, on a low-grade Sleep that left me frail for about a week after. I knew it was the cheapness of the tech that had overshot my nerves back then. The good-quality simulations weren't supposed to half fry you into the next life.

"This one has the classic catalog." He scrolled through the first set. Tom liked the solo-action ones, Matsuki explained. Sports, parkour, skydiving, and the like. Myrtle apparently was fond of anything that took place on a beach. "All the greats are here." Then almost wistfully, "Well, *almost* all of them."

He was referring to Daisy. All I knew of her career was the way people spoke of it. Happy Sleeps, prior to her stardom, were always loud, arousing, adrenaline-inducing experiences. But when Daisy had broken onto the scene, she'd embodied the very opposite. Quiet, stillness, vulnerability—a space for people not to run away from the things that plagued them, but to feel them all without consequence.

There was even a joke, at the peak of her popularity, that the fastest way to get a heartless criminal to confess their crimes was to hook them up to a Daisy Fay session, and they'd emerge an hour later swimming in their grief.

Matsuki leaned against the second terminal. "*These* ones—these are the beauties. The specs."

"Specs?" I'd thought Tom had been exaggerating. Spec sessions were private Happy Sleep recordings, custom-made, and could cost upward of millions. "Who ordered them?"

"Tom commissions them at Myrtle's request," replied Matsuki.

"How often?"

"At least once or twice a month, I'd say."

So Tom tossed away little fortunes on a regular array of fantasies for his mistress. The frivolity didn't surprise me, but through the last dregs of my sobriety, I remembered the depressing cloud that had formed over Daisy on the veranda. It was the first time that I felt a bit glad to be helping her. Perhaps the potential acquisition was in fact more personal to her than she'd let on.

"Want one for yourself?" Matsuki asked. "Maybe Tom can work something out for you. Though not many studios produce them."

44

"Like Daisy Fay's!" Mrs. Matsuki sighed from the love seat. At what point she'd teleported from her coffee-table stage, I didn't know. "Imagine what *that* would be like!"

"Daisy Fay's never done a spec in all her career, and she won't be coming out of retirement for *you*, darling," said Matsuki.

"But isn't that precisely what *makes* her Daisy Fay?" exclaimed Mrs. Matsuki. "She's a gem, isn't she?"

The question, for some reason, was addressed to me. "A gem?" I said.

"Yes! Like—like—a gorgeous crown in a museum that's never been worn ...," replied Mrs. Matsuki, sinking ever deeper into the heart-shaped cushions.

I blinked, and now Catherine had joined us too. "Can't be *that* much of a gem, can she?" she drawled. "Or else a proper man like Tom wouldn't get bored of—"

"*Who's* a gem?" Myrtle chirped, emerging from the bedroom down the hall with Tom. Her eyes swept across us disapprovingly.

Mr. Matsuki replied, "You, of course," which only made her scowl. Tom dragged her away to fix a drink.

After more forgettable conversation, I was wrangled onto the love seat, my back pressed uncomfortably against the dip of the heart. Catherine put a cigarette in her mouth, placed herself upon my knee, and coiled one of her arms tight around my neck. A metallic tang lifted out of her perfume. "Do you live down on the Eggs too?" she asked me.

"West Egg."

"Really? I hear a corpo or someone built a big tower there. Something exciting's happening soon. That's what all my friends are saying." She took out a lighter from her breast, holding the flame to her cigarette. "I've got fashionable friends."

I told her my apartment was right across from that tower. "Do you know what kind of corpo?"

"No one knows," she murmured in my ear, then nodded at Myrtle and Tom, who were arguing in the kitchen. Myrtle was slicing limes for a cocktail, her grip unsteady around the knife. "Neither of them can stand the person they're married to. Can't *stand* them." Her eyes were the same sour color as her hair. "It's really his wife who's keeping them apart. She'd scrubbed herself dry right at the end of her career, and Tom's too much of a gentleman to put her on the street. Got no money left—can you believe it?"

I was shocked anyone could believe that. Even without the royalties from her Happy Sleeps, Daisy's stocks in her family's biotech company had to be worth double whatever Tom had to his name.

The afternoon continued, I think. Tom and Myrtle were in a cycle of vanishing and reappearing, and each time, Myrtle emerged sporting a new look. Then the room waned into a hazy-edged vignette, shrinking ever smaller. Soon Matsuki was standing over me, cradling one of the spiders. "Have you made your pick, Mr. Carraway? What would you like?" he asked, and I murmured again, "Whatever you're having," and he was pleased by this too.

◇——◇——◇

Then—

A flash.

The marble rippled beneath our feet. We were standing in a meadow, a plain of verdant grass that stretched on toward an invisible horizon. A sky wrapped over us, bluer than blue. Then I blinked, and plush evergreens sprouted into view, followed by large pastel flowers, as if we'd stepped into one of Myrtle's kitschy oil paintings. Beside me—a light, carbonated voice. Chester's. We stared at one another and broke into fizzy laughter.

For a minute or two, I struggled to stay upright. My mind had split in half, and my body was dissenting. I think I must have moved to stand atop the love seat; my socked toes curled into the cushions. But I couldn't actually see the love seat—only the meadow, the enormous sky, and the flowers licking our ankles, their petals flat and wide like the tops of colorful mushrooms.

Chester refilled my drink. We toasted, drank, sighed, tumbled deeper into the meadow, where the figure of a famous Happy Sleep starlet faded into view, beckoning us. Her dress was a billow of white gauze, of smoke, moving through her and around her. She touched my cheek,

46

slid her lips from the corner of my mouth, up my jaw, and spoke words I couldn't hear, for half my brain was still awake in the apartment. Then she held out a pipe, which I accepted, and when I drew a long breath from it, the flowers at our feet grew towering stems that shot up into the candied sky, as high as the trees. We laughed again and weighed nothing.

So this is a spec, I thought. *A dream no one else has.*

We were in an ocean, swimming over the rest of the sorry world, made of money—Tom's money. I thought of Catherine and her metallic perfume. I inhaled, stuck my tongue out. I tasted it now too. Chester's hand circled my wrist, and the clouds were big enough to eat.

An eternity passed. We saw Catherine and Lucille, Myrtle and Tom, at the very edge of the meadow. Against the sky, Lucille was almost invisible in her blue dress, and Catherine threw her arms around her with a bright shriek.

Then—

"Daisy, Daisy, Daisy!"

Myrtle, from across the meadow. From across the room.

"You've no *right*—"

Tom shimmered before her, his vast body peeking through the canopy of oversized flowers. Myrtle was blond again, her hair pulled tight into a ponytail, long and stiff as a whip.

"I'll say her name whenever I want to!" exclaimed Myrtle. "Daisy, Daisy, Daisy—"

"No," Tom warned in a low voice. It rolled like thunder through the Sleep. "You won't."

Myrtle's expression darkened. "Won't I?" she murmured sweetly. Then she spun in a pretty pirouette, and when she smiled, something terrifying rose out of her.

It had clearer eyes, thinner lips, a rounder chin—and a sleek, warm, cinnamon-colored bob.

Short hair is off-limits, she'd said.

I froze in horror.

"Come now. Don't you know everyone adores me?" sang Myrtle, in an utterly acute replication of Daisy's lilting speech. I looked at Tom, who might have stopped breathing. "When we married, you know what they all said." Myrtle curled her hand over his still chest. "They didn't say *I* married Tom Buchanan, did they? No—they said *you* married Daisy Fay—"

Then—

Two decisive frames. A raised arm, a stream of blood.

The flowers shrunk back to their real pitiful size, and the meadow beneath us, the blue sky above, and the tall, tall evergreens fell apart like sand. We were in an ugly apartment again, suspended high over New York, back within ourselves, with late evening through the window and the muffled vigor of Harlem nightlife beyond. Everything was dull and flat and gray feeling. Resurfacing out of a Sleep, I realized, was a little bit like dying.

Tom had broken Myrtle's nose.

In the smoldering room, Catherine let out a shrill cry. Myrtle wailed, her Daisy-like bob morphing back into loose red curls.

She fell to her knees. Mrs. Matsuki fell with her. I watched Myrtle's mod glitch across her bloodied face as she tried, presumably, to right her nose. In the end, she only twisted it at a much more awful angle, to which Mrs. Matsuki stroked her hair in feeble consolation. Catherine reached over and yanked her sister back by the wrist, as far away as possible from Tom, who shivered in the corner of the room, looking at no one.

It was Matsuki who had broken the session for us, pulled the headset off, and steered me toward the elevator to escape the ruins.

He invited me to lunch.

"Where?" I asked.

"Anywhere."

I was still weak under the weight of the session. My nerves were tender; this time in a nice way. I couldn't feel my own feet. I thought I could still smell the flowers from the meadow.

He opened his mouth to say something more, and I saw that his tongue was stained green from his drink, which I realized meant my own tongue was probably green too. This made me laugh, and my laugh made me stumble. Matsuki steadied me. I leaned my heavy head against the wall of the elevator. His tongue darted across his lower lip. Our mouths would taste the same, I remember thinking. But I couldn't know for sure, could I? I wanted to know. Perhaps Matsuki had the same thought, for he moved first.

Then—

"What do you like?" he asked me for the third time.

"Whatever you—"

He stopped me. "What do you *like*, Nick?" The words were a whisper against my neck. He was underneath me, his cold hand scaling my thigh. "Isn't there anything you like?"

I shut my eyes. What I liked was simple. And didn't simplicity complicate everything? If only it were something I could hold in my hand—appearance or wealth, whether I was under someone or over them. No, simpler. Even simpler than kindness. Just a short string of meaningful attention, arranged without complexity, like notes in a nursery rhyme. . . . *What do you like?* One hand on my back. One smile in an airless room.

What I liked, maybe, was even being asked the question.

Then—

His bedroom cartwheeled around us. We drifted in and out of sleep, my leg over his, then his over mine. Hours passed, and our tongues weren't green anymore. He crawled over me to reach the stim-stick on his nightstand. I couldn't quite see his face in the dark, only the outline of his lean body and the blue gleam of his bio-ink. We took shots of something more bitter than the burning sugar of the night, and I watched the shape of the smoke curl out of his lips, as the earlier topic of lunch faded into a past life.

Then—

I was in West Egg, drunk and alone, tumbling out of the four o'clock train. The topmost windows of that grand tower were lit, and I carried myself toward it until, just outside its glass entrance, I saw an apparition before the doors, clad in white.

I tripped over my feet.

"Careful there."

The voice came from behind, and a pair of solid hands pulled me up. I raised my head. Through my dizzied vision, the fog-covered moon tripled in the sky.

I blinked, and a blurry, ethereal shape came into view.

"Allow me." The firm voice was attached to a firm body that helped me onto the sidewalk by the elbow. In the faint glow that washed onto the street from my building's lobby, I thanked the man.

"Good night—or—" I stuttered. "Morning?"

A laugh. Clear and pleasant. The cool mist of a waterfall, slicing through the heat. "I suppose it's both. It's whatever you'd like it to be."

He paused, as if it were really my choice to make, and not his or even the universe's.

I never trusted daybreak. The moon kept secrets, and the sun confessed them. So I decided it had to be night, and the stranger smiled.

"Very well. Good night, Mr. Carraway."

I staggered backward through the revolving doors.

Then—

His face almost sharpened, before unraveling again beneath the liquor.

Five

G EN WEALTH OWNED A MANHATTAN tower called the
Probity. The data science team, to which I'd been assigned,
comprised fifty contractors, tasked with sorting and
examining the multitude of databases that fed the company's predictive
genetic algorithm.

One enthusiastic AI oversaw the department, and at the end of the
first day's tour, I was informed that I had my own corner office.

"A *what*?" I asked.

"A private office," said the AI.

The office came equipped with a state-of-the-art diving rig,
set up in a dark, enclosed den that maintained a constant wintry
chill of thirty-two degrees Fahrenheit. This was standard—neural
strain made the body temperature soar in cyberspace, and the cold
helped impair sensory input, which made the dive smoother—
but the den also included a cushioned harness and a set of clean
compression suits. Even these were unlike any I'd worn before, the
fabric more breathable than skin, with bio-monitor sensors weaved
into it so that my vitals appeared on the holo-screen as soon as
I zipped it up.

I had been diving for many years, could never call it a comfortable
experience, and didn't believe there was such a thing as a "luxury" rig
until now. They had taken less care of us in the military.

At first, the rig looked incomplete, for I couldn't locate a single
interfacing cable or any hypo shots—the bare minimum components.
Without any body temperature regulation, I'd overheat within minutes,
and the dive would be impossible if there was nothing to connect to

my mods. I realized, however, once I stepped onto the marked metal ring in the center of the den, that everything was automated.

The rig moved on its own. The harness straps snaked around my waist and over my arms, lifting me one foot from the ground. Then a rope of cable slid out from a panel in the ceiling and clicked smoothly into the back of my neck. Two thinner cables came down a second later, attached with syringes—a premeasured hypo shot to counteract the heat spike and even a sedative to soothe the nerve-burn on the way in.

For the first time, I didn't feel a thing. The dive was as swift as blinking and just as painless. Within seconds, the den peeled away in papery strips, and I was unbodied, floating through the blank, airless void of cyberspace.

I expected that this contract wouldn't be as intense as security or counterintel, where intercepting breaches and reinforcing VINEs required much deeper submersion. Someone straight out of training could have just as easily sifted through these user records and psychographic databases, and I found myself working through tasks rather quickly.

In my boredom, I played nice with the other contractors and asked casually, to no effect, if anyone had ever seen Gen Wealth's C-suite. After an uneventful week, I reported to Bunsen that the job itself was stranger than the android and the letter that had brought me here. The lack of work made me uneasy, as did the office and its spoils, and though I'd gone through the motions of inspecting every corner, I couldn't help but feel like I was being watched.

It had been weeks of similar tasks when I decided to contact our department head.

"Is the work not to your liking?" the AI asked.

To my liking. As though it were a meal served at a fine restaurant. "It's not that. I've worked through my assignments for the week already."

"Outstanding! How efficient you are, Mr. Carraway."

"Actually, nothing new has come—"

"Exceeding expectations is always rewarded!"

"I was wondering," I said quickly, "if I might thank whoever it is that provided me this office."

The AI's shadowless hologram blinked wordlessly at me for thirty long seconds, and I knew that I'd stepped far outside the bounds of its repertoire.

"You are a valued member of the Gen Wealth family!" the AI exclaimed, and then it was gone.

◇——◇——◇

The first weekend of June, around eight o'clock in the evening, a hundred hover-cars flecked the dusty West Egg skies, gathering in a holding pattern over the neighboring tower's landing pad. As soon as one car flew away, a dozen more raced to take its place.

Below, the city made a runway of the cramped streets. In less than an hour, a line formed, shepherded around the corner and down several blocks by a string of dutiful bots. By nine o'clock, the lightless tower had morphed into a chromatic beacon, a golden arm grazing the clouds and casting all of West Egg's cold vitality into honeyed steam that lingered the whole night.

The dome over the tower roof retreated before ten o'clock. From the balcony of my bedroom, I spotted a wide, overflowing terrace, cutting beams of strobed neon through the black sky and bordered by a conveyor belt of elaborate foods and bubbling cocktails that never seemed to empty. At its climax came the fireworks and the gush of music, and perhaps one or two wonderfully besotted socialites aching to be remembered for something. On the first night, it happened to be a young man, naked down to his underwear, doing handstands on the roof of a flying hover-car.

Later, I'd learn that just about every variation of person bled into this colorful crowd—important corpos with their ties loosened, athletes and actors and Happy Sleep stars, politicians campaigning and politicians hiding, beautiful girls in taut latex, and rich women turning twenty-one for the tenth time. They all glided their way through the tower's open mouth, enchanted and high off a glittery splendor I couldn't quite see from afar.

Throughout the week, the tower remained dark and shuttered, save for early Monday morning, when I noticed a flurry of bots shoveling sparkling debris into garbage trucks.

On Wednesday, I returned home from the Probity to find a Klipspringer standing in the lobby of my building. He was about my height, with that distinct silvery coating and lidless black eyes. But it was the robin's-egg blue uniform that stopped me short—identical to the one that had washed up in Manila.

I approached the android with caution. He bowed, announced he was here on behalf of his owner, and handed me another pristine envelope before departing.

With unsteady fingers, I opened the delivery. It was an invitation to that weekend's illustrious party across the street. Unlike the previous note, this one was handwritten in heavy, lavish ink.

The host would be honored, apparently, if I could spare even a moment to enjoy the festivities on the coming Sunday. It addressed me once again by name, which disturbed me, but not as much as the signature that swept grandly at the bottom of the note:

With the warmest and humblest well wishes, it professed, *Jay Gatsby.*

◇——◇——◇

"He must know."

"I'm not sure about that," said Bunsen over the comm. "Could be an employee perk. An impersonal invitation."

Jay Gatsby of Gatsby Corp, founder of Gen Wealth and the most private billionaire in the Americas. Requesting my attendance at his famous skyscraper.

The invitation was ostentatious, terribly vague, and more suspicious than before. Corpo politics was always the worst kind of game, and if there were only players and pawns, I feared I was the latter.

"I don't like what I'm walking into," I said.

"Put a face to the name, that's all. If you can't, sniff around the tower." I heard the scratch of Bunsen's chin, fingers drumming against a table. "Do what you need to, but above all, don't get caught."

"How do I know I'm not *already*?" I asked, but Bunsen had hung up.

In frustration, I crossed the street on the appointed day around ten o'clock, determined to find something that could get me out of this unwanted errand quickly.

Floating through the tower's glass doors, my feet barely touched the ground, pushed this way and that by hordes of partygoers, their numbers swelling by the minute. In the round lobby, I counted no fewer than twenty elevators shuttling guests up and down at regular intervals. I was shuffled into one haphazardly, pressed between the wall and a large woman dressed in knife-sharp sequins, before the elevator barreled us upward.

Then the tower, in all its bared brilliance, opened before us.

We emerged into light. My ears popped. An awed gasp emanated from the guests. The walls of the elevator rippled to windows, and we could see through the glass, blurry streaks of each elaborately themed floor—casinos, dining halls, ice rinks, art galleries. Any imaginable pleasure had been collected into this untouchable city in the sky.

I didn't know where we were destined to stop. It seemed no one knew and no one cared. For a stretch of two or three floors at a time, the windows dimmed back into opaque walls, keeping parts of the tower shrouded in mystery—for what I could only assume was a ruse to encourage repeat trips down different elevators.

We weren't let out until the rooftop, where the party was climbing to its peak. A long milky blue pool extended across the terrace, where bleary-eyed men dove from the top of a ten-foot diving board and the girls reclining on the side shrieked gleefully in the ensuing splash.

I'd dressed in beige flannels, tie forgone so that no one could accuse me of any stuffiness. Though as I glanced about restlessly, I wasn't sure if there was much of a dress code.

Bright-haired men and women, clad in mesh bikinis, entertained a group of uniformed military folks near a fire pit. I saw the mayor, too, hugging the sides of the conveyor-belt bar, flushed and swaying, in raucous conversation with three of her most difficult councilors. Not far off, a woman I recognized as the CEO of the East's largest synth-meat operation whispered in the ear of an emerging Happy Sleep starlet. Amidst all the glorious light and free-flowing drinks, there were handshakes and business transactions, the flash of money beneath wrists, exchanged from one comm to the next.

I began my inquiries about the host and was met consistently with incredulous laughter or yet another obscene rumor. It became quite evident that Jay Gatsby's status as owner of the tower was uncommon knowledge, and after a while of meandering, I hesitated at the base of the steps that led back up to the elevators, reappraising the throbbing party.

I'd already noticed on the way up that the elevators were programmed not to stop at every level. If the tower was a residence, then a personal suite had to be tucked somewhere on at least one of the private floors.

And where there were locks, there were secrets.

The Klipspringers, however, were an unfortunate obstacle. I counted forty on the rooftop alone, which, combined with the serving-bots flying between tables, seemed excessive. I had to assume the androids' function wasn't reserved to carrying around trays of aperitifs. More likely, they doubled as surveillance too.

As I stood there, balancing the risks, a high voice cried out over the party, "Let *go*, you—hey! Suit!"

The derisive nickname could have been directed at any number of "suits" in this crowd, but I turned out of habit to see an unexpected sight—the strange young woman with the large oc-mods and her equally peculiar trio of friends.

I recognized them as the group who'd been milling around the tower doors last month, all four of them dressed head to toe in black leather jumpsuits as two Klipspringers attempted to shovel them into the elevators.

"Uh—we're with *him*." The woman shook her arm out of the android's grasp, waving wildly at me as her companions froze in terror.

I recalled the scheme they'd been yelling about on the street that first afternoon I arrived in West Egg. It appeared their infiltration had gone awry. That was a good enough reason to feign ignorance and move on—before it occurred to me that I'd just stumbled upon exactly the smoke screen I needed.

"What seems to be the issue?" I asked the Klipspringer.

"Nothing at all, sir. These scavengers were caught trying to take apart one of our serving-bots. They'll be escorted to the nearest precinct. Please enjoy your night."

There was a girl, shorter and rounder than the owlish woman. The other two might have been brothers, their hair dyed in two varying shades of raven blue. The woman's oc-mods were the largest and most elaborate, but the boys' eyes, I saw, were just as colorfully modded. Up close, I thought their brash mischief smelled like adolescence.

"I'm sorry," I said. "I do happen to know them. They won't be any trouble."

The woman grinned. Her companions sighed in relief.

"Sir?" said the Klipspringer.

I reached into my jacket and extracted the physical invitation. It had the intended effect. Both Klipspringers bowed in unison and left.

The woman gawked, stealing the paper from my hand. "This a holo? Shit, it's not. What do you know about the host?"

"Not a thing." I snatched the invitation back. The four of them, dressed in those matching getups, seemed a sorry attempt at whatever hardened criminal band they were pantomiming. "I see your big heist didn't go as planned."

"How'd you—"

"You weren't exactly quiet about it before."

The yellow light in the woman's oc-mods twitched in irritation. She swept an arm out at her companions. "Pigeon." She pointed to the other girl. Then, nodding at the boys, "Big one's Penguin. Skinny one's Parrot."

"And you are?" I asked.

She smirked, yanked me forward by the arm, and I realized belatedly that she had pressed our comms together, exchanging contacts.

"Let's see. . . . Mr. Nicholas Carr-a-way," she recited. "What kind of name is that?"

I looked down at my own wrist. The screen simply read, "Owl Eyes."

"Senior netdiver." She pursed her lips. "Gen Wealth? Gross."

"Gross," the other birds agreed in unison.

"I told you I don't know anything about the host or the tower," I said. "What I do know is that you could hardly make it through the door without being caught."

I was beginning to understand their dynamics. Owl Eyes had the air of a dictator. Penguin and Parrot swapped hesitant glances.

"Maybe—" Pigeon squeaked.

"Maybe nothing! We've made it this far, haven't we?" said Owl Eyes. "But—"

"You're not a diver, Pigeon. You're here for morale, and you're not really morale-ing." Owl Eyes sneered. "Penguin. Parrot. You want to be cowards, too, or what?"

The boys did not want to be cowards.

"Good. Well, Mr. Nicholas Carraway, this place is bigger from the inside. Could use an extra man. Here, floor plan. Bought it off an intel smuggler around town." She tapped our wrists together, and a screen flared up in front of me. It wasn't awfully detailed, but it marked all one hundred levels and the routes of the elevators. She circled the center. "See in the middle? None of the elevators stops at them. So what's hidden there? Best-case scenario, some rich bootlegger owns this place and keeps a stockpile of body-mods. We nab 'em. Flip 'em to the mod-docs around town. Worst case—well, we'll find something else. Crowd like this, there has to be something."

I had several other ideas for a worst-case scenario, which, on the mildest end, involved these birds getting tossed into a jail cell anyway. But if they were flaunting their illegal mods so brazenly, then that foolishness was theirs to shoulder.

I did have a use for their floor plan and even more so, their unrestrained passion, which I figured could keep the security well occupied. As it was, the androids were already wary of them.

"You don't know how to hack the elevators," I guessed. "That's why you need me."

Owl Eyes babbled through a denial before settling on an assurance that really, she was doing *me* a favor by letting me in on a share of whatever riches she was sure they'd find.

I waved the screen closer. "I came here to figure out why this invitation was sent to me. I don't care for your robbery, but if you set off every alarm in this place, you won't make my search easier. I'll handle the private floors while you scour the rest of the tower. Transfer me this—"

A squawk of protest erupted among the birds. Owl Eyes insisted on joining me.

"You'll slow me down," I replied. "Unless you can explain exactly how to override the locks without slashing through the tower's whole VINE."

As expected, no one spoke.

"That's settled, then. I'll crack the elevator, leave it open for you." I glanced behind us. The dance floor had packed tight in a vibrating, drunken mass. "The only thing I'm after is information. Anything else is yours."

"But—"

"Either I do the breach myself, or I hand you off to a Klipspringer right now."

The birds paled at the thought.

"Christ, you negotiate like a corpo." Owl Eyes shook her head. "Fine. But we're keeping you on comms so you don't scurry away. Now, let's see whatcha got." She stepped behind me, and with a leap, pulled back the collar of my shirt. "What—these look military as hell. Where'd you steal 'em from?"

"Nowhere. I was a combat diver."

The boys let out a low whistle. "Soldier to corpo. Figures," said Penguin.

"Now, now," said Owl Eyes. "Don't judge the fellow. He's valiantly lent his services to us for free. Wrists out."

She extracted a thin wire from the nape of her neck, pressing the heated tip against each of our comm-sensors. The light in our wrists pulsed, melting from green to red. A series of screens sprang up before us. Owl Eyes' fingers danced across them, dragging them together until their voices crescendoed slowly in my ears—indiscernible at first, before forming into solid words.

PIGEON: *How odd. . . . Is this what cyberspace is like?*

PENGUIN: *This, times a thousand.*

The wire retreated into Owl Eyes' neck. She clapped her hands together, dispersing her crew, and they each flitted away into separate elevators.

PIGEON: *I'm not sure I like this sensation. It's like—it's like I can taste everyone's moods. Someone's tastes like a sealed jar of farts.*

PENGUIN: *Parrot's for sure.*

PARROT: *You—*

OWL EYES: *Shut it. Gonna get a damn migraine.*

I made my way unsteadily down the neon-lit steps. Another half-naked drunkard dove into the pool, splashing water onto my shoes. Bunsen's warning came to me again, out of the screeching cheers and thunderclaps of music.

Don't get caught.

The thought reverberated with so much force, I couldn't catch it before it slipped through the slats in my mind. The birds all heard it, and I felt Owl Eyes' briny laugh crest over me.

OWL EYES: *Nerves? No use for them now.*

Six

WHILE THE BIRDS DREW UP their haphazard plans, I settled on a stool by the conveyor-belt bar, far from the dense pack of bodies on the dance floor, and examined the tower's diagram. The locked section was concentrated near the middle, spanning approximately ten levels between floors forty and fifty. I decided I'd get as close to either side as I could.

PENGUIN: *Everything from top to eighty is a write-off.*

PIGEON: *Lobby to ten's got nothing useful either. Though floor five is hot yoga if anyone cares.*

PARROT: *Hot yoga!*

OWL EYES: *No dumbfuckery. If you can't steal it or hack it, leave it.*

PENGUIN: *I'm headed to the casinos. East Egg prey.*

I stood up to exit the rooftop, but a familiar voice floated from down the bar.

It was Jordan Baker, holding the arm of a colossal male athlete. They spoke in careless pleasantry with a woman who looked to be a journalist. A camera-bot hovered at her side and flashed obnoxiously, photographing them mid-laughter.

Shit.

OWL EYES: *What is it?*

"Mr. Carraway. I thought you might be here," said Miss Baker, noticing me as her companion left with the journalist.

"Ah—yes, hello ..."

She reached for my hand. "I remembered you lived—"

Not five seconds later, a pair of women in matching baby-pink tulle appeared at our side.

"Jordan!" said the shorter one. "Sorry you didn't win."

"I'm not," replied Miss Baker. "It'll make for an interesting season. I haven't had one of those since I was fourteen."

I'd learned more about Jordan Baker's career since the Buchanans' dinner. She'd gone professional at age twelve, and until recently, had never placed less than bronze every year. Yesterday, she'd lost her third game of the season in a row.

"Do you come to these parties often?" Miss Baker asked both women, not letting go of my hand.

"I like to come," said the tall one. "When I was here last, I got miserably sick around the thirtieth floor. It's a Sleep lounge with a hundred terminals, if you haven't been."

"I haven't," said Miss Baker. "Have you, Mr. Carraway?"

OWL EYES: *Hey, suit! Don't go static on us.*

Stuck on the roof. Need a minute.

OWL EYES: *What d'you mean "stuck"? Can you do the elevators or not?*

I can. Just wait—

"Mr. Carraway?" Miss Baker prompted.

I shook my head. "I—sorry, no."

She eyed me curiously.

"Well, apparently some idiot had uploaded a cheap sim," the woman continued. "Of *course*, it had a virus on it. Ruined the entire catalog. Five minutes later, one of those Klipspringers was asking for my contact, and the next day there was a whole Sleep terminal on my doorstep with a *handwritten* apology! It was loaded with all of last season's greatest hits."

The short one giggled. "There's something funny about a corpo who'll do a thing like that."

The other shook her head. "You don't know they're a corpo. I have it on good authority they used to be a spy. Flipped sides during the war. Heard they've killed a whole lot more than the average gangster here."

PENGUIN: *Ehhhhh—problem . . . at the card tables . . .*

PIGEON: *Why are you panting?*

PENGUIN: *Tried to scan the account number off a drunk corpo's comm, and he caught me. Klipspringer's tailing me around the casino!*

PIGEON: *Can you stop panting? Makes your thoughts taste like sweat.*

PENGUIN: *Fuck—think he's trying to scan me.*

OWL EYES: *Take him down; just get out—*

Stop, stop, I interrupted. *Don't touch the androids. Too risky. Shut the lights off; crack the security cameras. But keep it local. You can't interfere with any other floor.*

Miss Baker pulled a stim-stick out from thin air, flicking it on. "Actually, I've heard the whole tower's just run by Klipspringers," she said.

I glanced at her. She winked.

"But *someone's* got to be behind it all," replied the tall woman.

PENGUIN: *How—how do I even do that?*

OWL EYES: *Come on, Pen. Find the floor's breaker. Connect your neck mod—*

It took an immense effort not to groan aloud. *For the love of God, do not do that.*

PARROT: *Huh? That's how they do it in The Rosenthal Legacy. . . .*

I wasn't surprised this merry band had learned everything they knew from a decade-old action film.

Run a remote subroutine. Much safer.

PENGUIN: *I—what?*

Thumb over your comm-sensor. Wait five seconds.

PENGUIN: *All . . . right?*

Is it blinking?

PENGUIN: *Yes.*

Get a visual on the nearest camera and share your feed with me.

While Miss Baker and the sisters traded anecdotes about their previous escapades here, I opened my comm. Almost immediately, Miss Baker glanced my way, as if she could actually see the screen sprouting from my wrist and was surprised that I was anything less than wholly engaged in her conversation.

I flicked through a series of programs before uploading one to the comm-sync. *Use this. Should see the controls.*

PENGUIN: *Whoa . . . this a pyrewall?*

Not as intense as a pyre.

PENGUIN: *A VINE-cutter?*

Even weaker. I modified it. More of a "scalpel." Just to get you far enough to jam surveillance.

PENGUIN: *Shit. It's actually working!*

In the center of the terrace, a crowd had collected under a large holo-screen. A Klipspringer, poised on a hover-bot above the whole party, introduced the musical act for the night—an exclusive rendition of Vladimir Tostoff's "Jazz History of the World," sung by a European pop star and accompanied by a full-piece orchestra. The holo rippled into the singer's beaming face, and the party erupted into applause.

The women broke off their passionate speculation to find a table. Miss Baker locked our arms together, tugging me along before I could excuse myself, and we found ourselves seated among a plethora of the season's top bullet-golfers, including the man Miss Baker had arrived with.

The rousing musical performance did nothing to stop the excited discussions around the host, however. I stayed for a moment longer, wondering if the athletes would divulge some insight amidst their gossip.

"You're all lost to the clouds," said one man. "The host's a tried-and-true gangster. Classic bootlegger. Being smart about staying in the shadows. You see all the mods here? Tons of illegal imports, and no one's hiding it."

That was true, at least. Outside the military and professional sports, which granted strict licenses after a rigorous application process, the Americas held a long-standing prohibition on noncosmetic mods. A cursory glance at the festivities and you wouldn't know it at all.

"No, no, listen here." Miss Baker's companion shuffled forward in his chair. "I've a friend of a friend who works as a secretary for someone on the International Space Council. *He* said it's one of the higher-ups there who must own this place, and you know why they throw all of these parties? It's a last hurrah! ISC is close to cracking that probe, and when they do, war'll be just around the corner."

The women gasped. "Close to cracking it? *How* close?"

"A few months. Maybe sooner. ISC thinks alien nukes won't be far behind. Media's trying to bury it, of course. Smother the panic."

The conversation dissolved into morbid conjectures about galactic war. Miss Baker, who'd been listening to all this with the tight lips of a perpetually stifled yawn, raised her wineglass. "To the apocalypse!" she said as "Jazz History of the World" climbed to a trumpet swell, and the whole table followed suit, toasting the end of the world.

With everyone reanimated by their drinks, no one cared about the host anymore. Miss Baker leaned toward me. "This is much too polite for me," she muttered, so we stood up, and as we roamed through the party, she didn't stop to entertain any more greetings, gracefully ending conversations before they could start.

"You're distracted," she said.

"What? Oh no—"

"I can tell when a man isn't giving me his full attention."

I was sorry she'd noticed. "It's not you."

"I should hope not. What is it really, then?" Her cold smile reminded me of our first encounter—the way she'd asked if I lived in West Egg and that she was acquainted with someone here.

"You *know* the host is Jay Gatsby," I realized suddenly.

She lowered her stim-stick in surprise. "Oh? And so do you, it seems. Well, that's no fun."

I reached into my pocket. "Only because I was invited—"

"*Invited?*" She plucked the paper from me and held it up to the light like a jeweler. "Oh my. You're serious."

I mentioned that she was the first person I'd met who even knew the host's name. Regrettably, she knew nothing beyond that.

"I'm going to keep trying elsewhere," I said.

"I adore an adventure," she murmured. After all the tired gossip with the bullet-golfers, I thought she'd be deterred from wanting to waste her night with me. Instead, she took a sharp drag of her stim-stick, and something in her smile flashed with welcoming candor. "Let's find out about your neighbor."

◇——◇——◇

Private entertainment rooms spanned floors ninety to ninety-nine. Following that were the art galleries, each themed to various historical periods—chambers filled with medieval portraits of sulking nobility and labyrinths of marble statues, the tops of which grazed ceilings holo'd into clear ancient Greek skies.

Ambling through a butterfly conservatory with Jordan—who insisted on my using her first name—a part of me didn't want to leave her company just yet, though it was nearing midnight, and we hadn't gotten closer to a clue.

> PENGUIN: *Lost the Klipspringer. They're calling up more. Think they caught the surveillance jam. Now they're scanning everyone who's coming in and out. I'm locked here, Owl.*
>
> OWL EYES: *Get him out of there, suit.*
>
> *Can't do anything about the Klipspringers remotely. Best thing is to sit tight till their guard is down.*
>
> OWL EYES: *What! And do nothing? You may as well make the most of it, Pen. Lotta money flowing on that floor. You can't intercept another comm or two?*
>
> PENGUIN: *Dunno. . . . That one subroutine's got me feelin' a bit—dizzy. . . .*

Parrot and Pigeon offered to regroup with Penguin at the casino. A fortunate turn of events. At least I knew three of the birds would be stirring up trouble on a different floor and wouldn't interfere. All that remained was Owl Eyes, but her disobedience made her the most difficult of the flock.

> OWL EYES: *If I get near the fiftieth floor before you do, Mr. Nicholas Carraway, I'm not waiting around on those elevators.*

> *Don't,* I warned. *The elevators are synced to the tower's core VINE. Remote subs will bounce and burn you if you're not careful.*

She grumbled an incoherent complaint.

Filtered rainforest sounds gargled through hidden speakers, and from above, the synthetic foliage imprinted patterned shadows onto the pathway. The lighting was orange-hued, the air very humid and floral. A bit of perspiration had collected along Jordan's dark collarbones. Her bio-ink was a muted red today, and it brought out all the warmth in her coppery gown.

"Do you like these large parties?" I asked.

"Is this a large party?" A holo-butterfly landed on her shoulder. She moved to touch it, but its image shuddered through her finger and flew away. "I suppose I've never been to a small one. Can't imagine it'd be very fun."

"We had dinner at the Buchanans'."

"People have to be enjoying themselves, I say, or else it's not a party."

The saffron lights deepened the farther we walked. A kaleidoscope of butterflies circled us like a ribbon, some as large as our heads, before disappearing again into the whispering foliage, and soon we were passing more than one impassioned couple stirring in the synth-trees. I promptly suggested we continue onto a new floor, which made Jordan laugh, and she wound our arms together tighter.

At the next level, we found ourselves alone in a space observatory. A holo-screen near the elevator flashed with a menu of different simulations. She selected one at random, and the room flattened to a dusty red. She sighed, kicked off her heels, and splayed out on the ground, which had flickered to Martian sand beneath our feet.

Tonight, her black hair was streaked through with blond and woven into long, thin box braids that spilled around her head as she starfished into the sand. "How is Gen Wealth?" she asked.

I sat beside her. "I have an office."

"I thought you were a contractor."

"I am."

"What use does a diver have for an office? Aren't you asleep all day?"

I laughed, though she was right about the office being unnecessary. "Diving is *not* sleeping."

"But you're not awake when you're under."

"Not awake, but not asleep. I daresay it's more tiring than being awake. Bullet-golf seems much more interesting anyway."

"Do you even know the rules?"

"I could learn."

"Come to one of my games," she said. "Maybe then I'll win."

We could see Earth across the room, a blue-and-white blip dotting the fake sky. The simulation was good enough that I could card my fingers through the sand, even if I couldn't actually feel its texture.

> OWL EYES: *Shit, just found a library. Books—first editions. Guaranteed we can flip these to some weird corpo art connoisseur.*

> PENGUIN: *You're gonna stuff books into your pocket?*

> OWL EYES: *No, idiot. I'm gonna figure out how to scan 'em. Even a hologram recreation of these'll be worth something good.*

I stood up. I was supposed to be working, and instead, had fallen for the tower's spectacles. "I appreciate the help. I should be off."

"What? You're leaving?"

The simulation disintegrated. The sand vanished around our ankles along with the cosmos, and I turned to her, suspicion twisting her graceful face.

"I stole you away from your date." I marched toward the elevators, but she followed in haste, then pinned me with a sly smile.

"I see why Daisy picked you, after all."

It hadn't crossed my mind before that Daisy would have made Jordan privy to her family's politics, but then it made complete sense.

"Picked me for what?" I said innocently, but the battle had already been lost. Lying to Jordan Baker was a matter of milliseconds. I learned this lesson that night and have never forgotten it since.

A light of intrigue sprang up behind her bottomless eyes. "I think I've changed my mind."

"About what?"

"Small parties." She smiled. "If that's what we're having now."

Seven

I OFFERED JORDAN THE FULL CONTEXT about the Gen Wealth contract, the equally unusual arrival of the hand-delivered invitation, and finally, the encounter with the birds. None of it deterred her from following me into the elevator. She watched me with that brimming light in her eyes as if this whole party had been made of paper before, and only now was it coming to life.

"Everything Daisy's told me about you is starting to make sense," she said.

I studied the elevator's nav-holo. Exactly twelve floors in the middle of the tower were missing. I cross-referenced it with Owl Eyes' diagram. "Should I even ask what that means?" I muttered, though I remembered how my cousin had called me "an absolute rose" without batting an eye.

"She told me you're unreadable. That you have this tendency to glance over your shoulder if someone so much as compliments your shirt." Jordan laughed. "But she also thinks you're a hard person to lie to, and Daisy's never described anyone that way. It's why I agreed she could introduce us at dinner. I've never gone along with her suggestions before."

I would have been flattered by this anecdote if Jordan had said it with an ounce of playfulness. Rather, it was phrased like a scientific observation.

I scanned the holo-screen with my ocular-mods. An acute pressure spiked behind my eyes; then my comm lit up above my wrist. I dragged it over to the elevator menu, and the two screens momentarily rippled into one.

"Since she retired, she's been more involved with Medica," added Jordan. "They've still got ambitions but haven't been able to do anything since that disaster years ago. Now their finances are locked in with Buchanan Group, who's too risk averse to invest much in them. It's why a new partnership could make a difference."

"Does she confide a lot in you?"

"Only some things. She never told me it was Gatsby Corp that they're in talks with." A stiffness briefly frosted over her voice, and I wouldn't have guessed that the two of them had shared as close a girlhood as Daisy had suggested. "She's too careful about matters of the self, though I suppose she's quite good at making you think otherwise."

I remembered how quickly Daisy's soft concern formed in front of me on her veranda. *I haven't anyone else to turn to.* The words were rather venerating, even just for a second. "Speaking of careful, this is your last chance to leave," I warned Jordan, but nothing I could have said would have made her turn around. The tower's private floors fascinated her, as did the actual process to get there.

To bypass the lockdown protocols, I'd have to make it look like the elevator was malfunctioning. "It'll help mask the breach," I said.

"Won't the system notice it anyway?"

"Eventually. I just need to delay it long enough that we're gone by then."

That was what the birds were for. A few suspected intruders would take priority over one broken elevator. According to their updates, Owl Eyes was still preoccupied with the library, and Parrot and Pigeon had made it into the casinos. Their newest scheme was to hijack the slot machines.

> *You know how to do that? Once I initiate the breach, my hands are tied, and I can't help—*

> PENGUIN: *Give me some credit! 'Course I can do it. Owl? You still alive?*

> OWL EYES: *Very alive. There isn't a soul in this library. Gonna scan as much of it as I can. You should all stand by until the suit's finished with the elevator.*

Don't linger too long—all of you. As soon as you tamper with anything in the tower, it'll trip alarms. You'll want to start moving quickly.

This was met with pointed silence.

I sighed. "All right. Diversions are in place. I'm going to shut the elevator down first." I pulled apart the holo-screens. With the scan completed, a compilation of cutters I kept handy in my comm hung in the air like a hundred bubbles. I pinched down the same one I'd shared with Penguin earlier in the night and dropped it onto the elevator's nav-holo. It shivered, dissolved, then reappeared—this time, with the controller on display, comprising a dozen smaller screens.

"How'd you know so much about the tower when you've never even been here before?" asked Jordan.

"Virtual Intrusion Network Executions." I flicked through the controller's commands. "It's the foundation of everything that's built in cyberspace. If you can get past it, it doesn't matter if it's guarding a bank account or a building. We run 'cutters' against them. Or pyrewalls if we need something stronger."

"*Pyre*walls?"

"Programs to burn the VINEs, or at least, parts of them. But they burn us, too, since they require a lot of processing power. Netdiving mods mitigate the strain, but there's always going to be a sting. Early divers used to die a lot that way. Hence the name 'funeral pyre.'" I glanced up at her. "Colloquially, we sometimes call our rigs 'the gallows.' Because of the way the cables attach to our necks and the harnesses keep us suspended," I explained. She looked horrified by this. "Well, it's just occupational humor." I pointed at the silver-ringed slot at my nape. "I suppose it makes more sense if you see it up close. Do amusement park rides make you queasy, by the way?"

Her lips pressed together, a dart-sharp throw of a smile. "I'm a bullet-golfer, Mr. Carraway. You wouldn't be asking me that if you'd ever watched a game."

That was now her second invitation to attend one of her matches. My skin sang with heat beneath my collar. "I'm going to trigger the malfunction. Brace yourself."

Jordan set herself into a wide stance, gripping the railings. I dragged the commands atop the nav-holo, and immediately, the golden lights overhead disappeared.

With the darkness came the plunge.

Jordan gasped but kept her balance well. I crashed forward into the wall as the air rushed from my lungs, and the elevator whistled, plummeting in rapid free fall.

It lasted ten long seconds before jolting to a stop. We caught our breaths. I guessed that we'd only fallen about two or three levels, but it was enough.

As I glanced at the controller, a red bead of light pulsed on the screen. A string of error codes flashed just below. I riffled through the pyres in my comm.

"These programs you're running against the VINE," said Jordan, "how do you know which ones to use?"

"For diving certifications, we have to memorize variations for different kinds of VINEs. The more variations you encounter, the more familiar the patterns become, and you can counteract accordingly." I dropped two pyres onto the nav-holo. "For a building like this, there's both a hard and soft lock on everything. As in a physical lock on the doors, but also a biometric scan that likely triggers full elevator access. It's a guess, based on what I've seen in standard building-security systems."

The nav-holo trembled vigorously before wiping itself blank.

"Are we—trapped?" Jordan stared uneasily. "Is that supposed to—"

The screen rippled back to life, and the twelve floors, previously missing, shimmered before us.

She laughed delightedly, as if I'd just pulled a rabbit out of a hat. The buttons were visible on the menu now, but still inactive. It would take another few minutes for the pyrewalls to fully sear it.

At that moment, Owl Eyes proudly reported that she'd scanned eighteen books in the library so far. The other birds didn't reply, which I took to mean their ploy to rig the slot machines was well underway.

"I've been wondering," said Jordan as the elevator bloomed with the dim white-blue light of the nav-holo, "What do you hope to find out about Jay Gatsby?"

"Who he is, of course. What he wants."

She smirked. "And what he looks like?"

I'd never exactly envisioned Jay Gatsby as a real person before. Despite the kind regards of his invitation, I had a hard time believing he was anything besides an ancient, arrogant socialite who had an android penning his missives for him.

"Anything. Corpos are at their most dangerous when you know little about them," I said.

She hummed pensively. "Assuming you meet him tonight, or if we find him on the other side and he asks why on earth you broke into his house, what then?"

"As far as his system knows, this elevator went haywire. It coughed us up somewhere we couldn't control, and we got lost."

The pyre had pierced halfway now. In steady intervals, the buttons on the nav-holo filled slowly with light.

Best leave soon, Owl Eyes.

OWL EYES: *No way. Barely feeling a burn on my mods. Could do another batch.*

The system will have registered your activity already. There'll be a Klipspringer headed your way.

OWL EYES: *Sure, sure. I'll move once I'm done with these.*

I frowned. *Move now. That goes for the rest of you.*

This went ignored, as my last warning had. A low beep chimed from the nav-holo, and I squinted to see a new pop-up pulsing at the corner of the screen.

"Problem?" asked Jordan.

I dragged the pop-up toward me. "Automated message. Core VINE flagged the elevator malfunction."

"Already?"

"We delayed it three minutes. That's an eternity." At least coinciding the breach with the birds had done enough to overwhelm the system, if only for a moment.

Now it was time to run.

Owl Eyes, I'm serious.

OWL EYES: *Don't tell me how to run my own op! I said one more batch, all right? Pen. Pen? Hey—meet the suit down on fifty so we can—*

PARROT: *Um . . . Penguin may have . . . run the wrong cutter on the slots?*

I startled. *He what?*

PARROT: *The—the subroutine bounced! Real bad. . . . He's burning up.*

He needs a mod-doc. Immediately.

PIGEON: *The Klipspringers caught him! Had to drag him into the bathroom to hide, but they're still—*

OWL EYES: *He's breathing?*

PARROT: *Yes?*

OWL EYES: *Take over, Parrot.*

PARROT: *What! Not a chance!*

OWL EYES: *You think there's time for cold feet? Subroutine's already started, so just finish it! We're leaving free cash on the table.*

PARROT: *I—I really can't, Owl. . . . Pen's veins. . . . They're—*

A wave of nausea rolled through the comm-sync.

OWL EYES: *Fine! Hole up in the shitter all you want, but I'm finishing these scans. We regroup once—once—once—*

Her voice broke off sharply.

PIGEON: *Owl?*

OWL EYES: *Once—the elevators are—shit! I—*

The comm-sync crackled like foil.
A choke, then a guttural shriek.
The pain rose quickly—reverberating through the sync in a sting of electrifying heat that started at my neck and flamed outward. I groaned, tripping into Jordan.
She grabbed my shoulders. "Nick? What—"

PENGUIN: *Can't—fuck—breathe—*

PARROT: *Owl, answer us!*

My vision dotted. *Leave the tower. All of you . . .*

PIGEON: *Owl's admin on the—losing—de-sync—can't leave—her—*

The breach.
In a minute, all the private floors of the tower would open for us, and we'd finally be standing on the doorstep of answers I'd been searching for all night. If I aborted the subroutine now, the chances of the same pyrewalls working again were next to zero.

The elevator tilted around me.

PIGEON: *Owl . . . Owl—are you—*

The echoes of Owl Eyes' scream clanged in my skull like an off-tune chorus.

I'll . . . find her. Get yourselves out; get to a mod-doc—

The comm-sync shattered.
Flatline.
Silence.
My head was my own again, empty and light, but my limbs were heavier than ever. I reached toward the nav-holo, clenching my fist through the screen, and it shivered away once more. When it reappeared, the menu had returned to normal, and the elevator droned awake.

Jordan's hand on my shoulder kept my knees from buckling. "What—why did you cut it off?"

"Comms . . ." I exhaled. "Just went dark." I punched the floor to the library.

"What's there?" asked Jordan.

"I don't know," I admitted, hoping it wasn't a corpse.

Eight

I N THE LIBRARY, THE HOLO-CEILING glowed in an expanse of small, hazy flames, as though the light were exuding from a thousand torches. We sprinted toward the sound of a low, pained wheeze. The packed shelves towered over us like the thicket of a great forest, curving endless trails through the darkness, and soon, we rounded a corner to discover Owl Eyes convulsing face down over a pile of strewn books.

Along with a lone uniformed Klipspringer.

He inclined his head. "The section will be cleared for your enjoyment soon."

I approached slowly. "What's happened?"

"A minor disturbance, sir." The android bowed lower. "We express our deepest apologies. Our security has been alerted to an attempted robbery. Rest assured, it has been contained."

"Have you sent for a mod-doc? For the girl?"

The android stared at me. "Once more, we express our deepest apologies."

I looked past him at Owl Eyes. No bruises or wounds across her skin. There was, however, a distinct smell—sharp, charred flesh.

I glanced at Jordan, and the same thought passed between us, as clear as if we shared a comm-sync.

I was closer to the Klipspringer, just the right height to hook my arm around his neck. Jordan bolted forward and, with a sweep of her leg, knocked the android to his knees—with an elegance that had me more curious about bullet-golf than I'd ever been before.

She held him down without a strain in her arms. I scanned the Klipspringer's wrist until his comm lit up and quickly pulled two cutters from my own—one subroutine to override his power, a second to block his security tag. It wasn't the most graceful solution. His VINE, I guessed, was a generation or two newer than the cutters I had on deck. A slight recoil licked my veins.

But the cutter pushed through, and when at last the android shuddered to the ground, I hurried to Owl Eyes, turning her over.

The smell made Jordan gag. "Oh!"

Owl Eyes' head tipped forward, neck sagging from the sheer weight of her oc-mods. The glass plane had dislodged slightly, and the light blinked in rapid, uneven bursts.

"Shit." The pulse in her wrist rose lethargically, her skin hot. "She's fried."

"Um," said Jordan, "what?"

"She's overheating. Help me prop her up."

Jordan kicked aside a heap of antique hardbacks. "Never seen oc-mods like that before." We set Owl Eyes upright against the bookshelves. Jordan bent over and ogled the mods up close. "Do you suppose they can see through walls? I mean, by the size of them, you'd think they could see right into the future."

I picked up one of the books, feeling along the spine until my thumb caught on a small indent. Peeling back the loose flap revealed a fingernail-sized microchip embedded within.

I sighed. "Tagged. She didn't even think to check."

"Tagged?"

I showed Jordan the spines. "Security measure. Shoots back malware when you try to scan it. Her nerve tolerance is awful if it hurt her this bad. Probably burned her, and the android came to clean up."

Owl Eyes coughed—once, then several times—and with it came a stream of blood.

"Hold her." I fumbled through my pockets for a hypo shot. "Quickly."

"What is *that*?" asked Jordan as I retrieved the hypo. It wasn't any larger than my palm—a silver pill-shaped canister with a four-pronged needle point.

"Regulates body temperature fast. Divers usually take it before going under," I explained. "Are you ready?"

She kneeled, ripping a slit in her skintight evening gown so that she could move her legs more easily. The sight very much held me in place for an embarrassing moment before I remembered myself.

She shuffled Owl Eyes to rest between her legs, the girl's back against her chest.

"She'll resist," I warned.

Jordan nodded, tightening her grip around Owl Eyes' waist.

I pinned her legs down with one hand, and with the other, pushed the hypo into her shoulder. The needles had barely made contact before another spurt of blood projected from her throat. She choked on a scream. I ducked as her limbs flailed, administering the rest of the shot.

She writhed in Jordan's arms, her lithe body seizing as if every ounce of air within her had been suctioned out. We held our breaths in severe silence as the rise and fall of her chest halted entirely, and Jordan lowered her ear to the girl's mouth, a shadow of panic darkening her face.

I reached for the girl's wrist again, scrambling for the hot, weak pulse—

My vision narrowed.

Then Owl Eyes, with a high gasp, sprang up.

"*See!* It's a bona fide piece of printed matter!" She stumbled to her feet, twirling groggily between the shelves and gesturing around at the books. "What—oh. Where's the crew?"

The pupils in her oc-mods spun around like marbles for several seconds before rolling to a stop.

"I . . . I told your birds to leave," I said. "Are you all ri—"

"What!" she exclaimed. "Why in the hell would you do *that*?"

My relief evaporated. Her negligence wasn't just obnoxious anymore but lethally idiotic. "No one ever taught you how to deactivate a *tag* before scanning something?" I grabbed a book from the nearest shelf, ripping the spine open. "If I didn't have a spare hypo on me, you'd be dead. Not to mention you would've killed your friends today. You'd better hope they don't go up in flames on their way to a mod-doc."

Her oc-mods flickered, and wisps of smoke leaked from the sides of the protruded glass. She groaned, keeling over, shaking her wrist as if trying to activate her comm. She tried a few calls.

"Fucking static …" She drove her toe into a pile of frayed paperbacks.

"Go home. See a doctor tomorrow—both kinds, if you can."

"A 'doctor,' he says! I look like I got that kinda money to you?"

"You have to see someone. And you're very welcome for the resurrection, by the way," I muttered, tossing the used hypo at her.

She caught it, then leaned toward me, and I smelled the burned tang of her skin. "Don't lecture me with your self-righteous—"

"I could have had those elevators opened if you hadn't decided to nearly kill yourself."

Don't get caught—the only instruction Bunsen had given me for the night. It was hitting me now how far my own judgment had swerved. I'd jeopardized everything for a common street criminal and a thankless one at that.

She stopped abruptly, as if she were prepared to express a grateful word but couldn't stomach the thought of being indebted to me. It was her own mistakes that had brought her whole operation crashing down. She did not acknowledge this, however, so I watched as her anger consumed her, and in a moment of frantic deflection, she said, "Here's the difference between me and you, Mr. Nicholas Carraway. Sure, you've got your fancy education and your fancy job, but you don't got the *soul* of a diver."

I tensed. "You have your … passionate ideologies. I see that. But you don't know me, and if there's anything you should be worrying about, it's your friends."

"I know you just fine. There're hundreds, thousands of you. Let me guess. Whipped up into a good military diver nice and young. Then spat out with the perfect skill set to be a good *corpo* diver—bred by the system just to give back to it."

"That's—" *Not true,* was what I meant to say, but even if it was, the world was more complicated than this girl's absurd idealism made it out to be.

She shook her head with a scoff, taking my hesitation as an affirmation of her point. "I'm not stopping until I've torched all the parasites razing the New East. And you—" She smacked her oc-mods several times, forcing them back into place, then brushed past me to where

Jordan stood, leaning against a half-emptied bookcase. "Wait, you're Jordan fucking Baker."

"Charmed," said Jordan.

I stepped between them. "Leave her out of this."

Owl Eyes shrugged exaggeratedly. "Happy to. Assuming you kept up your end of the deal."

"Haven't you heard a *thing* I've just said? The breach's already been detected—"

"So do it again."

She was too irrational to understand that another attempt wasn't feasible. "I didn't have time to slip out unnoticed. VINEs in this tower are smart enough to refortify," I explained slowly, though I doubted it made a difference. I might have had better luck trying to argue this with a nonsentient bot. "At this point, you'd need custom pyres—something stronger, something it doesn't already know. If you double dip, it'll burn you far worse than those books did. The fact you're alive at all is something you ought to be thankful—"

"Ah! Thankful!" Owl Eyes erupted. "Believe it or not, *I* don't have the luxury of walking away from this without . . . without *anything* to show for it . . ." The bite in her words tapered off uncertainly, trading her anger for guilt, but she held it in check with the last tendrils of her blazing pride.

I didn't want to pity her, but I saw a glimpse of what she might have believed herself to be. A leader who had failed.

It was Jordan who stepped forward. "All right. Let's all calm down. The girl needs something worthy to sell, and you, Nick, need to meet the host. It sounds like this is a sizable amount of work that could really just be solved the old-fashioned way. A bit of shoulder rubbing."

I stared at her doubtfully. Not all of us had the stardom of Jordan Baker that could be deployed upon people at will. "What are you suggesting?"

She crossed her arms. "I'm just saying you didn't even *try* putting that smile of yours to good use."

I didn't possess the confidence for that and even less so, the desire. But any further discussion about crashing the security was useless tonight anyway. There was a solid hour before the first guests would take their leave, and a handful more until dawn broke. I couldn't waste the remainder of the party. I'd have no report by the end of it.

"I'll keep looking. Let you know if I find anything," I said to Owl Eyes, in what I hoped was an acceptable compromise. "But *you're* leaving. You put all the androids on high alert, and doing anything in your state is suicide. Besides, if there's nothing to be found on those private floors—"

"'If'?" She huffed. "We both know people like this've got more than skeletons in their closet."

Her oc-mods let out a worrying spark. The wisp of smoke seeping through the glass thickened, and she cursed, staggering back through the maze of bookshelves.

"Owl Eyes," I said before I could think better of it. She stopped. "If you need to cover a proper medical visit—"

"I don't take corpo money unless I'm stealing it," she hollered. "Be in touch. If you go static, well, I know where you live."

She turned, disappearing into the library's crisp darkness and the dust of the old-century stories.

◇——◇——◇

In the stale elevator silence, Jordan folded her arms, her mouth pursed in a cool, tight-lipped smile.

"I'm sorry your party was derailed," I said. The nav-holo I'd over-ridden had disappeared, and the elevator was once again beyond my control. It began to descend automatically.

"No one comes to West Egg for a peaceful outing. I had a feeling spending the party with you would reap a surprise or two." She wiped at a spot of blood on my chin. "I like when I'm right."

We were nearing the bottom of the tower when, at that moment, the doors opened. On the other side stood her date, frantic. "Jordan! *Forward Sport*'s editor is on her way out!" He pulled her from the elevator. "Are you helping me get this cover story or *not*?"

She sighed disinterestedly, then told me to wait for her on the rooftop. "Don't worry. You'll find him," she said with the surest of smiles.

By the time the elevator recommenced its ascent, it was crowded again. At one of the casino floors, several older gentlemen entered in a rambunctious herd, chatting heartily with a younger fellow in a white pin-striped suit. He looked to be my age, though you could never really know.

After a few minutes, and many more guests piling in on the way up to the roof, the man and I were pressed shoulder to shoulder. I cast him an apologetic look when my foot knocked against his crease-less leather shoe, then felt a jolt of surprise when he smiled and leaned toward me. "Weren't you in the Third Division during the war?" he asked.

"Why, yes. I was in the Ninth Battalion."

"I was in Operations until June '69. Assisted many combat divers during my time."

I stared. He was exceedingly handsome—olive-skinned, with blond hair darkened by gel and a lustrous contentment that shone from his brilliant eyes. It was the sort of expensive grace that conjured up images of all the cosmetic mod ads that flashed on every holo-billboard. "Forgive me." I was sure we'd never met before, at least not in any cold military facility. I felt I would have remembered him. "I can't seem to ..."

"It's all right. The Ninth was for the best. There were so few of you and so many of us."

We spoke the rest of the way about the military base in Maine where our training had overlapped for three frigid months. He shocked me by sharing a very specific anecdote of a mission I'd led back in December of '68.

"You must have been one of my overseers at some point," I conceded.

He smiled before launching into a passionate story about how he'd aspired to be a diver, too, but had his plans diverted due to a nerve intolerance. Once we reached the rooftop, I made an offhanded comment about having seen little of the city. In turn, he mentioned that he'd just purchased a new hover-car, the latest model from Veluz Motors, and hadn't found time to dust it off yet.

"I was planning to take her out tomorrow," he said as we strolled toward some empty stools along the bar. "Want to go with me, old sport?"

"What time?"

"Any time that suits you best."

A recording of "Jazz History of the World" from earlier in the night was looping on the wide holo-screen, warming the party below. I realized I hadn't had a sip of anything yet, which seemed a great shame, so I plucked an oversized champagne glass as it cruised past on the conveyor belt. Before I could answer, Jordan reappeared.

"Oh good. You're both here," she said as the man, evidently not a stranger to her, offered his hand to help her sit. She squeezed it once impersonally.

"Always a pleasure to see you, Miss Baker," he said.

"I know," replied Jordan.

They chatted about the music and glowing drinks and upcoming fireworks display while I sipped my champagne until I was comfortably flushed. I looked around at the party, which felt gorgeous and important in a way it hadn't before. Everything was smaller, closer. The night sky was a plush black. Pyramids of glossy cake slices stood high at each table. Guests clung to each other in sweet lethargy, heads bent together like drooping flowers and conversations dimmed to a romantic flicker.

"This is an unusual party for me," I told the stranger. I explained that I lived across the street and wanted to meet the host who'd sent their Klipspringer with an invitation. "Jay Gatsby—would you happen to know anything about him?"

The inquiry appeared to send the man into momentary dismay. He looked to Jordan, then back at me, adjusting himself uncomfortably in his seat. "It seems this is all my fault," he said.

Jordan's haughty mouth twisted behind her cocktail.

"*Your* fault?" I asked.

The man held my gaze in earnest. "I'm Gatsby."

A beam of stark light whistled into the sky, then bloomed open.

I felt like a fool—and yet, at this precise intersection of my ignorance and embarrassment, Gatsby turned his keen attention toward me, smiling as if to banish any self-deprecating sentiment before it could even form. His eyes were alert, greener than the fireworks above us, and so imploring in their sincerity, it seemed as though he were asking a silent, solemn question of me.

86

It was a look of deep faith, a warm confidence of presence, and it carried the deferential promise that any apology between us was entirely his to offer and mine to forgive.

I was properly dizzy now. "I beg your pardon. . . ."

"I'm sorry; I thought you knew," he replied, a soft urgency weaving through his voice.

"Perhaps I would have." I set the empty champagne glass onto the conveyor belt. The party twirled around me in fresh colors. "If Miss Baker had made an introduction."

Jordan raised her drink in a mock toast, throwing her head back and emptying her glass. "I suppose it never came up."

I nearly glared at her, but Gatsby spoke first. "I'm afraid I'm not a very good host. If it's all right with you, I'd like to—" he said just as a Klipspringer stopped in front of us and whispered something in his ear.

He nodded once, stood up, then shook my hand with both of his. Before excusing himself, he assured me that if I wanted anything, I need only ask the nearest android, and if it wasn't too much trouble, then it would please him very much if I could wait a moment for him to finish his call.

"Not the unpleasant corpo you expected him to be?" said Jordan.

"Are you quite done?"

"I was going to say it sooner but—"

"Were you? You said you'd never met him before!"

"No. I said I didn't know anything beyond his name. Which I don't. Besides, how was I supposed to guess you were secretly shepherding around some criminals?" She stared up at the fireworks, insolently stoic, always sitting on the closed side of a secret. "I swear I was going to tell you eventually. But we were having so much fun."

I sighed. "Your fun was watching me chase my own tail?"

She smirked. "I haven't seen any more of this tower than the next guest. I was curious too." Her eyes narrowed at the cheerful pop star prancing above us. "Anyway, now you know how agreeable he is. As soon as you're at one of these things, you're sort of just his friend."

Men like him didn't keep friends. They kept resources.

"He did tell me once he was an Oxford man. However, I don't believe it," she added.

"Why not?"

"I just don't think he went there."

I looked at Gatsby again, who stood alone, observing the party from a high corner of the rooftop. He was taking a private call on his comm, and his lips moved in low murmurs as he watched drunken revelers sway into each other, though he himself was quite sober. That sobriety, for the slimmest moment, almost repaired my uncertainties, for his dazzling satisfaction swept across the guests with heart and an ostensibly silent gratitude.

But the moment dispelled itself just as fast.

A Klipspringer materialized at Jordan's side. "Mr. Gatsby would like me to escort you somewhere." The android's flat eyes passed over us. "He has a matter to discuss with both of you."

Nine

BELOW THE TOWER'S MIDPOINT WAS a level made entirely of two-way glass—both its ceiling and its floor. Looking up, you'd see the holo-aquarium above, and beneath, the crowded Happy Sleep lounge. Curled on velvet love seats, guests clutched one another in states of dazed unconsciousness, wafting like mellowed ghosts through erotic lights with headsets pinned over their eyes, lost in better worlds.

The lounge was one of the busiest levels in the whole tower, with hundreds gathered there at any time. For a moment, there really was something entrancing about spectating the dreamers underneath our feet, but the fascination only lasted a few minutes before I thought it was too voyeuristic to be lovely.

"Do you like it?" asked Gatsby.

"It's impressive," I said—without adequate passion, it seemed.

He looked unconvinced. "I wanted to show you the popular lounge here. The quality of our simulations is spectacular. Unlike anything that's on the market right now."

Jordan had fallen silent beside me, assessing this formal audience just as I was. He couldn't be boasting about his high-end lounge for no reason.

Other guests milled about the floor too; elegant couples seeking a moment of reprieve amidst the hilarity, as well as a handful of emotional drunkards who thought the semi-invisible quality to the glass floor meant they were surely levitating.

"You know, sometimes rumors can float around, unseemly kinds— about this tower or—or me." Gatsby wet his lips. "Anyway, none of it is true."

I glanced at Jordan.

"We've only had the grandest time, Mr. Gatsby. Isn't that right, Nick?" she said quickly.

The only thing to do was agree.

He nodded. "Well, that's good. I suppose I should just be direct about it."

Jordan and I traded another cautious look. "About what?" I asked Gatsby, bracing myself for a harsh questioning about the night's several disasters.

He said something rather startling instead. "I've been reviewing your work performance, Mr. Carraway. You must know that you're overqualified."

"Pardon me?"

"You're a netdiving *talent*," he said.

"Oh, well—"

"I'd be a fool to let you wander off at the end of your contract. I can offer you a placement anywhere you'd like. Full-time, of course, with a salary of your choosing and good benefits."

Full-time corporate placements were quite rare. If he only wanted to offer me a new job, it made little sense why he'd brought me here first. The night was continuing to contort in inexplicable ways, for I could have scarcely guessed where this conversation was headed now.

"I'm not sure I understand," I said warily.

"The system recorded the other week that you were unsatisfied with your tasks. That's why I began to review your file and invited you over. To speak with you. In fact, it's very fortunate to see you and Miss Baker already acquainted." He smiled. "Because I have a business venture that you both might like to hear about."

"What sort of business?" she asked.

"I've acquired a new Happy Sleep studio," he said. "Do you know Happy Sleep recordings use very similar setups to most standard netdiving rigs?"

I nodded, but Jordan shook her head. She looked bored now, at the mention of a business venture. Perhaps she was used to being ambushed with these proposals and promises.

"For Miss Baker's benefit, let's put it this way: cyberspace is like an underground building with many levels, yes? In the deepest levels, we build our infrastructure, our VINEs. But at the very top, in shallow space, is where you're skimming the virtual and real world at the same time. That's how Happy Sleeps are recorded. The actors aren't *in* cyberspace, so much as they are wading into it," said Gatsby. "Now, anyone who's spent time in *our* Sleeps can tell you our immersion is almost seamless. The small difference is that we record our sessions in a deeper level of cyberspace than other studios. Soon, we'll be creating perfect virtual experiences, one where the mind is so hooked to the Sleep that it's not aware it's a Sleep at all."

He stopped here, as if anticipating some impressed reaction from us. I believe both Jordan and I were so perplexed that neither of us could even attempt a nod. "We're looking for a good diving consultant to bring into our R & D," Gatsby continued breathlessly. "We've worked with a few already, but not anyone with as much experience in deep cyberspace as you, Mr. Carraway. Really, what we're researching is—is cutting-edge science. I'm offering a very coveted opportunity."

He spoke this way for a while, but I couldn't focus on half his words, still anticipating he might snap his fingers and accuse me of trying to dismantle his tower.

He proceeded to offer me an obscene hourly rate for a single afternoon of my time, and if I liked it enough, we could work toward something long-term. His mounting persistence only made me more hesitant.

"It's not the sort of role I could offer to—to just anyone. I have to pick someone reliable and competent, and I get the sense you're a humble sort too, Mr. Carraway." The fake aquarium water overhead cast whimsical, undulating shadows across his face. "Why don't you think on it? There's no rush—"

Another Klipspringer, dressed in a crisp white uniform rather than the robin's-egg blue of the others, came over and interrupted us. When the android apologized for his intrusion, Gatsby looked annoyed, as if he'd given explicit instructions not to be disturbed unless the sky was imminently falling.

"Can't it wait, Ewing?" said Gatsby.

The Klipspringer bowed. "I'm afraid not, sir."

They stepped several feet away, but not out of earshot.

"A breach?" muttered Gatsby.

"Yes, sir."

"Physical or cyber?"

The Klipspringer paused. "Both, sir."

Jordan and I feigned interest in the aquarium.

Gatsby sighed, examining a holo-screen balanced in the Klipspringer's hand. "Says here everything's restored. No data's been flagged as stolen, and the android can be sent for repairs. What's the issue?"

"The issue, sir, is that the intruders haven't been caught. We did have suspects, but they managed to escape in the frenzy."

"Surveillance?" asked Gatsby.

"The same cutter ran on floors seventy-two, sixty-three, and elevator nine. Remote subroutines, sir. Untraceable."

"That can't be possible." Gatsby frowned at the report, though he appeared more irritated than concerned. "It's showing elevator nine was a controller malfunction."

"Yes, but—"

"I'd be happy to take a look for you," I suggested. "If there's a security issue."

Gatsby looked up. I held my breath.

"No need," he said. "I assure you the tower is—perfectly *safe*." He waved his Klipspringer away sternly and turned to Jordan. "Now, Miss Baker. Beloved star of the East."

"*Fading* star, some might say," replied Jordan.

"Only fools! Though I do hear you've had a turbulent start to your season. I happen to know that when an athlete such as yourself slips into a losing streak, you might find yourself short on sponsors."

This displeased Jordan, not just in the unsubtle reminder of her poor performance, but in the indelicate suggestion that his money would save her. There was a cold slant to her lips. "You want to sponsor *me*?"

"Of course. You're Jordan Baker! You can have the top mods at your disposal to turn that season right around." There was more to it. We waited for Gatsby to circle to the truth of his offer. Finally, he said, "I'm hoping to work with the best in the Happy Sleep business, and I'm willing to accept nothing in return for my patronage. Monetarily, that is."

"If?" she said sharply.

"Well, if . . . among the lovely sea of stars and starlets you claim in your social network, you could pluck one or two down?" Another unsteady pause. "A simple introduction would do. Talent, investors, big media journalists, anyone."

Something visceral shifted in Jordan here. I didn't catch it then, only a while later, when the memory returned to me.

Her whole body drew tight, and the open humor in her face shuttered up. "Nick," she said, after a moment, "why don't you go enjoy the rest of the festivities? I'll join you later."

I was shocked that I was being dismissed, thrust to the exterior of a mystery that was blooming before my eyes.

"If you're sure," I said reluctantly.

"I'm *sure* this money talk will bore you to death," said Jordan.

Gatsby looked baffled, too, and I didn't want to leave her alone in such questionable company, but their conversation had halted, and I sensed that she'd refuse to resume it with me still there.

I left unwillingly, returning to the rooftop, which had begun to empty. The music had dissipated and the night was cold. Farther away, girls held up the skirts of their wrinkled gowns, heels off, whispering their final nighttime secrets to each other. Time had stretched under so much champagne, and I lingered for another half hour before piling into the elevators with the remaining guests.

Back in the lobby, I noticed an additional elevator in the corner, smaller than the others and guarded by a hover-bot. Just as I was about to ask around for Jordan, she emerged from this private elevator, holding Gatsby's arm. He shared another quiet word with her, and she nodded stiffly before bidding him farewell.

"I think I've gone mad," she muttered, taking my elbow.

"Are you unwell?"

Her chest swelled with a deep breath. "We have to meet. Soon. Privately."

This sudden distress of hers worried me. "Is something wrong?"

"Give me your comm."

I extended my hand, and she pressed her wrist to mine. Her name flashed in glowing letters; then her date called out from across the lobby, waiting impatiently with the other bullet-golfers and looking none too pleased that Jordan Baker had spent the whole evening on the arm of a nobody.

"I'll call you," she said. I had the impression she was restraining a whole flurry of tense words in her jaw. "I'm going to need your help with a certain matter. But you can't say a thing."

"What *kind* of matter?"

She embraced me, tipping her mouth into my ear. "We both need to find out who he really is. I can't speak about it here. I'll call you." As she turned to leave, she seemed to remember something and stopped, squeezing my arm one last time. "Nick," she murmured gravely. "Do be careful with him," she said; then she was swept away by her eager party.

I looked behind me to find Gatsby still here, shaking hands and patting shoulders. I walked over, waiting my turn to say goodbye.

"I feel awful about earlier," I said. "The misunderstanding—"

He clapped my arm. "Don't give it another thought."

"It's a splendid place," I offered, and it was only as the words left my mouth, and a radiant light washed over him, that I realized, despite everything, there'd been a moment where the laughter and the music had distracted me from work.

"I'm very glad, Mr. Carraway." With his hand on my arm, he escorted me toward the doors slowly, as if I were the last or most important of his guests. "Listen. I really would love to borrow you tomorrow. Take you to lunch in the new Veluz. Not to worry, of course—I'll have your assignments rearranged."

He said it like work was a thing to be eliminated at will, and I reminded myself that my livelihood, for the time being, belonged to him. There was no choice but to shake his hand now, and with the other, claw out whatever lurid truth lay undoubtedly within this invitation, in the locked floors of the tower, and in Jay Gatsby himself.

He wished me good night, and I went out into the dark morning, his fond smile trained on me all the while.

◇——◇——◇

Not a minute past noon the following day, I found Gatsby waiting outside, reclined on the driver's side of a cream Veluz, the car bulbous and iridescent, as if a giant pearl had washed in from the ocean and was misplaced on the narrow West Egg street.

Before I stepped out from the lobby, there was a moment where he hadn't noticed me yet, and in this oblivious state, he kept adjusting his cuff links, moving through a sequence of uncertain poses as if every nerve in his body were vibrating beyond his control.

When he spotted me, he leaped to full posture, and we both stepped into the Veluz. "It's pretty, isn't it, old sport?"

My palms brushed the hard viridian leather. "This is the one going to market in the New Year."

"It is. Are you a car man yourself?" he asked eagerly once the auto-drive switched on and we set off over West Egg.

I explained that my family owned a body shop in Minnesota. It started with my grandfather, who immigrated from the Philippines right when a cluster of barangays in Manila had been declared the first successful hover-community in history, just in time to spare millions from the wrath of a harsh flooding season.

Hover-tech had boomed into Southeast Asia's primary export, beginning with Veluz Motors, the largest global hover-car manufacturer. My grandfather had been a technician at their factories in Manila before packing his bags for the American Midwest. The body shop he started up had eventually passed down to my father, though we'd still been resigned to intense frugality compared to others in our suburb.

I didn't get far in this explanation, however, before Gatsby interrupted to tell me about every Veluz he'd bought in the last three years. Each car was conveniently attached to some brilliant adventure that took us through the enchanting Singaporean metropolis, into a small hover-village off the coast of New Oceania, and then a Hollywood-like scuffle in the Vegas desert.

"How did you come into netdiving?" he asked once we'd reached the edge of the district.

"I'd intended to become a mod-doc, but my professors suggested I might have a knack for diving, so I went through the exams. When the war came, anyone who scored decently was drafted."

I'd passed the body shop over to a cousin, and after the conflict ended, I was too antsy to return home. Contracting was a natural next choice. I was unmarried, could travel on a whim, and the corps always needed temporary bodies to do temporary tasks.

As my professors had informed me, diving was best suited to calmer minds and softer tempers—a difficult thing to teach in a classroom but considered necessary after one too many cases of divers burning through their nervous systems from split-second distractions or losing grip on turbulent emotions. In deep cyberspace, as the mind strayed farther from the body, the ability to stay focused—to remain human— was a matter of survival, or you might never resurface.

"Now, that's something." Gatsby fumbled around with several buttons on the dashboard-holo. The roof turned transparent, flooding the car with tides of white sun. "I climbed the ranks myself too. People think Ops isn't as interesting as diving, that all you do is set up rigs and monitor vitals, but it's more than that."

He plunged into a valiant story about saving a whole squad of divers from certain death by exposing a saboteur in his ranks who'd supposedly poisoned the hypo shots. The feat had earned him a lieutenant rank, and soon he was being stationed all over the East as a strategist. This was the plot of a thriller film, and I think I nearly laughed in his face before reining myself in. You couldn't chew on these stories, let alone digest them.

I saw the crumbling edifices of the valley's sad apartment buildings coming into view up ahead. Gatsby fidgeted with his cuff links again. "I don't want you to get the wrong opinion of me from all these stories you hear. I'll tell you God's truth. I am the son of some wealthy people in the New West—all dead now. I was brought up in America but educated at Oxford."

He then rattled off sporadic facts about the operations he owned. Gen Wealth was the largest. Other notable ventures included the Klipspringer android factories and this new Happy Sleep studio he hoped would solidify his footing in the entertainment scene.

We were soaring past the ad-drones over the valley now. "See these? They use revamped hover-tech. Licensed from Veluz, of course, best of the best in the business. I decided to invest in them since they were getting so run-down. I think it's a waste to leave them dark and unlit. Aren't they lovely now?"

"These ad-drones are *yours*?"

"Why, yes," he replied with the air of someone who owned countless wonderful things, and a sliver of the sky happened to be one of the simpler ones. "I'll show you something. I've never showed anyone this before."

He pressed his comm against the car's console, and the dashboard rearranged itself. With a secretive smile, he tapped one glowing button, and suddenly the holo right beside us—an advertisement for a new stim-stick brand—dispersed into a million pretty sparks, its light falling apart like the fireworks at his party.

"You're allowed to control them like that?" I said. "The whole ad-scape?"

"Of course. It was a condition of the purchase agreement," he replied, and though I knew there was no ceiling to frivolity in corpo matters, this was a disconcerting flavor of richness that outbid anything I'd witnessed at Yale or in a Buchanan home, or even in his own tower. "Now no one has to get bored of seeing the same old images cycling up there. Try it."

He was insistent, so I reluctantly tapped a button. This time, three drones sailed toward one another, circling together to flash a holo of a ten-foot-tall model posing for a luxury clothing brand. She materialized before us, and as we flew past her—or rather, square through her chest—the holo waved and blew a kiss.

I pressed the button again. She flickered, disappeared, and the drones flew back into place.

Dr. T. J. Eckleburg's bored eyes followed us as we glided out of the valley, and soon, we were flying alongside the great Queensboro Bridge. I saw up ahead a row of police cruisers diverting hover-traffic away from the city core as they did every morning during rush hour. To my shock, however, the officers took one look at Gatsby's license plate before waving us straight through.

"You do a lot of work around the globe?" I asked at a break in one of his harrowing tales—this time, of a trip he'd taken to the provinces of Cebu.

"Oh yes. I mean, as much as any business might," he said rather noncommittally, and if the bootlegging whispers were to be believed, this didn't surprise me. Body-mod regulations remained most stringent in the Americas, which only prompted gangs to expand their resources internationally, fostering an elaborate underground network to which I was still trying to determine Gatsby's proximity. "The Philippines is one of my favorites."

I supposed he was trying to forge some common ground with me. Considering he'd just transformed the sky moments ago, I wasn't sure what ground we could really share. "Aside from a couple childhood visits and my last contract, I haven't spent much time there. My father's side has been entrenched in the Americas quite a while."

"Your father is the Carraway?" asked Gatsby.

"Carraway is a recent name of mine actually." I watched all sorts of new questions flash across his face. "It's not for any scandalous reasons. It just makes the contracting game easier here."

"Of course," he insisted. "I understand. One must reinvent himself as the opportunity demands."

He was, in fact, reinventing himself constantly to me. Even though I noticed it then, beneath the broiling sun, his eyes set off another flare of astounding reassurance.

As his fluctuating holograms kissed the clouds behind us, New York unfolded beneath with open arms, and I felt for the first time that there was something imperceptible moving through us here—some fine cosmic dust filling the lungs and stinging the eyes until the whole of it wasn't visible. Only the tips of its corporate monuments, its sharp neon burn, and those ceaseless ad-drones with lights so fierce that surely they could outlive the stars. And perhaps we could too.

So could anyone caught in the blinding glare of Gatsby and his redolent laughter, and the great American nucleus below us, and all of it together, a pledge of sustained possibility.

Ten

WHEN THE FIRST BODY-MOD ENTERED the market, it ran smartphone corporations into the ground in three short years. This mod was the neural communication device.

The comm, as we know it now, was a European effort that produced a nickel-sized implant inserted under the wrist, and it would go on to change the way an entire society communicated and browsed the net.

The growth that followed in the cybernetics field was too rapid for the fracturing American governments to keep up. Once a blueprint had been laid out for the seamless integration between organic matter and technology, every imaginable body enhancement sprang up to meet the demand. Prohibition laws landed in the 2050s and stayed put ever since. It did little to quell anyone, however, and had the opposite effect of creating a flourishing subculture of body-mod enthusiasts who outfitted themselves with the latest and greatest.

But of all the significant cultural contributions that the body-mod movement birthed, one of the most absurd and well-known was the story of a certain Manhattan speakeasy, which, as the rumors went, was haunted with the fallen spirits of the New East's most infamous bootlegging gangsters.

It was here where Gatsby and I took lunch that day.

We arrived into a buzzing, low-ceilinged antechamber, where he announced himself to the automated voice requesting identification. I stood still as four bots crept out of the ceiling boards and glazed their bug-eyed lenses across us.

Gatsby shared a piece of urban lore about the dead gangsters. "The superstition around the regulars here is that all the prominent New

East bootleggers who've met their untimely demise live on within the club's service bots. I mean, of course it's sensational—'technological reincarnation' and all that. But nothing wrong with a little faith."

I thought that was rather the least sensational thing he'd said all day. It was an unkept secret that every biotech corp in the world was quietly working toward trying to solve death, and though it still belonged in the realm of ghost stories, I wasn't surprised to find Gatsby taken by the idea.

"You must be modded to gain entry. That's what the scanners are checking for," he explained. "Really, it's to honor the spirit of the place by keeping it a venue for enthusiasts only. Comms don't count. But you'll be just fine with your diving mods."

I didn't see a single mod on Gatsby, but I assumed he might have possessed some undetectable oc-mod or simple cognitive enhancement from his military days. Or perhaps, just as likely, the rules didn't apply to him.

The club was at a midday surge, as dark and delirious as the stories suggested—and its clientele as ornately decorated. More steel than skin stretched on through the sea of bodies. Limbs were doubled and tripled or swapped altogether for any manner of claws or firearms.

It was most congested at the entrance, and we shuffled our way through clusters of raspy-voiced guests, huddled together in rowdy gossip and cigar smoke. "Don't worry," said Gatsby in my ear. "This is neutral turf. Won't find a safer place in the city than right here." He was behind me, chest pressed against my back in the flux of the crowd.

Past the entrance, an archway emanated a dim yellow glow. Eclipsing its center was a short man in a paisley suit. As Gatsby strolled toward him, he looked up to reveal a charmingly mirthful face. The man's left eye was modded, twinkling like a maraschino cherry.

I waited as the two exchanged fond jibes and half-finished jokes. When their bantering concluded, Gatsby introduced me. "Meyer, this is Mr. Nick Carraway."

"Sir," I said politely. He appeared just above middle age, but I guessed he could have been much older than that. *Dear boy*, he'd called Gatsby, and he held himself with the relaxed demeanor of someone without a single important thing to do for the rest of his life.

"Just call me Meyer. I don't like the stuffiness of a 'Mr.' or a 'sir.' I'm a retired man," he said, then invited us to join him at a large corner booth.

Gatsby ordered from the holo-menu while entertaining Meyer's complaints about the club's being too popular these days compared to his previous favorite drinking hole that had shut down for good.

"We're talking about the old Metropole," Gatsby explained to me.

"The old Metropole." Meyer nodded somberly. "Filled with faces deader than the ghosts here. I can't forget the night they fried Rosy Rosenthal there. Let me tell you. It was a stormy evening many years ago now. We were sitting together in a nice Sleep, and at four in the morning, what do I find when I resurface? I see Rosy cut up and charred. Every mod on his body was hacked, burned him *right* to a crisp. They had to sneak up on him, of course, 'cause they'd never catch him any other way. . . ."

I knew this story. All netdivers knew it, and half the ones I'd met in my life had come into diving explicitly inspired by Rosenthal's legacy. As it happened, he was a prodigy of a previous generation who had materialized out of a backwater New West slum and made a vigilante name for himself hacking a swath of wealthy corpo bank accounts. No shortage of gangsters lined up to hire his services after that, until one disagreement inevitably led to the next, and he'd angered just about every powerful entity in the Americas short of the devil himself.

I'd always thought of Rosenthal like a folkloric character, not someone who had friends that I could sit across a table from at lunch.

Meyer's old tales enraptured me. I listened intently as a lush spread of synth-meats, cheeses, and breads arrived, along with two golden highballs. Gatsby filled my plate and handed me one of the drinks. I exchanged an uneasy look with the serving-bot, which lingered at our side as though it were eavesdropping. I wondered if it required a dismissal, but neither Gatsby nor Meyer said a word, and eventually when it floated away on its own, I began to see why that urban legend about the ghostly bots had endured so long.

As Meyer cut off mid-story to shake the hand of another friend passing by, Gatsby leaned into me, so close that I could pick out the spiced undercurrent in his cologne. "Look here, old sport. I know you might have some reservations about me. You were quiet in the car."

I wondered how often he took colleagues out to be fantastically spoiled, and of those colleagues, how many fawned over his ad-drones and golden drinks and close-hand accounts of Rosenthal.

I decided to be up-front. "I don't like mysteries. If this is just about helping with your Happy Sleep studio, then I can. When shall I start?"

"I'd say we can bring you on board in about a month." He reiterated that the project was very confidential. "We're just finalizing some tests on our new rig."

"All right," I said. "But I don't know why Miss Baker is involved in such an underhanded way—"

"It's nothing underhanded! Miss Baker is very upstanding. We met at my first little gathering this summer. She agreed to speak to you about something that's—that's important to me. It'll make better sense coming from her."

A light blinked under his wrist. He offered a hasty apology, leaving the table to take a call.

"Fine fellow, isn't he?" Meyer turned to me again, nodding at Gatsby as he faded through the club. "Never stops working. Handsome to look at and a perfect gentleman."

"Yes," I agreed, leaving out that handsome gentlemen were the most deceptive people I'd ever met in my life. "Have you known him a long time?"

"Many years. He was still in his adolescence when he started developing the idea for Gen Wealth."

"Are you business partners?"

"Once upon a time. Sort of. As I said, I'm retired." Meyer took a long pause. "But this is how it went. About fourteen years ago, I had a friend tell me about a young man out in the West making breakthrough progress in the predictive genetics field, and I was toiling away at that myself. So we came into contact with one another, and I'd spoken with him barely an hour before I realized he was special."

He nodded again to himself, or perhaps at the memory. "It's his grit that's turned him into such a success. You won't find any corpos like that these days. Jay's very careful about whom he acquaints himself with. It's an admirable quality, though I fear it's left him with few true friends. I do wish he had more of those—or any, for that matter."

Gatsby returned to our table with the grim fatigue of pending business on his face.

Meyer stood up, buttoning his suit. "I'm going to leave you two young men before I outstay my welcome." His farewell with Gatsby lasted another minute, then turned into a parting hug. "You two sit here and discuss your sports and your young paramours and—" He glanced between us with a humorous light in his eyes that seemed embarrassingly presumptuous. Perhaps Gatsby hadn't noticed—or he had, and didn't bother to correct him.

Meyer strolled away with his spirited, unfinished sentence. I searched for a different topic to move quickly toward. "How old is he?" I asked.

"Ninety or so, but I couldn't be sure. I've never had age-mods myself."

"He said you were once business partners."

"For a short time. The corporate hustle never suited Meyer. He still sits on the board, though." He paused, adopting that distant pensiveness I'd seen on Meyer's face not a moment ago. "Gen Wealth wouldn't exist without his contributions. You've peered into the system many times, yes?"

"Parts of it."

"See, I've always had a special fascination with family trees. How they start, grow, intersect with others, come together, then apart," explained Gatsby. "I liked the idea of finding your existence in the context of so many others, understanding what glorious layers of serendipity made *you* come to life in this world. What important people came before you and what important people could come after. Meyer and I shared this fascination. That's why he's a dear friend and a mentor of mine."

"How long was he involved with the business?"

"He chose to retire early—after he sold the patent. Now he enjoys himself over in East Egg. He's probably the only person there who wasn't born into great fortune."

"I see."

A pause ensued. This time Gatsby didn't rush to fill it with another dubious anecdote.

"This has been quite the excursion," I said. "But I like charity even less than mysteries. So if you've a business matter you'd like handled through Miss Baker, I can't fathom why, but it's not necessary to—" I gestured around at the club. "I mean, you can come right out and say it."

"Charity?" Gatsby looked alarmed. "You misunderstand me, old spo—"

"I work for you," I reminded him. "You needn't call me that."

A flush settled in at the base of his throat, just noticeable in the cloudy dimness, and I recognized the tense confusion in his furrowed brow, as I had seen it on corpos before; he had laid out a glorious morning, taken me to a legendary place, assuming I'd be delighted by the spectacle, enough to forget who he was. But this all had the same effect as his overzealous stories and "old sport" habit.

"I . . . apologize." He sat back in his chair, swirling the glass of his highball that I now noticed he hadn't drunk. "During our first meeting, I was too cavalier. Too quick to jump across formalities and make your acquaintance. Oh—do you remember it? It occurred to me yesterday that perhaps you don't."

I was sure now that he was mistaking me for someone else. "What?"

He went on to describe the remnants of a night I'd thought, up until then, I had dreamed—the fading moon and the stranger beneath it. In my own corroded memory, there were large gaps, and Gatsby, with a touch of amusement, began to fill them in.

I listened in mortified silence. Then I raised a hand, cutting him off. "If I happened to say anything indecent . . ."

"Not at all. You were full of great wisdom. You spoke of the moon and the sun, I believe—"

I grimaced. "I promise it wasn't an ordinary night for me."

That smile again—all at once, stamping out the fires of my shame.

"In any case," said Gatsby, "I had a difficult time trying to be polite with East Egg suits last night. When we struck up a conversation in the elevator, it was the first breath of air I felt I'd had in hours." I saw the color extend from his neck into his ears, fanning across his tanned cheekbones. "It's tiring, having to prove yourself to those old-money types." He appeared to be, of all things, embarrassed, and I remember feeling some sympathy, for I knew the discomfort of sitting at a Buchanan dinner table. "What I mean is, the business with the studio and Miss Baker—well, it's important, but it's got nothing to do with my soliciting your time this afternoon."

He peered up through an unexpectedly flustered expression; it held a certain bared vulnerability. I didn't know what to make of him in that moment.

Uncomfortable, I glanced across the club and spotted none other than Tom, brooding in the corner, a fist around his whiskey. The smoke wasn't thick enough to hide in. When he noticed me, his mouth fell agape.

"Excuse me. I've got to say hello to someone," I murmured to Gatsby and went to meet Tom at the bar.

I couldn't imagine seeing Tom in this place, though by now, I assumed he might have had this masochistic tendency to surround himself with the crooked sorts he claimed he couldn't stand, and yet simultaneously, envied. I had to wonder, though, like Gatsby, how he'd manufactured his own entry. I was sure that the closest Tom had ever been to noncosmetic mods was standing in George Wilson's shop.

We offered each other stiff, requisite greetings.

"Daisy's furious because you haven't called up. She's been insuffer-able, asking after you. All she does is laze about and ask after people." Tom stared into the depths of his whiskey glass. "By the way, Chester told me you were prodding about my specs for Myrtle. Is something going on?" he demanded. "That's not like you. Don't tell me you're in the pocket of some reporter digging for a headline."

His assertion of what I was "like" irritated me. "Of course I'm not in a reporter's pocket. But since we're on the topic of truth, don't you think you owe Daisy some of it?"

"Oh." He relaxed, leaning against the bar. "It was just her who put you up to it? Hell, you had me in a twist for nothing!" He waved down a hover-bot to refill his glass. "What are you drinking? I'll get your next—"

"She didn't put me up to anything, but I suppose if you don't talk to her about this, someone has to."

He looked around as if wondering who this someone was, for surely it couldn't be me. He straightened again, craning his neck downward.

He wasn't that much taller, but I noticed he had this tendency with most people, an unconscious habit of extending himself over a person like an awning against the sun.

"Come on, Nick," he said curtly. "Maybe Daisy's put some ideas in your head. She does it to everyone. She hasn't a kind word to say about me, but that's the thing about your cousin. You haven't spent much time with her, and I hope you never do. Then you'd see her true side. She's no angel. She's crafty and—"

A light pressure touched my spine, and Tom cut off, his eyes flitting behind me.

"All right, Mr. Carraway?" asked Gatsby.

Tom glanced between us with a stern look.

"Yes. This is Mr. Tom Buchanan. Of the Buchanan Group clan," I introduced them after a pause. "Tom, this is—"

"Jay Gatsby." Gatsby shook Tom's hand. "A pleasure."

I hadn't considered that Tom's adamant East Egg superiority meant that he didn't recognize the name as anyone significant. I hazarded a guess that he'd forget it immediately. He grumbled a reply to Gatsby, then resumed our conversation as if he weren't there.

"Chester wanted me to invite you to this nice trip we're all taking upstate," he said. "Luxury cottage on the edge of the domes."

I stiffened. "Work's keeping me quite busy."

I doubted rejection was an emotion Tom often had to parse. He threw Gatsby another glance. "Work. Right." He scowled and, after a cool nod, excused himself.

Gatsby watched him go with an inscrutable expression. "Funny, I haven't met a single cheery Buchanan in my life," he said once Tom was seated at a far table.

The words didn't come out meanly, and the lightness in his voice restored my mood. "We're not friends." I felt compelled to clarify that. "It's complicated."

Gatsby dropped his hand, leaving a thrum of warmth on my back. "I didn't mean to intrude. He just looked to be upsetting you."

I hadn't realized I'd lost such command of myself. Or that Gatsby would be able to notice it across a dark club.

We returned to our table where the bill awaited us on the holo-screen. I rushed to pay before he could stop me. He made a fuss about it all the way to the doors. As we exited, I glanced at a row of idle serving-bots, those bug-eyed lenses surveying us as we departed from the smoke and intimate dimness of the New East gangsters.

Gatsby followed me to the passenger side of his Veluz, blocking the door with his hip.

"Mr. Carraway—I hope you don't think ill of my character after the confusion of today," he said insistently. "Isn't there any chance I could make it up to you?"

My comm-screen lit up with a stack of messages.

> OWL EYES: Penguin's alive if it matters to you. Spinal fry. Can't move an inch. Got a man swapping his mods.

> OWL EYES: Opened a tab. With interest. Heaps of fucking interest. Sooner I collect, sooner Pen walks.

> OWL EYES: How's the shoulder rubbing going?

"I suppose—" I attempted a purposeful stutter. "Although, no—it's too much. I'd hate to put you out."

He leaned forward. "Just say the word."

"Well, the tower is such a marvelous place. I wasn't able to peruse it all. I do regret it," I said uncertainly. I wasn't proficient at this game the way Jordan was and felt embarrassed at the prospect of trying, but I hadn't gotten any closer to scratching the varnish off his polished exterior, and for the sake of the assignment, this seemed a good starting point upon which to reorient myself.

He smiled. "Oh, if you'd like to view the tower another night, the honor would be entirely mine."

As I watched a flickering excitement pull the nerves loose in Gatsby's face, it struck me with the same rushing satisfaction of a perfectly timed pyre—of locks flipped, doors opened, secrets thawed by a glance and a word.

I used to consider myself the most careful person I'd ever known. I know now that was never true. If it was, I would have run away from all of this long before, and whatever fallout might have arisen, I imagine it wouldn't have been worse than what had indeed come together, then apart, that summer.

I imagine it would have left more of us intact.

The auditor they send from Gatsby Corp asks me if I've ever stopped a robbery before.

Because I have, he says. *Hundreds of 'em. There's nothing like it. I used to do it all the time when I worked for—*

The banks, yes. As you've said.

The banks, he states proudly. *Best ten years, that was. Still miss it sometimes. Smart criminals try to snip and trim their way around the VINEs, but the real crazed ones—they're coming into cyberspace with more pomp, circumstance, and ego than you can imagine. I'm talking pyrewalls that'll blaze themselves half dead. I'm fried from hunting those types. Auditing's dry, but at least it works for an old-timer like me. Closest I'll get to retirement, huh!* His laughter shakes between my ears, tasting like spices and sharp mint. *Not as close as you, of course.*

I'm not retired, I say.

Oh. His surprise stirs. *Well, I heard some things.*

The auditor is silent, but we're sharing a rig, so I can sense his immense curiosity. It's poor etiquette to intrude on a fellow diver's thoughts, however, and in the end, the man is polite enough—or at least, not bold enough—that he doesn't ask a single thing more.

We resurface four hours later. I jump down, out of my harness, pull the cables from my spine, and dunk my head in a waiting ice bucket to bring me back to life. Climbing out of the den together, we strip out of our compression suits.

109

"All of that, just to come back empty," the auditor mutters. "Board's not going to like this one bit. They were *hoping* we'd find something, you know. Rather desperately, in fact. Something easy to patch up, tell the press, be done with it. Now they'll be more restless than ever." He walks over to a holo-screen and begins filling out our report. "What's there to say? Not a single hole in the VINEs."

"Intricate gang op." I towel my face dry. "Multiple crews, probably? Rebuilding as fast as they're breaking down."

It's a Saturday, but the counterintel floor simmers with panicked activity, all the dens loaded up with freshly contracted divers dangling from their rigs. The previous team, last I heard, had resigned in a panic.

"You used to work these gallows, yeah?" asks the auditor. "About two years ago?"

"Briefly, yes."

"Met Etty?"

"I did."

He rubs the reddened skin around his neck mod. "Can't believe they're trying to pin her for this. It's cruel."

I nod stiffly, then sign my name on the report before riding the elevator up to the lobby. When the doors slide open, an android greets me on the other side.

"Mr. Carraway, the board would like to speak to you."

I frown. "The report will be ready shortly."

"No—not about that," replies the android. "About your time in Mr. Gatsby's employ."

Part II

The Mind of God

Eleven

I WENT TO ANOTHER OF GATSBY'S parties the following week, in the hope that I might glean something about his interest in Fay Medica. They had done much to tarnish their reputation and were hardly profitable anymore. As far as partnerships went, there were more distinguished biotech companies to choose from.

We observed the roulette tables and rounds of blackjack together. Gatsby never participated but stepped in as dealer when a Klipspringer needed to be replaced, not allowing the happy gamblers to be without fun for even a moment. We sat through the orchestral performance afterward on the roof, where a dozen holo-aerialists swung between ribbons in the sky. It was a busier party than the last, and it was odd to spend it with Gatsby when previously I'd run around thinking he was some incorporeal wraith. Now I wondered how many times I might have simply not noticed him during my first visit.

He had a way of flitting around his own tower like a stagehand, imperceptible, examining everything with a sort of sharp clairvoyance behind his eyes, as if every night were already choreographed and he wanted each partygoer to play their hilarious role as rehearsed.

I still didn't know what my own role was. I could barely hear him over the roar of the roof. He ushered us through pools of guests, urging me along with a brief hand on my shoulder or a cradling of my elbow as we took a shortcut across the dance floor. I asked him if I wasn't keeping him from more important matters, to which he held my arm and laughed, full-throated, his eyes disappearing in a broad grin.

"You are," he said, as if this were a fabulous talent of mine, "which is why you must stay, or else I'll have to actually speak to these people."

Those who did know his face—which, early in the summer, were not many—halted their revelry to greet him with all the esteem of a pope, including the NYPD commissioner and the mayor of Paris. Whenever I tried to ask who "these people" were to him, he responded unhelpfully that they were associates he'd done favors for once or twice.

At one o'clock, when the West Egg bar hoppers showed up to finish the night at the tower, I decided to take my leave. We descended to the lobby, where a troupe of inebriated Happy Sleep stars from England had just arrived. Gatsby began to say a parting word to me before one of these giddy men collapsed into his arms. The man screeched "Ja-*ay!*" as if he'd done so many times before, kissed his neck gracelessly, and by then I was already being pushed like driftwood out of the tower's doors.

I watched as Gatsby, arm around the fellow's waist, looked out at the feral lobby with a stiff brow. It softened, or seemed to, when I nodded my farewell, but he didn't follow me out of the tower, and, of course, I shouldn't have expected him to. Right as I turned, I noticed him lowering his earnest mouth to the ear of his companion. Whatever was said curled the man's spine backward with laughter, and I realized I'd learned nothing inarguably true about Gatsby that night besides the cost of the teakwood shelves in the library and which famous engineers had designed the holo-landscapes in his space observatory.

As he guided the new guests into the elevators, his shoulders took on a spirited posture, and it seemed that perhaps my role was, as he'd told me, little more than to shield him from unwanted business meetings. Now the role had been speedily recast into a pretty celebrity.

He contacted me the next day to apologize for the abrupt farewell, and I was rather surprised when he invited me for dinner that evening—a weekday, when the tower was usually closed. At last, he brought me onto the locked floors.

As I expected, they encompassed his residence and private amenities. On his raucous weekends, it was easy to forget he actually lived there—breathed and ate and slept as a mortal. Beyond its noise and pageantry, I found the tower's silence to be its most fascinating quality, and it was the first time I could think of it as his home and not just a floating amusement park.

Despite Owl Eyes' confident suspicions, I didn't see any signs of illegal mods stashed inside boudoirs or under couch cushions. Relative to the rest of the tower, his private floors were surprisingly tame with a gym, a conference hall, a storage station for the Klipspringers, a pool smaller than the one on the roof, a movie theater, and his main suite, furnished with geometric, impractical furniture, along with art sculptures still encased in bubble wrap and unrolled area rugs, newly shipped from an estate of his in India.

He kept his suite very cold. He wore wool sweaters with long, cavernous sleeves. He drank only water, or black tea at boiling point, but always poured two glasses of wine when we ate. He wasn't even a full year older than me. His birthday was in December.

"An odd month for a birthday," he lamented as we sat one evening beneath the holo-aquarium, on the glass floor above the Sleep lounge where he'd taken Jordan and me before. "Winter. Full of endings."

I think before that, I had perceived him as rather ageless, for he was a clutter of contradictions—juvenile exuberance, telling tales with nonsensical timelines and a constant nostalgia that now seemed like an affectation he'd picked up from an old man like Meyer. But he was really only thirty. A round and solid age.

The lounge below was dark, the Happy Sleep terminals shut off. Without the glow of their holo-screens, we could only see our own reflections.

"I like winter," I said. "It's my favorite season."

Gatsby pulled his legs to his chest. "That's the Midwesterner in you. But your birthday is in August. Everyone's in their best mood in August." He smiled dimly, less in his lips than in the whole attentiveness of his eyes. "Long days, high sun, no one's too serious."

A holo-stingray swam over us like a cloud. It seemed odd to me that he'd perhaps learned that from my employee record, though even stranger that he'd commit it to memory.

"Why did you decide to invest in androids?" I asked in what I hoped was a tone of casual interest. "Rather than cloning, for example. I hear some biotech companies think androids will be a thing of the past."

He didn't answer immediately, and I worried that I hadn't brought up the topic deftly enough. A long, strained moment passed. "Human cloning is generations away," he said at last. "Androids have been developing for decades now and are far from obsolete." He stood up. "I've spent my whole life wanting to effect change. I don't want to spend another life waiting on things that *could* be." He offered his hand. I took it, and he pulled me to my feet, his smile resetting itself and pushing the rest of my inquiries away. "Shall we check if dinner is ready?"

On my third visit, I noticed matching pairs of things scattered about the suite. Towels, toothbrushes, dishes, house slippers. I asked him if he shared the tower with anyone.

"No," he said after a sip of his tea, then frowned.

I backtracked. "I suppose I just thought the man who greeted you at your party—"

Gatsby set his mug down. "Not at all." He said this with a vigorous shake of his head and a locked jaw, and that could have meant many things—"at all" as in "men" or "at all" as in "that particular man"—but I had no rational reason to clarify other than my own curiosity.

I thought after Yale that I'd lost my ability to find corpos intriguing, to want to know them at all, for they'd started to streak together into similarly insufferable characters to me. Like their invisible beauty mods, you didn't need to see their duplicity to know it was always there. Not in spite of their perfect faces but because of them.

But as Gatsby fidgeted with his sleeves, knees bouncing beneath the table so much that the water in his cup was shaking, it gave me the intimation that he was wearing his money like clothes rather than like skin. If conversations with Jordan were quick spars, then Gatsby's were long hunts. I never knew when a burst of exhilaration would pour forth from him, or when I'd find an opening to ask him anything meaningful, or when he'd shut himself off like right now at a small inquiry.

At the end of that week, I knew Gatsby liked to take his tea with a drop of cream, that he had a long Greek heritage on his mother's side, that he disliked winter, and that he lived alone, though perhaps not happily, in that skyscraper. These were not things that could be put in my reports, and yet I found myself, at night, turning these curiosities over in my head, holding them like jagged stones, thumbing

116

their crevices for answers. I wondered how many more guests of the thousands might have also called him "Ja-*ay!*" with that enamored vivacity and how many waists he held easily like a book nestled in his elbow.

◇——◇——◇

"What's the holdup?"

It was the last day of June. Aside from informing Bunsen about Daisy and Tom's sad marriage, and Gatsby's mysterious Happy Sleep project, I hadn't provided anything new for two weeks straight.

"You're the one who told me not to spook him with questions," I said. "He's not exactly forthcoming."

"I told you that you have to let him play out his hand," replied Bunsen, pacing his office through the holo-screen, crushing a cigarette, then lighting another. "That doesn't mean we can just wait for the luck of the draw. Medica's threatening to jump firms if we don't get this sorted by next quarter. Get me something to work with. A little dirt on him to quench their thirst."

My comm shivered. Gatsby's name appeared out of the corner of my eye. "He's calling."

"Good. Shuffle his cards a bit and force his hand," said Bunsen, blowing out a cloud of smoke. Before it cleared, he slapped his holo-bar off, disappearing.

I answered Gatsby's call. He wanted to go into the city together that day, but as we hung up, I knew another planned excursion of his would get me nowhere.

A little dirt. There were still the whispers of Gatsby's mod-smuggling operations. Perhaps that was worth probing. West Egg was the epicenter of illegal mods, and unfortunately, it wasn't a simple matter of asking around. There were cryptic rules about how to move through these streets during the day. If I wanted to verify that Gatsby had connections here, as every bootlegger in the New East did, a careless inquiry could land me in trouble.

This was how I found myself bent over my bathroom sink, holding a hot penlight to my left eye, softening the glass plate of my ocular implant until it loosened, then cracked. I winced, heat barreling through my skull. The vision in my eye shattered.

I gripped the sink, and a milky film descended upon the bathroom, smearing my vision, folding it inward, black pixels clumping together like gnats. With my good eye, I glimpsed myself in the mirror. The pupil flashed rapidly; then a red light enveloped the eye socket whole.

I took slow, deep breaths, adjusting to the pain, before teetering out of the apartment and onto the street, where Gatsby jumped out of his giant pearl of a car and led me by the shoulders into his passenger seat.

"What happened?" he demanded.

"It was giving me trouble when I woke up," I lied. "I shouldn't have touched it. I think I'll have to find a mod—"

"It's morning. You shouldn't go alone around here." He crouched between my legs, tipping my chin up, and the pressure from my eyelid dripped down through my chest in a spiral of heat. "These are still the military ones?"

"Yes." With enough luck, I had at most half an hour before the injury would cause actual damage to the optic nerve, and it seemed Gatsby was making the same calculation in his head. If he did know a respectable mod-doc—a legal one—then they wouldn't operate out of this neighborhood. I knew most docs didn't bother licensing anyway, unless all they wanted to work on was cosmetic enhancements for people like the Buchanans, not ex-soldiers.

Gatsby stared at me with apprehension. I wasn't sure if I had broken the oc-mod for nothing, incorrectly estimated his willingness to humor me, until he stood up and said resignedly, "I know someone nearby who's got the right parts."

He drove us to the edge of West Egg, bordering the depressing dirt road that led into the smart town, and to the rolling steel door of a warehouse around the back of a discount liquor store.

Gatsby kicked the door twice. "Mr. Chase," he called out.

The door reeled up halfway. An older, bald gentleman stepped out from underneath, with a woolly beard slashed down the center by a knotted scar. The top of his chest and both forearms were inlaid in a patchwork of chrome and exposed wires. The scar that extended from his chin to his neck was far less severe than the twist of his scowl, however, as if the wind had blown a foul stench his way. "Gatsby. Bet you don't know where I spent last month," he spat, "cause I can't imagine what business *you'd* have with me after that deal in Nevada you—"

"Do you have that last batch of optic plates in stock still?" asked Gatsby impatiently. His expression showed no indication that he knew anything about Chase's last month, nor cared to.

Chase's gray eyes roved sideways as he looked at my flickering oc-mod, then back at Gatsby. "Charging you double. Got a buyer lined up in an hour. Won't be happy about missing inventory."

"Call it triple if you work in silence," muttered Gatsby as we followed the man inside, ducking into the dark, echoing warehouse.

The shelves were stocked with mods of every body part, limbs hanging loose or peeking out of unlabeled crates. Most of the light panels overhead were shut off, or perhaps broken, so that only one little pocket in the center of the warehouse was illuminated—an exam chair with tattered leather upholstery and a stack of uneven cabinets, bunched together beneath a triangle of whirring lamps. There was a desk and an office chair, too, a few feet away, but Gatsby did not sit.

"Which crew do you—" Chase stopped, squinting closer at my neck mods. "Ah. Army man?"

"Not anymore," I said, climbing onto the exam chair.

"Got a name?"

"He doesn't," Gatsby interjected, his tone low and dry. "We're not here."

Chase looked at me with fresh interest. Then he wandered off between the tall pallet racks for a minute, waving aside a dangling bundle of steel arms hanging low from a metal rod like tree leaves. He returned, clutching a transparent optic plate—an inch-long petal of malleable glass. I stared up at the warehouse ceiling where the pixels of gnats were reproducing, encroaching from the corners of my vision toward the center. My eye throbbed.

Chase inserted a thin needle, filled with a numbing agent, into my brow bone. He waited only half a minute before prying my eyelids apart, peeling the broken plate out with a pair of forceps. My left vision crumbled into total blackness. "You still dive?" he asked.

"Corp-side."

"Figures." He lifted my wrist next, holding the new optic plate against my comm to calibrate it. I felt a pinch in my eye socket as the oc-mod shivered in response. "Enjoying yourself?"

"Your silence is very loud, Walter," said Gatsby, leaning impatiently against the desk, arms crossed. A table lamp beside him cast one side of his profile in a harsh white light. In my half blindness, he looked like a dramatic, overly shaded charcoal sketch.

Chase scoffed but continued without a word for the next hour, measuring the new plate to my oc-mod, reshaping it with a laser and a hand drill, shaving it down meticulously, and when it was finally the right size, reattaching it.

My vision returned to me in stages—light, shapes, details. That was when I noticed that Chase had a procession of mods down his neck that resembled mine, only far bulkier. A few generations old.

"You served as well?" I asked.

He grunted indifferently. "I serve myself now. As much as I can, anyway." He got up, tossing the used syringes into a trash can—eyeing me closely, or perhaps his handiwork. "Never too late to start, you know."

"Thank you, Chase," said Gatsby tersely. "I'll finish up here."

Chase offered me another considering glance, before disappearing somewhere into the warehouse shadows, and I shuffled up on the chair, swinging my legs over the side.

"You're quite familiar with the mod trade?" I asked Gatsby. He looked at me sharply as if I'd accused him of something. "Since you're in the android business, I mean."

That was not what I meant in the slightest, but it was safer to give him a way out. The vision in my eye was still vibrating, but it had resharpened enough that I was certain he looked upset, as if this was one enormous misstep in the tour of riches he'd shown me thus far—a window with a view he couldn't curate.

"Yes, I've learned things here and there," he replied vaguely, then paused as if anticipating I'd say something more, but I couldn't overextend his discomfort, or else it might tip into suspicion.

He pulled open a cabinet beside the exam chair, taking out a plastic bottle of painkillers that he dropped into my hand. I swallowed one.

Then he ripped open a bandage and a sealed alcohol pad. "You said you wanted to be a mod-doc once, right? How'd that come about?" he asked. "Diving pays much better."

I thought he was only deflecting now, but when he stepped close to swipe the soaked pad above my brow, his voice had reset into that warm, smooth key.

"At my family's body shop," I said, "there was a man who used to sell us old parts every month, using the money to buy cases and cases of this—" I held up the bottle of painkillers. "The ones they administer at the illegal clinics around the outer domes, near where I grew up, are highly addictive." I closed my eyes as Gatsby stepped closer, smoothing the bandage over the wound from the syringe. His hands stilled for a moment. Though my skin was still numb, I felt the heat from his fingertips. "My father explained there was a shortage of good mod-docs willing to work out there. But when I got into Yale, my professors pushed me hard to consider diving."

I opened my eyes. Beneath the stark lamps, Gatsby's face was bleakly shadowed, its gentle, rounded angles more tapered, more rugged than I'd noticed inside his tower. He pushed his fingers through his hair, and a curl sprang free from its gel. "I see. Do you regret it?"

Even regret was a luxury. When the war happened, they needed divers. "Maybe. I wish the circumstances hadn't stripped me of a choice."

Gatsby blinked. His hip brushed my thigh as he bent over and discarded the pad into the trash can at my feet.

He flashed the penlight into my eye a few more times, testing the sensitivity. When I insisted I felt all right, I hopped off the chair and noticed Daisy's name on my comm, scrolling across my inner wrist beside the green pulse of her incoming call.

"Thank you. I'd better rest today." I massaged the numb side of my face, hoping the feeling would return soon. "I can get home myself. You've done a lot for me already."

He led me back outside, where we spotted Walter Chase sitting on a stump of plastic, a broken bus-stop bench for a line that didn't run out here anymore. He was gulping from a beer can, staring solemnly at the blanket of holo-ads over the valley.

I waited for my taxi, and Gatsby cleared his throat. "If it's worth anything . . . I think a mod-doc like you would have saved many lives, Mr. Carraway."

Later, as I flew over to East Egg to meet with Daisy, the sun was a wild, raging light, consuming the whole sky and stabbing at the nerves of my oc-mod.

I didn't know whether the quivering smile on Gatsby's face had been a nervous one, or if my mod hadn't yet stopped shaking, but I think sometimes that my vision has remained forever half veiled since that day—one eye still endlessly fixed on the summer's chimeric visions, seeking unsaid truths within its obscurities.

Twelve

DAISY GREETED ME ON THE porch, dressed in her ivory silks. We walked across the soft lawn that stretched down to the beach. Even beneath the air of the fan-bots, I thought it far too hot to be outside, but Daisy had already ordered an elaborate picnic spread, and at the suggestion of moving into the house, she refused. I wondered if the whole place really stifled her.

She was curious, of course, about the progress I was making on her family's account. I had the sense that was why she'd called me.

"These things take time," I said, repeating a line Bunsen had drilled into me before I'd boarded my plane. "We're being careful."

She moved away from the topic unhappily, and I inquired about Tom's whereabouts instead. I knew this was the weekend he was traipsing upstate, but I was curious what kind of lie he might have invented in the meantime. It turned out to be a two-day golf excursion with folks from one of his executive boards. Whether or not Daisy believed it, I couldn't tell.

"Aren't you going to ask after Jordan next?" she teased.

"Would you like me to?"

"I'd like to think you're already the best of friends and so you needn't ask me."

"I do happen to know she has a game today."

Jordan and I had kept in close contact since Gatsby's party. It surprised me. I'd thought she might disappear for a few long weeks, as women like her had the habit of doing, but instead, she sounded rather urgent about meeting. Our schedules were difficult to align as her matches, training, and media commitments had escalated farther into the season.

"How wonderful," said Daisy. "She doesn't speak at all about you."

"Oh."

"No, it's a good thing." She stole the pot from the serving-bot beside us and took it upon herself to refill my teacup. "Jordan only speaks of people when she has something to complain about."

I relaxed. "Then I should tell her I'm honored."

"Don't do that. She'll be annoyed with me. I'm the only person who knew her before she was famous and mysterious."

"Hasn't she got family?"

"She has one aunt about a thousand years old. She went back home to Nigeria, so Jordan visits once a year."

Daisy smoothed the pleats of her skirt, then looked far off into the Sound. Even from this side, it wasn't a lovely view. The city dumped icy-blue dye into it every two months to mask the toxins, but the color retained its swampish quality that wouldn't be salvaged no matter how many ad-drones glittered over it.

"Jordan was my only real friend in Louisville," said Daisy. "She used to follow me around. I . . . adored her for it."

She smiled softly. I'd never seen her smile quite that way before. I was certain that every face she turned to the world was an illusion rather than an expression of true feeling, a graceful distraction from the inner workings of her heart—the depths of which I now honestly believe had never been traversed by anyone.

Under the fragrant breeze, without Tom's lumbering imposition to match or an audience to beguile, I saw this act of hers crumble like a fistful of wet sand.

"You wouldn't recognize her if you saw her as a girl," she went on. "She used to be quite short, shorter than me, and very quiet. When she spoke, she had this fairylike whisper in her voice."

They lived in the same biodome apparently, just a few streets apart. On Daisy's tenth birthday, her parents invited the whole neighborhood. "Business was good back then," she said. "So whenever we were throwing a gathering, it was always a big affair."

I did remember some of Fay Medica's prime years. It was an important player in the biotech space before it floundered a flagship project, left behind a string of dead test patients, and was narrowly saved by a well-timed acquisition by Buchanan Group. Daisy's Happy Sleep success then skyrocketed straight into her marriage to Tom, and the media abandoned any sensational headlines about Medica's abysmal business practices in favor of a great fairy tale.

She leaned back onto her elbows. Her silk dress fell across the picnic blanket, loose and luminous in the summer light. "Jordan was different from the other kids. She and her aunt were living off some dwindling family inheritance. I think they almost had to sell the home in Louisville. She only confided this to me many years after the fact."

"Is that what brought her to bullet-golf?" I asked.

"Perhaps it's what brought her to it, but I don't think it's what kept her there," said Daisy. "I think she always felt like she had something to prove. Even at nine years old, she was so serious all the time. At first, she didn't come to my tenth birthday party. I was sad about that until she showed up right at the end of it, sweaty and adorable. She'd sprinted from home, hoping to make it in time. She told me later she'd had an important appointment, getting outfitted for mods."

"At nine years old?"

"She was preparing to enter the New East junior division. Failed a few times. When she finally qualified, people thought she'd be in and out of the circuit right away. You see, everyone says now that Jordan Baker is a 'natural,' but it isn't true. Nothing about it came easy for her. Of course, that narrative ... it's not as dramatic sounding as *destiny*. There's much to—to admire about her." Daisy sat up straighter, whatever memory she'd wandered into fading away. "Anyway, she likes to keep people on their toes, doesn't she?"

I tried to imagine this small, adorable Jordan, but indeed it was a difficult image to reconcile alongside that disdainful posture and aloof smirk.

"Did she *like* the sport?" I asked.

"If you're good at something, I suppose it shouldn't matter." The sun flared behind the clouds, and Daisy held her arm up to block the sky. Her wedding ring glinted violently in the light—a massive thing that dwarfed her entire hand, encrusted in diamonds with a great emerald at its core. "What if she chose another path and realized

125

maybe she should have stayed right where she was all along? No . . . Jordan's too smart for that."

The veranda doors opened just then, and a maid stepped out, holding the hand of a little girl in a pink floral dress. She had Daisy's exact shade of cinnamon hair, curled in tight ringlets. When the maid let go of her, the girl stood at the edge of the picnic blanket, endearingly petrified, her small fists bunched into her skirt.

Daisy sighed and patted the empty patch of blanket beside her. The girl seated herself about as far from me as she could manage.

"Hello," I said warmly.

"Don't hide, darling. It's not polite." Daisy shoved her up a little closer. "This is Tito Nick."

At her mother's introduction, Pammy got back up to her feet and shuffled over, stopping right in front of me. To my surprise, she wrapped one of her tiny hands around mine, pulling it up until the back of my fingers pressed into her forehead. I'd greeted dozens of uncles and aunts this way myself, but I'd never been on the other side of it before, and it made me feel suddenly, terribly old.

I smiled. "And you must be Pammy."

Immediately she turned around to partake in a small basket of strawberries.

"Don't be offended. She *can* speak," muttered Daisy, "but she hardly does around me or Tom—especially him."

"How does she know how to do that?" I asked, referring to the polite greeting.

"I was raised by a Filipino grandmother, too, you know," said Daisy softly. "Of course, I ought to teach her *some* things. Or else she'll grow up uncaring and detached from it all."

"That's right. I forgot," I said honestly.

"It's all right; everyone forgets. Certainly, Tom does too. Even me." Daisy shook her head. "Do you know the first compliment that man ever gave me? He said, 'My, I never would have guessed! That *mystery* about you is just gorgeous.'" She laughed, humorlessly, and squinted very hard at the sun again until it disappeared behind a cloud.

It was easy to understand what Tom found "gorgeous" about Daisy. She had always kept herself artfully scarce. That was a steadfast truth of the business. The best Happy Sleep stars were the ones anyone could imprint their own desires onto. No one was better suited for that than Daisy—her petal-like softness, a liquid beauty that molded to the whims of its audience. And Tom was quite used to having things shaped to his liking.

A little exotic, but not too much so. Worldly, but a solid American. Excitable, but a shy southern belle.

I'd imagined he'd wanted Daisy like he'd wanted his varsity football championships, or any number of youthful accomplishments to collect and prop up for display in his vast house.

"I should tell you something I learned from Tom. When we went into the city together," I said.

Daisy tensed, and all the alarms went off in her face. I almost couldn't meet her eye, and then I felt rude and ridiculous for it. "I met his ... his woman." Wading through the mental fog of that night, I explained the spec Sleeps ordered for Myrtle Wilson.

It wasn't as though I were anticipating an outburst of tears, but Daisy's reaction to this was shockingly underwhelming.

"I see," she said.

"I'm sorry that—"

"That's a kind thing to share with me, Nicky. Thank you." She stretched her arms up high. "Let's give him a frigid shoulder for a week. That'll rile him up! Won't it, sweet Pamela?" She ran a hand through her daughter's hair, pulling her away from her strawberries. Pammy whined. "We'll make Daddy very—"

"Don't you care about—" I shook my head. "I mean, it's a great deal of money, and not a difficult thing to trace back to him, should the media decide to care."

"Oh, I know just the account he's pulling from. The one that holds the royalties from *my* Sleeps." Daisy scoffed. "It's uncivil. But that's to be expected of Mr. Buchanan. Tom and I—well, he detests me, every now and then. Not always, of course. Sometimes he smiles, and Pammy's not afraid of him. ..." At the sound of her name, Pammy glanced up at her mother again, but Daisy was not looking at her; her eyes were fixed on the murky water, a tension wavering between her brows. "Other times ..."

"Does he dislike your Happy Sleep career?" I guessed.

I saw the weight of the question deflate Daisy's posture. "He dislikes that it has legs. That it still walks. Follows me around no matter where we are."

I'd seen at the apartment in Morningside Heights, among Tom's own acquaintances, that this was true. Daisy Fay was an enduring entity, larger than anything Buchanan and larger than Daisy herself. Indeed, it would follow her forever, but nothing followed Tom around, and perhaps that perpetual nothingness haunted them both now.

"I used to play this game in my head, guessing all the ways his woman is different from me, lovelier than me," said Daisy. "Now I don't care to know. It wouldn't change a thing. I'll still be here, won't I? And the sun will still set, and—and he'll still be off somewhere with anyone else."

I wanted to say Myrtle wasn't lovelier, and that was likely the reason Tom entertained her at all, but I wasn't sure how much of a reassurance it would be.

"You needn't endure it," I said after a while. "I don't see why you should. I know there were business forces at play when you married, but your name means more on its own than his."

This made something quiver in her rosy face. "Oh, Nick. Do you know I care a lot about your opinion of me?"

"I can't imagine why," I replied, stunned.

"Well, I *do*. Ever since the time you visited Louisville."

I'd visited exactly once, as a child, for a distant relative's wedding. "When we were young?"

My only memory of that Louisville trip was a photograph my mother kept of it on our holo-bar above the fireplace. I might have been five years old. Daisy was six, a flower girl. In the photo, we stood next to each other with our arms entwined.

"Yes, you were so well mannered. That was what all the adults said," Daisy explained. "You never hid behind your parents. You spoke fluently and eloquently in two languages. During the ceremony, I was fussy and tired, and my lola pointed at you and whispered in my ear: 'That's Nick, your cousin. You ought to be *just* as polite as him.'"

I had no idea why Daisy was telling this story, or whether it was even true.

"If I did a horrible thing, Nick, would you dislike me forever?" she demanded.

I couldn't discern what words she wanted from me then. Somewhere amidst these strange vagaries was a plea for my unconditional approval of her. "We're all capable of horrible things when we're unhappy," I offered. "That's why I'm saying you don't need to resign yourself to any unhappiness."

Her lips formed a thoughtful pout, and then she let the matter fly away with the wind. The morning stretched on. We moved down to the beach together, along with a fan-bot. Pammy wobbled between us as Daisy once more declared her love for the ad-drones over the Sound. Then Pammy tumbled over into the sand, and Daisy lifted her up with some difficulty, but in her mother's unpracticed grasp, the little girl wailed.

"May I?" I asked.

Helpless, Daisy deposited her daughter into my arms. We strolled the rest of the beach, basking in the muggy midmorning silence.

Pammy tensed against my chest—quiet but not relaxed. When we reached the edge of the gardens, I stopped and scanned the fan-bot above us, running a subroutine to override its controls. A holo-screen lit up next to my comm.

"I'll show you a trick," I said to Pammy, and pointed at the bot.

She craned her head up. With my free hand, I pressed a button on the control screen, letting the bot fall rapidly toward us. Pammy squealed, covering her eyes, before the bot came to a hard stop just above her head, bouncing like the spring of a jack-in-the-box.

She giggled and reached out to swat it. Daisy scolded her.

"It's fine." I laughed, lowering the bot farther until Pammy could pet its metal wings with her hand.

"Birdy," she murmured.

"Yes, they are like birds, aren't they?" I agreed.

"Me—me *too*," she whined incoherently.

"She wants you to teach her," Daisy translated. "Each time she sees something new, she never lets it go."

"Well, first you must be good for your mother," I told the girl solemnly. "Then maybe I'll teach you."

Her curious fingers poked the hard ridges of my neck mod. When the nanny came out again to take her inside, it took much coaxing to unlatch her from me.

"She loves you already," muttered Daisy.

"Children just like to be treated as equals."

She stared, in a blank-eyed daze, as the nanny led the girl back across the lawn. "Maybe you ought to keep her."

I searched for a joke in her face, but there was nothing there except fluttering unease.

She walked me to the front of the house. I thought again of that old photo of us as children in Louisville—pressed together, strangers. We were still strangers, except now we were grown, shaped by the ways of the world and the quiet insecurities of adulthood that kept us an arm's length away from honesty at all times.

As we stepped onto the porch, she leaned against the smooth ivory columns. That gentle misery encased her again.

"After I gave birth, I became very unwell for a time, Nick. I was cynical about everything. I went months without holding Pammy. And, of course, Tom was off—" She waved her hand around. "I swear Pammy remembers all that time I couldn't stand her and detests me."

She tipped her chin up—not with the hard-hearted confidence that Jordan possessed, but with tense desperation, like she was holding her neck above water.

"I used to think the best thing a girl could be was a beautiful little fool," said Daisy. "But fools don't last two minutes in this world. Now I know I'd much prefer my daughter smart. Forget beautiful. And you can't be both, of course. No one likes a girl who's both."

The wind gusted across the porch, swallowing her words, but I heard them in all their unabashed despair. I almost reached out to comfort her, but a ping from my comm stopped me.

JORDAN: Come to the arena tomorrow after work.

Don't you have a game?

JORDAN: Yes. But I wiped my evening.

130

For me?

JORDAN: Don't get bold, Mr. Carraway.

JORDAN: Come alone.

I informed Daisy that I'd be attending Jordan's game soon, and she started explaining the rules of bullet-golf as though she were preparing me for an exam. I assured her that Jordan already knew of my ineptitude and had requested my company anyway.

Daisy squeezed my hand. "I see. That ought to count for something."

"Let's hope so," I said, squeezing back with no particular effort. But she winced.

Then, before she could hide it from me, I saw it—not large, but noticeable. A splash of purple bruising across her fingers.

I pulled her hand closer. "What . . ."

She frowned casually at the bruise as if it were a stray bug flitting about the room that she thought she'd already killed. "Oh, I slammed it in the veranda doors yesterday."

I remembered how I'd held her hand during that evening of our dinner—how I'd forgotten all about it by the time I returned home. Now I knew she simply modded over the bruising, and she did it once again before my eyes.

Unbidden, the image of Tom breaking Myrtle's nose in a forest of pastel flowers rose up in front of me.

"How long's that been going on?" I demanded.

"Oh, Nicky, you're making a sad face—"

"Daisy," I said firmly. "What use is that 'good judge of character' now if you choose to ignore it?"

She seemed almost upset with me, enough to scold or scream or banish me from her private beach forever, but it was only a glint. Then all the light flooded back into her body, and she breezed past the whole issue, as if it had never existed.

"*I'm* the older one here. That's right, I'm 'Ate' Daisy," she said, employing the older sister honorific in a way she never had before.

"Now that I think about it, why don't you ever address me as such? I'm imposing a new rule—"

"Daisy—"

"*Ate* Daisy!" she exclaimed.

I was stunned by her dismissal. As I stood on the porch steps with her, the sun was at its peak behind us, and it transformed the great Georgian mansion into an iron shadow.

"You can always call me," I said, for it was the only thing I could offer that wasn't an awful platitude. "If you ever need anything, I'll help you."

She blinked and her eyes shone, as if my words had streamed down to her in a torrent of light, from the sky into her chest—as if such assurance had never been spoken to her, or ever in history. She hugged me, and I felt the frantic gallop of her heartbeat.

Contrary to Tom's belief, I didn't need him to tell me who my cousin was. Even then, she'd never been an angel to me, for I'd never met her as he had—as Daisy Fay, the icon. It wasn't just her beautiful gloom that stuck with me that day, but the lingering notion that something troubled her far more than Tom's complete disregard.

Thirteen

I DESCENDED INTO THE BELLOWS OF a Brooklyn bullet-golf
arena, where a seat in the front row was reserved for me, according
to the expensive android who met me at the doors and led me
into the cavernous venue.

No pocket had been left vacant beneath these fiery lights. Seated
among tens of thousands of New York's most passionate bullet-golf
enthusiasts, I was now a visitor in their strange, turbulent world.

Traditional, unmodded professional sports had gone well out of
fashion around the time I was born. Filling their place was the splendor
before me—great spectacles of bended physics, offering its rare victories
only to the best bodies money could buy.

The gentleman beside me sniffed my lack of knowledge, for he
leaned over and provided generous commentary. Even with his insights,
I was lost amidst the intricacies of the shifting holo'd obstacle courses
and the speed with which each competitor tore across them like
meteors streaking the sky.

By the time Jordan stepped onto the stage, the arena's excitement
had surged into whistling cries. Among the most impressive of her
mods was a set of propulsion calves that I had previously only glimpsed
in the slit of a satin dress in the Buchanan sitting room. Now in its
intended setting, her beauty came alive to me in all of its true nuance—a
whole foreign language translated before my eyes.

Her modded legs barreled her within arm's reach of the dome's
ceiling. She twirled midair like a flipped coin, rotating on a serendipitous axis in the glinting light, then shot forth across the holo-
course. At the last stretch, she whipped her arm forward, as fast and

smooth as a catapult, and the ball sailed from her fingers toward its final hole.

There was a *ding*, a red light over the clock. I paused to gauge the reaction of the man beside me.

"Now, that's rotten luck for Miss Baker!" he proclaimed.

"Why is that?"

"Twenty-one point seven! Point three seconds less would've gotten her fifth place," he said. "I reckon she's done for if she can't clear in twenty by her next match. Her season best is seventeen, you know. Seventeen! But she's not done that in about a decade. . . ."

There were ten competitors per game. I understood that fifth was the middle of the pack. "Done for?" I asked.

"She may be out of the playoffs," said the man. "Her sponsors must be writhing in agony."

Jordan frowned at the sight of "21.7" glowing rudely above her head. The obstacle course evaporated. From somewhere in the lower stands, a slender, mustached man jumped down and threw sharp words her way. My seat companion explained this was Jordan's coach.

As the announcer's voice boomed over the speakers, declaring the final standings for the day, Jordan's eyes found mine, and she set off toward me, fleeing from her purple-faced coach mid-speech. All the way past the security bots separating the front row from the stage, she marched purposefully in my direction, pulling me up and away. I could barely utter a farewell to my neighbor, who watched me go— slack-jawed—in Jordan's clutches.

"I won't speak to a single one of them." She meant the swarm of jostling reporters who had closed in on us as we crossed the stage. In the ensuing scuffle, her lips grazed my earlobe. "Stay close."

Cameras and mic-bots hovered so low, they bristled our hair as we moved together toward the players' tunnel. Jordan smelled of sweat and the piquant burn of her mods. She didn't let go of me until we were alone in her dressing room, where she collapsed onto a pink crescent sofa.

"What was that for?" I asked.

"Sorry." She didn't sound sorry. "They're writing the most insane things about me these days. They need a distraction."

"Because you've been losing?"

"Losing," she muttered into the throw pillows, "and aging. The two greatest sins of all women and athletes. Unfortunately, I am both."

"What about your mods?"

"What *about* them? Useless things!" She sat up and scoured her cabinets.

The room was upscale but very untidy. A holo-bar had toppled onto the floor, its screen tuned to a children's program, playing a cartoon of a talking frog. Clothes lay about like area rugs, and makeup, used stim-sticks, and a few small mod tools littered a large vanity. I spotted spare bits of screws, cleaning fluid, and hand drills like the one I'd seen her using on her knee at the Buchanans'.

"Mods have to work harder the older you get," she said. "Doesn't help that competition gets younger every year. Now it's all anyone will talk about: 'Oh, Baker ought to fire her coach, her mod designer—no! Retreat down to the Euro-league as she might benefit from all those strict regulations and weaker competition.' The absolute *drivel*."

At last, she found what she was looking for—a pack of cigarettes. She lit one, then leaned over the counter of her vanity and took several urgent drags, scowling at her reflection.

"I quit," she said hollowly. For a moment, I thought she was refer-ring to bullet-golf, but then I saw her contemplating an ashtray on the counter before her. She held up the cigarette and stared at me through the mirror. "Take it away from me?"

"I don't smoke."

"Well, you ought to. You make the rest of us look bad."

Eventually, she stamped it out and retreated behind a long folding screen to undress, the glass panels scrolling slowly with the brand logos of her sponsors.

While I waited, I pulled up the news on my comm and saw my own face gracing the front of the sports section. There we were, me and Jordan Baker, her proud chin turned into my neck. I almost didn't recognize myself under the bleak camera flash—my shoulders pulled in rigidly, the brown of my skin drained of color.

She'd been right about the distraction. I scrolled two minutes before I caught any trace of yesterday's headlines reporting on her losing streak. I informed her of this.

"Good!" she hollered.

"I thought you had that man from Gatsby's party," I recalled.

"I *had* no such man. He's new talent at my agency. I was helping him court sponsors. Otherwise, he'd be out of the professional circuit before the season's even up," she said. "It's all theatrics. No one cares about *skill* these days. Only the freshest bodies and the newest mods."

I knew that sponsorships greatly funded an athlete's regular proced-ures, the annual sum of which was enough to bankrupt even the best in their field. Corp funding was crucial, and it came first from popularity and second from winning—both of which were fraying for Jordan as of late.

"There must be parade floats when Daisy comes to see you," I said as she shuffled behind the changing screen.

"She doesn't. Come to see me, that is." Through the lights and logos of the glass panels, I could see the faint ridges of her silhouette, the compact muscle of her shoulders, which stilled for a second, then relaxed again. "Everything here disturbs Tom."

I'd never mentioned Tom, but since their marriage, it was true that Daisy was almost never seen alone, if at all.

Jordan emerged from behind the screen, dressed in loose denim and a satin blouse that made deep, pleasing shadows of her waist. "Anyway, she's never offered to come." She smoothed her long braids back, spinning them into a tight crown. Her back was to me, but her face in the vanity mirror fluttered anxiously. Then her lips pitched at an irreverent angle, and she joined me on the couch.

She picked the holo-bar off the ground and replaced it on the coffee table. The screen shimmered away from the talking frog and into the image of us on the sports feed.

"There's one thing I love about rumors." Her leg slid against mine. "You get to pick and choose what's true. And they say many things about me: my training staff despises me; I'm unkind to my opponents; I rotate who gets access to my dressing room." She looked at me in a hazy cocktail of satisfaction and curiosity. "They say, with so much stress and adrenaline, it has to go somewhere."

In the notch between her collarbones, I saw a spot like a wine stain, deep Merlot in the center and rimmed pink. She wanted me to notice, and that realization seared through my skin. Her hand moved from her lap to mine, her gaze gleaming ferociously, a solar eclipse against the naked eye.

The dressing room door slid open just then. It was Gatsby in the threshold, in one of his flamboyant suits, flanked by two security androids.

"Mr. Gatsby," said Jordan unhappily. She did not stand to greet him, nor move her hand from my thigh. "Which one of us are you here for?"

Gatsby took in the clutter of mod tools, the unfolded pile of Jordan's undergarments by the changing screen, and the sports-feed image of me on the holo-bar. "I happened to be in attendance today. Thought I'd say ... hello."

"Hello," she replied, as if it might dismiss him. When it didn't, she frowned and said, "Sorry if you came about sponsorship talks. I don't fill my head with business on game days."

Gatsby dragged his eyes away from the holo-screen. "Mr. Carraway's not here for business?"

"Oh, Nick is always for pleasure." She placed a careless kiss on my cheek, and when she opened her eyes, it wasn't me she was looking at, but Gatsby. "You can't borrow him, I'm afraid. He's mine today." She walked to her vanity. "We have a date."

I still had no idea what this date entailed.

"Very well," said Gatsby, though there was a stunned, dispirited look to him as he retreated to the door. "Is the ... oc-mod doing all right?" he asked me.

"It is, thank you," I replied, and then he was gone, without a farewell or even a parting nod.

"That's interesting," said Jordan, pinning her ears with large golden hoops in the mirror.

"What is?"

Jordan folded her arms, nodding slowly to herself. "Have you been spending a lot of time with him?"

"Yes, I have to." I'd met Gatsby almost every day since his first party. Dinner at the tower, when it was empty on weeknights, had turned into a fairly regular occurrence. While I waited to be onboarded into his Happy Sleep venture, Bunsen demanded I do nothing to compromise my access. This meant no overt inquiries about the odd Gen Wealth contract, and absolutely no mention of the acquisition. Everything had to be volunteered by him, and though he volunteered a lot, more than half of it was hot air.

"Progress is slow," I said. "He told me he thinks highly of you, though. Says you're very upstanding."

"What's your opinion of him?"

I pondered for a moment. "Excitable."

"Excitable?" she exclaimed.

It wasn't as though I'd called *him* upstanding, but I saw that she'd expected, rather desired, a more critical assessment. "He apologized for being indirect at first."

"Of *course* he did. Let me guess—he was quite sincere too." There was some heated itch beneath her words. "I was worried he'd start to call on you like that." She considered the ashtray on her vanity again, looking vaguely regretful, then sighed. "Did he also tell you he and I first crossed paths at one of his parties?"

"Well . . . yes."

"It's not true." She procured a lilac clutch from a drawer below the vanity and took out a pair of oversized sunglasses. "Wasn't the first or even the second." She punched the Open button of the dressing room door, and I sat up hastily to follow her out. "The second time I ever met Gatsby was six months ago in a Chicago Happy Sleep lounge. It's a ravenous place. Lots of nepo kids and young celebrities and the like."

"What was he doing there?"

"What he's always doing. *Business,*" she said. "Sometimes that means throwing beautiful parties in a skyscraper. Other times, like in Chicago, he's sweet-talking the heir of some small-time op he's trying to acquire. Or sucking the cocks of wide-eyed B-list Sleep stars until they're half in love with him and weak enough to spill trade secrets." She regarded me over her shoulder. "You see, he never does anything without a reason."

I flushed at her directness. "Sounds like any other Saturday for a corpo."

"Yes, but Gatsby's a man who'll tear someone to shreds and not even notice the blood under his own nails." She frowned. "I thought we were in agreement about that, but maybe *your* blood's already under his nails. In which case, I can't confide in you further."

I realized that when she'd advised me to be "careful" about Gatsby, it wasn't because of his rumored gang affiliations. "That's not—" I started, but I couldn't sound defensive. There was nothing to defend, besides. "He's a liar who won't answer anything straight. I'm just trying to end my assignment quickly, Jordan. Whatever you have on him, I need too."

We reached the end of the corridor, taking an elevator to the arena's landing pad. Outside, in the rolling heat, she led me to a compact silver Veluz. It was an older model, scratched in spots as if bumped on more than a few occasions.

"All right. Are you familiar with Gen Wealth's databases?" she asked.

"Yes, that's the team I work on."

She leaned against the car's trunk, eyes hidden behind her large sunglasses. "There's probably information in there on everyone who's ever lived in the New Americas under every name they've ever used. Right?"

"More or less." Population data, both past and present, helped train the algorithms. I had a sense now about what her big idea might be. Still, it was a long shot and rather hazardous for us both.

She circled around to the driver's side. "Where are the servers housed?"

"At the company building. With backups in the old smart town."

She unlocked the doors. "To the valley, then."

Fourteen

THE QUEENSBORO BRIDGE HAD JUST faded behind us when Jordan reached over the dashboard and switched off the car's automated controls. I watched, aghast, as her hands settled casually upon the steering wheel and she accelerated over the gray waters of the East River.

"Either you ought to be more careful or keep the autopilot on." I lurched forward, gripping the sides of my seat. "How'd you even turn it off in the first place?"

She explained cheerfully that this was an older model a friend had hot-wired.

"Dare I ask why?"

"Because it's fun, Mr. Carraway. What other reason does a girl need? Besides, I *am* careful."

"No, you're not."

"Well, other people are." As if to demonstrate this, she rose quickly and at a terrifying angle, zipping over three cars. The hood of her Veluz clipped the taillight in front of us and earned her a string of creative, mother-themed curses.

"Suppose you meet someone just as careless as yourself," I protested.

"I hope I never do. I hate careless people. That's why I like you."

She grinned at Dr. T. J. Eckleburg's grim eyes, growing larger on the dusty horizon, and, at least for that moment, I forgave her for all the secrets she kept in the curve of her smart mouth. I knew she enjoyed trivial lies, bit into them like small chocolates, then spit them out before the sugar could rot her teeth; if this was another one of those, I was willing to be peacefully ignorant for now.

"How is that bird from the library?" she asked.

"Still chirping in my comm, unfortunately. In denial, she can't seek her thrills elsewhere." No bootlegger worth a damn would keep a stash in their residence. Still, she was convinced there simply had to be a treasure locked up in there. Having seen most of the tower's locked floors myself, I hadn't gotten a whiff of any exceptional contraband, and at the time, I didn't think I ever would.

We landed on the edge of the district and stepped out into the valley's muffled, gurgling noises. One of those ominous security androids stopped and stared at us before marching on.

We weren't far from George Wilson's shop. As we passed it, I saw the AI out front had been hacked again, her appearance altered. Today she lay on her stomach, arms dangling off the sides of an invisible surface.

"You again!" she screeched.

"'Again'?" Jordan lowered her sunglasses and inspected the disheveled holo. "Another friend of yours?"

"Barely an acquaintance," I replied.

"Ha!" cried the holo, neither an agreement nor a protest.

"Now, that sounds like a story," murmured Jordan.

While I paused to locate the Gen Wealth building on my comm, she attempted to strike up more polite conversation with the scowling AI. After a minute, a glowing pin flourished onto my holo-screen, and we set off toward it.

Like most buildings in the valley, the Gen Wealth facility went unmarked and had been assembled inside a mid-rise condominium, the floor plan of which I managed to obtain without trouble from company files, along with the facility's regular maintenance schedule.

The lobby of the building was round and barren. Several bulbs had dislodged from a miserable chandelier and left a lawn of shattered glass on the scratched tiles. An inch of afternoon sun sliced through an open slit of the boarded-up windows. While I scanned the ceilings for a camera, Jordan lit a stim-stick and waited inside the revolving doors.

One camera overlooked a pair of broken elevators. I paused to run a swift subroutine, rerouting the surveillance feed, and once it was safe to speak, I motioned Jordan inside.

"You don't think it caught a glimpse of *your* face?" she asked.

"My oc-mods are military."

"So?"

"So they're built in with signal jammers." I saw that she had no idea what that meant. "My face won't show up on surveillance feeds. Visual gets warped."

"Why've they got that reserved just for military folks? *I* need that for all the cursed paparazzi," she grumbled.

I smiled sympathetically. "That's not how it works. Cam-bots and security cams aren't the same thing."

"How disappointing." We entered the dim, mold-scented stairwell. "As far as the database goes, I'm trusting you have some method for getting in undetected?"

The security systems would shutter up at any breach. I'd have to use my employee credentials to skirt around that and hope I could work fast enough to erase the record of my entry before I resurfaced. That was, of course, if a dive was possible in the first place.

"I'm more concerned about the tech," I said. "I don't know how outdated it is, or if there are enough resources in there to even set up a rig. If there aren't, I can't guarantee I can access it."

Footsteps pattered above us. I peered up the stairwell. A line of fluorescent pot lights flickered unsteadily. In the dimness, I made out a tuft of dark hair and two large brown eyes that darted away at the sight of us. A child.

"Tenants?" whispered Jordan.

I explained to her that the area was still classified as a residential neighborhood, despite being used for business purposes, and corps took advantage of this unregulated technicality. Every corp that had purchased buildings had space to spare, however small, and if they could charge rent by the inch, they would.

"So these folks really will just—let us in?" she asked.

"Engineers come by every few months to do maintenance." A free-entry clause was standard for leases out here, and I could only hope the tenants would be accustomed enough to the routine that our presence would hardly be cause for alarm.

We made our way to the top level, composed of fewer units and fewer chances to be spotted by any more stray residents than was necessary, though as soon as we stepped out of the stairwell and into the corridor, we were faced with the length of an elderly fellow draped across the grimy floors. He was modded clean down the middle—the entire left side of his body wrapped in chunky, mismatched plating as if a huge procedure had started years ago and was subsequently abandoned.

"Hello, sir," I greeted him. "Are you a resident?"

The man shot up, then slouched against one of the apartment doors. Two cigarettes bookended each corner of his scowling mouth. His left eye was swapped for some white, bulbous contraption that might have been an incomplete oc-mod; his other eye, the organic one, roved this way and that before settling hazily on us.

"You'd know that"—he hiccuped—"if you were the *usual* corpses."

"Would you mind—" I couldn't voice the request before the door of the neighboring apartment clicked open.

"Are you all right, Mr. Edgar?"

It was the child, the same one who'd noticed us in the stairwell. Up close, they looked no older than nine or ten, with cropped hair and delicate features. A girl perhaps, though I couldn't be sure, and when I asked for their name, the old man growled, "Back inside!" He shook a thin arm in the air in what I assumed was a vague gesture at Jordan and me. "I said—the corpses are here! Don't speak a word to 'em!"

"Corpses?" said Jordan.

"Corpos," the child answered politely. "That's you two."

"Oh, your mother wouldn't want you in there alone with 'em while she's away! Go, go!" exclaimed Mr. Edgar between a fitful of coughs. One of his cigarettes tipped out of his mouth, and he fumbled through his trouser pockets to fish out another.

I turned to the child. "You live with your mother? When is she returning?"

They had no idea.

"A nurse," said Mr. Edgar gravely. "The kid's mom's a nurse. Good soul, good soul, *last* of the good ones, I'd say. Saves lives in a city that don't deserve any savin'. . . ." He paused, drew in a stuttering breath, but before he could speak, his body went limp, collapsing again, unconscious this time.

"He's all right. He always wakes up," said the child. "I thought you're not supposed to come till next month."

"There's a little something that needs checking on," I replied, "Mind if we step in? Won't take a moment."

The child's lip jutted out in contemplation. They seemed neither apprehensive nor irritated, but rather like I'd put forth a sales pitch and they were carefully considering it. After an extended pause, during which I couldn't deduce their criteria, they ushered us inside. I thanked them, then thought to ask, "That was a Mr. Edgar, was it? Does he live next door?"

"Not anymore," answered the child. "Mother says he got an e-vacation notice last week."

"Eviction?"

"Yes. But he hasn't another place to go, so he's just been out in the corridor until someone cares to move him." The child flashed us both a panicked look. "Oh—*you* won't move him, though, will you?"

I promised we wouldn't. Then I took inventory of the apartment. The servers were set up on a loft overlooking the modest living space. There was a kitchenette in the far corner, and a small hallway that led into one bedroom and a tight, square bathroom. Taped to the walls over a fraying couch was a collection of artwork—a child's painting, a few unframed photographs, and a line of film posters that I recognized from another netdiving action franchise.

Beside the posters was a paper calendar, marked up with crayon. One particular day, a week from now, had been circled emphatically.

"What are we counting down here?" asked Jordan. "Your birthday?"

"No, that's for Mother's shifts," said the child. "I can't go back to school until I get my comm, so I can pre—cipitate in class. And I can't get my comm until Mother works ten more shifts. At the hospital."

I exchanged a look with Jordan. Then she smiled at the child, pivoting smoothly to some story about how she'd always found school quite boring anyway.

I glanced up at the loft.

144

"You're a diver," the child remarked, turning away from Jordan. "I see it—on your neck."

"You've a sharp eye," I said.

"I want to be a diver too one day." They pointed proudly at the film posters. "But Mother cries when I tell her that. She says only two kinds of folks become divers—corpos or gangsters."

They relayed this with such nonchalant wisdom that it made Jordan laugh outright. Then the child was overflowing with questions: How long had I been a diver (seven years); did it pay well (decently enough); had anyone ever told my partner that she resembled the bullet-golfer, Jordan Baker (sometimes, answered Jordan, but she disliked that comparison because she was *much* prettier than Miss Baker, wasn't she? The child flushed.).

I climbed the loft, crouched in front of the terminals while Jordan continued to entertain the child below.

"What do you like so much about these movies?" asked Jordan.

"They're always helping people, even in secret. They do brave things for people who can't do things for themselves."

"What sort of brave things would *you* like to do?"

"Dunno yet," they murmured. "I just know Mother doesn't like it here. She says it isn't how it ought to be. I don't think it's so bad, but I want her to have those great houses like in the movies. Like a biodome mansion where the weather is always perfect! And where you don't need to wear those big filtration masks when the smog storms get awful, and there's no corpos coming in every month. . . ."

It was time to set up the rig. The child couldn't stay for that. I was sorry to dismiss them, and as they shuffled dejectedly out into the hall to tend to their sleeping neighbor, Jordan watched them leave with the smallest downturn of her lips.

"What's wrong?" I asked.

"Don't know. All of it." She pulled her sunglasses off. I saw a weight had deepened the lines of her face. I recalled what Daisy had shared with me about Jordan's past—being on the precipice of a lost home and her hasty push into bullet-golf, eclipsing her entire childhood. "So, can you do it?"

I examined the terminal again to which a set of old-gen monitors was loosely connected. After I fiddled with a batch of thick cables, one of the screens lit up.

The hardware was archaic. Not promising. From a glance, I knew the dive wouldn't be painless. I had half a mind not to entertain this mess anymore; I'd risked enough as it was trying to pick apart Gatsby's elevators. Now I was riding on nothing more than Jordan's intuition.

"We'll have to find out," I said. "What do you want to pull, exactly? If a man like Gatsby isn't who he says he is, then either there'll be no trace of him in public records, or whatever trace there is will be fabricated."

Jordan climbed the loft and squatted beside me in front of the flickering monitors. "That's why we're finding his real name."

My fingers paused along the tangle of wires. "You *know* his real name?" Uncovering a birth name could open several new avenues. If it ended up being useful enough, I imagined it might even end my assignment.

"I know that sometime in 2063, he might have been stationed at one of two Kentucky military bases. That's not very difficult, is it? I'd like to see a full list of the men."

Pulling names wasn't complicated, but there would be hundreds. I estimated that I'd have a few minutes at most to dive, retrieve, and resurface before my credentials registered in the system beyond my reach. At that point, my cover would be decimated. "Jordan," I said as calmly as I could, for she didn't seem to understand the gravity of the matter. "I'm breaching my contract. Rather, I'm committing a crime. How sure are you that you can review a hundred names and—"

"I'll remember it if I see it," she insisted.

Remember it. "So the first time you met him was—"

"A long time ago, yes." She inclined her head. "Maybe."

"Maybe?"

"Well, that's why we're here, aren't we? To see if I'm right."

Fifteen

DOWN THE HALL, I INSPECTED the bedroom. It was smaller than one of Gatsby's elevators, furnished with a plastic nightstand, two mattresses, two comforters, and a mound of pillows. I dragged them all out into the main area.

Bemused, Jordan peeked down from the loft. "We're building a fort now?"

"A makeshift rig."

"Made of—mattresses?" She held the cable I'd set aside. "I thought all you needed was this here."

"That provides the neural connection that makes interfacing possible once you're *in* cyberspace," I explained. "But it's the *getting* in that requires work. It's a matter of timing."

"Timing what?"

"At the precise point when the neural connection is made, the body must be weightless."

"As in"—she leaned over the railing—"you're going to *jump*?"

"Yes." It was the easiest workaround, given our lack of a harness.

"But why does the weightlessness matter?"

"You don't have a body in cyberspace. The feeling must be replicated right before you jump in; otherwise it's not going to work." I gestured at the faded movie poster across the room, where the artwork depicted a diver hanging dramatically in his harness, attached to the rig by the neck, arms spread wide in midair. His head fell slack in front of a glowing light, fanning his body in the fuzzy-edged shape of angel wings. "It's what harnesses are usually for. Keeps you suspended the whole time."

Her face soured. "I see why you call it 'the gallows' now."

The last order of business was to make the apartment as frigid and lightless as possible. We drew the curtains closed. While we waited for the temperature to lower, I reclined against the railing of the loft. Below me, Jordan made herself comfortable on the pile of mattresses and pillows.

She sat up on her elbows. "I want to know the whole storied history of how a rogue AI in an abandoned smart town knows you."

I proceeded to recount my whirlwind afternoon last month that began on the West Egg train with Tom, took us through Wilson's shop, and then ended in a double-stim at Myrtle's penthouse—drunk from green liquor and high off spec Sleeps.

"Specs? That explains it. Daisy was paranoid it'd be worse," said Jordan. "She'd noticed Tom's spending habits."

"Then what did she *think* he was doing?"

Jordan lay back down. "Can't say exactly."

"Can't or won't?"

"*Can't.* Look. Don't ask me about those two." Her eyes slipped shut. "All I know is Tom's got a way of sticking his nose in things, and Daisy's more of her own person than he'd like. I'd hazard a guess she was worried he'd hired someone to keep an eye on her. You know, a professional. Someone like you, except with her on the wrong end of it. You never know with Tom. He has money, time, and a petty streak that'll never break."

I was almost tempted to ask if that paranoia of Daisy's was built out of nothing, but I didn't want to endorse Tom's controlling manner in the slightest. Instead, I said, "Daisy mods her skin."

"I'm quite aware." Jordan folded her hands over her stomach. "Why do you think I agreed to spend my whole New York season in that awful house?"

"It's good she has you," I said, for I'd felt guilty leaving Daisy after our picnic. "She told me how she adored you when you met as kids."

I watched her throat bob. Her eyes didn't leave the ceiling. "Hyperbole, I'm sure."

It hadn't seemed that way to me. "Have you ever been in a spec?" I asked curiously.

"*God*, no. Can't stand Happy Sleeps, no matter how high quality they are," she replied. "I can't accept Gatsby's sponsorship. Aside from

148

how offensive it was, I wouldn't spend a second of my time in that industry. Did you know that when new performers are recording sessions, they won't even remember what they recorded? It's like that for the first five or twenty times, depending on their endurance." I didn't know that, in fact. She continued. "Having your mind detached from your body in such a way—it's never been appealing to me. Diving seems even worse. Just watching you now's giving me shivers. I wonder how you tolerate it."

Actually, it was just that sort of corporeal disconnect that I found peaceful about cyberspace. I couldn't say *how* it was tolerable, only that I was used to it and past the initial discomforts, I relished the quiet relief of letting the real world and all of its unpleasantness dissolve away.

As the temperature continued to plummet, I started to undress. I had never done a run without a proper compression suit before, but stripping down to the undergarments was the next best alternative. There was no time to be bashful about it now. Jordan stared at the water-stained ceilings again, presumably for my comfort more than hers. After I folded my shirt, jacket, and pants into a neat pile, I called her back up to the loft.

"You have so many." She stood behind me. It took me a second to realize she was talking about the extra ports along my spine. There were ten or twelve of them; I couldn't remember. I'd looked at them only once before in the mirror after the surgery, which I underwent four weeks after enlistment, and never again.

"I don't use all those anymore."

"They're from the army?" Her modded fingers—made colder by the decreasing thermostat—crawled across my back. Her thumb brushed a particular spot, a scar perhaps, and I felt her exhale. "You needed all these to interface with the military rigs?"

"Yes." I was too conscious of her in the dark—of our proximity, her touch, the floral twirl of her perfume. I worried my temperature was rising again. "If you don't like Happy Sleeps," I said, half to distract myself, "that means you've never seen a Daisy Fay session?"

I'd meant to say it lightly, but it had the opposite effect. Her hand fell, and she stepped away. "Have *you?*" she asked, a hard shift in her tone.

"She's my cousin. Of course not."

"Precisely. Happy Sleeps are for strangers." She paused. "Athletic mods enhance your senses. Make you hyperaware of yourself, your strength, the wholeness of your body. Diving and Happy Sleeps do the opposite. They eliminate all sense of your own physicality so that your mind *becomes* your body, and all you're left with is your thoughts. Some like to claim that swapping out your limbs makes you less human, but that's nonsensical. Isn't it *more* inhuman to cheat things like age or death? To live so much of our lives inside memories that aren't real? If you ask me, I like living in my own body. That's why."

She curled her fingers into a fist, and I was sorry I'd posed the question at all. I'd struck an unknown nerve.

From below, the thermostat beeped quietly, signaling it had reached its lowest possible setting. It wasn't as cold as I would have liked it. This worried me.

I turned to Jordan. "There's something you must do for me later."

"Something *I* must do?"

"You'll see a harsh climb in these levels when I'm about to resurface." I indicated a spot on the monitor. "Before I do, I'll need you to go into the bathroom down the hall and run a cold shower. Then disengage this cable"—I indicated my neck—"and bring me into the bathroom. I'll be slow to my feet, mind you. Won't have much control of myself. You need to get me under the shower quickly."

"How quickly?"

"As quickly as possible. The dive causes heat spikes. Not unlike how we found Owl Eyes in Gatsby's library. I've taken a small hypo shot, but it won't be enough. A cold shower will wake me while bringing my temperature down."

She hesitated as if she were just now taking in the intricacy of the procedure. "You're sure you'll be all right?"

Truthfully, I wasn't sure about anything, but if at the end of it was a shadow of truth, I couldn't walk away from it now. "It'll be a shallow dive. If I can get it to work."

I slotted the cable into my neck, holding my breath. It crackled, resistant, and with a sinking dread, I thought the whole endeavor had failed. I twisted the head harder, rattling the cable until the lock fastened and a familiar tension whipped through me, from my nape to the tips of my toes.

I smiled, nearly buckling with relief. "Well," I sighed, "at least I can get in." How much my nervous system would detest me for the frolic I was about to put it through was another question.

"All right. Shower," she repeated. "Undergarments and all?"

I pressed my wrist to the terminal scanner, and the monitor flashed briefly with my employee ID. "Don't get ideas."

When I glanced back at her, at the smooth planes of her face catching the blue lights of the screen, her smile was wild and brilliant. I hoisted myself up onto the railing. The pressure mounted between my ears, and the room dripped into streaks of wet paint. I sucked in a breath.

Then came the rubber-band sting—a snap, clean across my nerves—and I realized, with a surge of shocked satisfaction, that the rig was holding, launching me forth toward the soundless intensity of raw cyberspace, flooding my pores and my bloodstream.

It was the stimulation, often more than the money, that attracted people to the dive. There was a high to the pain, a giddiness to the jump, a scorching surge through the fall. Diving to me was perpetually associated with work, and so I'd never fully understood that exhilaration until this moment—until Jordan stood before me, the heat of her breath singing through my skin.

My eyes slipped shut. Her hands were on my face, her mouth against my mouth, and I surrendered to the chill and the haze, arms out, falling backward off the edge of the loft.

By the time my unconscious body landed on the mattresses, I was awake again on the other side.

◇——◇——◇

I resurfaced, shivering and wet.

"Mr. Edgar . . . was right about one thing." Jordan was on her knees, bent over the tub, panting. I was curled on my side, cheek pressed into the cold tiles. "You *were* an absolute corpse."

A crisp ache settled into my neck. I shifted onto my back and gazed up blearily at the running shower head. I was feverish.

151

"Names ...," I groaned. "Pulled them ..."

"Yes, yes." She sighed and stood up. "Get dressed."

She'd lowered my temperature in time, but the burn still sizzled my skin like small pricks of hot oil. The lights were too sharp, and it hurt to blink, so I lay there under the water, eyes closed, for a while. Entering cyberspace on a makeshift rig might have been vaguely amusing, but exiting was a whole different story. I waited, overstimulated, for the room to right itself. My breakfast was lodged somewhere between my stomach and my throat.

I managed to towel myself dry, slipped back into my clothes, and joined Jordan in the loft. She was crouched before the monitor with sharp concentration. "Anything?" I asked.

"You said he was born in '44?"

"Unless he lied. Wouldn't be the first time."

She jabbed her finger into the screen. There were fourteen names listed under that year. "Look at this: 'J. Gatz.'"

I might have laughed if I hadn't been so doubtful. "If that really is him, you think he would've picked a better alias."

"And how *should* one pick their alias?" she said.

Now it was a question about me. "You don't know?"

"Your real name? Why would I?"

"I don't know. Perhaps Daisy would have told you."

"She hasn't."

"Right." I chuckled tiredly. The delirious remnants of the dive hadn't melted away yet. "Because you don't ask after me."

"I don't. If I like you, why shouldn't I speak to you myself?" She said this without any trace of coyness, but somehow this elicited more of a reaction in me than when she'd made a joke about my undergarments.

"I didn't pick the name. I borrowed it from my grandfather," I replied. "When he came here, the only way to start up his body shop was to take out a loan. They told him an American-sounding name would fetch him better rates and a faster process. He went along with it but chose something entirely ridiculous. When my father was born, they made sure he inherited the real family name."

"Which you didn't keep."

"I did. Until I was discharged."

"How was the army?" asked Jordan. "You don't seem to speak about it."

There wasn't much to say. I couldn't scrape together enough to disqualify myself from the draft through back channels, as people like Tom and most Yale classmates had done. The war had been a tapestry of corporate conflicts, disguised as foreign cyber-invasions to justify pulling in government resources and heaps of military funding.

As Jordan began to set the apartment back in order, I remained up in the loft, sprawled out on my back. I wanted to say the whole experience was uneventful, but perhaps it was just that I never thought about it for too long.

"If you kill someone in cyberspace, there're no bodies, no faces, no blood. But you feel it as if you've just killed yourself too. The minds of divers are so connected." I stared at a particular spot of mold on the ceiling, waiting for my nausea to subside. "It was an intel war, anyway. Combat death was rare. Most injuries and casualties came from your own mistakes. Wrong pyres on the wrong VINEs, neural fry, that sort of thing."

Jordan admitted that the war had passed entirely in her peripheral, through news headlines she'd never stopped to digest. This was not uncommon, and yet it still reminded me how far apart our social circles could be—that a war that had entirely halted my early adulthood, and consequently redirected the rest of my life, had been little more than background noise to her. To most people.

"After the fifties, when the Philippines successfully erected several hover-districts, the West began to flounder for ways to replicate the tech themselves," I explained. "The Americas sent spies overseas. Eventually, it all led to a series of needless conflicts between dozens of American corps and the burgeoning ones across the Southeast. Veluz and some others."

With the exception of an attempted bombing at the Veluz headquarters in Manila, the conflicts had largely never left cyberspace. Divers on both sides were plunged to dangerous depths, trying to dig up and defend their industry secrets. The conflicts hadn't quite "resolved" but simply fizzled out, and a precarious truce settled in its place. Mostly because war was expensive.

"But that was years ago now," she said.

"Suspicions remain." I'd learned rather quickly that most American corps could only see me as a son of a Filipino family with generational ties to Veluz. The optics of this had rendered my résumé useless.

"So that's why it troubles you."

"What troubles me?"

"That you've spent all your career forcing some patriotism, squashing espionage suspicions," she observed. "Now Daisy's actually pushed you into it."

"No, I—" The prickling heat in my bones reignited. I felt a hot flash. "I don't care that much about it. I adopted 'Carraway' because it doubled my contract offers." I checked the time on my comm. "We should be on our way before the mother returns."

Jordan offered her arm for balance as we went back out into the small hallway where the child was seated on the floor, leaning their head against the shoulder of a sleeping Mr. Edgar. I apologized again for the inconvenience.

"I know you're not the maintenance team," they said.

Jordan tensed. I forced a smile. "Now ... why would you think that?" I asked cautiously.

We'd gone about the day too brashly. The trouble would catch up with me soon, but right then, I can't explain how I knew that the child would not be the cause of it, except that when they glanced up at us, limp and exhausted, there wasn't the faintest shred of suspicion or resentment.

"Corpses don't apologize," they replied.

It was just that—a mundane fact of nature, no different from the cycles of night and day.

◇—◇—◇

We retraced our steps back to the hover-car in silence. It wasn't until Jordan ignored Wilson's screaming holo that I realized she was deep in thought.

"Maybe I've got it wrong," she muttered. "I just ... I *swore* there was something familiar about him when we spoke."

154

"What did he say to you?"

She stopped us in front of her Veluz and bit down hard on her lip. "It's a long story. I shouldn't tell it in halves."

I was wrung dry from the dive, foggy headed, and still plagued by a terrible dizziness, and she didn't look much better. "It's already late tonight. I'll run 'Gatz' through some databases first," I decided. I couldn't say if it would do much, but it seemed the least drastic course of action for now.

"I don't suppose he's told you anything else about his past?" asked Jordan.

He hadn't, but I remembered Meyer from the mod club and mentioned that he was a chipper old man with a residence in East Egg.

"Could you get us an audience?" she asked.

"He's not *my* acquaintance."

"But we can orchestrate something, can't we? We both have the entry to East Egg," she said, and I couldn't argue with that.

Then she surprised me with one last unexpected question: "Would you be able to arrange an untraceable transaction?"

Considering it would be the easiest task she'd requested all day, I informed her that I could. "What for?" I asked.

"How much, do you suppose, the fanciest current-gen comm model costs?"

I had never imagined Jordan could be described as "gracious," and I don't think even she saw this as an act of grace herself, but it did surprise me for a second.

I hesitated. "What did you have in mind?"

We considered a few numbers, overestimating by an extra thousand or two, and once she was satisfied with an amount, I said I would track down a full list of the building's tenants as soon as I could, assuring her I'd get the money safely into the mother's account.

She glanced back at me before ducking into her vehicle and plucked something out of my expression. "'Charity is tape over a crack in a dam,'" she sighed. "That's what you're thinking, isn't it? Well, you did the same thing to your bird in Gatsby's library."

She was right. I'd done it, too, without realizing, despite how deeply I'd thought my pessimism had rooted itself.

Still, the age of "cracks in a dam" was long past—the age of working the system, climbing the ladder, choosing lesser evils, or choosing anything at all. Systems were broken, and ladders had turned to slides long before either of us. Lesser evils had leveled out into equal ones, burgeoning ones, inevitable ones. A place like the valley wasn't birthed from one legislative oversight, but from a spectacular compounding of societal failures, and, in the face of that, one spot of incidental kindness was only a bandage waiting to be bled through.

[LOADING]

.

.

.

[PLAY]

"Please state your intention for the record."

"What ... um, what intention? What is this?"

"Oh, it's just a formality. We're required by law to record all consultations. Don't mind it."

"A-all right. What shall I say, then? Like ... 'I—I would like to apply for a Generational Wealth Loan'?"

"Perfect. Tell us a bit about your background."

"Well, I'm a nurse? I'm afraid I don't know what else to say."

"I see your family's already in our system! You're a second-gen applicant. Your mother, before she passed, had an account with us. That's great news."

"Is it? I'm still paying off her balance."

"Means you're a legacy client. It'll fetch you a lower interest rate. You have a daughter as well?"

"Yes."

"How lovely. I see today's her birthday. You'd really like to get her a nice gift, I bet."

"A comm. She's the only one in her class without one. Can't keep up with the lessons, you know ... but I—I just can't afford the implant yet. Not a proper one, that is."

"We'll make sure you get it in no time. Here's what I've put together for you. Take a look."

"O-oh . . ."

"Is something wrong?"

"Is this the lowest it can go?"

"Let me see. . . . Hm. If you can provide us with another six thousand right now, then we can push perhaps two percent down one more generation? And there you go!"

"Oh my. Just like that?"

"Just like that. As I said, our legacy clients will always get the best rates! Now, factoring in your mother's balance . . . splendid! Your total amount owed is all the way down to—wow, would you look at that? $2,467,912."

[STOP]

[ERROR—]

[ERROR: ACCOUNT NOT FOUND]

Sixteen

O N THE FOURTH OF JULY, I went to see Gatsby, crossing our narrow street on an unusually cool evening. The heedless West Egg characters thronged the village in their patriotic colors, rushing toward the waterfront, where a gathering of light drones had amassed in preparation for a holo-fireworks display.

I was escorted into the elevator by Ewing, whom I'd come to know as Gatsby's closest attendant and favorite of the Klipspringers. He took me to the private pool, a stretch of turquoise quartz carved six feet deep in a rectangular Grecian style. The ceilings above were holo'd into a collage of Renaissance-era angels and cherubs.

Through the steam, I made out Gatsby's figure on bended knee, dressed in navy-blue swimwear, shorts fit snugly around sturdy thighs, and a loose matching long-sleeve shirt. The moisture in the air curved the ends of his hair.

My shoes lost their grip in the humidity. He smiled as he noticed me. "The water's just warming."

"Are you swimming?"

"*We* are indeed."

I paused to consider the extravagant pool. Gatsby prompted Ewing to bring another pair of swim shorts. Afterward, the android was dismissed until dinner.

Gatsby was already in the water when I came out from the bathroom, his shirt discarded on the floor where he'd been kneeling previously.

As I entered by way of the steps, he burst forth from the far end of the pool with a long pull of air. I saw another passionate story was about to pour out of him, surely one of his half-lie adventures, but as he blinked the water from his eyes, he glanced up, and his thoughts seemed to break off.

The steam curled between us. I couldn't be sure whether he was staring at me, or in my general direction, but I felt quite defenseless anyway, in nothing but his spare swimwear. It wasn't the physical exposure; I'd often shared netdiving dens in the military, the stripping of compression suits after long runs and the cold communal showers. But there was a decency to that, a self-consciousness summarily unlearned by its procedural nature.

This was not that. It wasn't even like standing before Jordan, in frozen darkness, with cyberspace to escape into soon.

As I sat on the last step of the pool, the water bobbed below my shoulders, just shy of scalding, and I felt heat sink through every taut muscle.

Gatsby swam half a lap, and when he resurfaced, he told me my photos with Jordan at the game were still top of the sports feed. "Quite the pair," he said.

I didn't think Jordan and I had stepped fully in that realm yet, but Gatsby must have believed otherwise, given the way he'd found us in her dressing room earlier that week. There was a sudden bloom of color in his ears.

"I'm not sure I know her that well," I said. "But I'd like to."

His expression was impenetrable in the steam. "That'd be very rewarding, yes. It can't be easy to hold your own against someone like her."

"Certainly the most lively person I've had on my arm in a while."

"Have you had many?" He smoothed his hair back. "Lively women on your arm, I mean."

"No." I stared up at a cluster of frowning cherubs. "A few more men than women. As far as the lively ones go."

A tinge of surprise emerged in Gatsby's face, and I saw that he'd made an assumption of me that he was now recalculating. I thought again about Jordan's story of him in that Chicago Sleep lounge. It drew my attention to the uneasy press of his lips, and to his still-flushed chest, half submerged in the turquoise liquid.

I could see the remnants of his military days—the wiry muscle, not firmly defined but more than noticeable, suggested a past of physical exertion. Perhaps it was true he'd meant to be a netdiver at some point. I remembered the conditioning required to prepare for the mods, how their intensity had disqualified most candidates before they even reached the neural-tolerance tests.

He rolled his neck to the side, as if working out a knot, and I wondered if there was some reticence that startled him too. "At least you have Miss Baker. When I first stepped out of domed walls into the unfettered churn of New York, I was alone. I felt lost and unsteady. Often I still do," he said.

It was an unexpected admission. He had everyone flying to his doors like they were temple gates, ready to bare their souls within his halls. I didn't know what more a man could need. I watched him as he drifted slowly on his back. He spoke about impersonal things for a while—trips to Europe and Happy Sleep stars newly signed to his studio.

"This is my first time using the pool," he said once he'd tired himself out and sat beside me on the shallow steps.

"Really?"

"Yes. It's not fun swimming here all alone. In a place like this, even the sound of your own breath starts to stick in your ears." A steady pattern of water droplets fell from his hair and caught on a particular jut of his cheekbone, before sliding to his shoulder, and lower perhaps, though I had better restraint than to confirm it. "I'm glad you've taken a liking to the place, because it's been a long project, and it means a lot to me that it's finally come together."

He said this in a short-winded breath. It was how he often spoke. I was quite transfixed by it, always waiting for that stutter step of honesty to reveal itself. Though every time it came close, it pulled away again, and he'd continue inventing tales of expeditions through rural Chinese mountains or ordering highballs he didn't even like to drink.

Through the water, I could see him holding his right arm in his left hand, sort of cradling it. I almost thought I saw a bump above his wrist, a spot of swollen skin or a scar. I thought it rude to ask, so I stopped myself.

His eyes lifted just then, glancing up at me through long eyelashes, stuck together and darkened with water. He stretched his legs out and propelled himself off the steps, and about two feet away, dipped into another graceful breaststroke. When he came up again, he stared at me, expelling a soft laugh.

"What is it?" I asked.

"You look as though you're trying to stay as dry as possible."

I attempted to ease my posture. "It reminds me of cyberspace. Being underwater."

"You don't like it?"

The water lapped quietly against our bodies.

"I just don't get many wakeful hours in a day. I have to make them count," I said. "If you spend too long unconscious, you start to get used to it. Starts to feel easier than being fully alive. It's hard to explain."

He swam back toward me. "I suppose that would be rather ... enticing." His voice permeated the thick steam. "It's why I wanted this tower to be a place that'd replicate the most vivid of dreams. Like something better than a Happy Sleep. You're awake—but you can completely forget yourself."

I stared into the speckled quartz beneath our feet, the water reflecting the holo-cherubs and the clouds. "Making paradise. That's quite the undertaking."

"It is. Everyone has their own idea of it, so I tried to ensure every possible scenario. I'm usually rather good at determining the best floor for a guest within seconds of meeting them." Fresh droplets balanced on the tips of his lashes. "I can't say I've figured out yours yet, though."

I wasn't sure I had one—a belief in any perfect, untouchable oasis. Then again, I had always moved through life a little too skeptically. I'd been raised to mind the gaps. The deceptively small ones. The ones you think you can jump, even though you know those that try never make it.

You can completely forget yourself.

It was a precarious notion to entertain in the presence of a man like him, and yet, beneath his diligent focus, I eventually floated away from the steps.

He smiled in surprise. "Have I tempted you, after all?"

There was no paradise to be found there, beneath those lyre-wielding cherubs, or in any of his holograms, but I returned his smile anyway, falling backward into the water as his laughter cascaded in my ears.

◇——◇——◇

Gatsby's bedroom was a sea of green-black walls—stylish, but austere. Heavy curtains covered the windows. A long carpet extended from the doors to the foot of the bed, which was draped in cool-toned cashmere. Intricate Victorian patterns were carved into the crown molding, and the only notable spot of warmth emanated from a two-tier chandelier casting a bronze gradient over the matte black tiles.

I availed myself of the oversized shower, lined with faux-tatami and a wall of synth-plants on one side, and when I exited his rainforest of a bathroom, I found him wheeling pressed clothes out from a corridor that hinted at an audacious closet. At his urging, I selected one of his fine cotton sets to change into.

I was taller than him. I noticed this for the first time that evening when the borrowed slacks stopped a few inches high on my ankles and he stepped close to help with the cuffs of the button-down. It wasn't a considerable difference, and yet somehow in that moment, it was all the difference in the world.

Standing before me then, without a smile or a story on his lips, he seemed much smaller than the person who could change the colors in the sky with just a button.

"There." He relinquished my wrist. "It's not too snug?"

I shook my head. He had freckles too. They were faint, perhaps recently emerged over the course of the bright summer days, as well as the light beginnings of crow's feet, which I was surprised to see he hadn't modded over.

Out in the dining room, faced with a floor-to-ceiling view of the Sound and the revelers below, it seemed that whatever ruminative mood overtook Gatsby a few minutes ago had vanished. He again adopted his animated abstractions about the world, its issues, and his place within it. I listened between sips of Riesling, and when prompted, offered simple answers to his questions about my family, Minnesota, and my short contract in the Philippines.

He asked, "Do you think you'd settle yourself in Manila?"

I wasn't sure. The Americas, for better or worse, would always match the frequency in my bones—the world I knew best even when I felt it didn't know me back.

I missed my mother most often, the clamor of her barangay, my cousins down the road, and the gated Pasig house I'd managed to move her into after my first three years in grueling, high-paying contracts. I couldn't call a city on the other side of the world home, but it was enough to say Manila was made of bewitching questions for me at every turn. All the multitudes of ways I could have existed had my mother not acquiesced to my father's dreams.

The domes of the Midwest, and their stagnant, suburban sprawl, had never suited her. She'd returned home a few years after his death, as soon as I'd received my Yale acceptance, hoping rather in vain that I'd eventually come around to shaking my American roots in a way my father never could.

"I'm too weak for the weather," I said, and took the opening to prod about Gatsby's own youth. "Do you miss the West?"

"Sometimes," he said gravely.

"You can always go back."

"Oh no. I could never—I mean, I've made it here after much difficulty," he replied without elaborating.

The fireworks began, whistling through our conversation, and Ewing served a dessert of tart pudding topped extravagantly with real berries. After a short while, the last florets of light poured over the Sound, in the shape of the old United States flag.

Then it was dim again, and I became aware of Gatsby in renewed pieces. His damp hair shone, burnished gold, his eyes holding the reflection of the holo-candles, and he looked over at me, starting to form another question, but he halted, and I realized—for no reason, except maybe the Riesling—that I'd been watching him too intently.

I decided to excuse myself for the evening.

"Are you sure?" he said reluctantly.

"It's gotten late." And I had a report due to Bunsen that night.

He checked the time on his comm and frowned. "So it has. May I call on you again soon?"

"It's funny that you ask." I rose from the table unsteadily. "That you always ask."

"Why's that?"

"People like you never need to."

"Is that a yes?"

I had the vague, startling thought that I was not in the right head at the moment. "Ask me again tomorrow."

A smile flourished across his face. He insisted I keep the borrowed clothes as Ewing had already pressed, folded, and packed away my own. We argued casually about this as we went into the elevator together, and after we were five or so levels down, he seemed to recall something and pushed a button for another floor.

"You know your way out, don't you, old sport?" he said.

"Of course."

He touched my arm as the elevator slowed to a stop. "I'll leave you here. Good night."

The doors opened. We were met with a wall of pitch-black, and I watched Gatsby retreat into it, an inexplicable tension in my chest.

It was only after I'd descended to the lobby and crossed the street that I realized that was the one floor he'd never shown me.

◇——◇——◇

Bunsen called promptly at eleven o'clock. "Got a ping on that bootlegging tip," he said when I answered. "The name 'Walter Chase' was helpful. Ex-military, mod engineer. He knows a thing or two about dodging the law, but he spent last month in a jail out West over a busted trade. Arm-blade extensions in a Klipspringer android transport. He wouldn't hand over the names of his contacts. Admirable, I suppose, but that's what integrity gets you."

I sat on the edge of my bed, staring out at the dark tower through my window. "He took the fall for—" I hesitated. "For someone?"

"Probably. That Klipspringer factory could be one way Gatsby Corp smuggles in black market mods. Parts ship in from all over the world. There're some weight discrepancies in the shipments."

"So, Medica'll be out, then?"

Bunsen laughed, too loud for the late hour. "Personally? I doubt it. It's not a pretty operation, but it's profitable. They might actually find that appealing. I know you're eager to get out of there, but Medica still wants answers about the acquisition."

"About Mr. Chase—" I pinched the bridge of my nose, staving off my exhaustion. "You won't move against him, will you?"

The audio wave on my comm flattened as Bunsen went silent for a moment. "NYPD pays a hundred thousand minimum to bust any unlicensed mod-doc operating within a year of conviction. So, yes, there's a bounty on him. We collected." He paused again. "Why?"

I pressed a hand over my left eye. "No reason." The wine was surfacing to my head. "Pero parang ... hindi siya—"

"Nick." Bunsen made a noise of forced sympathy. "Hindi mo kasalanan. All right?" he said, but it didn't release the pressure in my chest. "Fellows like Chase know what kind of business they're in. It was a good tip, and that's what counts. What led you to it?"

I almost brought up Owl Eyes, then stopped myself. "Whispers from his parties."

"Whispers," he muttered. "Nothing else?"

I hadn't mentioned the mess Jordan had roped me into in the valley either. I debated offering over the name that had caught her eye, but it was only her hunch, and my own attempts to scrape various records for the name "Gatz" hadn't led me anywhere.

At the last second, I swallowed it back. "Nothing else."

I heard the high clink of glasses, the unstoppering of a decanter. I fell into my pillows, unbuttoning my shirt that I remembered wasn't mine at all, but Gatsby's, the spice of his cologne living in the collar.

"Fine, then." Bunsen swallowed his drink. "Mag ingat ka."

The comm-screen blinked closed.

I sat up, stripped myself in the bathroom, and took a second ice-cold shower that night, my head spinning through the wine fog.

Seventeen

GATSBY'S NEXT INVITATION CAME AROUND seven o'clock the following evening while I was still at Gen Wealth. We were to have dinner at a restaurant, but that day was a Friday, and his parties always began on Fridays. As I understood it, his role as host was a rather sacred duty, one that I didn't expect him to abandon just to speak with me.

This was the first oddity of many that night. When his pearly Veluz came around the office an hour later to pick me up, we didn't speak at all the whole ride.

We arrived atop a busy hotel landing pad. The restaurant he'd selected had a six-year waiting list with a menu designed by a celebrity chef whom he'd befriended during one of his business trips. I didn't dare ask how we would be dining here tonight, for as we began to cross the landing pad, I saw a cluster of well-heeled guests, about a hundred of them, causing a chaotic scene near the doors. As Gatsby and I were led past the angry crowd, they paused their hurling insults to watch in disbelief as we walked by.

A procession of uniformed human servers bowed at the waist in greeting, and a sea of empty tables, draped in fine cloths, stretched out across the dining room, complete with a live five-piece band and a crooning vocalist. Artificial katmon trees wafted in the recycled air, beneath a ceiling that had been holo'd into a black sky and decorated with pulsing fake stars. The largest table was set and elevated upon a marble platform where the army of servers motioned, in unison, for us to sit as they rolled out a three-tiered drink cart.

Gatsby shuffled back and forth in his chair, ordering water and Riesling as I glanced at the empty tables, cleared in a haste to accommodate our last-minute arrival. Our own table, wide enough to seat a dozen people, felt like a propped-up stage in an unattended theater. Being spoiled outside of his tower was uniquely discomforting.

Service slowed after the first set of appetizers, along with our conversation, which began to chafe from the oversized venue, the minuscule portions, and their flat fusion sauces.

"I ought to tell you something, old sport," he erupted during the long break between courses.

He seemed now to be trembling. I set down my cutlery.

"You know the thing about Rosenthal," he said out of nowhere, "is that the man was a genius, and he knew it. Yes, he knew his skills were far above any diver who'd come before him, and everything he ever did was to expose all the layers of corruption from West to East. People like that, rare as they are, often find themselves tempted into morally questionable habits—not out of an ill character, no. Just boredom perhaps. Or a thrill!"

Gatsby stopped and drew in a breath.

"Sometimes," he rushed on, "it might begin in small ways. An inclination here and there. Then the idea pops into your head that no one can stop you. Then you act on it. Then you may find yourself somewhere you oughtn't be." The shadows shifted in his expression. "Like trespassing a facility and accessing protected servers—with a famous sports star in tow."

When he finally shut his mouth, clenching his teeth, I can tell you there was a different man sitting across from me, and I caught, very starkly, a flash of the corpo I'd suspected him of being before I ever met him. A man whose civility would melt off at the first indiscretion. Still, seeing it unfold up close snapped me back from any illusions, a dislocated limb forcibly reset.

I moved my hand beneath the skirt of the tablecloth, my thumb hovering over my comm-sensor. Why I hesitated, I didn't know. It was more reason than I'd ever needed before to force a swift discharge. Pierce the skin, activate a distress signal.

And yet, I couldn't move. Gatsby's intent eyes were strained.

"You can ask me forthrightly," I said.

"What's that?" he muttered.

Perhaps I could retrace my steps to where I'd faltered and carve a way out. There couldn't be any evidence of a breach because I hadn't stolen anything—I was confident of that. I'd erased any record of my entry and exit. The child was a factor, and so was the elderly neighbor, though considering the certainty of Gatsby's accusation, I suspected the more likely smoking gun was that the surveillance cameras had glimpsed Jordan before I'd managed to reroute the feed.

"You'd like to know if I was in the valley and accessed your servers," I said. "The answer is yes."

"You—what were you there *for*?"

I was intrigued by how nervous he was to be confronting me, as if he were actually rummaging for any hope I'd prove him wrong. "That 'date' Jordan mentioned to you after her match—she wanted us to go to the valley," I replied. "So that's where we went."

"A rather unconventional spot . . ."

"Miss Baker is nothing if not unconventional. But there was more to it." I took an extended sip of water. "She has a philanthropic bone in her, if you didn't know."

"Does she?"

"Yes, she wanted to see the neighborhood. Its unfortunate state troubles her." I picked up my cutlery and resumed my meal. "She thinks it's awful that all the space is rotting and unused when it could be a bustling district like any other. Something to rival both Eggs even." I looked Gatsby in the eye as I spoke, steadying the frightful tremor in my chest. "It's a project we're—*she's* interested in."

Gatsby leaned back in his chair. "But what on earth did you need to access the servers for?"

My mind shuffled through the events of that day like a slot machine. I swallowed back the pressure in my throat. "Jordan wanted a list of the building's residents. She was feeling sad and charitable. Perhaps a stronger man would be able to refuse her, but I wanted to help, as long as I didn't breach any sensitive information." I paused. "Which I didn't."

He nodded slowly at this, which at least confirmed that I'd been right about his not knowing anything else besides the simple fact that

Jordan and I had been there. His more pertinent question was about the rig.

"How did you even go about it?" he asked. "The whole reason there's no rig there is so that the servers *can't* be accessed."

"I made one."

"Out of *what*?"

I explained it to him.

He bent so far forward over the table that his silk tie grazed his plate. "You *jumped*—? As replacement for a harness ... that's"—he scoffed wildly—"a ridiculous improvisation!"

"I apologize, of course." If there was one thing I felt I was quite good at, it was acting contrite. "I know I've betrayed my—"

"So that's the extent of it?" He was almost smiling again, and it troubled me, the ease with which his hostility had overcome him, only to disappear just the same. "I feel as though ..." His fingers settled at the base of his water glass, which was sweating with condensation. "It's strange that I've spent so many weeks trying to know you, Mr. Carraway, and yet, I don't at all."

My stomach lurched.

A server came to apologize about the growing delay, which was no bother to me, considering I'd all but lost my appetite in the last few minutes.

"I was concerned the matter would need to escalate to the board," said Gatsby when the server departed. "I see no reason for that. However, perhaps I might still issue a warning." He lowered his voice. "The board—they're not easy people to handle. It's no big trouble to me if you'd like greater allowances, but we all answer to someone."

I could scarcely register that I'd just wriggled out of the line of fire with nothing but a few lies, resined in the thinnest wash of truth.

And yet—somehow I could sense it wasn't really whole innocence Gatsby saw in me. Rather, it was a satisfactory alibi.

I drew my hand away from my comm, but I didn't feel one bit of relief.

Why, I wondered, *is he choosing to believe me?*

"That trick you did to make a rig—I can't even picture it. I'd like to see it sometime," said Gatsby. "And I hope it all went well."

170

"What went well?"

He looked down, wiping his mouth on a napkin. "Your date. With Miss Baker."

"Oh. Yes." I forced my shoulders to relax. "I can only hope she entertains me another day."

"I'm sure you've nothing to worry about." He smiled wider—again with his soft, private faith—then jumped from his seat. "It's been a long wait. I'll have to go into the kitchen and have a word with them."

"That's not necessary."

"It's almost ten."

"Why don't *I* go on in?" I suggested. Sending Gatsby back there would cause a panic.

"No, that won't do—"

I went across the dining hall before he could stop me, shouldering my way through the kitchen door, and was struck, unsurprisingly, by a scene of devastation.

Three separate fires had erupted at the stoves. By the sink, a man was washing out a deep wound across his palm, while another blabbered on in tearful apology. A hundred conversations in Tagalog toppled over each other, including one hysterical argument about the horrors of serving synth-beef.

I moved farther inside, but no one noticed. The loudest argument seemed to be occurring between a line cook and the head chef—a short fellow with a graying beard.

"It's all madness!" cried the woman. "We had important people on the guest list tonight!"

The chef reprimanded her and struck his fist upon the counter, rattling a tower of saucers. I felt then was a good time to clear my throat.

Dishes were dropped. The chef whipped his head over. "Sir—!"

"It seems it's been a terribly long day, and you should all go home for the night," I said. "Mr. Gatsby will settle the bill. Extra for your trouble."

The kitchen ground to a halt. It seemed no one had realized whom they'd been serving. The chef, in his haste, knocked over a tray of shiny gelatin desserts. "Sir, we are perfectly happy to set things in order."

"Ayos lang," I reassured the man, then went to inform Gatsby that we'd be leaving and that throwing this whole place into shambles wasn't an exciting experience for me.

He stood up, a flurry of embarrassment. "You're not enjoying yourself."

I could never risk offending him. If the night ended now, my only accomplishment of the week would be to admit to Bunsen that I'd almost destroyed the entire assignment over a risky romp with a sports star that I'd previously omitted from my reports.

"We can go elsewhere," I decided.

The suggestion pleased him, and he went over to the hostess to handle the payment. I waited outside on the landing pad, emptied of its previous activity and the hundreds of people snapped away by a single phone call from Jay Gatsby.

After a few minutes, the head chef came out into the humid night with a stim-stick. There was no "sir" between us anymore. He had a guttural chuckle that reminded me of every mirthful, meddling tito I always met at family functions.

"Sorry you had to hear all that back there." He sat on the curb with a sigh. "You're not a corpo like him, are you?"

"No. I'm not."

The man nodded at that, and for some reason, it felt good to get his affirmation that I didn't exude the lofty entitlements he probably disliked. I had practiced, rather unconsciously, this chameleon behavior my whole life; that was, taking comfort in being "one of" whoever's company I was currently in. Sometimes it meant you'd go completely unnoticed; other times it was the closest you could get to acceptance or temporary camaraderie.

"It's a damn nightmare dealing with those types. One bad word from them and—*pfft!*" He mimed a knife across his throat. "We're one misstep away from having half the team replaced by androids, as it is. Can you believe we're the last American location with an all-human staff?"

I sat beside him, and he offered me a drag. My refusal made him smile.

"What kind of life are *you* living, huh? Seems a fun one, if you're not even a little stressed at all times," he muttered.

172

I didn't think a stim-stick could have saved me from the stress of the last twenty minutes. "It's not that fun. Just boring."

"You're bragging. I'd take a boring life any day." He laughed, knocking our shoulders together. Then his voice drawled out in those long, Tagalog vowels that somehow turned any benign question into a morsel of gossip. "Siya ba talaga?" He was asking about Gatsby now.

"Yes," I said.

"Really?"

"Really."

"Akala ko iba siya," said the man.

I'd spent so much time around Gatsby lately that I often forgot he was still a mythical entity to just about everyone else. "What *did* you imagine?" I asked.

"I don't know. But not that. Such a nervous fellow—for a corpo, that is." The chef flicked his stim-stick off. "If there's anything I've learned from serving those types my whole career, if a corpo's nervous around you, it only means two things."

The doors opened behind us, and Gatsby came strolling out.

The chef stood up. "Nagsisinungaling, o kaya"—he winked at me—"may gusto sa 'yo."

Of course, it was a joke, a very Filipino one, but I think I forgot to laugh. Before I knew it, the man returned to his professional stance, bidding Gatsby a formal farewell and disappearing inside the restaurant.

Gatsby watched me with raised eyebrows. "Ready, Mr. Carraway?"

I nodded, taking the driver's side of the car. "I know a place."

They're lying, or—

He tilted his head, smiling, and by the time we were airborne, I'd banished the rest of the thought from my mind.

Eighteen

T HE ENTRANCE TO ESKINITA HID within a series of narrow passages that broke away from the loud shops along Roosevelt before disappearing into a sharp, dead-end corner off Seventieth Street. I had actually never been to the Eskinita in New York, but I figured any Little Manila would have one, so touching down in Woodside, I asked the first local to point us in the right direction.

The venue was marked by a flickering sign, curled in neon calligraphy. In the car, I rolled the sleeves up on my shirt and advised Gatsby to leave his tie and jacket behind. I took another look at him, free of his outer layers. His throat moved visibly with nerves, and his eyes seemed to shiver in the cold streetlights filtering through the windows.

"Open your collar," I said. He obliged without protest, and something about this unquestioning demeanor of his struck me in a satisfying way. "And your hair . . ."

"My hair?"

It was gelled so immovably that not even the harshest windstorm would knock a strand out of place. At this rate, we'd never be let inside. After some hesitation, I reached over and ruined the careful styling myself, just enough for the front to droop down over his furrowed brow.

"Better," I said. He stared at me, tense and looking about five years younger. "But don't be so skittish."

Stepping out into the night, we could smell the smoke, spiced oil, and lemony aromas. At the doors, a group of chattering Filipino youths guarded the entrance. They squatted around a holo–card game, sharing a stim-stick and releasing puffs of yellow dust into the air.

One of them looked up, startling at the sight of us. "Nawawala ba kayo, corpos?" the young man hollered, and his group erupted into laughter.

I'd hoped we looked informal enough, but something gave us away—perhaps Gatsby's posture, his dipped chin as if he were always on the cusp of asking you for a favor.

"Not lost," I said. "Just hungry. Like any other paying customer."

The young man's demeanor shifted, as if he hadn't intended for his joke to be understood. He stared between us in deep consideration. "Fine. Pero walang gulo, okay?" Then he stood up and pounded a complex rhythm on the steel door behind him.

I glanced at Gatsby, wondering if he'd walk around all night with that wide-eyed discomfort, and rather worried that bringing him here was a mistake. Earlier, I'd wanted only to smooth over the tension, but now I remembered how far a luxury rooftop restaurant actually was from a back alley in Queens.

"You're still too stiff," I said, and before I could ask if he'd rather turn around, he made an honest effort to relax, then smiled, waiting for me to lead.

We went inside. The entryway was dark, with a heavy black curtain that led out into the venue itself.

"Where in the world have you taken me, old sport?"

"Eskinita," I replied. "It means 'alleyway.'"

There was scarcely room for the both of us to stand shoulder to shoulder, and in the dimness, I felt the warmth of his nervous breathing. A hover-bot bobbed in front, containing a box of compact headsets. I grabbed one for each of us.

Gatsby was at a loss now. "We're not about to go into a Sleep, are we?"

"Not quite. The headset will induce a synesthesia."

He had never seen this sort of dining experience before, so I explained to him that the idea for it had first been invented by a group of underground netdivers in Manila who'd decided to get into the culinary game. The business had gotten popular across major cities around the world, but its clientele still consisted largely of a certain younger, rebellious subculture.

"In cyberspace, all your senses meld together," I said. "These divers discovered that using a simpler variation of a standard Happy Sleep headset could replicate the same sort of thing, but with food." I fit a headset over my eyes, and then Gatsby's. "When you taste something here, you taste it with your whole body."

A calming sensation dribbled down our spines, thick and syrupy. Gatsby's breath hitched. He momentarily lost his balance.

"Just wait. It has to sync," I said.

He inhaled slowly. "What has to?"

"Your senses—with each other." The light beneath our wrists flashed. "And with mine."

A full-body shudder rippled through him; then I pulled the curtain back, and we stepped out together into a long corridor that had been simulated into an outdoor night market. Raucous food stalls lined the left and right of us, beneath a sea of holo–paper lanterns, and smoke billowed and hung in the air like a mystical fog. The headsets over our eyes disappeared as the simulation began to fill out completely.

We were pushed along into the swarming crowd, as if from an invisible river current, and it took a minute for Gatsby to find his bearings. Even eyeing one of the stalls made our mouths tingle, and the stimuli briefly winded him. He did a slow turn amidst the crowd.

I reached for a sample cup of leche flan floating past us on a hover-bot and offered it to him. The moment he ate a spoonful, I could feel his splendor—the giddiness—rising into his chest, and it rose into mine too.

"It's ... the best thing I've ever tasted," he said, awestruck.

I smiled. "That's the point. Everything will taste that way."

"You're all pink! And orange at the edges ..." He laughed. "I see sparks around you like little fireworks."

I gestured for him to come farther inside, but he stopped me, holding out the sweet custard. I obliged.

"What do *you* see?" he asked.

The leche flan melted on my tongue, and I shivered. A light rippled behind Gatsby's dark golden hair. But it wasn't quite like fireworks to me. It was softer, subtler.

It was the same faint warmth always reflected in his inquisitive eyes—green with life and early spring, crisp air fading into mild sunshine, morning dew upon a blade of grass, the earthly wonder of seeing a season turn in real time.

◇——◇——◇

It wasn't long before we found ourselves separated. Gatsby had wandered off ahead of me, lost in the spectacle. A rush of bodies came between us, flooding toward a busy junction where a crowd was rallying to watch a rapturous food display.

A pair of cooks flew around on hover-bots, their entire stall elevated as they roasted long slabs of synth-pork—lechon, specifically—so that it appeared as though a dozen glazed pigs hung suspended in the air. One cook tossed a pig up and skewered it onto a metal pole as it fell. His modded hand opened, and from his palm extended a blowtorch contraption that he ran across the length of the skin, charring it golden brown. The crowd broke into applause.

"Hell, they let you in here looking like *that*?"

The voice tasted sour, a vinegar punch. I whipped around.

Owl Eyes' appearance had shifted dramatically since the party. Her ice-white hair had been dyed charcoal, chopped shorter to her ears.

"I hope you haven't been following me," I said.

"Don't flatter yourself. I'm scoping for a new crew. This is the best diver hideaway in town."

"New crew? You said your friends were all right."

"I said they were *alive*," she muttered. "Only so much our usual guy's willing to do till we pay up. And even then—shit, I dunno." She gnawed at her lower lip in contemplation. "Anyway, I'll square up the money once you help me hit that tower. Pigeon's made me her sworn enemy already. Says I went 'too far' this time. That I'd better clear the debt to our mod-doc, and if Penguin ever walks again, she'll make

177

sure all of 'em are walking far away from me, even if it means they gotta crawl. Wordsmith, that one."

Her pupils flickered. A low pang resounded in my chest—a quiver of regret she couldn't hide. As quickly as it had come, she shoved it away. "And that's that! They can *crawl* all they want. I'm trying to fly."

"Far too close to the sun, it seems. You'd better listen to your friends."

"They don't have the stomach for this life. But *you*—" She plucked a stick of synth-barbecue from a stall and brandished it in my face. "I had a good feeling 'bout you."

I leaned away from the meat stick. "Did you now?"

"First time I saw you, I thought—this is a corpo who looks bored out of his damn mind. Then at the tower? Now, that's when I saw how right I was." She bounced back and forth on the balls of her feet as if warming up for a sprint. "You almost sliced the damn place open! With that kind of skill . . . why work for *them* when you could do so much more?"

As I stood there, watching her gesticulate madly, the more I saw flashes of my life appear before me like pins on a map, all the precise places where that path to her world could have opened for me.

But from the moment I'd set foot on Yale's hallowed grounds—a rare lottery acceptance among a sea of legacy admissions—my course had been set. Every day since had become a tireless exercise in gratitude for receiving opportunities that few others were afforded.

I wanted to tell this girl there was no point in agonizing about every injustice around us, that it was enough for anyone to manage the feat of escaping it, and I wouldn't throw it away for whatever joyride she was undoubtedly proposing.

"How old are you?" I'd never thought to ask before. "Twenty?"

"Hey! I could be a century." She sobered a little. "Twenty-*one*, thank you."

"Learn diving the proper way. You'll live a much longer life."

"Exactly. A mentor's what I need."

"I—"

"Look here, Mr. Nicholas Carraway. I know what you see in me. You think I've watched a movie too many, just chasing my next high." Her voice carried deeper into my head; a bloody, salty fragrance in its wake. "But I'm not after the high, or even the money. It's *actual* change I want." She stepped back, arms wide and chin upturned, the lanterns reflected in the glass of her oc-mods. "And you want it, too, don't you? You *act* like one of them"—she waved vaguely at my clothes—"but I can tell you're brighter than that 'cause you haven't tricked yourself into thinking you'll ever *be* one of them. Otherwise, you'd have let those androids throw us straight into the bin without a lick of remorse."

I protested, but she swatted at me with her barbecue.

"People think Rosenthal himself has to rise from the dead before any change'll happen. But I don't care about dead heroes. You're close enough, and you're alive," she said earnestly.

I looked around at the growing masses, gathered in awe beneath the flying pigs. She'd offered me a compliment—a kind, if rash, conjecture about my character—but it wasn't as though I could accept it. Perhaps those chameleon inclinations I always retreated into had worked against me this time. I simply wasn't the diver she insisted I was.

"You've misjudged me," I replied. "And many other things besides."

Her eyes narrowed, daggers of light.

"I hear your ... grievances," I fumbled. She stood rigidly, arms crossed. "But clearly, you've not seen the inside of a corp. Nor do you understand their place in the world. They're more than just a few buildings and servers of data." I thought absently about Gen Wealth— every life caught in its tendrils, wriggling in its grasp, both living and yet to be. "The power they exert over people's lives, dictating who gets to have what and where, exactly when and for how long." I looked up through the smoke of the food stalls. "I'm saying, there are hurricanes less destructive than that. You understand, yes? You can't dismantle a storm. But you *can* weather it if you're sensible."

Owl Eyes grew quiet, the flames of her imprudent zeal dampened by whatever "grievance" I had evidently let burrow and fester in my own conscience. She looked for a moment, somehow, even younger to me then.

Worse than a child—lost.

"So ... that's all? I turn around, keep rolling the dice until I get fried? And what's left for *you*?" She sat atop an empty plastic table, one knee tucked to her chest. "Advise some board about diverting a pittance of funds to a couple socially minded initiatives and pat yourself on the back for it?" She laughed dryly. "Well, I'd rather do something *real*. Build something good out of everything that's been broken. Maybe then, I don't know, history might actually remember us as more than some—some empty shells 'weathering' the storm in our separate holes along the Hudson! Maybe our generation could actually be worth a damn."

I couldn't understand what sort of enduring remembrance she was chasing, or what was even possible in this age of intangibles. Information and money, dreams and desires—they were formless things now as they'd never been before, packed into our wrists, crumbs of data in cyberspace. Those old ages of hope and invention—Science, Enlightenment, Industry—when life itself could still feel like a frontier, were behind us.

Above, I thought I almost saw a glint of a star amidst the lanterns, but I knew that was impossible. The sky was holo'd; we weren't outside, and even if we had been, it wouldn't have made the stars any more visible.

Somewhere ahead, a soft, invigorating tune began to play. I couldn't make out the exact notes, but I felt the edges of the melody.

The Jazz Age. That was one too.

Owl Eyes handed me half her skewer. I accepted it. "There was a moment during that party where I thought you might be one of those intel-scout types," she said.

I'd taken one bite of the flamed pork and coughed. "I—" I ran my tongue over my teeth. "Why would you—"

"I know. Poor stereotype. And obviously you're not. You chose to save my life in that library. You didn't have to ... but you did." She took a dejected bite of her synth-meat. "By the way, what have you found out about the tower?"

I didn't see the point in tempting her curiosity further. "Nothing."

She glared at me. "Huh."

"It's the truth."

"Sure it is. I get it." She hopped off the table. "Protect your own and all that."

"Look. Just because you *want* to find a treasure trove doesn't mean you can manifest its existence," I argued. "I'm sorry the tower isn't what you wished it would be, but I hope you—" I didn't know what more to offer her. "I hope you find your small revolutions elsewhere. I've said I can't help you anymore, and that's that."

She stepped several paces away from me as if being pushed toward a ledge. "Know what? I changed my mind. You're worse than one of them," she decided. "'Cause you're more skilled than the average diver, but you won't do shit with it." She scoffed. "No such thing as a *small* revolution, Mr. Nicholas Carraway. If that's what you tell yourself, then enjoy standing in that hurricane."

She leaped toward me, squeezing my wrist, and I watched in disbelief as my comm-screen winked awake, twelve hundred dollars dribbling into my account. I sputtered. "What is this?"

"Your cut." She spit out a pork bone, yanking her arm away when I tried to exchange the money back. "That's from the casino. I said you'd get a piece of whatever we hauled that night, so there you have it. Unlike you corpos, I think a promise is still worth something. Now I don't owe you a damn thing."

She fixed her owlish gaze on me then, as if she were trying to reconcile the person in front of her with the person who had saved her life.

I clutched my wrist, digging my nails into my skin. "Did you get yourself to a doc at least? Your oc-mods look . . . well." The glass pane of the front, though still scratched up and crooked, seemed otherwise restored to healthy function.

"Did it myself," she said, to my surprise. Perhaps I'd been too fixated on her rashness to consider such ego could be channeled into actual ingenuity.

It was at this moment that Gatsby returned, having fought his way back through the crowd. I saw him try very hard not to react to the sight of Owl Eyes' uncanny appearance. "Um, hello! Miss . . .?"

"The name's Owl Eyes."

"That's nice," he replied clumsily. "And you're . . . friends?"

"Strangers! Complete and utter strangers." The animosity was directed at me, but then she took in Gatsby's expensive attire. "Who are *you*?"

181

Gatsby, careless as ever, began to speak the truth. "I'm—"

"This is my husband," I interrupted before Gatsby could out himself like a fool. "Good night to you then, miss."

Her oc-mods flickered, and she looked between us skeptically. She stood up with a terse "Good night—Mr. and Mr. Carraway," and shrunk into the crowd.

I turned to Gatsby, who looked very distracted all of a sudden. I saw that my small lie had rendered him speechless. I wondered if it offended him and began to apologize.

He blinked. "Oh no, it's not that."

But something was worrying him. I sensed it, with our moods synced through the simulation.

"You shouldn't make a habit of that," I explained.

"Of what?"

"Going around, telling just anyone who you are. Corpos have a reputation around here, and it's not beloved."

Concern nestled between his brows. I was supposed to be pretending that my opinion of him was uncorrupted, but we weren't inside his tower now, and the real world didn't carry those infinite protections of self-sufficient androids and an automated security system.

It wasn't something he could grasp right then—that his utopia didn't simply follow him wherever he went, and that down here, nothing was sacred. Him, least of all.

Nineteen

NEARING MIDNIGHT, A PROCESSION OF dancers and musicians strutted down the middle of the crowd so that we found ourselves lurched up against a siopao stall. It was run by a cheerful tower of a woman with an extra set of modded arms rapidly folding buns along a conveyor belt as her real arms arranged them in the steamers. When she made eye contact with me, I had no choice but to order one, to which she insisted no one ever orders just one.

"Tama na, 'po. Sobra na 'to," I protested.

"On the house! Para sa 'yo at sa partner mo." She nodded at Gatsby, who, in the jostle of the crowd, had decided to glue himself to me or else we'd get separated again. Our hips pressed together, he was listening to the conversation with vacant, uncomprehending politeness. "Pareho kayong gwapo."

I gave up and took the extra portion, paying for it anyway, which seemed to be her rather effective sales tactic.

"What'd she say?" asked Gatsby.

"To eat it while it's hot."

"Is that so?" His laugh was soft, disbelieving. He might have guessed I was lying, but after the awkwardness with Owl Eyes, I thought I was doing him a favor. He accepted the siopao with both hands. We'd reached the end of the strip where the crowd was at its thickest. The holo-lanterns hung lower and larger, bobbing like sailboats. The musicians had begun a vigorous performance, playing through an energetic OPM set list that had everyone corralling to form a dance floor.

At the edge of the crowd, we settled on two foldout chairs, the armrests sticky with spilled drinks. He peeled the wrapper of his siopao carefully, as if opening something expensive.

"'Mr. and Mr. Carraway,'" he muttered under his breath.

I was mid-bite through my own bun and stopped. "What?"

"I think it has a funny ring to it."

"Yes, well, I told you it's a fake name."

His amusement threw a sugary mist into the air. "We're like—two fresh characters here." He wanted to know more of how "Carraway" came to be, so I shared it. My grandfather's stubbornness drew a laugh from him. "A wise man, by the sound of it," he said.

"He was. Passed when I was young, though, so I didn't know him at all. But if he hadn't built up the shop, I don't think our family would have had much." A candid, stony image of him reclining in front of the body shop on its inaugural day once hung in a frame in my childhood home. Supposedly, I resemble him most, more than either of my parents. I have my mother's deep-set eyes, I think, but his height, the squareness of his face, and darker skin had skipped over my father and onto me. "My relatives say I'm exactly like him, though not bull-headed as he was. I have my father's disposition. Very ... compliant, I'm told."

Gatsby's hesitation spiraled between us. I felt the precise shift where he considered holding his tongue but decided to speak anyway. "You've never seemed that way to me," he said, then between the folds of his doubt, a supple warmth spilled through. "I quite like the name."

"If you want to borrow it, then be my guest."

"Should I?" He grinned. That smile was doing astonishing tricks again, sucking in so much light. His delicate irresistibility, I believed, didn't come from any of his arresting features but from the glowing layer just beneath—the concentration in his eyes as if he were always searching for you in a crowd. "Actually, I've always wanted to know what your name was before that."

"Let's trade," I said. "Have you always been 'Gatsby'?"

He halved his bun. The steam rose up into the air. "Yes."

"Really?"

His smile dimmed. "Yes. Why?"

A weight pooled in my chest. Whether it was his nerves or mine, I couldn't quite tell.

The way that name, *Gatsby*, curved on the tongue animated the murmurs of West Egg on its own. It fit him like a coat spun from gold thread but had never quite seemed like a name one was born with. Still, a part of me wondered if Jordan's guess about him was off the mark.

"That's not a fair trade, then," I said lightly. His laugh was uneasy, pink bleeding into the edges of the spring green haze. "'Carraway' works well for tonight. A name made for hiding. Since that's what you're doing right now."

"Is that all an alias is good for? Hiding?"

"How would *you* see it?"

He paused. "Rebirth."

"That's too romantic for me. But it suits you well enough."

He snapped his head sideways, studying me. "I keep wondering why you seem to go about your life with such pragmatism."

"Occupational hazard, I suppose."

He licked his fingers clean and stared out into the dancing crowd. "Maybe that's why I could never be a diver. You can't be emotional or indecisive. I failed all the exams for it. Apparently, my thoughts just wander too much." He must have been in a good trance by now because he normally didn't speak about his shortcomings like that. "Do you think you'll stay in the field a long time?"

"I'm not good at anything else." I would have to make a living somehow. At least diving didn't depress me, and the same couldn't be said about my colleagues, many of whom were still rather tied up with ladder-climbing, so much that competition stymied any true fellowship. It'd been a while, in fact, since I'd bonded with someone in a new city, so I mentioned how relieved I was to have met Jordan.

Gatsby sat quiet for a moment. "She knows many shades of you, doesn't she?"

"I don't have many shades at all."

"That's not true. You talk much more when you aren't sober, for instance."

I tossed the paper wrapper of my siopao into a passing trash-bot. "Don't remind me. Does that explain why my glass never empties at your table?"

"You caught me." He chuckled, and I couldn't tell if he was joking. "Your voice, too—it lightens so much when you switch languages. You sound less formal."

"That's not the language," I said. "That's just you."

It was now karaoke hour. Out on the dance floor, a microphone soared over the crowd on a hover-bot. There was an amiable tousle among a group of friends before the microphone was claimed by a giddy young man who rushed to join the band onstage.

"What do you mean by that?" Gatsby leaned to make himself heard over the ensuing cheers. "That your formality is—just me?" The soft halo around him dithered.

"I mean that you're Jay Gatsby, and how's one supposed to act around you?" I said.

I realized how often he couldn't see the distance between us, or rather, refused to. Looking back, I think he wanted to believe he wasn't ever taking advantage of me, and perhaps in turn, I'd wanted to stow away the bubbling guilt about my own deceits. To me, he was an assignment. To him, I still didn't know what I was, and in a stirring, ignorant way, disregarding my inhibitions just enough, I could have been anything.

I remember having another of these willful lapses in judgment as a rush of euphoria blew through him, like a lazy summer wind.

He stood up with a smile. "But as we agreed, I'm not Gatsby. Not right now."

With that little joke, he welcomed me into a brief hallucination. He wasn't Gatsby.

Not for that indeterminate stretch of time as the young singer's voice—rough, but full of soul—drew us toward the dancing horde. The orange lanterns swayed there in simulated reality, and the glow of their lights lit fires in his evergreen eyes.

He took my wrist through the crowd. I tasted his trilling delight as if it had sunk its teeth into my thoughts, bursting with sweet juice. Pulled through the melancholic force of the acoustic guitars and the aching violin harmony, we spun, him and I, in transient ecstasy, our arms locked together, and our arms locked with strangers.

He smiled his smile of a thousand promises, and when we fell into each other's laughter that night, the consequences blew up like sparks, lifetimes away.

We spun, pretending we were both strangers, too—unknown, even to ourselves, and to our truest desires.

⬦——◇——⬦

Outside in the neon-washed night, we emerged with all our senses pulsing and overstimulated. The silence itched as we walked back to the car, and I was trying to figure out a way for Gatsby to let me onto that last locked floor of the tower, when he spoke, his voice hoarse from screaming over the music and merriment. "At the restaurant, when you brought up Miss Baker's interest in the valley, you almost said that her idea of reconfiguring it was something you were *both* thinking about. Not just her."

I was surprised he remembered. "It does seem like a project worth investing in. Maybe you've never seen the extent of the trouble there."

We reached the Veluz again, but neither of us got inside. "The truth is . . .," he said. "I came from nothing. All the important people I descended from out West, well, it was more than an exaggeration."

After all the weeks he'd spent bragging about his pedigree, this was his first time confessing that he'd lied to me.

"I mean that places like the valley—they remind me awfully of my difficult upbringing. It unearths memories I've tried to . . . put away," he shared. "I worked so hard to escape it all and to return seems impossible. Like it might suck me in again. I know it's naive."

He'd opened up a window into the revenants of his past. So he hadn't grown up poor in the average way; his shame and reluctance seemed to suggest it was more destitute than that.

My strange argument with Owl Eyes earlier in the night came back to me, in which she had insisted, with such ardor, that no good could come about on this side of the game—that corpos couldn't solve things, only ruin them, and that chaos was the only way forward.

But right then, I refused to believe her, for I'd never before stood in front of one of the most powerful men in the Americas, with his heart and humanity bared so clear. Surely, something more meaningful than one-off charity, and yet more reasonable than reckless crime, had to be possible.

"I've chanced upon a few people who really live there," I told Gatsby. "Of course, you know Jordan doesn't want your sponsorship. I think a better investment would be to look into restoring that place. It's famously one of Buchanan Group's greatest failures, but you could set things straight."

He leaned against the hood of the car, listening intently. "What are you thinking?"

"To start, buy up the land and restore the buildings as proper residences. Help a true community form, not just another big bunch of investors," I explained. "Provide grants for businesses to get started there." I caught myself. "Anyway, it's just a thought—"

"All right," said Gatsby. His gaze was still hazy, shaking off the residue of the simulation, and his hair had begun to curl from the humidity.

"You'd really think it over?" I asked.

"I can't promise anything. There's a lot to navigate with the board, but—" He stopped and smiled. "I'd like to try."

I was so stunned that I thanked him for considering it, and for everything else too.

"If I've ever come across wary, or overly pragmatic, as you say"—I paused, shuffling a bit in place—"it's only because graciousness like yours is rare, and I've never been . . ." I didn't know what I was trying to say anymore. "It's just very new to me."

His eyes widened, though he didn't say a word in response and, rather awkwardly, offered a single nod before moving around to the passenger side.

I tried hard not to steal swift glances at him in the car. I observed him fiddling with his tie, doing it up a little too tight, his throat straining against the silk. I wondered now if I'd done something to trouble him, or if the market had simply sapped his energy. The whole way home, the fog in his eyes only thickened.

By the time we reached the tower, he'd put his suit jacket back on, smoothed his hair—becoming Gatsby once more.

GENERATIONAL WEALTH INC. DATA BREACH
INVESTIGATION (CASE STATUS: OPEN)
TRANSCRIPT: NICHOLAS PAULO CARRAWAY (AGE: THIRTY-ONE)
LOCATION: HEADQUARTERS, GATSBY CORPORATION
(NEW YORK CITY, NEW YORK, NEA)
DATE: JUNE 22, 2077

[LOADING]

.

.

.

[PLAY]

"You were employed with Gen Wealth from May to August of 2075."

"I was."

"And you understand why we've called you in?"

"I understand. Though I'm not sure how I can help."

"There are few who can provide true commentary on Mr. Gatsby's character. Even we, as the board, have little insight in this regard. However, it's clear that he gained a less-than-stellar public opinion in the aftermath of what occurred in August of that year, wouldn't you say?"

"Indeed."

"And the fallout of that incident might have been a catalyst for the mess we have on our hands now, yes?"

"I attended Mr. Gatsby's parties, as the entire city did that summer. As did you, Mr. Chairman, and all of you in this room. He and I became acquainted personally, but I can't speculate beyond the inform-ation you already know."

190

"It's not my desire to accuse you of lying, Mr. Carraway."

"Then don't."

"Given what he's entrusted you with, you can't expect anyone to believe that you were simply 'acquainted.'"

"As the board mandated, I completed a full security check of the Gen Wealth systems this morning. Scaled every VINE. No signs of an attack. Your auditor accompanied me. It's all in our report."

"The fact remains that someone wants to drive Gen Wealth into the ground, and we *need* to find out who."

[PAUSE]

Twenty

GATSBY'S HAPPY SLEEP STUDIO OCCUPIED a windowless basement in Chelsea. He led us past an android receptionist and into a narrow hallway of glass-paned offices. Peering inside, I caught glimpses of stylish silhouettes and smooth profiles bent toward wide holo-screens, tense and grim, or in one room, utterly sobbing. According to Gatsby, this was where talent met with management to discuss contracts, scripts, and performance metrics.

"As I told you before, the sensory feedback tech in the current Happy Sleep market isn't without its flaws. Those who partake in Sleeps gradually become more aware of that 'fourth wall,' so to speak. It dampens the quality of the immersion," he said. "We want to improve the experience so that blurred line between virtual and real becomes invisible. That's why a seasoned diver is invaluable for our research. If we can induce solid immersion on someone as accustomed to cyberspace as you are, it'd be a considerable advancement. Then if we get ahead of the curve on this, there are certain applications that could be revolutionary in the medical space too."

"What part of the medical space?" I asked.

"Memory," said Gatsby. "The tech holds untapped potential. We've mostly used it as a means for entertainment, when really, it opens us up to all sorts of interesting memory augmentation. For instance, everyone's been trying to address Alzheimer's for years, and we're closer than we've ever been before. And that only scratches the surface."

Farther inside was a smaller waiting area. A glittering trio, done up in bold makeup, shivered in the corner, wearing thin white gowns and sharing a stim-stick for warmth. I could only assume they were preparing to record something, though I couldn't, for the life of me, deduce what the theme of the session was supposed to be; perhaps somewhere between tropical and disco.

I found it all unnerving. Up close, this glamorous industry had the sterility of a hospital and even its sharp, septic scent.

Soon, a horde of lab coats appeared, perhaps ten or twelve of them. Gatsby shook each person's hand before they led us into a red-lit antechamber and then through an imposing triple-locked door.

The studio was a frightful sight. If netdiving required near darkness, then the recording space was like stepping into the blinding white of an overexposed photograph. Several hundred wires dangled from twenty-foot ceilings, the ends of which were attached to round micro-cameras. It resembled a jungle or perhaps a sea of black spiders spinning down from their webs.

Introductions were made, and then it was my turn to shake all the hands. I caught none of them except for the leader of the research team, an excitable and heavily modded person called Newtonia Orchid. The name, I recognized as a longtime player in the film industry. Apparently, they were the outcast of the Orchid empire, having jumped from film directing to Happy Sleeps.

Their eyes were matte black, with white crosses in place of irises. They explained this was an expensive and irreversible oc-mod that allowed them to easily interface with all the cameras at once.

"It won't *feel* like diving. Not exactly," they said after I'd changed into a thin, loose gown like the ones the performers wore in the waiting room. "Happy Sleeps are recorded in shallow cyberspace. The most significant difference is that you'll be conscious. If you've ever been double-stimmed, it's rather like that, but more intense. Your mind's going to try to drag you fully under, so you have to resist it. Now, I'll show you how to—oh, you have it."

They were about to secure the harness for me, but I'd gone ahead and stepped into it. It was a lower one than I was used to. The tips of my toes grazed the cold tiles.

"We'll be monitoring and recording your synaptic feedback." Orchid circled behind me with a bundle of cables tucked under their arm.

They measured each against my neck port and then selected one, which they handed off to Gatsby. "I'll prepare the calibration."

They joined their team, sitting in a line behind the thicket of wires and facing a vast holo–control board. After they rattled off a few commands to their crew, all the lenses on the dangling cameras flashed red.

"Nervous, old sport?" murmured Gatsby. His fingers brushed my neck.

Some strange dizziness momentarily coursed through me, but I blamed it on the hot lights. "No," I replied.

His hands moved in a practiced way, and I remembered that he'd supposedly been an Ops man in the military, that he knew his way around netdiving rigs. The cable slotted in with ease.

"Feels good?" He stepped back for a moment, then toward me again, flattened his palms on either side of my waist, and readjusted the harness so I was about half an inch higher.

"Fine." I cleared my throat. "Yes, it's fine."

"Calibrating." Orchid's voice shuttled in my ears, echoing as if through a tunnel. They relayed a set of instructions—raise my right arm, now my left, inhale, exhale. I waited for the familiar tension to pull my muscles taut. Instead, the opposite occurred; my heartbeat slowed, my spine liquefied, my lips numbed. I'd been warned that it wouldn't feel like diving, but somehow it still surprised me.

I didn't realize I'd gone slack until Gatsby's arm curved around my back and I slumped against him. Orchid said, "We're going to give you a relaxant, along with the usual hypo shot for body-temp regulation."

"Just the hypo is all right," I said weakly. If I relaxed any more than I was, I feared I'd go unconscious, or worse, that I'd lose my tongue like after four shots of strong liquor.

"There's a burn on the way in. Not like the one you're used to," warned Orchid.

"Why not a half dosage, at least?" Gatsby suggested.

I shook my head. "No, that's—"

"You shouldn't hurt yourself," he said in a decisive tone that left no room for argument. Another dizzy wave crashed over me. "Please. For my peace of mind, if not yours."

I must have nodded, for one of Orchid's assistants appeared before me to administer the shot.

Gatsby, still hovering at my side, added, "You can let us know at any time if you're overstimulated." Then I watched him fade through the jungle of spidery cameras, and not a second later, I was falling, inch by inch, toward a blazing light.

"Close your eyes for us, old sport."

◇——◇——◇

As Jordan had told me, Happy Sleep actors do not often remember their first recordings. I myself have no memory of the session from that day. Only having watched it back on many occasions since, I can relay it as follows:

ORCHID: "Mr. Carraway. Can you hear me?"

I blinked. The cameras were there, and then they weren't. The harness around me was gone, too, and the room, a shadowless white void.

ME: "Mm."

ORCHID: "Can you speak?"

The numbness around my lips spread to my tongue.

ORCHID: "You're half awake, Mr. Carraway. We'll pull you down farther. Let yourself relax for now, and the numbness will fade."

I relaxed as best I could.

ME: "Mm—yes ... I can speak."

ORCHID: "Stay lucid. We're administering a serotonin stimulant. It's a little bit more than what you'll find in an average stim-stick."

GATSBY: "If you need a moment—"

ME: "I'm fine."

ORCHID: "Now you'll feel the first pull."

A heaviness nibbled between my brows. Then it poured down into my neck, chest, toes. One moment, I was sure I was going to fall over;

the next, I was floating. After a stretch of immeasurable time, I let out a breath.

ORCHID: "Good. Excellent."

GATSBY: "How does it feel?"

ME: "Like we're ... swimming in your pool again."

A pause.

GATSBY: "That's a good thing, I hope."

ME: "Mm."

ORCHID: "You'll feel a swell next. That's the endorphins. As they're rising, we're going to pull you deeper. We'll be layering in a visual afterward. Describe it as best you can. It may be difficult at first—your brain will start trying to map any visual it sees to one of your memories. Try not to get swallowed up in it."

The sky filled out first—a harsh, oversaturated blue, uneven in spots as if from a child's marker drawing.

ORCHID: "Stay with us, Mr. Carraway."

ME: "I'm here."

ORCHID: "What do you see?"

There was grass, dotted with flowers, a spotting of trees in the distance, birdsong and wind.

ORCHID: "Your other senses have activated already? That's good. Walk forward a bit until you're in the meadow up ahead."

I walked. A sturdy oak tree sat in the middle of the clearing. The grass stood taller, the flowers cartoonishly bright, the sunlight glaring. And then—

GATSBY: "We're registering a temp spike. Do you need a break?"

ME: "No, I—no."

ORCHID: "Describe the scenery for us, please."

ME: "Meadow. Tree ..."

GATSBY: "You're doing well."

I smelled cologne. Something floral, with a bourbon depth. A shadow developed behind the trunk of the oak tree. The sunlight shifted, stretching the shadow all the way to my feet. It moved, and there was a figure—pale and long-limbed, with lines of glowing blue curled around his arms.

ME: "Chester ...?"

ORCHID: "What was that?"

The wind was cresting in my ears.

GATSBY: "Mr. Carraway?"

Silence again.

GATSBY: "Nick? *Nick*—are you with me?"

I shivered, but it wasn't cold. I was sweating, in fact.

ME: "Sorry, it's—I'm having a memory bleed."

ORCHID: "A heavy one?"

It was the meadow.

ME: "Could you ... cycle the interface?"

The grass dissolved into water, miles of it on all sides—shallow, just halfway up my calves and pleasantly warm. I exhaled.

GATSBY: "Better?"

ME: "Yes."

ORCHID: "Bringing you deeper, then."

GATSBY: "What else do you feel?"

ME: "Your voice ... it's sticky."

GATSBY: "Sticky?"

ME: "In my ears. Like you said about being in your pool alone. Except I'm not alone. You're here. ..."

GATSBY: "Is there too much stim on the audio?"

I believe Gatsby may have been speaking to Orchid here, but I had answered.

ME: "No. Just ... it feels tender. Warm. Like laughter. Or like summer, but without the heat ...? I—"

ORCHID: "This is great. The pleasure chemicals are steady, and these visuals are so clear. Shall we pull him deeper?"

GATSBY: "Nick? How are you?"

ME: "Just splendid. ..."

GATSBY, TO ORCHID: "You may. Slightly. Don't be rough with him, please."

ME: "Mm—Jay?"

GATSBY: "I—I'm here. Your heart rate is high. Are you sure you're all right?"

ME: "Yes. It's you, I think. It's just ... 'cause of you. ..."

GATSBY: "You're dipping again."

ME: "Mm."
GATSBY: "Nick?"
ME: "M here. . . . I'm . . ."
ORCHID: "Shall we push one more—"
GATSBY: "Stop. Bring him out."
ORCHID: "He says he's all ri—"
GATSBY: "I said, bring him out."

◇——◇——◇

By the time I regained consciousness, I was no longer in the harness. Voices hung in the room like dust motes. The rig had been disassembled, the red eyes of the spider-cameras turned off, and I lay on the cold floor with my head resting on a folded blanket. Gatsby was crouched beside me.

"Sorry." I sat up, lightheaded. "I didn't last very long, did I?"

"Actually, you lasted far longer than any of our other divers." He held something in the palm of his hand—a vial, containing a tiny smooth bead, delicate as a raindrop, prismatic as it caught the light. "This is a memory diamond. Not *real* diamond, of course; that's just what we call it," he said. "It's a thirty-year effort created by Newtonia and their talented team."

"What does it do?"

"Stores memories. This is just a test subject." His excitement mounted. "Happy Sleeps are like films—scripted and impersonal. But with these diamonds, one day, you'll be able to watch back your *own* memories. You can relive moments of your life, heighten the sensations, make them feel even more wonderful every single time." He gestured to the smiling lab coats. "With your tolerance so high, the visuals you produced were quite vivid. The team's pleased with what we collected today. More than improving our Happy Sleep immersions, we're getting close to finalizing our research. We have plans to partner with a good biotech venture to bring it to market soon."

My head was a vicious stampede, but I pulled myself together just enough to ask, "A biotech partner? Do you . . . have one in mind?"

"We do," said Gatsby. "Talks are stalled at the moment because half the board is still reluctant to divulge the research externally. It's a delicate matter, deciding whom to trust. No one wants a second corpo war so soon after the last."

He pressed the bead into my palm, and I stared at it, quite astonished that such a tiny thing, not larger than an old penny, could take three decades to create and subsequently cause so much uproar.

This was it.

This was what had spurred powerful corpos to action and mobilized an entire espionage effort in the shadows. This was why I'd been plucked from my desk in a Manila office and dropped, flailing, into New York.

"How—" I relinquished the bead to him. "How impressive."

He unfurled the crisp pocket square from his suit jacket. "Here. For your nose."

I touched my nose. Indeed, I was bleeding. "I feel fine. You didn't need to pull me out."

"I didn't want to push you," said Gatsby.

"I'm glad I could be of help, then."

"You were. You did well." He took the handkerchief from me and dabbed an extra spot under my nose. "If you want to join the project full-time, the offer is still on the table. I know you might want to think on it with a clearer head."

I nodded, gulping a quarter gallon of fluids as Gatsby went to thank his team. Afterward, the lab coats retreated, and Orchid shook my hand before rushing to their next session.

Half the spotlights had mercifully been shut off. My vision was starting to clear.

"Who is Chester?" said Gatsby as he helped me into a chair and gave me my clothes.

I almost fell over. "Sorry?"

"You said that name while you were under. Memory bleed." Gatsby turned a holo-screen on with a wave of his hand. That seemed a little horrifying, and I wondered what else I'd said. "Was it a positive memory? It'd be helpful to note for our research," he said as I stepped out of the white gown and into my slacks. "We want to ensure the tech's inducing exclusively positive output. It'd be a massive oversight if a negative memory could accidentally leak into the sim."

In my feeble haze, it took a moment longer than usual to process his spiel. "If it's a matter of endorphins, then I suppose it was positive."

Gatsby looked up from the screen. "You suppose?"

"It was intimate," I said, shrugging my shirt on, too tired to find more tactful words and still too unbalanced from the session to care. I would regret that extra relaxant later.

I was doing up my shirt buttons when I noticed Gatsby was not typing but staring at me—with intense focus.

"I have the impression that I—" He halted. "That you, perhaps, can't feel at ease with me because of the way I went about . . . introducing myself to you. I mean, I hope you're not still upset with me at all."

I wasn't, not right then, but it would be the last time in a long time, for soon the summer would begin to rot, and I'd never look at him the same way ever again.

In the moment, however, the question struck me only as rare honesty, so I was honest in return. "Well, I suppose—there are far more fascinating folks you could have plucked from your parties and persuaded into friendship. I still can't work out why you chose me, of all people," I admitted. "I guess I'm not upset with you more than I'm upset with myself. For breaking these rules I have—"

"Rules?"

I was dangling too close over dangerous waters now. "Never mind. I'm quite tired."

It took some effort to get to my feet. He offered me an arm for balance. We were halfway through the long, dim antechamber between the studio and the waiting room when he stopped us.

"The thing is . . ." He was strangely agitated. I didn't recognize this coiled voice of his, as if these words had somehow been fermenting for a long time. "You know, people aren't fascinating for the things they own or the work they do. Not you, anyway. You are—something else."

I stared at him. Blood surged to my head.

He said, in a single, dazed breath, "I don't know why you make yourself the smallest thing in the room. Or why you bite your genuine thoughts and hold your judgments unless they're pried from you. Why you say you're 'compliant' when it's not true at all. Why you leave space for others to be their whole selves but never leave enough room for *your* whole self." He swallowed. "I could give you a thousand more invitations, I think, and I'd still wonder what it would be like to receive yours one day."

I wobbled backward, still holding Gatsby's arm, and his grip tightened, as he stumbled forward in a grand attempt to keep me upright. My back pressed up against the cold wall, and then he was only inches from me—his smooth face creased through with concern.

The harsh red lights of the antechamber deepened the shadows beneath his eyes and the hollows of his cheeks, and I wondered if this was how he'd met me that first night.

Holding me steady through my own stupor.

I saw a tremor in his throat. I smelled the lace of vanilla beneath his gingery cologne, sweetness through the spice. His lips parted, birthing and killing a sequence of unvoiced thoughts, shallow breaths saturating the silence as his hand traveled from my arm to my waist, and at the end of that eternal second, the only sound that escaped him was a low, fevered whisper.

"Nick."

I might have still been attached to a rig, floating and incorporeal in cyberspace.

Of all the striking reveries and delusions Gatsby could fashion out of thin air, I didn't think there was one more impossible than this.

His eyes were dark. He leaned closer. His lips moved again. "I want—"

"I appreciate the offer, this opportunity," I muttered, and he stepped away from me with a start, "but perhaps I'm not cut out for your team here. My head's a bit ..."

I turned, marching to the exit, and I heard him calling after me, offering to fly me to West Egg, but I insisted I'd take the train.

Out of the city, past the ghosts of the valley and Dr. T. J. Eckleburg, somehow I made it home and fell face down into my couch. I was hovering outside of my own body, all my thoughts addled with the taste of his voice as the room twirled and twirled, a pinwheel in a hot breeze. . . .

When I stumbled into the shower, I didn't know why the ground wouldn't straighten beneath my feet.

But I knew one thing most definitely.

I'd gotten my ticket out of this assignment.

Twenty-One

BUNSEN'S EXCITEMENT PULSED THROUGH THE holo-screen. Straight from the shower, I'd rung him up and given him a report of the afternoon, as thorough as I could manage. The lethargy of the session had settled in, and my nerves were chittering like cicadas.

"You see!" His hand struck his desk. "You pulled through, Nick. I fucking *knew* you would. You're a natural—haven't I always said so? This kind of research, it's everything Medica's interested in."

I shuffled up on the couch, toweling my hair. "How so?"

"They ran themselves into the ground trying to create a little thing called 'memory transplantation.' You remember that? Killed a thousand cancer patients in the process, bad headlines, terrible PR mess." He gulped his coffee, cringed, then called in a secretary to fetch him a new mug. "The short of it is that they were the closest ones to ever detach mind from body, you see. Close, but never successful. It's the *re*attaching they couldn't ever figure out. But this could be the right step forward. A perfect partnership."

All corpo conversations led back to money and death, and all of them sounded the same to me. What I wanted to know was if I was free now that the acquisition was green lit.

"Better than free," replied Bunsen. "You want a promotion out of contracting? I'll get you on a plane to Manila. There'll be an office waiting for you by the time you land."

I stared through the holo-screen, at the Sound wavering in a dull gleam beyond my windows. "I can't leave Gen Wealth before the end of the contract. The timing would raise questions."

I thought it was the careful thing to do, but Bunsen considered it for a long minute. "Right. We'll work out a way to cut it short for you." There was a wrinkle in his brow that, in better light and a more sober state, I might have thought was suspicion. "Don't spend more time around these sorts than you have to."

The screen vanished, and my living room darkened, washed orange from an encroaching dusk.

I rubbed my eyes, rose from the couch, and walked halfway down the hall to the bedroom, when the doorbell chimed.

It was Gatsby, out of breath, floundering in the entryway for a moment. "I tried to—" His eyes ricocheted in a hundred directions, before I remembered I hadn't fully dressed yet. "Your comm was busy."

I widened the door, slinging my towel around my shoulders. "Building's yours, isn't it? But you still knock."

The joke didn't crack a smile from him. He took one step inside and not another inch more. "You left in a hurry today. I hoped you weren't sick."

"I'm not," I said. He plunged his hands deep into his pockets, holding himself tight as if he were standing against the bite of a winter wind. "Did you need something?"

"No, that's all." He shook his head, relaxed his shoulders, tensed again. "I know you said you wouldn't like to work with us at the studio. But when your contract ends with Gen Wealth, do you plan to stay in New York?"

In his fitted button-down, that swollen bit of skin on his right forearm caught my eye, as it had in his pool. He took his hands out of his pockets and rubbed this spot through his sleeve as if it were a nervous habit.

"If I had a good reason," I said carefully, "I suppose so."

The earlier afternoon in the studio's antechamber wafted between us.

He blinked. Sheets of setting sun fell west across his taut face, and I remember stepping toward him, close enough that a droplet from my hair landed on his arm.

The only thing that ever kept or moved me anywhere was work. Neither my hometown nor an ancestral land, or any of the places in between, had effectively tied me down before.

But for centuries . . . wasn't New York, the racy thrill of its lights and shadows, always the exception?

"The tower," he murmured, his voice congealed in his throat. "Would you come to the tower tomorrow?" He wet his lips and turned to the door. "I need to show you something."

For the first time that summer, I could have declined his invitation without consequence. Still, I found myself agreeing, and there's little else for me to say in my defense except that a string of indecisions had defined my whole life up until then, but here, in the conclusion of my assignment, I thought I'd heard a strange, tempting freedom beating beneath the war drum of my self-preservation.

"Good night, Jay," I said.

He left, and I leaned my forehead against the closed door, startled and half embarrassed by my own informality. As I listened to his footsteps trickle uncertainly down the hall, my attention drew to my comm-light, blinking beneath my wrist beside Daisy's name.

◇———◇———◇

"How thrilling. It's like a movie." The gloss of Daisy's lips was almost the only thing I could make out in the bar's dimness, glinting in excited little movements as she laughed. "You seem to suit the village now, Nicky, I hate to tell you."

She wanted to meet here in West Egg, which I thought was a horrid idea, but her own house was out of the question. Apparently, Tom disliked being in public with her these days, so it'd been a while since she'd left the grounds, and she wanted to experience something different from a living room. It seemed unkind not to oblige.

"Actually, I've warmed up to it some," I said. "It's not all bad."

The bar was a cramped hole down the block, resurrected out of a demolished factory, its upper level an industrial catwalk-turned-mezzanine from which we'd stuck ourselves against the wall, spectating the first wave of the evening crowd. Until the midnight rush, it was about as serene a place as one could find in West Egg.

"Is it Jordan?" she said.

"Pardon?"

"Your smile, darling."

Sometimes I thought she sounded just as archaic as Tom about Jordan marrying off. "Why do you care so much about her prospects?" I asked. We both knew Jordan could wed someone tomorrow and without much effort.

"Why, she's my dearest friend." Daisy clutched her daiquiri with both hands, holding it to her chest like a bouquet of flowers. "I told you, I—I've always looked up to her."

The sapphire neon strips along the walls buzzed in the suffocating air, and a clanging beat rattled deafeningly from the speakers, but I swore I heard Daisy's every word correctly.

"Sometimes, she used to let me watch her train, and I'd listen to her explain bullet-golf plays, as if a perfect death to her would be beneath those lights and nothing else. It's a gorgeous thing to see that kind of ambition in someone. I never felt that way about Happy Sleeps. The lights in a studio ... they're so different from an arena. So much colder." She smudged the lip gloss imprint on her glass with a swipe of her thumb. "Every athlete's world is sort of destined for apocalypse in a way and ... well, you've seen Tom. It can be a depressing thing if you're not ready for it. I don't know where Jordan'll seek her next purpose, but I can only hope it's in—something worthy."

Around us, the stim-stick dust seemed to prickle her eyes. She blinked, and in the soft blue darkness, I saw Daisy's face in shades that I'd never seen before—older and heavier.

"But, Nick, I *heard*! That's why I called you up!" She swallowed her drink, discarded it onto a hover-bot, smiling brilliantly as ever. "I heard you've gone and done it. My father says everyone's excited now."

"I'm glad it's ended well," I said.

"Yes, and ... I have to ask—oh, I know you have rules, but can't you tell me now?" she insisted. "Did you meet him?"

The jeers of the bar and all its cacophony leveled out into a low, distant whine.

I tilted my head. "Meet who?"

She smacked my arm. "Mr. Jay Gatsby, of course. You must have met him, yes? What was he *like*?"

The question knocked me off balance, but Daisy assumed it was the gin in my hand and attentively relieved me of it. "Like?" I muttered.

The image of Gatsby in my living room just a few hours ago came to me first—not the keen introduction in his elevator, not the smile on his rooftop, nor the dramatic sales pitch about his Happy Sleep studio.

What was he *like*? Nervous, vivid, singular.

What I said aloud was "Why do you ask?"

"I'd—well, I'd just like to know. Was he pleasant?" she blurted out. "Perhaps . . . cheerful and handsome?"

Before I could form another thought, someone with good oc-mods across the mezzanine saw through the misty dark and gasped in our direction, whispering something to their companion. I didn't want to summon a mob, so I took Daisy's arm and we slipped down the sticky metal stairs, out the back, and down a damp alley that curved around to the maintenance entrance of my building.

It was night now, and a thin fog was beginning to coat the air.

I recalled Jordan's nagging hunch that she couldn't shake—that she'd met Gatsby before, in Louisville, and suddenly Daisy's "trust" in me, her cousinly appeal, her insistence on my appointment to this sensitive family matter came into sharp focus upon a fresh scene.

"Did you . . ." I inhaled, tasting the metallic breeze. When my lips moved again, they were numb as they'd been at the studio. "Daisy. Did you ever know a man named Gatz, by any chance?"

"Oh! Nick . . . are you saying it's really him? It's—" Her hand tightened in mine—shock and hope and longing in a single squeeze. "James?" she whispered. "Did he *speak* of me?"

Her voice stirred marvelously, and between the bright, sharp teeth of the West Egg night, the whole summer peeled its skin back.

Interlude

O NE DAY IN 2063, I returned to Louisville, following the victory of my first bullet-golf championship title. I was seventeen and went on a tour of some biodomes. There were crowds outside my childhood house. Everyone had come out to congratulate me. Everyone, except for Daisy.

When we were girls, she and I had strung our pinkies together one night under the canopy of her pink blankets. She'd promised to stand right beside me the first time I brought a trophy home.

"And soon after you'll have thousands," she whispered. "I'm sure of it."

She was more sure of it than I was. Back then, I was always nervous, but Daisy found me endearing. She was popular in that way wherein if she liked you, then just about everyone did too. I felt I owed her a lot for that. Otherwise, my early years there would have been lonely and even more unbearable.

I realized, however, standing in the parade that was in my honor, that Daisy most certainly had forgotten about our strung pinkies all that time ago. The reassurance she'd offered me in her childhood bedroom—words that had propelled me through a bone-crushing sporting season and into glorious victory—to her, in fact, had held less weight than her fading laughter.

I shall tell you this as well—and only once. You ought to take it to the grave. I swore to myself that I would, but I suppose you're really a professional since you worked it out.

Daisy was always coveted, which was why she withheld her kisses longer than anyone imagined. Until she was sixteen, to be exact, and the first one she ever gave wasn't to the new boy who moved in across the street. That was just the story she told at sleepovers.

Everyone laughs about their first, and all its unbearable clumsiness, but in truth, every moment with Daisy in Louisville was like an extension of our long, effervescent first kiss that she reignited in each breath. When she borrowed my clothes, held my hand during mod appointments, taped my bruises after practice—these things lived within me, feeding a hearth hot enough to burn me.

It was just before that first championship title, in fact, that she'd thrown her arm around me in her bed and talked about how boring marriage sounded, that she envied my life, and that she'd miss me while I was away like she'd never missed anyone before.

I went to search for her after all the fanfare dissipated. I took a long walk in the early evening to her house, a redbrick mansion that was the largest in our gated community and crowned the end of a cul-de-sac. The bronze lights in the windows were lit, and I crossed the soft lawn, carefully stepping over Mrs. Fay's expensive tulip bed.

All of a sudden, a giggle rang through the street like church bells. I turned and hopped down the porch.

Around the street corner, I found her in the driver's side of her white Veluz. It was an old-school roadster style, very fashionable that year. Daisy was the only young woman who had one.

In the passenger seat sat a military man. I knew she didn't let just anyone in her car, and that was the first time I'd ever seen someone in that seat aside from me. The two of us used to go on spontaneous trips; that was a thing Daisy liked to do—just up and go somewhere. Her parents never made a fuss if I went with her, so she'd beg me to join her until I obliged. I always did.

It was clear she had gone on a drive that day. Her round cheeks were wind flushed, and her eyes filled with the mirth of new experiences; she'd gone and lived so much life in the time I'd been away.

The young man beside her was a lieutenant; as I drew nearer, I saw this denoted over the left breast of his tan uniform. His hair was shaven underneath a tight military cap, and he was about Daisy's age, nineteen, though at the time, I thought him a shade younger. His boyish face glowed, utterly absorbed; you'd think, looking at him, that he had witnessed Daisy paint the sunset onto the sky with her own hands.

When she finally noticed me, I expected her to spring up from her roadster with surprise, delight, or else sudden guilt to find how quickly the day had escaped her.

She did not, however. If she had, I would have been all right, for I knew many people were calling on her that summer. Our biodome hosted service centers and events for the nearby military bases, and as a descendant of Fay Medica, she was at those functions a lot.

I'd never thought much of these aspiring suitors until this moment when Daisy's joyous gaze fluttered, mothlike, toward me, and she called out from her car, "Hello, Jordan. Please come here."

I approached. She said something to me about the Red Cross. It was where she volunteered some evenings, preparing care packages for soldiers.

"Are you going there tomorrow?" she asked.

I was; I had a photo op scheduled.

"Then could you tell them I won't be coming?" she said, then turned her whole smile back to her lieutenant, who hadn't lifted his gaze from her, and just like that, I became as inconsequential as the synth-trees down the block.

I did not speak to Daisy for months after. I fled Louisville again and went to a training center out West to spend my off-season among athletic equals, out of the confines of suburbia. I competed in the less-prestigious Western circuit as a way to keep busy, won some trophies, and returned home in the winter to find Daisy depressed beyond repair.

I discovered her on my aunt's porch, sobbing, and she leaped into my arms the way I thought she would when I'd won the East championship. But, of course, she wasn't congratulating me on anything.

She was heartbroken.

Heartbreak is a parasite most of us flush from our systems in our adolescence, or at the very least, in adulthood, we have learned to live with its poison. To Daisy, however, this pain was raw and overstimulating; she was a newborn faced for the first time with the harsh, cold lights of existence.

I held her in my aunt's kitchen as she wept, and she didn't stop until it was nighttime. Then she crawled under my bedsheets, as she had for years, except it wasn't to pull my chin toward hers. She spoke longingly about her handsome lieutenant, his enchanting words, and his solemn devotion. Before he received his new assignment, he had done the unthinkable—asked to marry her.

I understood then that Daisy had fallen in love with him, too, so hopelessly that she couldn't even bear to utter his name.

"But perhaps we can find him," I said.

"It's no use. He's poor, Jordan," she whispered. "Medica might sink soon, Father's said, and he'd never approve a match like that. . . ."

The next morning, you couldn't have guessed Daisy had been sobbing her whole soul out in my bed. We went out around town together, shopping and driving like we used to, except we were both rising celebrities now; Daisy, at this point, had signed her first Sleep contract, and the two of us always felt important as we strolled arm in arm into places. With our lovely new clothes and trinkets piled in our laps, flying here and there in the hot afternoon, the previous night and all of its sorrows had already been forgotten.

The years passed, and Daisy became unfathomably famous, and I wasn't far behind. Occasionally, we'd hear things about one another whispered through the haze of parties. Daisy, during her career, was fussy about what she attended, only deigning to go places where she knew she would be the most interesting thing there.

She had a revolving door of beaux and so did I, though by then I respected myself enough that I no longer held myself to the slow standards I was raised in. I was seeing beautiful women, just as much as the men, and when Daisy and I met for tea, we'd laugh hilariously about all our conquests. Pretending our own names had never once belonged on each other's lists.

Every few months or so, she'd swear to me that she was close to an engagement, but it always fell through. I never assigned much meaning to this; to marry as a Happy Sleep star was most often equivalent to retirement.

That was out of the question for Daisy. Her status as a beloved entertainer was the only thing that had salvaged the remains of the

Fay Medica name; if she had to marry into retirement, then it was clear she had to marry upward.

A while later, there was a corpo she met in a New Orleans jazz club, a fellow from Jamaica who owned several Caribbean hover-districts, and she was dazzled by him. But he was new money, which wasn't remotely interesting amidst the "respectable" crowd, so her father wasn't pleased. Ultimately, they broke it off before he could even buy her a ring, but not before she threatened to jump off the balcony of her hotel. Or so the rumors went.

Then she was twenty-six, lonely and famous, floating absently around Chicago. One evening, at some fundraiser at the Palmer House, her heels had snapped, and she was running around the whole party barefoot for the rest of the night. Certainly, you've seen those photographs; there's one in particular of her standing at the base of a golden staircase, with foreign dignitaries and half of the East's corporate world fanned around her like spectators gazing up at a hallowed artwork.

You've probably seen this other photograph too—of how Daisy was escorted to her car at the end of that night. She was carried, rather sweetly, by a vivacious gentleman—Tom Buchanan, no less—who couldn't in good conscience allow a lady to walk barefoot across the street. She and Tom were not strangers to each other; they'd crossed paths every now and then at these sorts of events, and he'd wanted her for years, but that was the day their courtship solidified.

In a matter of months, an extravagant wedding entourage descended upon Louisville. That's right, you weren't there for it; you're lucky. It was grotesquely posh. I'd say the attendance was in the thousands. The whole world had seen that image of Daisy barefoot in Tom's arms, and the whole world now felt it held a stake in this gorgeous fairy tale. Tom invited every Buchanan he could, all his football teammates from Yale, and any socialite he'd ever shared a cigar with. He brought colorful light drones and one hundred android servers, and some contraption the size of a car that emitted holo-landscapes into the air so that the whole area around the ceremony shifted into a new nature scenery every hour.

I was her maid of honor. I couldn't say no when she asked, but I admit I almost wanted to.

"It's going to be the happiest day of my life," she murmured to me, about a week before the ceremony. "And you ought to be there beside me."

A well of anger I hadn't felt since I was seventeen surged unexpectedly in my gut. I doubted she remembered my own happiest day, and I realized something then, with the starkest clarity.

If Happy Sleeps make far-flung fantasies feel like memories, that was the moment I realized Daisy could do the opposite out of sheer force of will. Forgetting is its own death, and in ceasing to remember those years, they had never happened.

She insisted on having her bachelorette party the night before her wedding. I invited her Happy Sleep colleagues and the other women from our neighborhood, and we drank ourselves silly at a local bar, then again in my backyard around a spitting bonfire.

That night, Daisy was in such a state that I couldn't take her home. She was vomiting all over the place, and it was past 3:00 a.m.

She curled over the toilet in my bathroom, wearing a string of pearls Tom had publicly gifted her at their engagement party. She tore it from her neck, and the pearls scattered across the tiles. A cleaning bot flew over to try and suction the necklace away. She wailed and wailed.

I was terrified of her that night, and exhausted too—from the prolonged years of her unloading her heartbreaks into my arms. I called the Fay house, and her mother rushed over in the dark light before daybreak. Together, we stripped Daisy and put her in my tub until she'd calmed some. An hour passed, the sun rose, and she fell into a fitful slumber.

Her mother returned home before Mr. Fay would notice her absence. We kept Daisy in my bedroom. I didn't sleep at all. Sometime later, she roused on her own, and the only coherent words she could string together were lamentations for her lost lieutenant.

It was the first time in seven years she'd spoken of him. I was stunned she had remembered him so deeply. Daisy couldn't even remember all the places we had gone together in the last few months or the names of all the awards she'd won throughout her career.

But she recalled all of this—the height and glow of the moon on the night she'd snuck the lieutenant into her bedroom, how blond his

213

hair turned under the softened biodome sunlight, the roughness of his hand in hers, and how each one of his scars against her smooth palm was a reminder of how far they really were from one another, even when they were wrapped up in each other's arms. Apparently, he promised that he'd come back for her, and she had promised, in turn, to wait for him.

You'd laugh, hearing them exchange such solemn vows neither of them could keep. They're a funny sort, these kinds of people, who will shatter things and close their eyes and then be shocked to find all those bits of glass don't just disappear. They'll take their shoes off when it's romantic, and they won't care for that mess they made, will they, because they know without a doubt someone will emerge from the crowd and carry them over it.

Later, in her ball gown studded with teardrop diamonds, Daisy was the perfect bride everyone wanted.

In all the years since, I could never make out the name of that soldier, but the more I've tried, the more I swear I can hear it in Daisy's voice—*James*, the desperate sound she had choked on that night in my bathroom, like so much shattered glass, ripping her open.

Twenty-Two

JORDAN RECOUNTED THIS THE NEXT day when we took breakfast at the Plaza's Palm Court. I'd called her that morning to tell her that I'd met with Daisy, then demanded she release her grip on the rest of these irrevocable secrets. When she finally reached the end of her impossible story, having emptied two decanters of chilled synth-coffee on her own, we left the Plaza and flew deep into the East Egg village to meet with Meyer.

In the car, she wouldn't look at me, and I decided it was best not to speak, for my own thoughts were circling in a disordered mess.

Now I knew why she'd suspended her hunch for so long. It must have taken an astounding effort for her to admit everything. I'd latched onto those severe pauses between her words, the same ones that had locked Daisy's jaw tight in the bar, except Jordan's had been bruised with time and bloodied with honesty.

I was surprised she still cared to speak with Meyer, but she insisted upon it, and so we touched down in front of a brilliant tri-toned mansion with ornate trim and stained glass windows.

An android took us through an entrance of marble columns and chessboard floors. Tall mahogany doors were flung open on both sides. I spotted a gray-haired woman knitting on a veranda and just barely stopped myself from staring outright. It wasn't common to see anyone of wealth wearing an age past forty these days.

Muted afternoon light shifted through the stained glass, and our footsteps clicked evenly through the hall until we reached a carpeted staircase at the apex of the foyer. We climbed. Tinny music washed out from a room that appeared to be Meyer's study. I recognized the song as "Jazz History of the World," but this version was unaltered, nothing like that rendition we'd heard at Gatsby's party.

"A century and a half!" exclaimed Meyer, standing in front of an impressive fireplace, dark hair askew and beard neatly trimmed.

"What is?" I asked politely.

"This very recording. That's how old it is." He marched to the corner of the room, where there stood, amazingly, what looked like a real phonograph. "It's—"

"Tostoff, yes," I said.

Meyer grinned. "So you know it!"

"That's my aunt's favorite of all 1920s jazz standards and mine as well," said Jordan.

"What an honor to have you, Miss Baker." Meyer shook her hand, and they talked about Tostoff for a minute more. Jordan, as it turned out, was knowledgeable on this subject.

"This song was one of just three musical compositions included in the time capsule back in the 2020s. The one they launched with the probe," said Jordan.

Meyer gestured at the leather sofa in front of the fireplace. Laid out across the coffee table was a tray of three steeping teapots and a spread of delicacies. There wasn't a serving-bot in sight, and his android had disappeared from the room entirely.

"I keep one around just to tend to the gardens and all that," he explained. "My wife—perhaps you saw her. Well, she's been sick awhile. I'd have the place loaded up with more bots, at least, but she won't allow it. We lived modestly for so long that she enjoys doing a lot of housework herself. When Gen Wealth took off, I made it my dream to move out here and give her her very own garden."

Jordan and I dispensed more perfunctory comments about how lovely the grounds were, though having passed enough time with Gatsby, I found that the grandeur of it all now grated on me more than anything.

"So, Mr. Carraway, how's business with Jay?" He turned to Jordan. "I hear you're a friend of his too."

"Sure, if he says so," replied Jordan.

"I don't work closely with him," I corrected.

Meyer nodded slowly. "But you help with which part of the operation? Imports or . . ."

"Sir?"

"I mean, do you oversee the merchandise?"

Jordan, who was quicker than me, set her teacup on her saucer. "Nick is a diver at Gen Wealth."

"Ah!" Meyer clapped his hands. "Forgive me; I'd assumed otherwise. Since he'd brought you to that club."

"Do *you* help him with that?" I asked.

"Not at all." He shook his head urgently, as if he'd never dream of being confused with an illegal mod smuggler. "But I support him with his successes; you know, he's like a son to me."

"That's right," I said. "You knew him when he was an adolescent. What was he like?"

"Well, I mentioned that he was still a young roughneck when he started tinkering around with predictive genetics. I left a professorship at Princeton to go west and meet the young man. He had a guardian named Dan Cody at the time; God rest his soul, an old friend of mine. Our research halted when the war started and James—" He caught himself. "Jay, that is. Jay was drafted. I continued on developing the algorithms. Then one day, he came home after being stationed . . . ah, can't for the life of me remember."

"Louisville, Kentucky?" offered Jordan.

"Yes, Louisville, and oh, he was a changed man," replied Meyer.

All at once, everything Gatsby had ever said was thrown into purgatory—every word withering in my hand, like the dying frames of a Happy Sleep.

"We'd barely said our hellos when he marched over to me and declared, 'Meyer! One day, we'll run the Americas, the whole sorry lot of it!' I laughed at him then, but he turned out to be right, as he always is."

"Why didn't you stay on to help with Gen Wealth too?" asked Jordan.

"Oh, well, you know." Meyer reclined in his armchair. A whole story seemed to lie within those four short words. "Gen Wealth was Jay's brainchild. I wasn't thinking at all about business. I just thought—well, it seems so naive to say now, but people love family trees, tracing back to see who their ancestors are. What great people they're descended from. I figured, why does the tree have to stop?"

He took a long sip of his tea. "Of course, Jay was already racing to make the idea something life altering. He'd started pitching our work to any important folks who'd lend him an ear. That was how he secured funding, and then Gen Wealth became what it is—an innovative way for *anyone* to move up in the world!"

Jordan frowned, and I could tell she was in enough of a mood that this hypocrisy annoyed her. Meyer seemed to keep himself a casual distance away from Gen Wealth, so as to wash his hands of it—so that he couldn't quite call the operation his, though it existed on the foundations of his work. He held none of its glory the way Gatsby did, but also none of the guilt. A multibillion-dollar payout upon selling his patent had provided him this slow, enriched life in a stained glass mansion.

Meyer's eyes darted between us. "And . . . it's done a lot for people. Tuition, medical bills, rent. So many important things that would otherwise never be possible for—for less fortunate folks. . . ." He trailed off into his teacup, which was empty. "No endeavor is perfect, but if it wasn't Jay who developed Gen Wealth, it would have been another brilliant person down the line. Anyway"—he brushed off the topic as if it were lint on his collar—"he can work anyone, can't he? That's why the business was better off in his hands."

"Yes." Jordan glanced at me, then away. I gripped my knees hard. The room began to shrink. "Though for all that charm, he doesn't speak at all about his paramours to us, does he, Nick?"

I shook my head innocently.

"I *have* been so curious about that," said Jordan. "Would you happen to know, sir, about Gatsby in that regard?"

"Paramours? No, he was focused on growing Gen Wealth and all his other operations." Meyer refilled our teacups. "He did always enjoy Happy Sleeps, though. He has a foot in the industry himself now since it's always been one of his passions."

"Was there a performer he liked best?" Jordan pressed.

Without pause, Meyer nodded. "The Buchanan girl, I believe. Yes, wasn't she everyone's favorite before she went and married?"

"Daisy Fay," I said hollowly.

"That's the one!" Meyer wiped a spot of sugar off his thumb. "Daisy Fay. A sweet name indeed."

Then the glazed memories that Jordan had recounted over breakfast sharpened into the full truth, beyond a shadow of a doubt and a disembodied name pulled haphazardly from old public records.

The shattered glass of Daisy's broken sobs came together like two sides of lost history, reuniting.

"And did he ever say more of Miss Fay?" Jordan continued. "Perhaps they met or, at least, wanted to make contact in all that time?"

Meyer looked perplexed by this inquiry; he'd never heard anything of the sort. I didn't know what Jordan was hoping to learn from him, but after several more dead-end questions, she flashed me a disappointed look and I knew it was time to take our leave.

When we stepped back outside, she walked to the edge of the driveway, lighting a cigarette. Against the dense wreath of fog, Gatsby's tower was hardly visible except for the delicate contour of its shadow.

"Gatsby wants to know," said Jordan, "if you'll invite Daisy to your place some afternoon and then let him come over."

It was such a simple revelation, such a simple request, and perhaps it was just this simplicity that disgusted me, crashed against my lungs in a repulsive wave.

Gatsby had built an empire, a lighthouse to stand guard over the bay, to scrape heaven's dust and, from it, fashion a name for himself that tasted like money in your mouth—all to reach for the hand of this lovely girl.

"Did I . . ." I looked out at the fog. "Did I have to know all this before he could ask such a thing?"

"He wants to make it all seem—natural." Jordan recoiled at the word. "Yet it's all staged like some glorious production because he's afraid to come out of nowhere and frighten her." She contemplated the sky for a moment. "Men have always tried to get to Daisy through me. I suspected that was his angle when he started talking about the studio. As soon as we were alone, he mentioned her. Told me she was a girl he'd met in Chicago before she'd married. He had the *gall* to

219

request that I 'mention this in passing' to you, assuming you'd be endeared by it."

"Why didn't he ask *you* to arrange a meeting?" I asked, and Jordan looked at me as though she was shocked I'd missed the most obvious part.

"He wants her to see the tower," she said. "And you're right next door."

So I was—because Gatsby had put me there.

◇——◇——◇

I escorted Jordan back to Tom and Daisy's on the other side of the village. We walked silently, in the middle of the wide empty roads. All around us were the bourbon lights through the fog from the windows of other mansions, and above, a canopy of trees—centuries-old oaks holding so much history. East Egg was still luminous to me in this way. It was filled with stuffy billionaires, and it would be filled with them for far longer than their mortal bodies were due, but some nature was always meant to outlive humans, and I had no doubt these majestic trees had borne witness to many unworldly secrets like Gatsby's.

Jordan lit another cigarette and held it out to me. This time, I accepted it, coughing through the first several drags. I told her about the restaurant debacle, the night market, the studio. But I couldn't confess aloud how I'd gone home that day, paralyzed by his sincerity.

I finally asked her, "When does he want this all to happen?"

She froze under the yellow haze of a streetlamp. "You're not seriously—oh, but why on earth would you even *consider* it?"

"Jordan," I sighed.

"You *finally* get to the bottom of his cruelty and—"

"And what, do you believe, would I gain by refusing this modest request?"

"Modest!" she exclaimed. "What's modest about it? You're not in New York because of your merit, and you definitely weren't invited to his parties because he is *gracious*." All of it was rising out of her now. "He's a corpo down to his bones, isn't he? He thinks he can do anything

220

he wants—drag you across the world, make you feel important, befriend you just to utterly manufacture a storybook meeting. Maybe he didn't know you were assigned to appraise him. Or maybe he did but still didn't care one bit because he knew he could persuade you anyway. Is *that* modesty?"

Once it was spoken, in her unfettered brashness, the full force of it dropped anchor in my stomach.

I thought of Gatsby's glorious layers of serendipity, and I'd wanted to believe in it. But of course, serendipity was only meticulously designed, for there was no use in happy coincidences when you were rich enough to control fate, to own the sky above the Sound, or to stumble upon a lost love on a simple afternoon.

I was at Gen Wealth because I was Daisy Fay's cousin. The invitation, the dinners, the adventures, the swimming pool, and the *you are something else.*

"I met with Daisy. She talked about you. In a lot fewer words." I crushed the cigarette under my heel. "She hasn't been all that wonderful to you either, has she?"

Jordan's face twisted horribly. "What's *that* got to do with it?"

"I mean that Daisy brought me into this too," I said. Even if she wouldn't admit it, she was curious about him, and they were playing the same game, deploying the same pieces, and appallingly, I was chief among them. "They rather deserve each other."

"That's all you'll say about it? Try being furious!" Jordan stepped out of the glow of the streetlamp. "Be anything, Nick, instead of infuriatingly *polite* about it." She stopped herself. Then her eyes softened and so did the frustration in her voice. "All I'm saying is . . . don't you detest it?"

"I detest it, but what does it change?"

Jordan's mouth snapped shut.

I turned, continuing down the deserted road. After a moment, she followed, keeping her distance.

This matter had been festering within her for far longer than the bounds of this summer. She wanted me to share her indignity at being lied to, and even more than that, this poisonous heartbreak that hadn't, despite her own words, been flushed from her system.

"We need to go to Gatsby's tower this weekend. He can't know we're there," I decided. Jordan quickened her pace, walking alongside me. The whole season had confounded me. Now all I wanted was to rip down every curtain of this production, and I was through talking to corpos, taking them at their word. "He's still hiding something."

"So is Daisy, I believe." We reached a bend in the road where the Buchanan house lay just beyond the trees. "I'd hoped Meyer would confirm something I've always thought—well, I don't know if it exists for sure. But I think it'll be in that tower. Someplace not open to the public."

Gatsby's name illuminated my comm. I remembered I'd agreed to see him that night, but I declined the call, waiting in the thrumming darkness as Jordan bid me good night and I watched her shadow disappear into the willow drapes.

Twenty-Three

A
S THE SULTRY THROES OF July climaxed, what had months
ago been a vague, unsettling headline about the return of the
space probe now dominated every casual dialogue, comm-
feed, church congregation, and beyond.

The ISC spokesperson was a haggard fellow who made media
appearances every few days to provide nonupdates about the state of
the decryption. By then, you couldn't go two minutes without seeing
some strange new theory in the news. What little spaces of our attention that remained were filled by nearly every denomination of religious
figure, nihilistic orator, or fire-spun anarchist, attempting to overtake
the governments' reassurances on the safety of humankind. Press
conferences offered nothing but abstractions, and so the future
continued to shrink before us.

What hadn't shrunk at all, however, was the revelry at Gatsby's
parties; on the contrary, it had only grown. It was something about
this imminent sense of doom that must have made everyone headier
and reckless.

Jordan and I entered the tower after midnight on the second to
last Saturday of July. The party was wildest at this hour. We found the
entrance clogged up by a couple of pretty girls who had commandeered
four serving-bots and were trying to balance atop them, presumably
so they could fly around drunkenly.

Once we'd made it through the crowd, we went straight to the
private elevator, where a scanner ran across the length of my body.
From my previous visits, Gatsby had set my biometrics to auto-approve,

223

and this slipped me through the thickest part of the VINE. The breach was fast this time.

After I ran a swift cutter, the menu for the whole tower lit up before us.

◇———◇———◇

Daisy Fay had never recorded a spec Happy Sleep in her entire career.

This belief had draped her with unmatchable mystique and pushed her close to divinity, for even the richest and most powerful beings that ran the world couldn't buy a private memory from her.

"It's not true," said Jordan as the elevator ascended. "I believe she's recorded several."

"Recorded them for Gatsby, you mean."

"For her 'lieutenant,' yes." And so she explained it all. "Daisy and Tom had been married less than a week when I went to visit her in Chicago one night. He wasn't home. She was in bed, loopy in that way she used to get after a long recording session. Afterward, every once in a while, an incident or two would stick out in my mind. Snippets of calls with her old manager, for example. I wondered what they were still keeping in touch about."

She continued. "Then there was the time she had a horrible night out with Tom, and she rang me up, intoxicated as much as she'd been the night before her wedding. She couldn't stop rambling about Louisville, and the drives she'd taken with her lieutenant and how she couldn't wait to go on more with him soon. I asked what she meant, and she said she'd been in Louisville with him just the day prior. I assumed it was all drunk nonsense."

"You never thought to ask her about it?"

"Of course I prodded. But this is Daisy we're speaking about. She doesn't just deflect unwanted topics; she scorches them." Jordan scowled. "When we were girls, you know, we once saw a big fire burning in the distance in our biodome. The only thing she thought to say was that the glow on the horizon was *gorgeous* with the sunset."

The elevator opened into darkness. Several feet from the doors, I realized I was near a wide, curved window, which had been set to full

224

opacity. I dragged a hand along the glass until I reached the edge of it and then felt my away around for the manual switches.

The opacity faded, and the lights of West Egg poured in.

We looked around. The room was rather small, cut in a semicircle. Opposite the windows sat a spacious reclining chair, and beside it, a sleek black table that propped up a few unlit holo-bars. At the foot of the chair stood a pristine cube of frosted glass—an upscale Happy Sleep terminal. I walked toward it, and a holo-screen with the Gatsby Corp logo lit up.

"Look there." Jordan pointed across the street. "It's your building."

The view was level with the top floor of my apartment. Not only that, I noticed with a start, but this very room faced my bedroom, and I could see it from here. Curious, I brought up my comm-screen and turned the lights on. Sure enough, the window straight across from us brightened.

So it really had been Gatsby and not a phantom of my slumber—the figure I'd seen through this window on my first night in West Egg.

The terminal let out a tinkling noise. As the holo-screen pulsed steadily, waiting to be connected, I realized the green light that had swallowed Gatsby whole was this all along.

The glow from the Happy Sleep terminal.

I went over to the holo-screen. The logo rippled under my finger and disappeared into a session menu, far less populated than the catalog of hundreds I'd seen in Myrtle's apartment. This one couldn't have had more than ten sessions loaded onto it, all of them untitled with their descriptions blank, except for the dates they were ordered. The years ranged from '68 to '73.

Jordan stared at the list, the glow of the holo-screen shimmering in her eyes. "Can we—" she stuttered, "I mean, can *you*?"

"You want me to watch them?"

"We won't know for sure otherwise." The Happy Sleep headset was attached to the side of the terminal. She ran a finger along its prongs and shivered. "But I detest them—the sensation."

"I thought you said you'd never tried it before," I recalled.

"I . . . I have," she admitted. "Just once." A flash of shame cracked across her face before she sealed it over again.

I pulled the headset out of its case, lifted it over my eyes, and settled back into the chair—waiting for the green light to drag me heartfirst toward a luminous mirage. . . .

◇——◇——◇

And then I was dressed in the beige canvas of a military uniform, and the sky was liquid sunset.

There were people all around, faceless—soldiers dancing in the middle of the street with bold men and with beautiful girls in summer dresses. Jaunty music showered down from hover-bots above, and I stood alone, among all the hilarity, intent on fleeing, until an arm strung through mine and pulled me toward the boisterous crowds.

When I looked up, I saw a girl like no other, sunny and enchanting with a smile like a rosebud. She instructed me on how to move my feet, in a gauzy voice that made me lean toward her. I leaned and leaned until at last, she leaped up onto her tiptoes, and on the tail end of her delicious laughter, she whispered her name. *Daisy*—like the summer flower, like the promise of warmth after a long winter.

The sunset fell apart into the night sky.

I was in a white roadster, speeding down an empty freeway, choking on the wine of my own stupendous joy. There was Daisy beside me in the driver's seat. Her dress was ink black, flecked with constellations of glitter, and the fabric flapped around us in the wind as if the night itself had lifted out of the sky to drape her in its embrace.

Then I was standing between two trimmed bushes outside a redbrick mansion. A string of hover-bots carried me to a third-floor window, through white curtains fluttering apart like the gates of a divine after-life. In the center of this immaculate room was a canopied bed, whereupon Daisy sat waiting for me, crowned by the moonlight. She took my hand. As we collapsed onto the mattress together, the bed dissipated beneath us into a cloud of steam, and then we were free-falling through the heat. . . .

We fell and we fell and we fell—

through the dog days and beyond, we fell—

226

through the marvelous shifting of seasons, past this life, into the next, and into all the lives we never had—

we fell, and she clung to me all the while, fragrant and alive.

So I had entered the mind of God, where time was not a path, but an ocean.

Our lost futures stretched around us, an endless painting. At the crossroads of each brushstroke, I was consumed by the exhilarated certainty that as long as I never let go of her moonlit hand, the horizon indeed did not exist, and the sea of reality needn't ever touch the skies of our glorious dreams.

In this space, we would fall together and forever. In the blooming heights of spring, across blankets of pure snow, beneath Earth's immortal trees ...

Each time, Daisy Fay reincarnated in my arms, our heartbeats in time with our footsteps, and we walked hand in hand across this world that had fallen silent for us, as if even the stars didn't dare hum their celestial songs to sway us apart. ...

◇——◇——◇

There was smoke in the room.

For a moment, I wondered if the tower was on fire, but when I came to, I saw it was just Jordan's cigarette. She sat atop the terminal, looking grimly out the window as the holo-screen flickered across her torso.

When I roused from the chair, she looked up at me.

I nodded.

I remember quite vividly this expression she made, for even to this day, she hasn't shown it to me again. It was there, and then it was gone—a glimpse of something rare, helpless—doused in the green heartbeat of Gatsby and Daisy's fake memories.

We stared at one another. Perhaps it was the yearning debris of the Sleep that had put me in a trance, but I was sure I loved her in this moment. It flared in the pit of my stomach—the certain desire to dispel all the piercing thoughts that had clipped her wings. Indeed, I'd seen this woman fly across a stadium; she was shrewd, scornful, and sharp.

She was dishonest and, in the end, human too.

I knew I'd finally stepped through the last door of her fortress, staring past at the light that cast its shadow over her heart.

I looked at the glowing terminal and realized Owl Eyes had been right. Except Gatsby's treasure was nothing more than his simple, private world with Daisy—a bastion of his soul, collected somewhere beyond Earth itself.

I regained my balance. As we took the elevator back down, goose bumps pebbled Jordan's bare shoulders, and I put my jacket around her. She didn't let go of me as we crossed the street to my building, and I guessed she had no desire to return to East Egg that night.

I pulled spare clothes for her and a clean towel. While she showered, I lay on my bed, staring at the ceiling. When she emerged from the bathroom, I moved to sit up, but she placed a steady hand over my chest and pushed me back down.

A long time passed, and I was on the verge of sleep. The party roars from Gatsby's tower had faded to static, and Jordan was warm, her heat carrying through her modded limbs. She smelled like my soap. I held her close, her body firm and sharp edged, and her skin softly damp. The amber glow of her bio-ink illuminated the dark room.

"With the sessions he ordered," I said, "he was re-creating their past, their time in Louisville, but . . . not just that. There were fantasies of what their life could have been, I suppose, if they'd stayed together. It was like nothing I'd ever felt before." I didn't have the words for it; it was wonderful and disturbing all at once. "She and Gatsby, they've not seen each other for—why, over a decade. And yet, going back and forth like this in these Happy Sleeps, it's like they've always been together. They've lived countless lifetimes in their memories, haven't they? Or rather, in their dreams."

I didn't know if Jordan wanted to hear any of this, but she listened quietly. Then she said, "Arrange it if you want."

"What?"

"Let them meet for tea—it's your decision. Doesn't matter what I think. It never did." She closed her eyes, and it occurred to me that she might have wanted to be wrong this whole time. "I just had to know if it really was him. And I felt you deserved to know too."

My heart stuttered. With her head on my chest, I knew she could hear it.

"Daisy's always been more mischievous than anyone gives her credit for." She made a soft, dry noise. "That fire I mentioned in our dome when we were younger? She was the one who started it. We were fifteen. It was an accident. To this day, she'll claim she doesn't remember it at all. She's broken so many things over the years, and . . . when she smashes things up, in the end, I'm the one who's carrying her over all those broken pieces. But you see, I didn't care much when she married Tom. Or nearly married that other fellow, or anyone else. She's never loved any of them wholly, and . . . there was still room for me. So I took it." Her throat bobbed. "But the one exception was her lieutenant. I never imagined they'd find each other again."

"You warned me," I recalled. "Even on the night I met him. You said to be careful. It's like you knew."

"You can't blame yourself. He has a knack for it." She hesitated. "They both do."

Indeed, there was some dangerous, lightning-strike luster in the wake of their footsteps and their fancies. You'd see the flash before you ever heard the thunder. Both Jordan and I stood too close, wanted too much, never jumping away in time.

But at least we weren't alone in the crippling shock.

I threw my arm around her waist. Her fingers danced along the buttons of my shirt. I touched the waistband of her underwear. She didn't move, and I almost pulled her face to mine and kissed her. But her heart was hammering, and her eyes were distant, and so we watched the moment rush past us like a missed train. Perhaps I regretted it then, though looking back, I knew it would have ruined us.

She turned her chin into my shoulder, lips grazing my neck, and at last when I fell asleep, I dreamed Gatsby's dreams.

[LOADING]

.

.

.

[PLAY]

"What we can do is spread ten percent of the interest across three generations. That ought to get you to the finish line quicker—five years instead of eight! Or else, if you'd prefer, we can consider an alternative rate, factoring in your husband's income—"

"No. Not Henry."

"Are you sure?"

"This is my debt. Not his."

"Given your health, there's a chance—well, not to be morbid—but if anything does happen to you before you've paid it all off, then your husband would have some of it fall on his lap anyway. He's listed as your next of kin, after all."

"These are my only options?"

"Ma'am, if you'd like, we can take a short break—oh, you seem rather feverish. I'll call—"

"*Don't* call anyone. Don't bring me anywhere. If I set foot in a hospital again, the bill will send me right back here."

"Gosh, you really are looking a bit pale."

"I'm perfectly—all right. . . ."

"Well, let's see. Your husband happens to be a Gen Wealth netdiver. We offer a great employee discount, in fact! Why don't I play with the numbers again while you go fetch some water?"

"I . . . I don't think so. . . ."

"Ma'am?"

"I think—perhaps I'll be stuck in this office forever, won't I? Ha . . ."

"Ma'am? Ma'am! Are you—oh my!"

[STOP]

[ERROR—]

[ERROR: ACCOUNT NOT FOUND]

Part III

Deathless Song

Twenty-Four

O N MONDAY, I WAS MOVED temporarily to the counterintelligence team. A senior diver had thrown himself in front of a train, so they were understaffed. Unfortunate timing, I was told, as Gen Wealth was dealing with an all-out cyberattack at the moment.

Four levels beneath the Probity, there were fifty divers spread out in dens across the frigid floor. From the catwalk above, it looked like the honeycomb pits of a beehive. I didn't see much sunlight during this time, and I was assigned to the dead man's old station. I didn't know him myself, only that he was a likable fellow whose wife had apparently passed about a month prior.

The department head was a judicious woman named Mrs. Etty Anand. Though she looked hardly older than me, her résumé suggested she was about as old as netdiving itself. She welcomed me to her gallows by throwing a compression suit at my face.

"Dive in, Yale! Know how to set up a rig?" she barked. I knew it was a joke, but I assured her that I did. She passed me a case of hypo shots. "Putting you in deep. No choice. Take whatever dosage you need to—" As I began to undress, she stopped, inspecting my neck. "Hang on. What the hell did you do in the army?"

"Intercepted pyres."

"*Well*, fuck me!" She let out a relieved laugh. "What do they have you doing up in Algorithms?"

"Not as much as you all are," I admitted.

She made me work the night shift for two days, but I didn't mind. On Wednesday evening, we resurfaced together, and she hopped into my den to help undo my harness. "You have stamina." She yanked the cable from my neck port with force. "Thought you'd be some incompetent nepo freak—no offense. Heard something about a fancy office."

"Is it always this hectic?" I asked.

"Oh, if every day was like today, I'd have followed Henry to the afterlife ages ago." Anand hoisted herself out of the den. I climbed up after her. "No, we get a handful of these coordinated attacks every year. Lots of money in the system, so sometimes a hacking co-op gets cocky. It's a safer job than cracking the banks. We aren't authorized to kill on sight. Like you saw, all we can do is block and trace the attacks as best we can, kick it over to the police. We're airtight. And I'm not just saying that because *I* was the one who built half the VINEs."

Overlooking the floor was a ten-foot-tall holo-screen with a map of the entire New Americas, small green dots scattered across it like clusters of stars; each dot represented a few dozen Gen Wealth accounts.

"Existential dread makes people bold. End of the world is nearing, right?" she joked.

"Has any breach ever succeeded?"

"God, no. System's impenetrable from the outside." She swept an arm out at her floor of divers, dangling unconscious and hard at work. "It has to be. Or *we're* the ones that go down."

"Must be a lot of pressure." I studied the constellation of dots for a moment longer; then I helped her complete our reports for the day. "I'm sorry about your man, Henry," I said as we were finishing up. It came out a little stilted.

Her fingers paused for a second over her keyboard. "Yes." She blinked rapidly, and for the briefest moment, she looked her age. "We all are."

The next day, I didn't resurface until ten o'clock. It was raining hard when I left the office, but it subsided by the time I arrived in West Egg, and the pavement shone, making a glossy mirror of the evening streets. Walking from the station, I saw Gatsby's tower ahead, all its windows ablaze.

I'd managed a whole week without seeing him. Every day since the studio, he'd invited me over for dinner. I'd ignored his messages, so he'd sent over a Klipspringer, whom I'd dismissed. Tonight, there were no messages and no androids, but Gatsby himself.

He paced urgently along the sidewalk in front of my building. When he noticed me, he smiled wide and gestured up at the tower. "Doesn't it look like the World's Fair?"

The lights stirred through the glass in fiery hues; it resembled an oversized lava lamp. "Not really," I said.

He took me by the elbow. "Let's go to Coney Island—"

"It's too late."

"Well, suppose we take a plunge in the swimming pool?"

"I've got to go to bed."

He stared back, crestfallen, and it irritated me that he had some of the most talented divers in the country holed up in a subzero basement, working fourteen hours straight, and all he could talk about was Coney Island.

"Gen Wealth's been fielding attacks all week," I said. "Don't you know?"

He nodded in an absent way, like I'd brought up a news story that was mildly interesting and quite irrelevant. "You must be exhausted. I can have—"

"My tasks rearranged. I know."

He studied me. "Is everything all right? You never . . . came to the tower after we spoke."

For a moment, I didn't even remember what he was talking about. I'd gone so astray that day, in the hangover of the recording session, superimposing the idea of a man over the truth. Even when he'd listened to my suggestions about restoring the valley, I'd thought far too highly of him.

"I talked with Miss Baker. I'm going to call up Daisy tomorrow and invite her over for tea," I said.

The swift deployment of Daisy's name stopped him short. He flushed bright as the lava lights in his windows. "What? That's—you don't need—"

"Should I not?" I wasn't in the mood for this disingenuous humility. "It's what you wanted Jordan to ask me. It's why you gave me a job and everything else."

"You have the wrong idea—"

"I assume you found me easily. Tossed a good contract my way, with a coveted invitation, learned all about me to speak to me at your party." I walked past him. "Must have taken some work."

He followed me, grazed my arm with his hand, but I flinched back. He startled. "Please listen. I can explain it all."

"What's there to explain? That you brought me over an ocean so you could"—I released a sharp, cynical breath—"talk to my cousin?"

He didn't say a word. His lips fluttered. All the pairs of things I'd seen in his tower, everything I'd noticed or borrowed at his dinner table and in his bedroom, began to make sense to me.

"What day," I said through my teeth, "would suit you best? Sunday?"

He chewed his lip.

"You want to put it off?" I demanded.

"Oh, it isn't about that." His gaze slid tentatively to the exterior of my building. It was stylish by most standards; next to his skyscraper, however, it was positively decrepit. "I know something that might interest you. It happens to be a rather confidential sort of thing."

I didn't want anything more from him, least of all money, and when I realized this was his roundabout insistence on trying to compensate me for this arrangement, I felt physically ill. "I have *no* interest in your smuggling op."

He froze, as if he hadn't thought I'd speak into existence his dishonest second life, but his facade meant nothing to me now. "Well, how about—"

"You turned a blind eye to my trespassing your facility. We're even." I wiped the sweat from my neck, felt the stark heat of my overworked mods. "Besides, you tolerated so much of my company for this, even at a place like the market."

"Tolerated? Nick, that can't be what you—" He shook his head slowly. "We were synced. I couldn't have lied to you in there."

Except I wasn't sure about anything anymore. The whole summer had been fashioned out of his fantastic tricks. Even my name on his lips was now a foreign word. There had been a moment at the studio where the sound of it in his warmest voice had reverberated in my head, knocking every sensibility out of place.

"If you had just asked," I said, "instead of . . ." The rest of those words, if ever they had mattered, crumbled in the coarse air, but foolishly, I knew they were true, for when had I denied anything he had asked of me?

His eyes widened. "Nick—" he said, but he'd already become a corpo to me again, a harbinger of trouble to board my windows up against, his thoughtless extravagance a cruel glare amidst the plights of the real world.

"It's a favor. Good night, Mr. Gatsby." I went inside alone, and his lava lamp of a tower burned bright until sunrise.

◇——◇——◇

Daisy was stunned that I'd called her the next morning—and for tea at my place, no less.

"Don't bring Tom," I said before we hung up.

"Who is 'Tom'?" she said delightedly.

Sunday came, and the sky broke open, summoning forth the harshest rainfall of the season. In the middle of breakfast, a Klipspringer came to my door to tell me that he was going to mod my windows at Mr. Gatsby's behest, presumably because the rain had made the view wet and ugly.

Within the hour, the androids multiplied. There were two inside my kitchen, arranging tall heaps of golden pastries, breads, and marbled synth-meats. Another scrubbed the floors to a reflective shine, and the one from earlier in the morning had finally finished modding the last of the windows so that glancing outside, the view appeared brighter and warmer than it actually was.

Out in the living room, a whole garden had exploded with colorful bouquets bobbing midair, balanced on hover-bots. Soon, Gatsby burst through my door, wearing a white suit, gold tie, and a grim expression. His overgelled hair was plastered to his cheek on one side. "Is everything all right?" he exclaimed as he marched into my living room and sent the Klipspringers away.

I didn't know why he was asking me that when he was the one who looked frenzied. "The view looks fine, if that's what you mean."

"What view? Oh, that one." He narrowed his eyes at the artificial sunlight. No amount of modding could mask the sound of the rain, however, and its heavy drumbeat pounded on as the clock crawled glacially toward late afternoon.

I sat on the couch, reading the news headlines on the coffee table holo-bar. Gatsby placed himself at the very edge of my armchair.

"Listen, Nick, I . . ." He trailed off.

The silence stretched on for a whole minute. I frowned. "Aren't you glad to be seeing her?"

He started to pace around the living room. For a moment, I thought he really would leave, but eventually, he sat back down. When he gazed over at me through lidded eyes, I guessed that he hadn't slept much since last I saw him. "I just mean—thank you for this. I realized I never even thanked you."

His voice fell into that certain low register where he sounded tentative, unsure of himself. I rose from the couch and walked over to the windows. The modded sun had soaked my whole living room in a strange hue of dandelion yellow.

"It's just tea," I said.

"But the other night—"

"The other night, I said we're even." I turned. Gatsby was on his feet again. That one side of his hair was still askew from the rain or perhaps because he'd been pulling at it. "Stop fretting. Daisy won't be pleased to see you like that, and you'll have wasted everyone's time."

"Yes, but—you haven't forgiven me after we last spoke."

"Forgiven you?" I didn't even know what that meant to him except that perhaps he wanted me to clap his shoulder and tell him I was just ecstatic about the entire disruption he'd brought into my life all along.

A ping came from my comm, signaling Daisy's arrival, and I was grateful for the interruption. I went to the door, waving at a hover-bot to follow me.

Downstairs, one of the Buchanan Veluzes was parked out front in the fierce rain. She had one foot out the passenger side by the time my hover-bot expanded quickly into an umbrella, though not quick enough that the shoulder of her lilac dress was spared. She didn't seem to mind, grinning splendidly up at me from beneath the shadow of her matching hat.

"Is this absolutely where you live, my dearest one?" She took my hand as I helped her from the car. Her eagerness glittered today, more so than usual, as if she believed something wondrous lay within my modest apartment, or that she'd will it into existence otherwise. "And why'd I have to come alone?"

I smiled. "Tell your chauffeur to go far away and spend an hour."

"An hour or several, Ferdie!" she called to the uniformed man behind the wheel.

Inside the apartment, I led her to my floral bomb of a living room where there was no sign of Gatsby. She glanced around in a daze—at the food, the flowers, the modded windows.

Then a delicate three-act knock came from down the hall.

I rounded the corner and went into my bedroom, where I found Gatsby soaking wet on the balcony. I opened the door, and he spun around. The harrowing weight in his eyes made me wonder if he wasn't staring down the barrel of a gun.

"I just stepped out for some, ah, *fresh* air . . . Maybe—" He loosened his tie, blinking away fat raindrops. "Why, maybe it's best to call off—"

I gripped his arm and dragged him inside. He looked pathetic, dripping puddles onto my floor, and still all I could think about when his eyes lifted up at me was that his lashes were stuck together in almost exactly the same way as they'd been when we swam together in his tower.

I threw him a dry towel. As he stood before me, shivering, I reached over to straighten his tie.

"I really meant it, Nick," he muttered.

"Meant what?"

"I enjoyed our excursions. All of it," he rambled. "After today, it's not as though we ought to be strange—"

"Go out there, or else I'm calling her in here." There was a delirium about him now. I would have accused him of drunkenness had I not known of his alcohol aversion. I stepped away from him, opening the bedroom door.

He hovered a second longer, but I pushed him forward as if he were an anxious toddler, and at last he squared himself, marching out into the living room.

There was a bright gasp, the clattering of cutlery.

And then Daisy's voice, two semitones sharp: "I certainly am ... awfully glad to see you again."

A corpse might have materialized in my apartment. It was this kind of panic that infused my living room as I joined Gatsby and Daisy.

I found him leaning his hip against one of the food carts, sort of hiding behind it. Daisy sat in the armchair across from him, her back very straight, heels up, with just her toes touching the floors as if she might flee.

"We've met before," said Gatsby—to me perhaps, but I couldn't be sure. His gaze bounced off the walls, and his voice rang as artificial as the dandelion sunlight.

"Not for many years. Or at least—" Daisy cut herself off into a tragic silence.

It was an awful tableau. The oversaturated flowers and decadent food turned to plastic before our eyes. There was no warmth in the room, none of that reverent intimacy that had flooded the sessions they'd shared indirectly for so many years.

Now, with just my coffee table separating them, nothing they could say to each other's face felt quite as appropriate as their fabricated memories. It was like a painting that wouldn't dry, the air chemical and sticky, smeared by the slightest word. Somehow, I managed to get Gatsby to sit on the couch. I took up the other end, closer to Daisy. For several minutes, she and I talked stupidly about the creaminess of the synth-milk I'd poured into her London Fog, which got her on the topic of London, then to the bane of all conversation, the rain.

I could sense Gatsby decomposing beside me, and since he hadn't offered Daisy so much as a greeting, I hopped to my feet. "I'm sure you have much to discuss, about the acquisition and all."

"Where are you going?" he said, seemingly dismayed.

"I'll be back."

"I have to speak to you about something before you go." Gatsby was on my heels all the way down the hall and to the front door, where his knees nearly buckled. "This is a terrible mistake. A terrible, terrible—"

"You're acting like a little boy! Not only that, but you're rude. Daisy's sitting in there all alone."

This did little to sober him, but I spun him around quickly and escaped through the door.

Outside in the rain, the only thing I wanted was to see Jordan. Just as the thought came to me, her name flashed across my wrist. I accepted the call.

"Coffee's very much run the world for centuries," she said before I could voice a single word.

I smiled. "Has it?"

"Of course. Coffeehouses have always been the preferred venue of enlightened company—music, chess, scholarly debates. No one does that over *tea*. It's always under the bitter, rich stimulus of coffee. Then the Europeans got their hands on it, and the church called it the devil's drink, and four hundred years later, with agriculture in shambles, what did food corps rush to replicate in a lab? No, not meat or vegetables—coffee! Because we'd all be nothing without it." Jordan took a dignified pause. "Tea sits so stiffly in the mouth, doesn't it? Makes you think of unpleasant conversation and—oh, what else? British imperialism. And wars."

"Why, yes." I laughed. "It does."

"I hope you're not off having *tea* at the moment."

"No, in fact, I've just left it all behind in search of a better beverage."

"Good," she said. "Then come join me."

Twenty-Five

WEST HARLEM IN THE EARLY evening. I dropped down from the hover-taxi and onto the piers, where the Jersey skyline across the river was faintly obscured by the ad-drones bestowing a Technicolor blush over the Hudson.

I went to meet Jordan in an unmarked basement. It had a name once but was now invitation-only in the aftermath of some illegal mod raids that had torn across the neighborhood's entertainment scene sometime in the fifties. Ducking inside, I had the heartened feeling that I'd descended into some family gathering. It was loud and intimate. Jordan sat in the far-back corner, golden stim-stick in hand, chatting with a handsome saxophonist. She was overdressed, draped in a red ankle-length ensemble, and I guessed that she'd come from some sort of media event.

When I reached them, he rose from the table, clapped my arm as if he and I were already acquainted, then joined a group of other musicians across the room.

I took his seat. "Who was that?"

"Are you jealous"—she smiled—"or interested for yourself?"

I was pleased she was in good spirits. "Neither. You seem to know him."

"I know lots of people." She ordered two Americanos from the holo-menu. "My father used to run this place. Way back, before I was born."

Our coffee flew over on a serving-bot. She mentioned that she was born two blocks down from here before moving to the domes of Louisville as a child to live with her aunt.

"My mother was an early netdiver. You ask why I don't like the field and keep away from it, that's why. It makes me think of her." She frowned. "She moved to the New East from Lagos to head security for a bunch of hospital corps. Then she met my father in this very club."

Jordan shared this with concealed nostalgia, as if she'd never spoken all these words aloud before. We finished our coffees and ordered another round.

"They died in a raid, my parents. I'm not the only one who lost family and friends around here," she said. "You know about those?"

I did—the raids hadn't been specific to New York. Most cities had suffered during the early boom of the body-mod scene. Police task forces had been hastily formed and then sent out to nightclubs so that politicians had something to posture about.

"The mods here, tame as they are, don't technically count as *cosmetic*, so they're illegal. That was used as a basis for the raids back then." Jordan swapped her stim-stick for a new one. "Of course, there're all sorts of crazier clubs than this, but police wouldn't so much as blink in their direction as long as the folks inside them could pay them away."

Gatsby had taken me to one such club on our first outing. That place hadn't just withstood the start of the prohibition—it had thrived off it.

This basement, by contrast, was far more inviting. I didn't know enough about live music to recognize all the mods, but there were a few obvious ones like the drummer with an additional set of metal arms extending impressively out of her back. There was the saxophonist, too, Jordan's friend, who, upon second glance, had two extra fingers modded into each hand.

Another rather interesting mod was on display as well, though I didn't understand it without Jordan's explanation. It happened when the singer onstage paused to turn a small dial at the side of their neck. Their entire jaw, in fact, was constructed out of steel, with their mouth covered by a barred frame.

"It gives them range," said Jordan. "You'll see."

The next song began with the languid trumpet squeal of "Summertime" from *Porgy and Bess*, and though the singer went into the first verse adopting a slight replication of Ella Fitzgerald, the top of the second verse dropped right into the gravelly depths of Louis Armstrong. I startled in my chair.

Just like that, they were performing a perfect solo duet all on their own—two distinct voices flowing from the same mouth.

"That's marvelous," I said.

Jordan, amused by my curiosity, shuffled her chair closer to mine. When our legs brushed under the table, I noticed her right thigh swaddled in tape. I didn't have the chance to bring it up before she asked me, "You play anything?"

"I learned some piano from my mother."

"Ah. You do seem capable with your hands."

She was attempting to thaw me for something, and as always, it was working. "I don't play *well*," I said, but she wasn't listening, preoccupied with the holo-menu.

"More coffee?" I asked.

"No. Something stronger."

"What for?"

"Summertime" was fading into its final note, and two shots of whiskey landed on our table. Jordan threw her drink back, and I followed suit. Then she was on her feet, and she pulled me to mine, and soon we were weaving through the club—toward the stage.

"Jordan!" I exclaimed in a panic. "We *can't*—"

Really, I meant that *I* couldn't—I was no pianist and even less of a performer—but she was stronger than me and more persistent. When she spun around in the middle of the jubilant crowd, she threw her arms around my neck and murmured, "Trust me."

I'll always be glad that I did. Even now, I think of that basement as the last spot of goodness in that catastrophic season. Indeed, the city was crowded, lonely and cold; it was full of cruel people, tired people, good people too—corrupted by their circumstances and, still, teeming defiantly with life.

In a daze, I let Jordan set me down on the piano bench, slipped a headset over my eyes, and synced my comm with hers, along with the rest of the band's. A soft current dribbled through me, slow as honey.

246

It was just like the one at Eskinita, but I had never experienced it in this way before.

Jordan's mischievous mood coursed through me, alongside my own nerves. The four-armed drummer brimmed in fiery excitement; the alto sax was cocksure; the bassist scrappy. From the headset, a holo-sheet of music scrolled before my eyes, and my hands fell immediately into place over B minor, as if I'd played this song a million times, though I didn't even recognize it. I laughed, awestruck.

At the eight-count, Jordan opened her mouth, and the first fluty verse filled the room. Her mischief moved to pride and then to pleasure, and just beneath it, a scar of unwavering sorrow. I looked up at her, illuminated in the heat of these privileged spotlights. Her voice broke out from somewhere deep within, rich and undis-guised, each lyric a pared secret she knew everyone in the crowd would keep, for a rebellious joy infused these walls—a majesty I was sure no curated floor in Gatsby's tower could ever hope to simulate.

◇——◇——◇

An hour later, Jordan and I stepped outside and shared a cigarette on the curb. The rain had stopped, and an alluring mist buzzed over the slick pavement. I took her hand, and we walked a block until we reached her car. I wanted to stay with her, but she reminded me that it was probably best to check on the strange scene I'd left in my living room. Truthfully, I'd forgotten about it.

She set my address into her dashboard-holo. "You didn't come to see me just because of that, did you?"

"Of course not."

"It's all right if you did."

"I didn't," I insisted.

"Well, all right. I didn't either. How was the dreadful tea?" She said this with a furtive smile, like we were both still on the better end of a fabulous joke, but the edges of her sharp mouth were dull, and a quiet solitude pooled behind the umber gloss of her eyes. She was wandering away from me again. Manhattan was disappearing beneath us, and so was the splendor of the basement.

"It wouldn't have been dreadful if you were there." I touched her thigh where the slit of her dress revealed the bandage. "Tell me about more important things. Like this injury."

She stared at her leg reproachfully. "Had an appointment yesterday. My body's been rejecting every new mod all season, so I have to finish with the old ones. Doesn't matter. I'm out of the playoffs already. First time since I was sixteen." She smacked the steering wheel. "By *God*, I'll win next year, though."

"You could—"

"I won't retire. Not yet. That's what everyone wants."

"Well, maybe it's because everyone doesn't want to see you hurt."

"Oh, that's just you." She collapsed onto my shoulder. "No, everyone thinks I've outstayed my welcome. They want someone new and shiny to adore. The way they see it, I'm just standing in the way, blocking the light."

I studied the bridge of her nose, the sheen of her sweat-slicked skin, the way her eyelashes—spotted with glitter—fanned shadows over her cheeks. I'd been staring at her all summer, I realized, but never from this angle.

"Don't make that face." She straightened. "Like you're trying to figure out the kindest thing to say right now."

"What's wrong with that?"

"Nothing." With slow purpose, she rested her hand on my knee—a chord's first inversion, the dangle of suspense. "Nothing's ever wrong with you, and that's the problem." She tipped my chin sideways appraisingly. "You're just—too *good*, aren't you?"

As with all things, Jordan moved first—no shy pecks, just the decisive parting of my shuddering lips with her tongue. Tasting each other, it seemed, wasn't all that different from when our minds had been synced onstage, and so, as she seated herself in my lap, I felt her anguish rise into her breath and meet my own.

We couldn't hide from each other like this, but that was fine. Our pain didn't matter today; at least, not the way it had when she'd held me in my bed like a life raft. Now we just wanted one another, and if the pain was still there, then it wasn't close to the melody tonight—only the steady, forgettable percussion that made our kisses sweeter.

She went to work on my shirt, then immediately my slacks, before taking both my hands and placing them right where she wanted, at the tantalizing curve of her hips. Then she moved like that for a blissful moment, rocking us together with her mouth on my neck. I trembled beneath her, and when she took me solidly in hand, a sharp curse withered in my throat.

"What else is hiding"—she brushed my hair back with her other hand—"beneath all those manners?"

I pulled the skin of her throat with my teeth and finally drew a beautiful noise out of her too. But she would not be beat. After some murmured direction and a playful joke about my piano fingers, she had pushed aside her undergarments and sunk onto me. I sighed, falling back into the headrest, and closed my eyes for a perfect moment, unable to breathe.

"Jordan, you'll—" I said, strained. "You'll send me home in pieces. . . ."

Her dress was wrinkled, slipped off one shoulder and catching the city lights through the windows. The silk shone, a stream of glittering ruby, and her movements were fast, assured.

I reached up and cupped her face; perhaps that was too tender, but she smiled anyway. Then she curled herself toward me, nipping a trail from my collarbones up to the very visible high points of my neck.

I gasped. "I know—what you're doing."

One spot next to my throat was already bruising; when she kissed it delicately, it was sore. "Does it upset you?"

"It'll make no difference," I said. "To me or to him."

"I don't care," she said, carving a fresh mark below my jaw.

I held her waist as she moved. "You and your games, Miss Baker."

"Yes," she said, "and I don't like to lose."

I suspected as much. In all other things, she was obsessed with winning, and I realized if I was to be a consolation prize, then she would mold me into a victory with her own hands.

"I'm used to sharing with him, you know." Her breath came up in shallow bursts. "But after all these years—well, I don't feel quite so generous today."

"Jordan . . .," I muttered as she placed her hands on my chest, pace quickening.

"He's never seen you unraveled before." Now her voice was higher, coming from that rare place that birthed her performance in the club. Her mischief had returned, and with it, an invigorating hunger. "I bet very few people do, and I get to be one of them."

I shattered first, another victory in her eyes, and through the singed tremors, felt my way beneath her dress and between her legs, sending her along with me. She bent in half, blooming like a stubborn late-spring tulip, and when a lazy hum had settled between us, she pulled herself off me, but not out of my arms.

"Come back with me," I suggested once we drew closer to West Egg.

I could tell she was considering it. In the end, she said, "I'd better not."

We chatted pleasantly about nothing until we landed in front of my building. She redid my shirt buttons and pushed me from the car with a chaste kiss.

A dainty silence greeted me when I entered my apartment, and I wondered if they'd already left. Then I turned into the living room.

Vignetted by the floating flowers, Gatsby and Daisy sat together on the couch, so close they shared the same cushion. Daisy's round face was wet and fresh as a sliced peach, and Gatsby held her hand while she laughed and cried at once. In her other hand was his scrunched handkerchief. I was only a foot away when they noticed me.

"Oh, hello, old sport," said Gatsby, glancing around my apartment as if he'd transcended to an ethereal plane. Daisy smiled up at me through her tears.

"It's stopped raining," I informed them. They wouldn't know; the windows were still modded with fake afternoon sun, though the real sun had already begun to set. Time hadn't moved for them at all in this room.

250

Gatsby paused as if he had to recall what this phenomenon of "rain" was. "Has it?" He pulled Daisy to her feet. "What do you think of that? It's stopped raining."

"I'm glad, Jay," she said, ripe with joy.

"I want you and Daisy to come over. I'd like to show her around," said Gatsby when she excused herself to the bathroom. A redness stained his cheeks, as if perhaps he'd cried, too, but all that remained of that overwhelming emotion was moonstruck exhilaration. "She *was* pleased to see me. Can you believe it? But she's in a fair bit of shock, and she'll be at ease, I think, if you're there."

He asked this with at least some apprehension, and if I'd been even half a shade less pliable from my time with Jordan, I would have declined him. But I decided there was something half lovely in his earnestness again, and, perhaps masochistically, I agreed to chaperone.

"Where'd you disappear to?" he asked. "You look a bit ..."

"I had coffee with Miss Baker," I replied, stacking dirty dishes onto an idle hover-bot.

His gaze lowered. Jordan had left me just a bit improper, probably out of devious pride at her handiwork, but no matter what greedy things she'd said in the car, I didn't believe Gatsby would notice.

I was surprised to be wrong. His eyes latched onto my neck, my untucked shirt. "Coffee. Right." His voice was a little dry, perhaps from hours of talking, and he wandered toward the windows, lost in a thought I couldn't follow.

"Nick, I—" He began to speak again, but Daisy came out of the bathroom.

"Nicky, you're coming, aren't you?" she asked. "Please say you are."

I said I was; then we all went outside together. Gatsby led us across the street. "See how it catches the light on all sides?" he said, restless.

"That huge place *there*?" exclaimed Daisy.

Gatsby's nerves rose off him. "Do you like it?"

"I love it," she declared, "but I don't see how you live there all alone."

"I keep it always full of interesting people, night and day. People who do interesting things. Celebrated people."

I was behind them, following at a respectable distance, and Gatsby glanced back at me as he said this. It was a flitting look, almost nothing, but the weaker part of me would remember it forever.

I watched them enter the lobby, and I swear that when Daisy's foot stepped over the threshold of those glass doors, the whole place sighed and transformed for her. And she transformed, too—back into that girl, Daisy Fay, the tower's fabled sovereign, whose memory alone lit up all the windows and Gatsby's languished soul.

Twenty-Six

THROUGH THE CASINO FLOORS, EERILY grand in their emptiness, Daisy hopped across the card tables like they were giant lily pads, and the holo-marble in the sculpture rooms, unsurprisingly, moved at Gatsby's command. We strolled through art galleries and gardens, beneath the shade of Mesozoic trees, between the quiet enormity of prehistoric wildlife and any other landscape Daisy could imagine.

They had dropped their reservations and were now so captivated with each other, it felt as though their precious spec Sleeps were finally coming alive. Witnessing them, I thought, was in itself as unbelievable and stunning as all the attractions before us.

We reached the middle of the tower, the private floors, and though Daisy couldn't be tempted into the swimming pool, she threw off her shoes and splashed her legs in the turquoise water, pointing cheerfully up at the cherubs as Gatsby's smile burgeoned beside her like the first rays of morning.

A feast was set in the dining room, and Daisy took a delicate bite of each glistening dish before following him into his bedroom. As they went, I pretended to be particularly enamored with a platter of crab cakes. Once I was alone, Ewing came over to the table with chilled Riesling, the same one I always drank here, and wordlessly filled my glass.

"Please leave it, Ewing," I said. "The bottle."

The android obliged and parted with a bow. I listened to the excited peaks and valleys of Gatsby's and Daisy's voices from around the corner. With the Riesling emptied, I was lightheaded and renumbed and went to join them.

Standing just before the threshold, I saw that everything in the bedroom was levitating about four to six feet off the ground—bobbing midair like a silly aquarium of Gatsby's antique possessions.

"Nicky!" cried Daisy.

In the center of the room, she and Gatsby were a hair's breadth from the chandelier, laughing hysterically as if they'd swallowed a mouthful of bubbles. Daisy swam over to the door to drag me inside, and soon, I was floating, too, consumed by a hazy weightlessness.

"It's a fun trick, isn't it?" exclaimed Gatsby. "I've a friend of a friend on the ISC, and he gave me this zero-grav mod! I'd like to have it implemented soon as a new attraction on other floors, don't you think?"

"You *must* drape the whole tower in it, Jay," said Daisy, soaring across the room to chase the gold candlesticks and vases drifting in all directions. Flying suited her, I thought, as she twirled me in circles, taking the lead and my waist like I was an old southern debutante.

We floated into Gatsby's colossal closet, where his fine English shirts had lifted out of the shelves. The folds came loose, too, sleeves spread open, and they hung in the air like thousands of colorful clouds. There were jeweled tears in Daisy's eyes again. She reached for the shirts with so much joy—until a vast and inexplicable sorrow rose up to strangle her.

"They're such beautiful shirts," she whispered, cradling one made of fine blue cotton. "I've never seen such—such beautiful shirts before."

When she began to sob, the sound climbed to a violent howl, before dissolving into broken whimpers that washed the room like the low tide. They weren't the pretty kind of tears anymore, and though Gatsby hadn't once drawn his forlorn gaze from her, I believe in that moment, a certain veil had been lifted for him, one he hadn't known was there. Behind it was the wholeness of Daisy's emotion—more complex than he'd likely imagined—and it must have surprised him that, at its core, it did not sparkle.

◇—◇—◇

At last, we fell into Gatsby's enormous bed. Somehow, I'd ended up between them, with Daisy's arm loosely entwined with mine. Gatsby and I had landed with our hips pressed together, and we stared up at his Victorian ceiling in sober silence. The air had shifted—the bedroom a windswept mess, the shirts no longer clouds, and we could no longer fly. Gravity had returned.

It was past midnight. I knew this because a dull glow seeped out from the bottom of Gatsby's drawn curtains; the fireworks had begun as scheduled. The emptiness of the tower caused me to forget today was a Sunday and Gatsby had shunned the whole city for Daisy's arrival.

She rose to her feet, moving curiously toward the windows. At her absence, the bed suddenly felt too small and Gatsby too close, so I rose as well and followed her as she folded the curtain open. The light poured into the room, and she marveled at its bright vitality, the color as stunning as the gem of the wedding ring she wasn't wearing tonight.

"Well, that's just gorgeous," she observed, placing her hand upon the window.

Gatsby sat up. "Is it?"

"Why, yes, it's a lovely shade."

"I had the color modeled, you know, after—well, the light on a Happy Sleep terminal."

The words moved through him like the wind, stealing his breath, and Daisy spun around in shock. It was the first time either of them had mentioned their sessions, and it cast a sort of disillusion into the room.

That vivid light had tethered them across great gaps of wealth and time, and he'd followed it all the while like a supernal compass. Though now that she was here, real and material, I witnessed his realization that he'd reached the end of this long road without considering what lay beyond it.

Daisy reached for Gatsby's hand, and they stood together between the curtain folds and fireworks. I wandered across the room, sidestepping his scattered belongings, among which was a ragged photo album. It had fallen open to a portrait of a serious white-haired man in a sailor's cap, hands clasping the shoulders of what was doubtless an adolescent Gatsby.

"Who's this?" I asked, referring to the older fellow.

255

Gatsby walked over. "Mr. Dan Cody. He's dead now." He pushed back the photograph's faded corners fondly. In it, his freckles were more prominent, and his hair was thrown up in a dated style. "He helped me in so many ways, funded my work, and believed in me before anyone else. He plucked me out of—well, he made me into the man I am today."

Daisy pointed to the young, ruddy-faced Gatsby. "I adore it."

"Look at this. Here're a lot of clippings—of you." He thumbed through the rest of the album, which was indeed filled with other printed materials, many of Daisy. He'd followed her career diligently— all the awards she'd won, and snapshots of her most iconic public appearances, including the famous one of her barefoot at the Palmer House.

Gatsby held her as she began to cry again, and after a while, we returned to the rooftop, where he switched on the conveyor belt, devoid of its usual drink parade. Daisy seated herself upon it, letting it shuttle her around the roof for a lap, her laughter ringing out into the night. Gatsby beamed with pride, as if this had really been the conveyor belt's intended purpose all along.

His smile cut off into a frown as a call blinked on his comm. He stepped a few paces aside and answered it.

"Yes ... what about?" he snapped. "Oh, that. Well, I can't talk now. ..." He caught me staring, and I glanced away. "Well, sure. Indeed, it's very green, but half of East Egg's got themselves in on it, too, so what's the fuss? Call Meyer about this, if you must."

He hung up brusquely.

"Business?" I asked.

"Come here *quick!*" Daisy interrupted us. "Look at that." She hopped down from the conveyor belt, pointing in the distance toward the ad-drones that stretched from the edge of West Egg and across the valley. "I'd like to just get one of those drones and put you in it and push you around," she exclaimed.

Gatsby smiled. "Would you like to see something splendid?" he asked, and of course, she said she would.

So he showed her. He fetched Ewing to bring a holo-bar from his study, and when he navigated through a series of screens, the intricate menu he'd revealed to me on our first car ride appeared before us. Then, as if tapping the keys of a piano, Gatsby rearranged the sky for her.

The advertisements shimmered. Holo'd clothing brand models twirled, glasses of bourbon tipped over into pancake syrup, stim-stick smoke ballooned into puffs of perfume, and logos exploded into golden sparks like so much stardust, the holograms at the mercy of Gatsby's fingertips. Daisy's face brimmed with fresh wonder. Soon, she joined him, and the ad-drones bent gloriously for them both.

I watched the spectacle in silence, thinking about the valley's saddest souls—all the other George Wilsons and Mr. Edgars hidden away in the corporate storage units they called home—who'd stare out their dusty windows at this very moment and wonder, like thunder and lightning, whether this great flickering sky was an act of God too.

But if God was real that night, then he was crafted in the image of Gatsby's and Daisy's mindless joy.

"We'll have Ewing play the piano," declared Gatsby once the ad-drones had settled into a neon rainbow.

Ewing left and returned with a sleek baby grand, and with great fervor launched into the jolting glee of "Ain't We Got Fun." Daisy swayed with me for a verse, and then I sent her, giggling, into Gatsby's arms.

As the misty air held them in place, they waltzed against the backdrop of their shifting ad-drones, and I made a turn of the terrace. The cool night bit through my clothes. It reminded me of the first time I'd set foot atop this tower, staring out over the hollow, overpopulated city and feeling so alone amidst the thousands.

When I completed my ambling walk, the music had trickled away and Ewing was gone. Gatsby and Daisy had taken to the piano bench, murmuring softly as their fingers stumbled through an offbeat tune, never quite forming a melody. The ad-drones in the distance had now morphed into a school of pale, glassy fish.

Tangled together, with their backs turned to me, they had made themselves into their own lovely photograph, a scene as faded and intimate as the ones in Gatsby's album. I wasn't numb anymore, and it seemed rude to interrupt them.

I began to climb the staircase back to the elevators, but he noticed me and came over in haste. "Won't you stay?" he asked.

"I'm intruding."

"You're not." Gatsby shook his head.

"I agreed to arrange tea," I said firmly. "I've done that."

My favor was over, and I ought to have been free of them both now. I turned, stepping into the elevator before I could allow Gatsby another word. He returned, sullen, to the piano bench, taking Daisy's hand reluctantly.

A short silence passed, perhaps filled with all those swaths of unfinished memories billowing between them. There had been many silences all night, in fact—short gaps where they appeared completely overwhelmed by the sheer impossibility of each other.

I saw Gatsby look over his shoulder, our eyes meeting, just before the doors slid closed.

Twenty-Seven

T HE TOWER STOOD DARK FOR three scorching August weeks. Great mayhem erupted throughout West Egg in the wake of this, hover-cars swarming his landing pad like enraged wasps. By now, it should also be noted that Gatsby's parties had grown famous enough that his status as host became an open secret. This caused hungry journalists to camp outside not only the tower's doors but the Gen Wealth offices too.

I learned later that the whispers around his character had moved out of the simple realm of gangster or war spy. Now he was a government android gone rogue or perhaps a sentient AI whose parties had stopped due to some bug in his code. The speculation rampaged on. Under those brutal days and restless nights, everyone was more ravenous than before. Gatsby had stripped them all of the drug that was his tower, and the summer's unrest had nowhere to go.

I spent most of these weeks with Jordan, attending the last stretch of her games and accompanying her wherever she allowed me to. Eventually, this included her mod appointments.

"Take my arm," I urged as she stumbled around her dressing room. Her left calf was bent sideways after today's game, and she hadn't been able to complete the course. She was in a foul mood.

"Don't be sweet now," she said.

"I thought that was why you keep me around."

"Not today."

A part of me was glad that I was privy to this imperfect side of her, though she was obsessed with winning in a way that terrified me some. Against the advice of her coach and trainers, she simply couldn't be talked out of anything—even if it ended in disaster. This had always been rather charming to me, but now I could see the cracks where her courage walked the line of folly.

We made our way to the athletic training wing. She allowed me into the room as her mod-doc swapped her leg-plates and, at her urging, replaced her joint-screws too.

"It's not your joint-screws that caused your mishaps, Miss Baker," said the doc.

"Tell me I'm washed up and beyond my prime in plainer terms, why don't you."

"I'll tell you every mod in your body is running too hot—"

"Then it's a good thing I've never been scared of fire, isn't it," she snapped.

It went on like this for two hours, needling and unpleasant. We dined later on a Harlem hover-terrace, where she surprised me by reaching for my hand across the table.

"I thought you didn't want me sweet today," I said.

"I didn't mean it," she relented. "Not with you. People tell me all the time that they care about me. They're always lying. It's not me they really care about. The bigger you are, the more investors you have, and the more investors you have, the more money they lose when you fall. That's what matters to them."

"Well, I'm not an investor," I replied.

She laughed. "I know. I like your naivete. It's the most sincere part about you."

The ad-drone lights in the sky burst warmly behind her. There was nothing quite left to be embarrassed about between us, and I felt comfortable enough to speak my mind to her now.

"Perhaps your mod-doc is right," I said.

She stole her hand back. "Oh, you don't understand, Nick."

"Then help me," I insisted. "Exerting yourself—is it truly worth never playing again? Or damaging your body beyond repair? Legacy only controls you if you allow it."

I'd overstepped. She retreated into herself again. "You don't know a thing about legacy. I envy you for that. You might not see it, but it's true."

"What do you mean?" I said, incredulous.

"You have no honored persona you're trying every day to live up to," she muttered. "The world doesn't hold the image of your youth in their eye, and so you needn't ever live the rest of your life measuring yourself against the brilliance of what you accomplished when you were twenty."

I'd soon understand the difference between us as she wanted me to. I could shape-shift as any contract demanded, disappear from a city, or hide away in the quiet domes if I so desired. Even my name, fake and silly, held no responsibility or expectations. But everyone else who'd had a golden stretch of youth would try to spend the rest of their lives re-creating that cursed decade—their twenties, or the moment just before, when the whole world opens up.

If I'd become sure of anything since then, it was that I'd cherish my anonymity over this suffocating pressure of excellence that drove the rest of these people insane. That was "legacy" perhaps—a thing that followed you around, in Daisy's words.

A ghost you built with your own hands.

◇——◇——◇

Ewing was outside my door when I returned home. I lamented whatever outlandish task Gatsby was fetching me for this time.

"I've not been sent, sir," replied Ewing. "Mr. Gatsby has dismissed the staff."

He explained Gatsby's wishes for a security overhaul in the interest of protecting his new guest, Mrs. Buchanan.

"Then where have the others gone?" I asked.

Most of the Klipspringers were given away as gifts to various business acquaintances. The rest were sent back to the factory to undergo firmware updates.

"Where is *your* new placement?"

"Here, sir."

I had no use for an android, but Gatsby had once again thrown something expensive in my direction, hoping it would stick.

"Wait here," I said to Ewing.

I went straight to the tower that night. It was already late, but if I put it off until tomorrow, I knew I'd be too polite about it. A harsh rain started up as I crossed the street. In the lobby, I found not a single android or hover-bot roaming around. In fact, aside from the initial scanner outside the main entrance, it seemed that the whole security system was offline.

I shot up to the private suite, and when the elevators opened, the most unusual sight revealed itself on the other side.

Perched atop Gatsby's dining table, surrounded by platters of vibrant desserts, was none other than Pammy. She sat all alone, scrunching her fists into a bowl of cranberries, and as I rushed over, she clambered unsteadily to her feet.

"Hello, Tito," she said mildly. "I am eating fruits. Do you like?"

I carried her down from the table. "*Where* is your mother?"

Just then, Daisy came waltzing out in a loose burgundy slip dress. Her hair hung pin straight around her face, her pink lipstick faded and smudged. "Oh, Jay. Nicky's here," she called over her shoulder. "What a wonderful surprise."

I set Pammy in a chair and wiped her hands clean with a damp napkin. "Not as wonderful to see a child unattended."

"But she's Miss Pamela Buchanan, the sharpest child you'll ever meet," said Daisy. "She's perfectly fine."

"She's three."

"Our mod-doc says she's so good, she'll be ready for her comm in just five years," replied Daisy proudly, and there wasn't a chance to tell her that was very much beside the point.

"Mr. Carraway . . ." Gatsby ambled out from the bedroom, barefoot, dressed only in pajama bottoms and a robe of black silk.

He moved to take my coat, but I told him I wasn't staying long. "I didn't mean to interrupt your evening."

A flush extended all the way down his neck and chest. "Not at all."

"I was just leaving," added Daisy. "Jay and I are done discussing business."

I doubted what sort of business was being discussed in bedrooms and silk robes, but to my surprise, Daisy wasn't being coy. She shared a screen from her comm with me, boasting the headline: "Gatsby Corporation to Acquire Biotech Company, Fay Medica."

"Announcement's running in a few weeks," she said. "Isn't it great?"
I stared at the screen.

This whole summer, the thing that had uprooted my life so thor-oughly, that ran me in circles like a dog—reduced down to a single sentence, an uncited footnote of Gatsby and Daisy's unworldly affair. To see their names sitting boldly together in that way was almost disconcerting, their union nearly complete. The glow of the holo-screen illuminated their faces, rosy with excitement and tired bliss.

"That's fast," I said.

"Daisy helped move along everything that was stalled," said Gatsby. "With a bit more work, we'll be unveiling the first memory diamond prototypes to the public as early as this year."

Daisy nodded, encircling their arms. "Everyone's very thrilled." She rested her head on his shoulder, and Gatsby tensed before attempting to loosen his posture.

I closed the screen, and it dissolved into a shower of pixels. "I'm sure."

"Then once everything's sorted, she and I will, um—we'll go ... west for a while." He looked at her as if in confirmation.

Daisy smiled encouragingly. "That's right. Then take a trip over to the new domes in France."

Gatsby blinked, as though even now, he couldn't quite believe she was a warm-blooded body and not another one of his realistic, state-of-the-art holos.

Afterward, Daisy took Pammy's hand, and Gatsby walked them to the elevators. I could see the presence of the little girl confused him, for she mirrored a great deal of her mother's features and even the subtle inflections that tugged at the edges of Daisy's murmurs.

As Gatsby said his farewells, I stepped forward. "I'd like a word alone with my cousin. Family matter."

"Oh—sure ...," he replied hesitantly, and retreated to the dining area.

"Alone! How scandalous." Daisy slipped into a long periwinkle raincoat. "I love scandal. But what's the matter? I don't like when your brow creases, Nicky. It makes your handsome face very sca—"

"This acquisition—I hope you're planning a future and not just an escape route," I said in a lowered voice. "Especially if it's only taking yourself into account."

263

Her fingers stilled around her coat buttons. When she glanced up at me, the bright stars in her eyes were banished in favor of that arrow-sharp scrutiny she once again notched to full attention.

The longer I exposed myself to Daisy's radiance, the less I was sure of her. I didn't question only this supposed French elopement but where Pammy would fit into all that. I had half a mind to believe Daisy didn't know either and that she simply saw in Gatsby yet another spotlight to keep trained on herself until she could hop to a new one. I recalled how lightly she'd uttered those words about her daughter too: *Maybe you ought to keep her.*

Daisy's mouth fell open, and it seemed as though she was about to impart a word on me that might have dramatically shifted our thin bond forever, but then Pammy tugged my sleeve with her sticky hand. "Tito. Show me—another trick," she said.

I lifted her up. "Have you been good since last time?"

She glanced sideways at her mother, then burrowed her face into my shoulder.

Daisy cleared her throat. "Say goodbye to your tito now."

"Tito," Pammy whined. "Show me—"

"*Don't* ignore me, Pamela," interrupted Daisy, harder and louder.

Now Pammy didn't want to return to her mother at all. She clutched my neck tighter, and I patted her back in reassurance. "Another time," I promised, setting her down. She kissed my cheek dejectedly before letting Daisy pull her into the elevator.

I returned to the dining room to find Gatsby wearing a glum expression, staring out his enormous windows.

"You dismissed Ewing," I called out to him.

He spun around. "I'm rebuilding a whole new staff. Replacing all my bots while I'm at it. The firmware's one generation old."

"But you'll take Ewing back."

"I thought you liked him."

"I don't want your gifts anymore. Haven't I said that already?"

He began crossing the long stretch of marble between the elevator and the dining room but stopped mid-step. "Not in so many words, I suppose," he murmured. I fought the urge to apologize for my tone, and he went on. "Daisy said she'll be comfortable with new staff.

There's always a reporter hiding in the shadows, watching my doors. Can't risk it. The Klipspringer third line can be far too chatty. I've got the 4.0 in beta as we speak."

"I walked straight here, and you weren't even alerted," I pointed out. "What happened to your robust security? You'd better put something back in place right away."

"And I will! This weekend in fact," he said. "Speaking of which, while I have you here ... Daisy's never seen the tower in all its brilliance, and she ought to, don't you think?"

"If it's what she wants."

"What I mean to ask is, why don't you and Miss Baker come 'round next weekend? We'll throw open the doors altogether."

"Miss Baker's occupied with the end of her season," I replied shortly.

"Of course." He paused. Somehow, I knew he was about to grovel before the words were even spoken. "Listen. I know I still haven't done enough to apologize for not being forthcoming before. It was never my intention to upset you."

I didn't know how that could possibly be occupying his mind still, but then I had the infuriating thought that he assumed it might make me more likely to help him again.

"Your great plan has come together just as you envisioned. You don't need either me or Jordan now. I'll be returning Ewing. Please don't send anything else," I said. "It'll go to waste when I leave New York."

Next contract, next city—that life had served me just fine for years. It was a wonder I'd ever thought otherwise.

I went into the elevator, then back out into the rain. Later, Jordan called me, her voice low and urgent. "We *must* go to Gatsby's this weekend. If we don't, there'll be trouble."

"Trouble?" I demanded. "What's happened?"

She recounted her evening—how Daisy had returned home from the tower and begun to invite Jordan to the upcoming festivities. And then, "Tom overheard us." Jordan sighed. "He's insisted on joining, of course."

265

Twenty-Eight

I T WAS A SHAME THAT the last of Gatsby's famous parties would be remembered so miserably. About every three steps, Tom expelled an unpleasant observation about the gracelessness of it, the glaring lights, the hysteria. His purposeful resentment set my teeth on edge, and it had a visible effect on Daisy as well, her nerves clinking around like ice cubes. After so much time in the quiet tower, I imagined the squealing music and limpid-eyed guests seemed to her a frightful extension of Gatsby's varied holos.

She leaped from Tom's arm to mine as we moved through the bulging rooftop throngs. Gatsby chose this time to emerge from the shadows and greet us. Obligatory handshakes ensued.

"I believe we've met somewhere before, Mr. Buchanan," said Gatsby to Tom. "About two months ago."

"That's right." Tom nodded slowly. That club, and all of its implications, reached convergence behind his alert eyes. "You were with Nick."

There were many guests that night, more than ever before since the doors had been shut for three weekends prior. Gatsby made a show of pointing out all the most famous attendees like they belonged to some sort of exotic collection of his.

"We don't go around very much," was Tom's perfunctory reaction. "In fact, I was just thinking I don't know a soul here."

"Perhaps you know them." Gatsby gestured to a pair of women beneath the white glow of a holo-plum tree. The smaller one was a famed Hollywood director, and the lanky girl leaning over her was her muse. She donned a holo-layer of "translucent" skin, which gave her the ethereal effect of being, quite literally, made of glass. Even Tom couldn't feign ignorance and was forced to be impressed.

And yet, Daisy was still the most improbable creature here. When the fawning commenced, we had to have a Klipspringer follow us around to keep everyone at a safe distance. *The* Daisy Fay! It was so remarkable that people began tripping over themselves to get close. It wasn't really to speak with her, just to ogle and shout in her vague direction.

Under the severe attention, I looked over every few minutes, seeing her through the eyes of the masses—not my capricious older cousin, but that "gorgeous crown in a museum that's never been worn." Forbidden and inhuman.

Tom's introduction around the party was less stellar. What was he known for? Gatsby asked him this with mordant politeness, to which Tom floundered through a list of his executive boards until Daisy mentioned that Tom was somewhat of a polo player, or at least an enthusiast.

Tom didn't want to be a polo enthusiast while his wife was the retired Happy Sleep icon, but it caught on as we completed our turn of the rooftop. Gatsby stopped by the conveyor belt to pass us long champagne glasses. When he handed one off to Tom, he said, "I know your wife."

It was a good thing I hadn't sipped my drink, for I'd have surely choked on it. Jordan and Daisy, standing nearby, downed their glasses and pretended smartly that they hadn't heard a thing.

"That so?" said Tom with narrowed eyes. "She is known by many, as you can see."

Thankfully, the musical act for the night started up on the holo-screen. It wasn't the same European pop star from the previous party, but this one was no less famous, and Daisy became distracted enough by the full-piece orchestra that she relaxed a little. While Gatsby accommodated her eager questions, Tom slid himself between Jordan and me.

"Who is this Gatsby anyhow?" He swapped his untouched cham-pagne for a darker, shorter glass. "Some big bootlegger?"

"Where'd you hear that?" I asked.

Tom sniffed the drink before deeming it passable enough to ingest. "A lot of these newly rich people are just big bootleggers, you know."

"Not Gatsby," I said rigidly.

Jordan didn't correct me, and perhaps she and I had fine-tuned our telepathy.

"Well, he certainly must have strained himself to get this menagerie together," said Tom.

He emptied his glass and reached for another. At this time, the mid-tempo ballad from the pop singer shifted to something foot-tapping and lively. Daisy wanted to dance, so Gatsby offered his arm.

"Isn't it odd no one knows a *thing* about him?" continued Tom as Daisy and Gatsby jostled together happily in the crowd. It wasn't the first time I'd seen Gatsby dance like that. He danced well. I recalled—from that one unspeakable night at the market—his sure rhythm and fluid body, the way he held a graceful beat.

My chest tightened. I glanced away.

Tom was still speaking. "I keep hearing that name, Gatsby, but apparently no one knows—"

"Nick knows him," said Jordan.

Tom looked at me. "Right. How'd that happen?"

She shrugged. "Nick's special like that."

"Actually, I work for him," I said. "And I just live next door."

This was the wrong thing to say. Clearly that telepathy between Jordan and me had stumbled some. She shook her head at me, just as the suspicious light in Tom's eyes intensified. "And here I thought this Gatsby fellow might be to blame for your breaking Chester's heart," he muttered.

"Well—" I started, but then Daisy returned from the dance floor with Gatsby, who, a minute later, excused himself, citing a business call.

In his absence, Tom's prickling derisions started up once more. The party, in his opinion, was uncouth.

"These West Egg sorts." He eyed a passing Klipspringer distrustfully. "Rowdy men, indeed. Anyone can buy a tower, but something that *can't* be bought is proper comportment."

"He didn't buy it. He *built* it," said Daisy shortly.

"I'd like to know who he is and what he does. And I think I'll make a point of finding out," declared Tom.

"I can tell you right now," replied Daisy, a high note climbing into her voice. "He broke out into finance—all on his own, in fact; he didn't *inherit* a thing."

The musical act concluded in a furious climax, and in that short silence before the applause thundered, I swore a sort of bloodlust detonated behind Tom's eyes.

I knew Daisy to be daring—I'd seen it plenty of times—and I was rather certain Tom feared his wife more than she feared him. The problem was that Tom didn't, of course, know what to do with that fear.

But it was not a fear to be laughed at; I knew it was capable of breaking someone's nose with a single strike or bruising Daisy's hands. Jordan knew this, too, and acted decisively, dispersing us until we could all attempt civility again. She accepted the saintly act of chaperoning Tom across the party, which I took to mean that Daisy would thus be my responsibility.

As Jordan and Tom went off into the crowd, however, I turned around to find Daisy had vanished.

◇——◇——◇

I searched the Grecian sculpture rooms first, then the art galleries and gardens. When that led me nowhere, I tried her on the comm several times with no luck. I began to think she'd fled the tower and almost sent for a hover-car to take me across the bay, when I remembered there was one important floor I hadn't thought to check.

I went quickly to the private Happy Sleep room.

And there I found her, crumpled to her knees in her twinkling gown. I caught her expression only in glimpses, between the flashes of the terminal's blinking green light, shivering and sobbing in the cold darkness.

"Daisy—"

"He loves me," she whispered. "So much—I ..."

As I approached her, I noticed the headset lying at her side.

Her chest seized, and true terror blanketed her face, as if she'd only just reached this revelation herself and couldn't breathe through the weight of it in her lungs—Gatsby loved her.

"I'll tell you why I made the specs, Nick," she said, wiping her eyes. "You must know why we left Chicago. Tom was spending every weekend with a different woman, and it made an absolute *joke* of me. No one could look me in the eyes in that city. So when those spec orders kept coming through, I—I don't know."

"You couldn't resist it," I said.

"Yes, I ... liked making them." She set her head between her knees. "But the truth is that I didn't *know* he was James! I swear I didn't. I used to have spec requests come through all the time. My manager ignored them. That was, until he told me someone offered ten million dollars, and so I read the request brief myself—a summer festival in Louisville. Ordered by a man called Jay Gatsby." She recounted this in a winded, rambling daze. "I missed James dearly. I'd had no way to contact him all those years. But I was engaged then, to an absolute brute of a man, Tom." She shuddered. "This year, you know, I noticed all those big purchases he was making. I was sure he was having me investigated. Of course, I overestimated him. Then my father told me about the acquisition. *Gatsby* Corp. Oh, I just had to know it wasn't a coincidence ... but I never thought he'd seek me out too—through you. ..."

The terminal thrummed in the silence, its steady light flooding through the room, across her body and over her head.

I can't recall how long I sat there with her, but she went on for a while, recalling all the sessions she recorded and how each time, she'd done it for the same reason—retreating into them like a cave.

But to Gatsby, they'd been blueprints.

He'd drawn up his desperate visions, reaching frantically into this rewritten past as if it might bend toward a new future. Now he was holding it all out for her, waiting for Daisy Fay to accept the heart he'd clawed out of his own chest.

But that Daisy Fay did not exist.

"He has a way about him," she murmured. "You feel so ... important, holding his attention, as if you've done a marvelous thing by existing before him."

"I know."

She looked at me pointedly. Perhaps the tired frankness in her words had simply coaxed too much sincerity out of me, and I could see a question steeping in her eyes. But she did not voice it. Instead, her lip quivered, and she burst into tears.

Indeed, Gatsby loved her.

Beneath the showers of stardust that draped his tower, he loved her—and she didn't know what to do about it.

◇——◇——◇

"She didn't like it," said Gatsby, once the night had screeched to an end like the last stutters of a dying engine. He had asked me to stay back, and just he and I were left on the ravaged terrace. He turned to me as if expecting a reassurance that perhaps Daisy really had enjoyed it after all. When I said nothing, he frowned, shivering in the wind. "She didn't have a good time. It's hard to make her under-stand. . . ."

"I wouldn't ask too much of her." I contemplated my next statement for a long time. "You can't repeat the past."

"Can't—why, of course you can!" He crossed the space between us in three quick strides. "You've helped me so much, Nick. I want *you* to understand too. It's—"

"I understand perfectly."

"You do?"

"You're acting as if you want miracles out of her, but I'm saying you can't ask that of a person."

I'd soon regret invoking the cosmos like that. *Miracles.* That word transformed him.

"I'll tell you the funny thing about miracles—no one believes them until they happen. But they *do* happen. I'm living proof of that, you see, because I could have died a hundred thousand different ways as a child," he declared. "I almost ... almost had my eyes sold to a mod-doc for nothing but my father's favorite rum. And yet here I am. Against every odd." He spun with his arms out, gesturing at the gutted remains of his party and the acid lights of West Egg blazing below.

271

"Miracles aren't a suspension of natural law, old sport. Miracles are an *execution* of a higher power. See, that's how great fortune works. And isn't it also great fortune that brought *us* together, you and me—"

"Jay," I said through clenched teeth.

He glanced around as if he didn't know at first who had called his name.

"*You* brought me here. And *you* ordered those spec Sleeps from Daisy. *You* built this tower and threw these parties. None of those things are miracles," I argued. "They're expensive decisions."

The mention of the specs stopped him short. "You . . . watched the Sleeps," he realized. *"When?"*

I was past the point of lying to him—past the point of even tolerating him. "When? Ages ago. You wouldn't tell me the truth, so I had to go find it myself. Did you think Jordan and I were utterly brainless?" I made a bitter noise in my throat. "You started this whole thing by *flying a Klipspringer* across the world. I didn't trust you then, and I never have since."

Against any rational thought, all the foul honesty I'd been swallowing back came out. I was through being afraid to make an enemy out of a powerful man, for in that moment, there was nothing powerful about him, and his earnestness ceased to enthrall me.

"Who did you think tampered with your tower that first night?" I asked. "Why do you really think I would trespass your facility? When you confronted me about it, I thought it'd be the end of my life. But even *then*, you weren't truthful." I laughed coldly. "I know that you're really just a poor nobody named James Gatz. You've thrown all of this together for a girl who says she'll take your hand and run to France, but you can't see she's just tepid about you."

The name "Gatz" made him flinch. He stared at me—rigid with shock but not anger.

Looking back, I think I'd wanted him to be angry, hoping he'd become a real, ruthless corpo who'd toss me from his ranks and release me from his delusions once and for all. It was almost funny to think I'd ever feared him or anticipated he'd find out about Trimalchio's investigation, when really he was too self-absorbed to comprehend his own weaknesses.

"You knew. Everything. And yet you . . . you accepted all my invitations." His breath quickened. "You helped me anyway. Why?"

A holo-bonfire crackled somewhere across the terrace. This simple question burst between us like an insult.

"You—" I could have struck him now. "You *know* already, Jay. How can you even ask me that? The afternoon at the studio, I almost thought you . . ." I pushed the memory away to a dark recess of my mind where I hoped it'd perish for good. "Jordan wanted me to be careful around you. And it turns out I just wasn't. All right?"

A series of conflicted thoughts tumbled across Gatsby's expression. Then he looked at me with wide, clear eyes, as if he were seeing me for the first time.

It was more than I'd wanted to admit aloud. I don't think I was quite prepared for the way his understanding, the confirmation of those words, would glint like light on all the sharp points of his face. His lips moved, but no sound came out.

I turned, crossing to the edge of the rooftop. The aftershocks of the party whistled through the air. I went to a far spot against the railing and leaned my head out. The conveyor belt around the terrace droned on, cycling empty cocktail glasses, and revelers in every extreme emotional state shouted their unwanted farewells through the streets.

"Nick," he said, and his voice had fallen nearly to a whisper. For a tense, unending moment, I could only hear the staggering of my own heartbeat.

His vast selfishness had begun the moment he'd donned "Gatsby" in Daisy's name and decided everyone else was collateral on the way to his dreams.

Jordan, myself, all the millions shackled to Gen Wealth.

Everything was coming apart at the seams simply because Daisy "didn't like" the festivities.

At last, I looked at him again. "Couldn't you see how Daisy was so unwell with the crowds pawing at her? She was overwhelmed, and you were not helping."

Still, his infuriating optimism didn't waver, even that night. "She doesn't love Tom," he said irrelevantly. "He hurts her. And someone has to help her get away, but she's so afraid."

"You can't *force* her to do anything."

"If you saw our Sleeps, then you saw how we trusted each other. How she was with me in our youth." He nodded to himself, drifting away again into his misplaced resolve. "She'll listen to me. I *can* make her understand. Miracles are everywhere, if you just—just know where to look. . . ."

He and I would disagree on this to the end. Just like the other things he refused to see, he wouldn't open his eyes to this either—that no higher power had carried him to this rooftop and that all his miracles were made of money. It was the singular energy that propelled civilization forward, the axis upon which this offensive planet spun, and in such grotesque amounts, it delighted and deluded in equal parts, fashioning dreams proportionate to nightmares.

So we argued uselessly through the night, as the skies above us melted toward a sore, purple dawn.

GENERATIONAL WEALTH INC. DATA BREACH
INVESTIGATION (CASE STATUS: OPEN)
TRANSCRIPT: ETTY ANAND (AGE: SEVENTY-ONE)
LOCATION: HEADQUARTERS, GATSBY CORPORATION
(NEW YORK CITY, NEW YORK, NEA)
DATE: JUNE 15, 2077

[LOADING]

.

.

.

[PLAY]

"Where was *I* on that day? I won't ever forget it. It was the hottest day of the summer. I was in a hover-car, flying over West Egg when it happened. Heard the sirens. Watched the fires blaze on for hours."

"Is that why you and so many of your team left Gen Wealth, Mrs. Anand?"

"What?"

"You felt a certain way about working for Mr. Gatsby after all that happened?"

"I never said any of that! Don't put that on record. What's this got to do with the investigation, anyhow? As for Mr. Gatsby, I won't sit here and be interrogated about that man. He ought to vanish from all our minds."

[PAUSE]

Twenty-Nine

O N THE HOTTEST DAY OF the summer, Gatsby called me up out of the blue.

I wondered at first if he was calling about the abrupt end to my Gen Wealth placement, which Bunsen had followed through on. He set his divers loose, falsifying a deposit issue in my bank account. It was enough to create the illusion of a contract violation. Gen Wealth was forced to pay me out, and I gratefully seized the clean break.

Something had corroded me in the wake of my argument with Gatsby last weekend; I was ready to leave New York behind and had begun packing up my apartment.

As it turned out, however, Gatsby didn't know or care about my early departure. He was calling on behalf of Daisy, whose voice fluttered vaguely in the background.

"Would you have lunch at her house this afternoon?" he asked. "Miss Baker will be there," he added, probably because they both knew I wouldn't come otherwise.

They sounded panicked. I tried to call Jordan after, but she didn't answer, and I was sure something awful awaited in East Egg.

I was sad that my hunch was right. At the edge of the Buchanans' driveway, I spotted Gatsby coming out of his Veluz in a light pink ensemble, suit jacket and all, far too overdressed for the weather.

"What are you doing here?" I demanded.

"Lunch, old sport." The nerves I'd detected over the comm still clung to him. He smoothed the front of his jacket several times before taking in my much more casual attire. I was dressed only in my shirtsleeves; still the heat was unbearable. I was shocked Gatsby hadn't fainted yet.

I led him inside and down the corridor of Tom's college accolades. "Look here," I whispered, "I don't know why you've come or why Daisy's invited—"

"It's not Daisy; it's Mr. Buchanan who's extended the invitation."

Even worse. "You have to keep your head. You understand? No matter what."

Gatsby nodded, but his unhappy focus was on Tom's football paraphernalia.

In the sitting room, the windows were modded to half opacity, dimming the sunlight, while a flock of hover-bots blew around stale air. The chaises had been pushed against the wood-paneled walls in favor of a lavish couch whereupon Daisy and Jordan lay together, pretty and immovable beneath the billowing wisps of their white dresses.

I walked over to squeeze their hands in greeting. Jordan sat up and dropped a swift kiss to my cheek.

"And Mr. Thomas Buchanan, the athlete?" I asked.

Almost exactly when I spoke his name, Tom's voice rumbled from down the hall. I hoped he wasn't speaking so roughly to his house staff.

"He's on the comm," explained Jordan.

I made out some words about a mod sale and guessed he was speaking to Wilson, but his hushed tone seemed to convince Daisy that it was his mistress. She scowled at him when he lumbered into the room, his imposing body passing over us like a shadow.

"Mr. Gatsby! I'm glad to see you, sir." He shook Gatsby's hand and even smiled. Then he turned in my direction, pulling me into a bizarre embrace. I smelled the weight of his sweat and leathery cologne. "Nick. How's Gen Wealth?"

"My contract is up," I said.

"Why's that? Has Mr. Gatsby been an unkind boss?" He chuckled. The noise fell like stones in the silent room.

I said something about planning to return to Manila, but no one heard it. Daisy stood up hastily from the couch and told Tom to make everyone a drink.

He was barely out the door when she walked over and kissed Gatsby square on the lips—a quiet vengeance against her husband—and it took Gatsby by surprise; he tensed visibly.

I looked away, taking Daisy's spot on the couch next to Jordan, who glanced at me and then at Gatsby. She frowned. "You forget there's a lady present."

"*You* kiss Nick too," replied Daisy, irritable.

Jordan would have never kissed me like that in respectful company—and neither of us even had husbands. She sighed, resting her hand on my knee.

Daisy made a petulant face and crossed the room, falling defeatedly onto a chaise. When the doors opened again, it wasn't Tom but one of the nannies, leading Pammy inside by the cotton candy sleeves of her pastel summer dress.

Daisy gasped and spread her arms wide. "Come to your own mother who loves you!" she hollered as the girl padded across the room, seating herself calmly in Daisy's lap. "Say your greetings."

Pammy went to me first. I offered her my hand, and after she'd pressed it to her forehead politely, she said, "I got dressed before lunch, Tito."

I squeezed her hand, smiling. "And you look lovely."

She went to Jordan next, who patted the girl's cheeks with fondness. Last was Gatsby, who still seemed frightened by the child, but at least smiled when she curtsied once before him. Afterward, she retreated back into her mother's skirt.

"She doesn't look like her father," said Daisy proudly. We heard Tom's heavy footfalls from down the corridor. Pammy flinched. Daisy spun her daughter around, and that was about as much indication as the nanny needed to take the child away.

Pammy stared over her shoulder at us as she was carried through the door. At the same time, Tom returned with a hover-bot, carrying gin, limes, and tall glasses of ice. He passed his daughter without the slightest glance, fixed us each a cool drink, and once we were all refreshed and nursing a second round, he offered to show Gatsby the grounds. The women stayed put, but exchanging a look with them, I stood up, following Tom and Gatsby onto the veranda.

"I read somewhere that the famous hover-districts off the coast of Manila are doomed to fall into the ocean one day. It has something to do with poor quality-assurance processes. Everything's done very hastily. The education's different there," said Tom. "I like to read those sorts of things. There's also a fine piece from a man called Goddard about the dangers of Southeast Asia and the brain drain. Businessman like you ought to find it enlightening, Mr. Gatsby."

At this, Gatsby shot me a troubled look. I sipped my gin rickey and shook my head at him.

Gatsby cleared his throat. "Look there, I'm right across from you," he noted to Tom, nodding at the great shadow of his tower on the other side of the Sound.

For a second, Tom's disdain bled through his composure, but then he hid it away again.

We couldn't stand out there for much longer, so we ducked back inside, ate lunch, then settled into an anxious lethargy around the table. We were all tired, pumped through with cocktails, and yet, no one was relaxed.

"What'll we do with ourselves this afternoon?" Daisy whined. "And the day after that, and the next thirty years?"

"Don't be morbid." Jordan lit two cigarettes and handed me one. "Life starts all over again when it gets crisp in the fall."

"Not if there's war, or a space invasion, or—or apocalypse—" Daisy waved at one of the fan-bots to lower itself closer to her head. "Let's all go to town!"

Across the table, Tom had Gatsby trapped in a conversation about polo. "I was asked many times out of college if I'd go professional in a number of sports," said Tom, "but nowadays, even the gentlemanly activities mandate invasive body-mods."

"Invasive," repeated Jordan blithely.

I reached for her hand below the table. Her lips pursed around her cigarette. Tom scowled.

"Who wants to go to town?" asked Daisy again. "Ah," she murmured, meeting Gatsby's eyes tenderly. "You look so cool in all that. You always look so cool. . . ."

She was referring to Gatsby's many-layered attire that had hardly caused him to sweat, but the yearning in her voice shaped those mundane words into a confession, and suddenly, whatever bomb that had been rigged up since the party last weekend began to plummet to the end of its timer.

Tom, in speechless anger, looked quickly between his wife and Gatsby as if observing the climactic end of a tennis rally.

"I meant that you resemble the holo-ad of—of the man—" Daisy fumbled.

"All right." Tom's chair scraped the floors as he rose. "I'm perfectly willing to go to town." When no one moved, he barked out, "Come on! If we're going to town, let's start."

◇——◇——◇

With a suite booked at the Plaza, Tom showed Gatsby the quartet of Veluzes parked in his driveway while we waited for Daisy and Jordan to powder their noses.

"Yes, it's a nice collection. For a man with such reservations about the Southeast, you do enjoy your hover-tech, old sport," said Gatsby.

"You do a lot of business over there, don't you?" I asked Gatsby, cutting Tom off from what was sure to be a devastating reply.

Gatsby nodded. "Any *forward*-thinking businessman knows some brilliant innovations are coming out of the Global South."

Thankfully, Daisy and Jordan came floating down the porch steps then, and with all of us gathered outside, there was much discussion around the car arrangements. Gatsby mentioned that his was low on charge.

"Well, you take mine and let me drive yours to town," said Tom.

Gatsby shook his head. "I don't think—"

"I'll stop for charge in the smart town. I don't mind. They have everything there, you know. Even mod-docs. Maybe you know them too, Mr. Gatsby."

And then blood was drawn.

Gatsby's face swam with an unplaceable emotion as Tom, evidently pleased that he'd landed a good blow, gripped Daisy's hand and pulled her forcefully toward Gatsby's car.

"You take Nick and Jordan." Daisy tore her hand free. "We'll follow you."

We watched them go, Tom with his jaw open, as she tugged Gatsby by the sleeve of his jacket. I followed Tom and Jordan to Gatsby's Veluz. It took Tom some fumbling to acquaint himself with the dashboard-holo, but once we were in the air, he turned to us. "Did you see that?" he exclaimed.

I fixed my eyes toward the beating sun. "See what."

A humorless laugh startled out of him. "You think I'm pretty dumb, don't you? I decided to start investigating him, you know. I have a—a sixth sense for this sort of thing."

"Do you mean you've been to a medium?" asked Jordan dryly. She glanced at me, and our shoulders shook with poorly contained laughter.

"No!" Tom frowned at us. "Investigating his business practices and how Daisy knew him before we were married."

Jordan nodded. "And your investigation found he was an Oxford man."

"Like hell he is," protested Tom. "There's word going around that Medica is going to cut loose from us—for Gatsby Corp, no less!" He looked at me again, almost imploringly. "Be honest, Nick. That Gen Wealth business is a horrible operation, isn't it? Something about endless moneylending to sorry folks?"

The sight of the valley opened below us. Tom tapped the acceleration on the dashboard.

He wanted me to do nothing short of denouncing Gatsby's whole existence—hand over the Holy Bible, before a grand jury. But then Jordan reminded us about the car, so we made a stop at George Wilson's shop. The holo-woman outside offered us a prompt greeting of curses.

"Let's have some charge!" Tom called out. There was no answer at first, probably because the hum from the fans drowned out everything. He yelled a second time, before a pale Wilson stumbled out into the sun.

"Been sick all day," said Wilson feebly.

Tom grunted. "Well, shall I help myself?"

Wilson disappeared into his shop and came out hauling the charging cables. He looked worse than sick. Tom, downright intolerable now, barked out at him to hurry along. Taking pity, I reached over

Jordan, opening the door, and climbed out to help the man. I took the cables from him, slotting them into Gatsby's car.

Wilson's breath heaved. "Why, thank you, Mr. . . ."

"Carraway." I eyed his blistered skin. Where the metal plates of his arms met flesh, he was red and chafed all over, like he'd had some recent procedures done and they hadn't healed well. "You ought to have someone look at your mods. It'll improve your health."

"Oh no, it was God himself that bestowed me these blessed parts."

"Pardon me?"

He pointed off in the distance, and I turned to see Dr. T. J. Eckleburg glaring back at us from the sky. "Right there. He speaks to me— through—through there. Shows me the way, comes to me in my sleep. . . . He's been there a long time. I pray to him every morning and night. He tells me I've got this gift, tells me which mods I gotta—"

"Enough chattering about," grumbled Tom.

Wilson apologized. "I didn't mean to interrupt your lunch, but I need money pretty bad. My wife and I want to go west. She's been talking about it for years. Not enough business around here."

Once the car hit full charge, I detached the cables and passed them back to Wilson, who hadn't noticed the darkness brewing in Tom's eyes—much less that his admission about Myrtle was what had caused it. She was going "away." Just like that, as if into obscurity.

Wilson hovered awkwardly for a moment. Tom was staring, vacant eyed, at the steering wheel.

"What does he owe you?" I asked Wilson.

"Um . . . one hundred twenty," replied Wilson.

"Tom," I said. "One hundred twenty." He didn't show any signs of life until Jordan gave his shoulder a good shove.

Absently, he put his arm out through the window. Wilson tapped their wrists together, and I climbed back into the car.

Tom's face was grim. "I'll let you have that mod," he muttered at Wilson. "I'll . . . send it over tomorrow afternoon."

Wilson smiled, visibly heartened, and waved farewell to us as we soared up, for the last time, through the blinking eyes of Dr. T. J. Eckleburg.

Thirty

JORDAN DUG HER HEAD INTO my collar as the heat rolled on through the lazy city. By the look of it, no one was roaming outside in this harsh daylight, instead tucked away in their cool apartments like sane people.

"I love New York on summer afternoons when everyone's away," murmured Jordan. "There's something very sensuous about it—overripe, as if all sorts of funny fruits were going to fall into your hands." She popped her head up with a condescending smile. "Don't you think so too, Tom? Isn't it very sensuous?"

I rested a hand on her back placatingly. They'd been throwing barbs at each other all day, but between Daisy's jetting off with Gatsby, and the discovery that Myrtle would soon escape, too, Tom's ill temper required no additional assistance.

"Those aren't fruits; those are ad-drones," grumbled Tom. "And there's nothing sensuous about *those*."

We reconvened with Gatsby and Daisy on the Plaza's landing pad. At reception, we synced the access code to our comms, then gathered in the parlor of the suite, which was far too cramped for the five of us, and made worse by our irritation.

"How swell," said Jordan dispassionately.

"Call for another fan-bot," suggested Daisy, though it was unlikely the hotel had any to spare.

"The thing to do is forget about the heat. You make it ten times worse by crabbing about it," said Tom.

He ordered a bottle of whiskey from the holo-menu that rose up from the coffee table, around which we all tried our best to relax.

The women shared the couch, while I claimed a little bench in a dark, cool corner of the room. Gatsby hovered by an open window, and he decided right then to turn around.

"You're the one who wanted to come to town, old sport," he said to Tom.

The whiskey rattled through the chute, and the hover-bot whirring quietly at my feet flew over to retrieve it, then deposited it into Tom's waiting hand.

"All this 'old sport' business," he shot back at Gatsby. "Where'd you pick that up?"

"Order some ice, Tom," said Daisy.

Tom occupied himself with the holo-menu again. From outside, we heard the faint bellows of an organ song, accompanied by a bride and groom leading a whole boisterous wedding procession onto the street.

The sight offended Jordan. "Imagine marrying anybody in this heat."

"I was married in June," said Daisy. "Louisville in June! Somebody fainted. Who was it, Tom?"

"A Bernardo or Bautista. One of *your* very many uncles."

It was just enough unprovoked animosity that Daisy's patience splintered. "Yes, I do have very many of those. What's the matter with that? At least my half of the guest list attended because they cared about *me*—"

"It must have been Bernardo," I interjected. "I know him too. Tito Boy Bernardo—with a Veluz dealership in Memphis, isn't that right?"

"That's right," agreed Daisy.

"By the way, Mr. Gatsby," said Tom, "I understand you're an Oxford man."

Gatsby straightened. "Yes."

Now the ice bucket came rolling down the chute. The hover-bot went to scoop it out, but no one else in the room moved a muscle.

"I'd like to know when," said Tom.

"It was in 2066. I only stayed five months," replied Gatsby as if he'd rehearsed this rebuttal many times. "An opportunity they gave to some of the accomplished officers during the war."

Daisy sighed, almost in relief. She reached over to pick up the ice from the hover-bot. "Open the whiskey, Tom, and I'll make you a mint julep."

Tom twisted the bottle open, poured himself an inch, then downed it. "Wait a minute," he said in a low, taut voice. "I want to ask Mr. Gatsby one more question."

"Go on," prompted Gatsby, eyes gleaming.

Tom took one dignified step toward him, empty glass swinging between his fingers. "What kind of a row," he said viciously, "are you trying to cause in my house anyhow?"

The ice slipped from Daisy's hand. Jordan reached out to grab it before the whole bucket could clatter to the floor.

"He's not causing a row," Daisy fumed, "*You're* causing a—"

"I suppose the latest thing is to sit back and let Mr. Nobody from Nowhere," Tom spat out, "fuck your wife."

Outside, the joyful cries of the wedding party faded into oblivion as the guests piled into their hover-cars. Tom looked at each of us in turn, a crazed light flooding his face.

"Everyone wants to demerit the Western nations these days," he went on. "To destroy prestigious American names for *fake* ones." He waved a hand at Gatsby. "Well, as soon as we do that, we let the Americas be run by any common swindler, or any third-world corporation. Or perhaps—"

"Perhaps we'll have intermarriage between races next," said Jordan sarcastically. "Or imagine if we let men kiss one another in the street."

Tom gaped. "You think you're hilarious, Miss Baker."

"Not hilarious, just logical, considering the rate you're going—that is, back about a hundred and fifty years."

"I know my opinions aren't very popular out here." Tom bristled. "I suppose you have to make your house an amusement park in order to have any friends—in the *modern* world."

"Please let's all go home," Daisy implored. She rounded the couch and clutched my arm. "Why don't we all go home?"

I stood up. "That's a good idea. Come on, Tom—"

"Your wife doesn't love you," proclaimed Gatsby. And then, categorically destroying any chance we had at ending the day with a morsel of peace, he added, "She's never loved you."

"You must be crazy!" Tom seethed.

"She only married you because I was poor," Gatsby persisted, "and she was tired of waiting for me."

The whirlwind of the argument swayed Daisy like a flimsy reed. I guided her back onto the couch, where she wouldn't let go of my hand.

Tom swallowed another inch of whiskey. "What's been going on?"

"Going on for five years—and you didn't know," added Gatsby.

Tom glared at Daisy, who wouldn't lift her eyes. "You've been seeing this fellow for five years?"

Gatsby answered for her. "No, we couldn't meet. But it was something far more beautiful than meeting. I used to laugh sometimes, knowing that what Daisy and I had across so much distance was more than you two ever pretended at."

A burning certainty fueled these words, but it had none of the intended effect on Tom. He looked, of all things, satisfied. "Oh. That's all," he said. "So you're nothing more than a rabid fanatic."

Gatsby trembled. "Fanatic!"

"You're just obsessed with her. You watched her Sleeps for years, and you think that means she *loves* you!" Tom made an ugly, derisive sound. It was a laugh. "You know how many folks around the world have watched those Sleeps? Millions. You're no one; that's what you are. Daisy Fay comes home to *me*—"

"Oh, you don't know what you're saying. They were specs!"

Tom almost dropped his glass. I doubted he even comprehended this at first, but once he did, the revelation tore a high, furious color up his neck. *"What?"* he screamed.

"They were *specs*," repeated Gatsby with pride. "Daisy made them. For me alone."

"Daisy, you never—" He whirled on her. She couldn't bring herself to speak, but her silence blared a deafening admission. Tom's face reddened, his eyes bulging, as if she'd squeezed her hands directly around his throat.

"It's true, old sport. She was nothing but depressed being married to you, and the fact is, that hasn't changed at all." Gatsby paced around the room. "She may 'come home' to you, but you'd be crazy to think it's anything like love. Not with the disgusting marks you leave on her."

Tom's breathing stuttered. "Daisy loved me when she married me, and she loves me now. The trouble is that sometimes she gets foolish ideas in her head." He set his glass on the coffee table, and in a thick, dulcet tone that sounded like an off-key note in the scale of his gruff voice, he murmured, "What's more, I love Daisy too—"

She was on her feet in a flash, across the room, where she threw open all the windows, and the oppressive summer engulfed us again. "You're *revolting*—" she gasped.

Tom hurried on. "Once in a while, I go off on a spree, but I always come back."

She was bent so far over the window railing, it reminded me of that disturbing New Orleans rumor Jordan had mentioned—that Daisy had threatened to jump once. "*That's* what you call those horrible years in Chicago?"

Gatsby rushed over and took her shoulder. "Just tell him the truth—that you never loved him—and it's all wiped out forever. You never loved him."

"I ..." She shook her head. "I never ..."

"Not that night I carried you from the Palmer?" asked Tom, again with that misplaced tenderness. "And we stayed on the comm until sunrise, falling asleep together?"

"Please don't," murmured Daisy, closing her eyes until her tears finally overflowed.

"Daisy. Remember that last spec you recorded for me," said Gatsby. "Remember how we sat together beneath the foliage and—"

"Are you insane, Mr. Gatsby? That's a *fantasy*—not a memory!" Tom cried out.

"It's a memory as long as we both *shared* it!" Gatsby roared. "Tell him, Daisy!"

She wrangled herself out of his embrace with a sob. "I did love him once! But I loved you too. ..."

It wasn't what Gatsby wanted to hear. It wasn't what he'd erected his tower for, burned his old name down for, nor why he'd mauled his way to the top of the Americas' corporate kingdoms.

287

"You loved me—" he stuttered, "*too?*"

"Even that's a lie," Tom cut in. "There are things between Daisy and me that you'll never know. Things that didn't happen simply because I dreamed them up in my head. Things that are *real.*"

Gatsby shrugged out of his suit jacket, sweating at last. Daisy stole Jordan's cigarette case, and after failing to light one, threw the whole thing across the room.

Tom went over and collected her in his arms. "I'm going to take better care of you—"

"Daisy's leaving you," announced Gatsby. "It's why she's been helping us acquire Fay Medica. To sever all ties to you—"

"Nonsense!" shouted Tom.

Daisy wrenched herself free. "Oh, please, let's get out!"

There was a perfect amount of whiskey in Tom now, so a ferocious boldness possessed him. "Who are you, anyhow?" He rounded on Gatsby. "I know why you do such *worldly* business. You have yourself a nice smuggling operation on the side—importing illegal mods and distributing them to all sorts of nefarious folks, isn't that right? Bet you don't separate the common mod enthusiast from the violent gangster. It's all about money—to fill out that circus of a home you have. Well, it's people like *you* who are running this country to filth. And let's not even get started on your loaning scheme!"

"A scheme? It's done more for people than anything you've done with your own two hands, Mr. *Buchanan*," retorted Gatsby. "What a name to have and nothing to show for it."

"Don't insult my name—"

"Not your name. Just you, old sport." Gatsby chuckled dryly. "I've helped millions of good Americans afford to put food on their dinner tables. And what have *you* done? Failed to become a sports star because of your own useless vanity?"

"At least I'm a proper East Egg man, and I'm not playing dress-up—poorly as you are," muttered Tom. "So what if I won't defile my body? I'm perfectly happy with that choice."

Daisy tensed. *"Tom!"*

"No, Daisy, I'd like to hear his feelings about such defilement." Jordan rose slowly from where she'd been stretched out on the couch

288

like a bored royal upon a throne. "He's been biting his words about it for so many years. Go on. Remind us why you never made it into the professional leagues."

"You've no right to be smug, Jordan. I've tolerated it too long. Your career's washed up now anyway, so you have nothing to talk about!"

"Smug? Oh, *you* may have been too cowardly to work for your dreams," she snapped, "but that doesn't mean you can make it everyone else's problem. You're a sorry man—"

I can't tell you how I ended up between them. I only remember the pit of anger that opened inside of me as Tom lunged at Jordan with a scream and an open hand, and I shoved him back. It managed to stagger him—mostly from the shock.

It was the last thing he'd expected from me, as if I were a bot that had suddenly spawned a brain.

"Even *you*." He stared down his nose at me with a contempt I'd only seen him direct at others. "Perhaps you're the worst of us all along, Nick."

"Get ahold of yourself," I muttered.

"Ah! Good, virtuous Nick! Ever the picture of innocence." He clapped his hands. "Someone ought to have told you there's nothing more intolerable than a man who thinks so highly of his own morals— who acts as if reserving all his judgment somehow makes him a superior being instead of a downright liar!"

"I suppose I should be just like you, then, and not have any morals at all," I retorted without thinking.

"What! I let you set foot in *my* house, and you went ahead and aided this whole ruse to ruin my marriage?" he countered angrily. "And how does Mr. Gatsby feel about the fact that you're a Trimalchio wolf in sheep's clothing? Shipped over here to audit him, isn't that right?"

Silence dripped like hot wax over the room.

"You—" said Gatsby from somewhere behind me. "What does he mean, Nick?"

Tom nodded in satisfaction. "Christ, it took my own man three days to find out Medica had your firm on payroll. That's easy math from there. Though clearly, Mr. Gatsby's too slow to count sums. So where's the morality in *that*, Nick? Fellows like you only know how to wander around aimlessly, taking orders. You'd best stay out of this."

A charged silence suffused the room; hardly a second or two, but it could have been hours. Tom must have thought he'd shut me up.

But then I began to laugh from the stupidity.

"What makes you think that I've yearned for any part of this? That I'm falling over myself to sit at *your* table and endure your insufferable non-insights?" I spat out. "How sad must it be for you? To not have anything worthwhile to your name so you put all your excruciating effort into obtaining Daisy Fay, only to realize she won't just sit in your house and shine for you!"

I spoke it all in one breath, without remorse or hesitation, and a thick vapor formed in the air between us—a flash point upon which Tom's insolence had struck me perfectly alive, incinerating those chameleon colors of mine to unsalvageable ashes. Never again could I withdraw into the shelter of false belonging. Though in this realization came a relief, too, for I knew I'd rather die than return to his table.

Tom squinted. He took one deliberate step toward me. "It seems you've gotten some skewed ideas in your head about your own importance. But there's a natural ... natural order to things." He stuttered here, from the whiskey, but also because it seemed he usually only said that sort of thing in his head, and now he'd gained a swell of confidence to say it aloud. "There's always been one. Because the right sorts ought to run the world and make the right decisions." He tipped his chin high. "And those people won't ever be Mr. Gatsby, the swindler, and it certainly won't be you, or your people."

Daisy wilted onto the couch. Tom drank straight from the bottle this time.

Your people. He'd said this with the full arrogance that he'd previously tried to swallow on things like "third world" and "jungle." Tom was clinging, with brittle claws, to an order that had never been natural, only set forcibly in place.

But the world of a Buchanan was false and small. A snow globe made up of spec Sleeps and mansions, human servants, and money from businesses he had no part in operating.

My nerves prickled, my veins burned, and Tom bent his neck down as he stood over me. The liquor wafted from his breath.

"What are you going to do? Will you 'fry' me out right here? Be my guest, Mr. *Carraway*," he goaded. "But I know you won't do a thing because you're not worth a damn, and neither is that invented name. All you have are those ghastly mods. *That* is weakness. Nothing beats real strength—"

He leaped forward, seizing my wrist, and pushed me against an oaken bureau. A vase shattered to the ground. I lost my balance, tripping forward, my cheekbone bouncing against the hardwood floor. Daisy cried out from somewhere in the room.

I surged to my feet, grabbing the front of Tom's shirt. He squeezed my wrist again—harder, until my whole hand turned white. With a sharp groan, I drove my free arm into the hard wall of his chest. It did little to move him, though it loosened his grip, and I reached for his left wrist. I scanned his comm with my oc-mods, and for a moment I thought I could run a paralysis pyre against it, enough to slow his movements.

But Tom didn't need to stop and think. He was wider, taller, with old football instincts, and he hunched himself down in a bullheaded stance, arms encasing my torso as if to tackle me.

"Don't touch him."

It took everyone a moment to realize it was Gatsby who'd spoken, for his voice had fallen into a low, shuddering tone. He was speaking through his teeth.

"Don't you move or say another word, Mr. Buchanan, or you will regret it," warned Gatsby.

Tom let go of me and stepped away. Through frenzied eyes, he surveyed the scene, which had somehow left him alone on one side of the room.

"I see . . .," said Tom quietly. "Yes, it's you four against me. And I know *exactly* why."

His gaze roved studiously from me, to Gatsby, and then down—where Gatsby had reached out and pulled me back by my arm. Finally, he stared between Jordan and Daisy, their hands locked. His lip curled horribly. "Aren't we all just in *love* with the worst people?"

Jordan drew her hand back and turned around, her back to us. I touched her arm gently.

"You still want to avert your gazes? Well, fine, but don't call *me* the dishonest one." Tom glared at me again. "What did Mr. Gatsby shake up in that good head of yours, Nick? I knew I was right in thinking he bent you over—"

There was another clamor, glasses falling off the table, and from the corner of my eye, I saw a glint of light. I thought at first that it had come from the windows where the sun was setting behind the skyline and artificial greenery of Central Park. But it was not the sun; the flash was cold and shiny and silver.

A blade—and its sheath was Gatsby's arm.

The mod was a ten-inch length of hard steel, and it ripped through his cotton shirtsleeve, extending out from that slit of raised flesh I'd noticed before, halfway up his forearm.

Jordan jumped back. A gasp started out of Daisy's throat but shattered halfway into a scream.

In that moment, Jay Gatsby had finally shed his most coveted lie, as swiftly as he'd shed his suit jacket, and as he threw Tom into the coffee table, that pure exterior he'd so meticulously designed was no longer. Now he was exactly the man from the whispers of his most perilous gossip—a commander of West Egg's shadows, of crooks and gangsters.

A growl rose out of Gatsby. For a second, true fear shot across Tom's face as he stared down the blade, and in turn, Gatsby's rage boiled over in the sweltering room, pinning Tom hard against the table until it snapped beneath him.

The blade tipped right up to Tom's throat—hovering, shaking, but not breaking skin—and that was when Daisy began to sob.

Gatsby hesitated, loosening himself just a fraction, but it was all Tom needed.

"Ah. There it is," he said, his laugh starting up in a storm, "old *sport.*" Then he grinned, savagely, for he knew that against all odds, he'd won today.

The victory was in the crackling fear of Daisy's eyes. Just like that, the whole spectacle of Jay Gatsby was extinguished, and with it, the blazing summer too.

"This is ... this is an old ..." Gatsby hobbled to his feet, struggling and groping for reassurances, but it was lost forever. "If you'd let me explain it—"

But she wouldn't even look at him. She'd stumbled all the way to the doors, breath heaving.

"You two start on home, Daisy. In Mr. *Gatsby's* car," said Tom happily. "Go on."

The blade retracted into Gatsby's arm, and as Daisy flitted out of the room, he reached for my wrist, which had begun to develop into a particular shade of red.

"Are you ... all right?" His hands moved, trembling, up to my face, and he turned my chin to the side to get a look at whatever welt was throbbing on my cheek.

"Go check on her."

He hesitated. There was desperation in his eyes, too, and it rattled my chest—a hopeless, dangerous urge to move into his touch.

But I didn't. "Go," I insisted, afraid for Daisy to be left alone in that state.

Slowly, he moved away and out the door. In his absence, a chill descended upon us. Jordan set the room back into some semblance of order. I registered faintly that Tom was still drinking and rambling under his breath, but it flattened to nothing in my ears. I'd forgotten, until right then, that it was the end of August.

I walked over to the windows.

"What is it?" Jordan came up beside me, holding my shoulder.

"Today ... is my birthday," I muttered.

In an instant, I was thirty, staring down the long, graceless denouement of youth. Observing the city from up in the Plaza, where the skyscrapers hung against a darkening sky, I was struck with the same odd sentiment that accompanied such things as the ironic calamity of the space probe.

How strange, I always thought, that our civilization had sent that thing out into the universe for signs of alien life, and when it had returned with precisely this evidence, hysteria had consumed us.

The shock and dread of the inevitable.

293

In quite a similar way, I knew I was never going to be twenty-nine forever, and so the arrival of the next decade shouldn't have ruptured me open. And yet, the passage of time has a way of creeping up on us all, implanting us with renewed anxieties and regrets, as if from here onward, the future would hold nothing but smoke.

When we were back in the car, Jordan leaned against me. It wasn't a casual touch; there was misery and meaning in it. I circled an arm around her, traded my melancholy for hers, and for that brief moment flying away from the Plaza, I set aside any lingering lamentations for what I couldn't become or never was.

But the evening was cooling, and something worse than smoke lay ahead.

Thirty-One

THE VERY JOURNALISTS WHO AVAILED themselves of Gatsby's hospitality that summer would go on to win awards from writing profound dissections of his sins. When inevitably they would report about what happened in the valley that evening, the most referenced account would be that of a café owner called Mr. Michaelis.

According to Michaelis, every ad-drone in the sky began to flicker.

It intrigued many residents, for a similar event had occurred some weeks before when the holo-ads had malfunctioned, or turned somewhat feral, and no one knew why. This coincided with what I remember to be the first night Gatsby had brought Daisy to the tower, but some of the more superstitious sorts in the valley had taken that violent light show to be an ill omen—a heralding of celestial doom.

One such man was George Wilson, Michaelis's neighbor across the road. He was known to be rather peculiar, but ultimately kindhearted, and his financial troubles had worn terribly on his marriage. Michaelis would thus bear witness to many of the Wilsons' spats over the years.

They were trapped in another one of these arguments that fated evening. As for Michaelis, he'd been trekking back to his shop after delivering unsold pastries around the neighborhood. Upon returning, he saw Mr. Wilson chasing his wife onto the road. Their quarrel frothed more intensely than usual, trading insults that echoed through the streets. They were so consumed by themselves, they didn't notice the drones vibrating above them.

Until, one by one, the holo-ads went dark.

Michaelis halted, just as other residents had come out to observe the bizarre spectacle too. At first, there was no cause for panic—simply mild confusion. But Michaelis sensed something was not right.

Rarely anything of note happened in this forsaken district, and a shared curiosity passed among them as they basked in the sight of the darkened holos and the rare unobstructed view of the full, clear night. For that moment, it was even peaceful.

Then the drones fell—dropping hard and fast like a thousand dead birds.

They plummeted through the dark sky, crashed into buildings, broke off into a million pieces of debris, and crushed a whole family before Michaelis's very eyes. Hail the size of a hover-car.

It was like this, several times over, across a span of sixty seconds, after which not a single ad-drone over the valley remained afloat. Blood spilled, bodies flattened, cries cut off in people's throats—dead before they could even expel a horrified shout.

The last drones to fall, in Michaelis's memory, were the ones that hovered almost exactly in the center of the valley—the eyes of Dr. T. J. Eckleburg, a mod-doc of a bygone age, whose holo-ad was as old as the place itself. It was the largest advertisement of all, with the most condensed cluster of drones required to hold it up, and so when they, too, finally dropped from the sky, it destroyed an entire building on its own.

Michaelis was certain he would die, too, for he'd been standing out in the open, unmoving, and barely managed to pull himself together, just enough to remember the Wilsons. He broke into a sprint, but it was too late.

Myrtle Wilson had been crushed from the waist down. The force severed her in two distinct pieces. Her legs, detached from her torso, were pinned beneath two large wings as her distraught husband cradled what remained of her head and chest, entrails scattered across his lap.

But it was her face that Michaelis said he would remember forever, for she possessed a unique beauty-shifting mod, and when Michaelis crouched down, he saw the woman must have been mid-shift at the point of impact.

Her hair shone half-red, half–cinnamon brown. The set of her eyes was unevenly parted, her nose bent, jaw sharper on one side and rounder on the other. She would be stuck, forever, in the middle of a glitch, buried like that—caught between herself and whatever she was trying to transform into.

When the last vestiges of her life rose up with the smoke, Wilson wailed so loudly into the night that it took Michaelis a second to hear the police sirens crescendo in the distance.

Air medics would eventually recover forty-two bodies, though this number only includes the corpses found mostly intact; it is believed the real death toll was much higher. We will never know exactly, for any demands made to investigate the incident thoroughly remain unsuccessful.

Even days after the incident, Michaelis would tell me himself later, Wilson didn't leave that spot on the street where the asphalt was darkened with his wife's blood, and he continued to gaze up, entranced, at the swath of sky where Dr. T. J. Eckleburg had abandoned them once and for all.

◇——◇——◇

Coming out of the city, we discovered a swarm of police hover-cruisers blocking out all air traffic, so we were grounded, crawling slowly for about an hour. From the Queensboro Bridge, we saw the voluminous columns of black smoke and the copper glow of what looked to be a rabid fire in the distance.

"Wreck! That's good," said Tom, once we were finally allowed to fly again, though at a lower altitude so as not to block emergency services. "That sorry valley will have a little attention at last."

But I suspected it was far bigger than a car wreck. There were twenty cruisers in front, and more blaring their sirens behind us, leading a convoy of air medics. That was when I noticed, through the thick smoke and rising flames, that the sky seemed to be unnervingly dark up ahead, as if the valley's holo-ads had all been dimmed.

"Try Daisy on the comm," I told Jordan. We'd rung her and Gatsby almost an hour earlier to inform them about the traffic, and neither had answered.

"Still nothing," confirmed Jordan.

"Let's take a look," I said. "Make sure they're not caught up in it."

Tom glanced apprehensively at the engorged smoke. There was much clamor around one spot in particular, and we were low enough to make out that it was George Wilson's street.

"Just a look," decided Tom, changing the address on the dash-holo.

We had to land carefully, so as not to be turned around by any stern officers, and once Tom's dominating elbows parted the hysterical onlookers, we found Wilson folded on the ground, in a state of total demolition. It took no less than five men to hold him steady; he was flailing, screaming incoherences that might have been holy tongues.

"What's happened to him?" demanded Tom.

"It's his wife," replied a young man standing next to us at the edge of the crowd. This was Michaelis; we'd learn that later after seeing him on tomorrow morning's news cycle.

"His—wife?" Tom choked out. "Where in God's name is *she*?"

Michaelis nodded at a medic hover-craft parked in front of the shop.

"We just came from the city," said Jordan. "What's all the mess about?"

Michaelis shook his head. He wore a white apron—or what I guessed to be white. The whole front of it had soaked through with blood. Even in that moment, I picked something precisely awful out of the grim hollowness of his face; this man had seen hell.

"They just—they shut down," he stated.

"*What* shut down?" I said, bewildered.

He gestured up, through the smoke—at a blank expanse of nothing. It wasn't that the holo-ads were not lighted, we realized. The drones themselves were gone.

Tom turned a distinct shade of green. We glanced around at the burning ruins. Jordan's hand flew to her mouth.

Wilson ruptured with another one of his cries.

"I'm a friend of his," insisted Tom to one of the officers, and when Wilson didn't refute this, they allowed us closer. Tom kneeled. "You've got to pull yourself together." He shook Wilson roughly. "Sober up, would you! Hey! Were you with Myrtle?"

298

Her name destroyed Wilson all over again.

"I told you," said Michaelis. "They've packed her away already."

The callous phrasing made us finally understand, and it was Tom who reacted last, staring far off, unresponsive, in disbelieving horror. I called his name several times, but doubtless he heard nothing. He turned wan, shaking with each breath, and wobbled toward the hover-craft, dispelling his authority upon the busy medics who made way for him.

They had stowed Myrtle Wilson in two translucent bags—her torso stacked atop her legs—and by the time Jordan and I saw it for ourselves, Tom had already curled over, emptying his stomach of the afternoon's whiskey. He vomited like that for about a minute, his hand hovering hopelessly over Myrtle's twisted face as if he were afraid she'd decay entirely with a single touch. It took both Jordan and me to bring him back to his feet.

"Gatsby drones," said one medic, watching on with distant pity. "Nothing'll come of it. I can tell you that much."

At the mention of Gatsby, Tom regained some sentience. "What was that?"

"Gatsby Corp—they acquired the whole ad space last year," replied the medic. A grave sympathy passed over the man's face, just for a second, before it dulled into plain exhaustion.

Another medic stepped around us, dumping an armful of remains into the hover-craft.

I looked down, next to Myrtle's split corpse, and saw the rusted steel and gentle old face of Mr. Edgar, peaceful in death as he hadn't been before. His cracked lips were parted, nearly smiling, as if he were still staring at the sky, the drone having crashed so quickly, he'd been spared his own fear.

I swayed. Jordan's eyes sprang with tears. She spun around.

The medic kicked the doors of the hover-craft closed. Then, like an afterthought: "If you'd like to make funeral arrangements, there are some sales associates on their way. Just ask, and they'll be glad to tell you about their discounts."

Tom retched twice more. I stared at the hover-craft until it flew off, my vision crackling, my breaths caked in my chest like cement.

Afterward, we returned to Wilson, who'd somehow been coaxed into an upright position. He was leaning against his broken nav-holo, the AI woman's image frozen still, her bluish light scarred with dead pixels.

Tom slapped a shuddering hand against Wilson's back. Then his mouth fell open with the start of some tragic sentiment, but in the end, a heavy guilt seemed to eclipse any attempt at expression. He turned away sharply.

"If somebody'll come here and—and sit with him ...," Tom called out in the general direction of the crowd. Michaelis, who'd been speaking to a bored-looking officer, broke off mid-speech and went. Then, to Jordan and me, Tom whispered, "Let's get out."

"Go without me," I said, squinting through the smoke. I couldn't see that building owned by Gen Wealth from here, but if Mr. Edgar had been caught in it, then the child—

Jordan stopped me. A flurry of panic emerged behind her eyes, and she said, almost desperately: "It's a mess, Nick. There's still debris falling everywhere. You'll upset the medics and police."

I didn't believe that was what was really on her mind. I had a gut-wrenching theory about how exactly this had all happened, and I saw that Jordan might have been forming the same thought.

She wouldn't let me run off, so we all trekked back to the Veluz, and though Tom reclaimed the driver's seat, the tremor in his hands proved too much to start the engine. I reached over him, across the dash-holo, and set the autopilot on.

It wasn't until we were halfway over the Sound that his sobs broke free, soft and fresh as raw yolk.

◇—◆—◇

There was no sign of Gatsby's car when we returned to East Egg, but the whole mansion was aglow, and there was movement in the windows.

"I ought to have dropped you in West Egg, Nick," said Tom, unexpectedly demure. The disaster at the Plaza, along with every profanity he'd thrown my way, was abandoned in the face of all that death. "I'll call for a taxi to take you home."

300

He offered to have some dinner served in the meantime, but I couldn't fathom the concept of food. I accepted the taxi and waited outside.

Jordan took my hand. It shocked me, how suddenly foreign her touch was; not even a day ago, I could have been swayed to propose at a moment's notice. Now, East Egg and its rich sins felt like a rash.

"Won't you come in, Nick?" she pleaded.

The smoke from the valley wasn't visible from here, blocked out by the large canopy of trees.

And these trees—how strange that I couldn't stand them either anymore. I once believed they were East Egg's last redeeming beauty, unmarred and rightfully preserved, but they were nothing more than an accessory now for these intangible billionaires, sheltered by the leaves' grand curtains. By their money and their names.

"No," I said.

The emotion in her eyes hardened. "Whatever righteousness you're turning over in your head, you'd best forget it," she warned.

I looked past her, inside the foyer and into the dining room, where Daisy sat motionless at the table, a cigarette between her fingers. Tom took the seat across from her, laying his hand gently upon hers.

"She doesn't need your protection," I told Jordan. "I'm not sure she even wants it. Or ever will."

I'd said something horrible—I'd wanted it to hurt—but when Jordan's anger struck me like a whip, I regretted it. She ran inside, slamming the door closed.

Grimly, I retreated down the porch. Jordan had never turned her back on Daisy her whole life. I shouldn't have expected that she'd do so now. Whether it was a dead body, or a hundred, Daisy flew above it all—and Jordan would fly with her, as long as it kept Daisy from falling.

I walked all the way to the edge of the driveway, and I remember something compelled me to pause and glance at the shadows behind the broad trimmed bushes, as if I might look over and find Gatsby hiding there, gazing forlornly through the Buchanan windows.

But he wasn't, and as I stared into the wicked darkness that stretched over the miles of blue synth-lawns, I knew I couldn't hold myself above the events of this night the way I'd held myself over the rest of the summer.

I knew if I took this or any other grotesque corpo secret to the grave, then I'd surely cosign my place in hell.

◇——◇——◇

When the hover-taxi began its descent upon my street, I spotted him—a flutter of sad pink fabric seated on the curbside. He'd forgotten his jacket at the Plaza, so he was left only in his shirtsleeves, drenched with sweat and ripped through on the right forearm.

He lifted his head as I came out of the car, rushing to his feet.

"What are you doing?" I demanded.

He had the gall to look at me wide-eyed. "Just standing here. . . . Say, did you see any trouble on your way back?"

His reduction of the valley's devastation appalled me.

"Yes," I said.

"Did anyone"—he lowered his voice uselessly—"die?"

"They've recovered about ten or fifteen bodies so far. No one's sure; in fact, they're still counting."

He slumped against a streetlight, shaking as if consumed by a wave of fever chills, before his breaths came up in panicked bursts.

"So how did it *happen?*" I snapped.

His Veluz was parked a few paces away, nearly over the curb. I guessed that he'd probably been out here for at least an hour.

"When we . . . when we left New York, Daisy was very nervous," he explained hoarsely. "We were still arguing, and she said she couldn't even stand the sound of my voice. I tried to calm her. We were flying through the valley and . . . she screamed that the holo-ads were unbearable—ugly, bright, and horrible, she said. She screamed at me to dim them. That was all I was going to do—*dim* them! But then she protested that I was too slow, so she reached over . . ."

The phantom burn of the valley's smoke stung my eyes and nose. It was exactly what I'd assumed, and yet hearing it confirmed was sickening. "She shut them off. Say it, if that's what you mean."

302

"I—I shouldn't have even let her touch the controls in that state," said Gatsby, ashen and distressed. "It was my fault. She didn't mean to, and she was horrified with herself immediately!"

"One of the drones ripped a woman—"

He paled. "Don't tell me."

"It ripped a woman in *half*—literally. She was packed away in two body cases like butchered meat." I marched toward him. I didn't care if it made him retch or sob or crumple on the street. "It brought people's living room ceilings crashing over their heads during dinnertime."

"I—I understand, Nick." He covered his mouth. "Please."

"No, you don't. None of you understand anything!"

Gatsby gulped, but it turned into a gag. West Egg throbbed around us like an open wound.

I had read somewhere that all this land was once a modest fishing village. When it hadn't yet been capitalized, it was just a sea of small cottages for folks who weren't quite fashionable enough for the mansions on the other side of the Sound. None of West Egg's historical quaintness had survived, however.

There were only the gangs now, and Gatsby's tower, and this new, infernal tragedy no one would answer for.

"I *know* it's my name on those drones. I . . . I'll make things right. . . ." Sweat dripped down his forehead. To think everything could simply be righted was a ridiculous corpo instinct that made me shove past him, but he snatched my arm first. "Nick, you've hardly looked at me since that evening you agreed to arrange tea," he murmured. "Won't you please just *listen*? For once?" As his gaze latched onto my wrist, I saw him staring intently at the half inch where the edge of my sleeve slid up—where Tom's grip had bruised me. "About Trimalchio. Was that all true?"

I scoffed. Even now, we were still squaring out our lies and secrets. "Yes. I didn't do it because of your stupid hand-delivered offer to Gen Wealth. Daisy saw the same use in me as you did. It's absurd that you never noticed."

He shook his head. "I didn't notice a lot of things." He rested his thumb gently atop the bruise. "But . . . I'm noticing now."

303

He set those words free in the hot air—so simply, so quietly—and it was as if even he were surprised to have spoken them aloud. A slow, pointed light moved through his eyes.

After all the things he'd used me for, I couldn't be used for *this*.

I tore my hand free. He was flailing now, for his tower was emptying, his girl was vanishing, and soon, he'd have nothing left. "You're feeling sad, Jay."

"What? *No*, I—" He pressed on in determination. "I just—I planned *everything* with precision. All right? For years!" He let out a choked breath. "Gen Wealth took off, the tower was built, Daisy moved across the bay, you took the damn contract, and still it all fucking crashed! Because of *you*." He held his head between his hands, hair damp and curling. "You . . . you threw off every calculation. . . ."

The suffocating edifice of his tower loomed like a sentry against the high moon, cutting a strip of shadow over us. Around the bend, at the corner of the main intersection, a bar with its windows open blew a forlorn melody out into the night.

I detested the heat that punctured every nerve in my body, how his desperate, lucid face pulled me right back into that studio antechamber—into the memory of his darkened gaze, his lips, my desire imprisoned by my distrust. A distrust that had anchored my own calculations.

That I had disobeyed to my own demise.

He reached for me. I stumbled several steps back, nearly tripping on the curb. "You're sad," I repeated hollowly. "You're anxious and scared. That's all."

"You do that a lot, don't you? Decide how people must feel, refuse to see it any other way." His mouth set in a hard line. "You never came to the tower that day . . . and I thought I'd read you wrong. Then suddenly it was too late—"

I was horrified and abruptly turned to leave. Him and his plans, his minute calculations. I refused to be blamed for them.

"I'm sorry we didn't get around to celebrating your birthday," he called out.

That shouldn't have halted me in my tracks, but it did, and I ventured a glance at him over my shoulder.

"I'd wanted to give you something," he admitted. "That is, I had a small thing prepared, but you said you wouldn't accept another gift."

I was nervous to know what his idea of a "small thing" was. I was ashamed to even be curious.

I left him there without another word. The sirens from the valley wailed on for hours, and when the sun rose to steal away the remains of my birthday, I knew I shared my life now with those burning corpses and their abandoned souls, whose lives had been so wholly stamped out on a glittering whim.

Thirty-Two

I N THE MORNING, A WEATHER alert appeared in the corner of my comm-screen, forecasting a stretch of bad air ahead, followed by the usual advisories for filtration masks.

I hadn't slept that night, but the exhaustion hadn't caught up with my adrenaline. Bunsen called me shortly before noon, informing me of some dissent between half the Fay Medica board and that of Gatsby Corp. In light of the news coverage, the acquisition was again jeopardized.

"There are some important people who think Mr. Gatsby himself ought to face a camera for the first time in his life and step down," explained Bunsen. "I know I promised you were off the account, Nick, but I don't suppose you could massage a change of heart, could you? Since you're still there?"

I sat up on the couch, rubbing my temples. "That'd be ... a big confession on his part." Moreover, it would be a lie.

But I knew the truth didn't matter. Fay Medica would mobilize at lightning speed to protect its esteemed daughter, and any hint of what truly happened would die beneath the ash.

"Well, yes," said Bunsen, "but reputation's everything, as are the demands of the shareholders."

Acquisition, reputation, shareholders. It was all ruckus, indistinct noise. I couldn't stop thinking about Mr. Edgar's serene, dead face, and when Bunsen and I hung up, I cared about nothing except making my way back to the valley.

I surveyed the view from my living room—across the bay, through the building smog and heavy clouds, the dome over East Egg had been erected. So the storm was here to stay.

◇———◇———◇

I flew a rented Veluz to the valley that afternoon. The poor visibility from the smog proved a fortunate thing. A handful of hover-cruisers still circled the skies, though not enough to spot me, and when I landed—not far from Wilson's shop—I found most of the medic teams were gone too. The only stragglers left, I assumed, were some displaced residents without any place to return to.

At the Gen Wealth facility, I saw a whole smoking drone had smashed through the revolving doors, but the rest of the structure stood quite intact. It was here, in front of the rubble, that I noticed the café owner, Michaelis, speaking animatedly with someone on his comm before he hung up in a shout of anger.

I approached him. He remembered me from the previous night and could tell I didn't live around here. He started to accuse me of being a reporter.

"I'm not," I insisted. "I came back because I'm looking for someone—a child who lived in this building? The mother was a nurse, I believe."

At this, the man became more polite and confirmed he knew them. He knew most people in that building, in fact, because he regularly delivered leftover breads and pastries around here.

"The kid's all right—physically, I mean. I have 'em sheltered up at my place with some other survivors. But you see," his voice wavered, "the mother didn't make it. A lot of folks came outside when the drones started flickering and ..." He gestured needlessly at the devastation. Then he explained he was on the comm with emergency services. "They won't come back. Won't even spare a single unit to come pull out and ID more bodies till they get some budget approved. Plus, there's a corpo-looking fellow who ran inside an hour ago and hasn't come out."

◇———◇———◇

I found Gatsby on the top floor, standing inside the unit with the loft. He had opened the small window in the kitchenette and was now leaning over the sink and breathing heavily.

I paused in the doorway and pulled my mask off. He turned. I saw that he was dressed in yesterday's clothes and his eyes were bloodshot. It was the most dreadful state I'd ever seen him in, and I felt at once a surge of pity—and then cold vindication. A single night had aged him, annihilated him, and it was still less than he was due.

"Nick." He stared as if I might have been an apparition. "I figured—I mean, I had hoped you'd come here."

He waved me over. I went reluctantly, and he shared several screens with me from his comm. I didn't know at first what I was looking at.

"I'd gone and put your ideas in motion," he said. "Went behind a lot of backs to get these approved."

I squinted at the holo-screens, stunned. They were, in fact, purchase and sale agreements.

"I was able to obtain five properties so far. Well, this building we already own, but I'm working on more—all of them. The whole land. We have to contact the individual investors, negotiate with them," he explained. "But now that most of the buildings have been destroyed, it'll be easier to get a fair price, seeing as they've lost a great deal of money. They'll want to recuperate the costs, set up their farms else-where." He swallowed. "I won't stop till I've rebuilt everything from the ground up."

Nothing about this destruction could be fixed, though it seemed he was still clinging to his impossibilities. His voice was ragged, but steady, as if perhaps he'd been standing around all morning, inhaling the smog and thinking about this. As I scrolled through the documents, I saw the earliest ones had been dated all the way back to July. Only weeks after I'd first asked him to consider it.

I gave him another hard look. "You came out here like that?"

A crown of dust motes twirled around his hair in the midday sun. "What?" he said, startled.

I shut the window. "Smog warning." By the look on his face, he hadn't even noticed the alert. "This is no biodome. Ruin your lungs another day."

I was about to throw him my own filtration mask and tell him to leave, but then he stepped out of the kitchenette, glancing up at the loft. "I always wanted to see how you made that rig." His eyes drifted

308

back to me. "Will you finally tell me why you've come all the way out here?"

"Depends. Will you finally report me to the board?"

"I'm in the process of trying not to be ousted myself." He grimaced. "Meyer thinks I'm better off pleading at their feet right now, but I know it'd be a waste."

I glanced around the apartment. It hadn't changed much since my first visit. The child's film posters and marker drawings still lined the walls, but the printed calendar was blank, no longer counting down to anything. It was odd—and dreadful—to stand amidst these small details of a home, to know the stories, to be their final witness.

But no one had cared for the valley's residents in life; it only made horrible sense that they were being abandoned in death.

"Someone has to make sure the victims get burials. It won't be the city," I told him. "Even if all the bodies can't be recovered, if they have a name and an address here, I should be able to locate them on the Gen Wealth servers. Find out if they have family and notify them."

I could see the light on Gatsby's comm blinking with incoming calls, but he ignored it for several minutes before they grew too insistent. When he went out into the hallway to answer them, I began to prepare the rig the way I had the first time I'd done it—dragging out the mattresses and pillows, lowering the thermostat. I'd brought two medium hypo shots with me and took them both.

I expected Gatsby to leave soon after, but instead, he followed me up into the loft and shared that he wanted to pay for funeral costs, as well as contract a private search team to salvage the lost bodies.

"Is that your contrition?" I kicked the monitors awake. "Throw money down until you feel better?"

He didn't answer, but silence was less grating than denial.

I stripped down to my undergarments, attached the cable to my neck. "You're right about the board. They want you out. It'll make folks on the Medica side happier." The last thing their reputation needed was more mass death. "Since you already know what my actual job is, there's some truth for you, if you care for it. You've struggled with that all these months."

"And *you* haven't?"

I stared at him. *"What?"*

"Accepting my invitations, digging up my identity, just to record them for some intel reports?" he muttered, and there was a flicker of real hurt behind his eyes. "You knew my name. I *still* don't know yours. How are those not lies too, Nick?"

The apartment grew colder as we waited, but the heat of his body simmered like a furnace beside me.

"They were." I ran my thumb over my wrist, the comm-light winking. "But I couldn't control my assignment. The moment it was finished, I wanted to start over." I felt the weight of his eyes move across the bare expanse of my back. "You brought me here in the first place. You could have told me who you were at any time."

"I was going to," he insisted. "When I came by after the studio—"

"You came by," I recalled, "and you still put it off."

His face blanched in the harsh light of the monitors. "It began dishonestly, but it didn't end that way. All of it was true to me. I can't stand to have you think otherwise."

I thought back to the last time I'd been here, with Jordan, under such different circumstances. I'd known nothing about him then; I almost hadn't wanted to, for perhaps he could have remained like that forever in my mind—nothing more than the attentive stranger I'd met in an elevator, cramped between East Egg men, unburdened.

"When you took me to the studio," I admitted, "I asked why you'd care for my company. You told me all those—things." *You are something else.* Had I been damned ever since? Perhaps I was compromised all the way back then, even before Tom had shouted it in the hotel. "You told me you'd like to receive my invitation one day. I would have liked to offer it. If you had meant it."

Gatsby moved toward me. "You think I didn't?"

It was an absurd question, but he was full of these absurdities, even now. "Daisy took up all the space in the room. All the air in your chest. What else was I supposed to think?"

The apartment had grown frigid, and soon our breaths were forming soft clouds.

"The thing about Daisy is ... she has all these faces, and you can't ever be sure which one's true," he murmured. "Sometimes you love someone like a bad habit. You love them because it's all you've ever known how to want, and you don't know who you'd be otherwise." His chest heaved with each inhale. "And suddenly when you realize there's something else you want just as much—if not more—you try impossibly to have both. Only to ruin it all."

The words fell from him like plucked flower petals, delicate and helpless.

By the time the thermostat beeped, it came as a relief from my own swirling thoughts. I hoisted myself swiftly up onto the loft railing, jumped, and the mindless calm of cyberspace washed over me.

⟡—◇—⟡

I scarcely remember the following weeks. I spent most of that period in the cramped loft, floating through the valley, collecting names and cross-referencing who was alive or dead with the help of Michaelis. It proved a larger task than a single dive, for the strain of the make-shift rig took a harsh toll on me, and I couldn't handle more than a few short bursts at a time.

Protestors came in droves to West Egg, staking out Gatsby's tower. As everyone had stayed caustically silent about the valley, there was nowhere else for people to put their rage and grief. After a series of riots broke out on our street, police officers had been stationed around the neighborhood and in the skies, keeping nonresidents out. Too much of the public was starting to question the quality of all hover-tech—in ad-drones, in cars, in the floating coastal districts.

It wouldn't amount to anything worthwhile. Soon the corps bullied protests off the news cycle, and days later, coverage of the incident ceased altogether.

Gatsby shadowed me, mostly in silence. He refused to be dismissed, so he sat around and made his calls. From my eavesdropping on a few of them, it sounded as if his friction with the board was reaching irreconcilable levels. I didn't care for his business matters, but he kept his word on the funeral payments and the private search team.

In a strange and unspoken way, he'd also fallen into the habit of helping me in and out of the rig.

One night, as he was detaching the cable from my neck and handing me my clothes, I saw him staring at a spot on my face, and I realized it must have been the bruise from my scuffle with Tom, still sore. I hadn't glimpsed myself in a mirror for a while. I wondered if the mark had swollen into its worst color.

I poked the tender skin. "I should mod it over."

"No. It's healing." Gatsby moved my hand away. "It's good to see it heal."

They were the first words we'd exchanged in a while. I decided to finally ask him about his arm-mod. He seemed to carry some shame about it, which didn't surprise me, given how badly he wanted to be an East Egg man. After a careful pause, he told me the long story anyway—of how he'd fallen into a certain crowd in his adolescent years, to care for himself and his parents, how the mod was a rite of passage, and so was using it.

That night, for the first time, "James Gatz" became something more than an unwanted figment of Jay Gatsby's past.

"Killing because you have to ... and killing because you want to— they're two very different things," he said.

Neither of us had eaten all day, and we sat together on the dusty apartment floor, picking at a few day-old rolls that Michaelis had offered me that morning.

"I swore once I left that life behind, if I were to ever unsheathe this thing again, it would be out of necessity. After all this time, there's only been one exception—where I was sure I could have killed a man from my own anger and nothing else," he confessed. "It surprised and terrified me too. . . ."

I watched, holding my breath, as his gaze shifted from the bruise on my cheek to the one on my wrist.

◇——◇——◇

I don't recall falling asleep that night, but I distinctly remember waking up before sunrise. A long pile of unanswered messages from Bunsen lit up my comm, demanding a progress report.

312

Gatsby lay beside me on the mattress, out in the living room, just inches away. I'd forgotten to adjust the thermostat, so the apartment froze like the cruel chill of a December night.

I sat up slowly and noticed a fine suit jacket had been draped over my shoulders.

I stared at him. He lay on his back, making soft noises and shivering. His eyes moved erratically. His lips fluttered. One particular section of his fringe curled down over his forehead like a dewdrop.

After a long moment, I returned his jacket, settling it across his chest. His body relaxed into itself.

"James," I whispered, tasting the shape of it.

Thirty-Three

THE SEASON SHIFTED WITHOUT WARNING, fogging up windows and diffusing the sunlight so that a bleak veil loomed over the autumnal dawn.

My mother called, demanding to know why I hadn't returned to Manila. The news of the drones, and their proximity to me, disturbed her. She wanted me to leave right away, but the valley was far from restored and I couldn't abandon what I'd started.

She informed me that my "boss" had reached out to tell her about my promotion.

I hung up and rang Bunsen. "You spoke to my *mother?*"

"Fuck, Nick, you can't go static. Marcelo thought you turned coat!" A flurry of noise gargled in the background, as if he were marching briskly through a chaotic office. "It's been three weeks. Why's that Gatsby not done anything yet? He's been soft on you all summer, and *now* you can't get through to him?"

I swore I'd heard an insinuation like that in his tone before, but I'd always convinced myself otherwise. "Bunsen," I snapped. "Whatever the hell you're trying to say, sabihin mo ng derecho."

He sighed. "I've done this job, too, all right? Sometimes we play the role too well—I understand that. But no matter what a corpo tells you"—his voice sharpened—"huwag kang magpapaloko."

I bit the inside of my cheek, leaning against the balcony railing, taking in the tower's vast, dark windows ahead. There was nothing to say, for I'd done just that all along—looking out for myself, disbelieving everything that fell from Gatsby's lips.

And yet, I was still here, staring out at that monument across the street, as if waiting for the lights to come on again.

"Look, I'm speaking as a friend," said Bunsen tiredly. "I'm the only thing keeping Marcelo from benching you—by force. If you won't run point, you'd better come back." A door opened and shut; the background clamor hushed to a muffle. "Mag ingat ka."

A flight itinerary appeared on my comm-screen.

◇——◇——◇

The next day, I heard a great commotion coming from Gatsby's. Looking out, I saw several hover-crafts were parked on his landing pad along with a procession of bots. He was emptying the tower.

I remembered that I still had something of his—the clothes he'd loaned me the night we went swimming—and I packed them up, then went across the street.

I found him standing right in the entrance, stone-faced, dressed in a wrinkled pajama set. Around us, the bots flew in and out of the elevators, carrying furniture and confetti machines and the rest of his ritzy props.

He startled when he saw me. "I'm just selling all the knickknacks. They're worth a great deal, and the money could be put to use." He called them "knickknacks" in that impersonal way, as if up to now he still didn't know what things he owned exactly.

We went to the rooftop, where the dome was up to keep out the persistent smog. The pool of neon milk had been drained, the conveyor belt torn from the railings, and all the light fixtures disassembled. Never again would actors and politicians kiss beneath his holograms or dance to explosive arrangements of "Jazz History of the World." It was so unremarkable in its barrenness, I could have been convinced that his parties had been a hallucination all along.

"The board has grown quite upset with me, but I fear I need as much sway as I can get to fund the reconstruction of the valley." A conflict tore across his face. "I don't know if I can do that if I step down now."

315

I finally informed him that I was leaving for Manila early in the morning.

He blinked. "Leaving?"

"I'm supposed to persuade you to step down, or else I'm compromised and they have to pull me from the assignment," I said. "Do what you want. Just be warned there's a battle ahead."

"I see. Perhaps I'd hoped this restoration project would have been your good reason to stay." He cleared his throat. "Here. Or I meant in New York."

He hadn't phrased it as a question, but it settled between us like one. I realized it *was* my good reason to stay, but I couldn't cross the firm unwisely. "They've got my comm on lock. They could fold me any minute. If I tamper with it, it's a contract breach, and someone will be on my tail. More importantly," I said, "most of your security system is still offline, isn't it? All the androids are gone except for Ewing. I don't think you should remain here, given the state of things."

He promised he'd address it soon. I offered to take a look at his surveillance system at least.

"This floor is still perfectly locked," he insisted. "I'll be fine."

For some reason, I couldn't bring myself to leave yet. He might have sensed some of my reluctance and shared it, for we both loitered a little longer. I knew he'd been in and out of some Midwestern domes during his formative years, but it shocked me to learn he'd spent so much time in St. Paul. In our early lives, we'd never been more than three domes apart.

"We could have met so many different ways," I said.

He smiled at the thought. Then he finally told me about the financier, Dan Cody, who had chanced upon him in his youth and lifted him into salvation. "That's why I believe in miracles," he reminded me. "Meeting Mr. Cody was nothing short of divine intervention. What are the chances, you'd say, that a corpo such as him would have plucked me from the streets and made his ward? Taken me out of the gang life of the outer domes? Shown me all the ways to be a convincing gentleman?"

I understood now why Gatsby loved his miracles, his fairy tales, his splendor. The strings of fate had danced for him once, and he'd spent all his years after trying to make them dance for him again. Despite the severity of his idealism, I certainly couldn't deny such rare luck.

His parents—in his words—had been "mod junkies," addicted to all manner of cybernetic procedures and the painkillers administered for them. Gatsby had sworn he'd never turn out like that himself. He hadn't, though in the end, he'd turned to bootlegging. After things began to fare well with Gen Wealth, he never meant to continue on with the business, but by then, his empire had become its own addiction.

"When you mentioned you'd wanted to become an outer-dome mod-doc, it reminded me of them," he said. "My parents—well, perhaps there are many things that could have turned out differently."

His family, I could tell, was the most painful bit of his past to share, in full-color truth.

But listening to him recount his whole life, I had the impression he'd been performing a card trick all summer, a sleight of hand, and though I knew it the whole time, he'd finally revealed to me the secret about how it was done. It was strange to observe—not because I believed in magic, but rather because a part of me, right up until the end, had still believed in "Gatsby."

◇——◇——◇

His private suite hadn't been touched by the moving-bots yet. In his bedroom, I finally relinquished the clothes.

"I'd like for you to keep them," he said.

"I won't."

"Then return them when you're back."

"I don't know when that will be. Or if returning here"—I waved around at the room, signifying the whole tower—"would be a good idea."

"'A good idea?'" he repeated blankly. "What do you mean?"

"I mean you have work to do. So do I." I frowned. "Let's leave it at that."

"You're doing it again." The tension in his face ruptured, scattering all his emotions out like light through a prism. "Deciding how things *must* be."

317

It stunned me that he could still make space for anything despite the guilt and regret of all that had happened. What he was asking of me wasn't just another small favor. In his desperate eyes, I saw he wanted my trust again, even after we'd already obliterated each other's.

Optimism was its own kind of defiance, and if there was anything I'd learn from Gatsby, it was that he'd swim perpetually in the bottom-less ocean of his own longings, while the rest of us were treading water in our cynicism. He made it seem so easy.

"It could have been different," I replied, and he was staring back as if he could see inside me. "Perhaps if you ... hadn't built 'Gatsby' for someone else. If I'd met you another way." I set the clothes on the edge of the bed. I could tell he hadn't slept here in a long time. The sheets were made up perfectly.

"All I've wanted is for you to believe me." His words picked up speed. "What do *you* want? Can you even tell me that? After I've told you everything there is to know about me, I can't even know your name? *I'm* still the liar?"

I closed my eyes. "Jay, it doesn't—"

"'Matter'? But it does." Around us, the silence vibrated, and I sensed the hard snap of his insistence right before he cried out, "I'm trying to tell you I was wrong, Nick." I heard him cross the room, and the dark floors began to spin. "How many different ways should I say it?"

I stood there, paralyzed, unable to look at him.

"You made me question everything the moment I met you," he continued. "And the night you brought me into your world—at the market—I didn't want it to end. And the evening I had tea with Daisy, and Miss Baker dropped you home in that disheveled state, I lost sleep for days because I ..." His voice broke. "I wasn't supposed to want you like that."

He took another slow step toward me, and I turned—fractionally, unthinkingly—to meet that terrifying earnestness of his.

A herd of police lights flared through the windows.

The world beyond still burned; it beckoned and it screamed. They were the sounds of our nightmares, and yet, in a single instant, it all receded into another realm, flung far away by his foolish devotion. I felt the pressure of his hand on my back.

"Have I used enough words yet? I'll find more. I'll invent languages—"

I hung my head. "You can't mean that."

"Why not?" he demanded.

Because of Daisy. Because of this tower. Because we were standing in a heaven he'd created for one concentrated shot of a dream. Because, because, because—

"Why *not*, Nick?" A murmur. A plea.

There was always a reason, a way out.

But he was cradling my face, and I knew then that I was trapped, and the reasons had already coalesced into one frightening truth.

Because I want you too.

He stole the confession from me, bending forward, our lips crashing, and I felt it move through his whole body in a violent shudder, a storm of desire taking shape in the room, as thick as the smog outside and just as lethal. The taste of him, impossibly, was familiar, like stepping into an ancient memory, freshly remembered—as if he had kissed me a thousand times before, in other lifetimes and in other ways.

I tumbled into the velvet bed. He chased after me, his knees hugging the sides of my hips. I made a sound that might have been his name, and he ground harder against me, tearing open my shirt and the buckle of my slacks. His teeth found my jaw, throat, collarbone, whispering unheard secrets into my chest, down my stomach. The Victorian ceiling blurred, and I became boneless, immaterial.

He pulled my knees apart, palms sliding up my thighs, with a feverish impatience in his movements and—I realized with a high keen—in his mouth, too, as he took me in.

I felt a hum in his throat. He drew himself up. "Of course you'd be so ... proportionate," he muttered, his voice a quiet rasp, as though he were speaking just to himself.

I swore I heard him wrong, or perhaps I was imagining him entirely. I wanted to drag him onto me again. "Proportionate?"

He blinked slowly, cupping me where his mouth hadn't reached. "To the rest of you," he said; then he was staring at me in a way that one stares at a piece of commissioned art—as if in surprised satisfaction that the final product matched the specifications in his head.

"Is that—" I couldn't even attempt to summon any levity, to say it as a joke. There was nothing light in his own gaze. Only a dark, intense focus. "Is that what preoccupies you?"

"You can't even begin to imagine." He pulled my slacks down the whole way, kissing the inside of my knee. "Since that terrible mistake I made, inviting you to the pool."

I writhed beneath him, but he held me in place, gently determined, and I remembered the night we'd flown around this room together, zero gravity, and still it was nothing like this—the heat of his tongue or the consoling pressure of his hands on my hipbones.

I stroked my finger along his face, at the perfect, tempting jut of his cheekbone, and then I felt, almost immediately, in a surge of inexhaustible pleasure, the way his throat relaxed, eyes alive like melted stars. I moved my hand from his face to his neck, pinching the fine hairs at his nape. His breath caught, and he pulled away as if completely under my command, and it was all over for me then.

I'd reached the final state of a permanent, carnal evolution that had started, perhaps, the moment he'd smiled at me in his elevator.

I sat up, crawling over him. He gasped, surprised, his mouth raw and glistening. I grazed his lip with my thumb, my knee pressed to the hard warmth between his legs as my hand dipped below his undergarments, around the curve of his waist, and lower. He groaned, and suddenly I knew, with the certainty of a god, the depths and contours of my own desire.

I kissed it into his neck and up to his ear—*can I take you like this?*—and he rolled his hips against me, expelling a noise from his throat that would follow me absolutely to the ends of the earth.

"Can I?" I said, aloud this time.

He couldn't manage a word. I stared, entranced, as the last of his great, unflappable persona liquefied beneath me, from nothing but my hands and mouth. Was it that simple this whole time? The thought turned my blood into heady wine. His chin lifted in what might have been a nod, but it was as if every thread within him couldn't weave into coherence.

320

"Jay." I touched his cheek. His eyes fluttered, struggling to stay open. "You need to say—"

"*Yes* . . .," he panted. "Yes, but I don't—" There were teeth in his next kiss, his thirst violent and exquisite. "I . . . don't know how I'll survive you."

He wanted me to believe him. Now I had no choice, for I could see it with my own eyes as he gazed up at me, pliant and beautiful, and I'd never known I was a greedy man until then.

I had taken Jay Gatsby apart, and I didn't want to put him back together for anyone.

He lay there, shuddering as I undressed him, whining into the first stretches and low praise, and when he relaxed just enough to let me inside, the room flooded with the gold rays of his want, until he fractured inexorably against the dark velvet.

He was a magic trick, I thought again. A holy spirit, a close encounter, a miracle.

◇——◇——◇

I stayed with him into the night. As we lay together, I felt a strange buzz of nostalgic euphoria, as if longing for a memory that hadn't even formed yet, that I was still living in.

He settled himself between my thighs, and I let him lick a stripe across my jaw, up to my ear. "I can't stand it," he whispered. "It infuriates me."

"What?"

He kissed the bone at the junction of my neck. "No one's supposed to be born like this, just so—"

"At the studio, in the antechamber, when you stopped me," I recalled, "what did you really 'want'?" I'd done a poor job at forgetting that, despite my best efforts.

"What do you *think*, Mr. Carraway?"

At the corner of my mouth, he pulled my lip between his teeth, and then I could hardly think at all.

"You know"—he brushed my hair from my forehead—"I'd step down if it meant freeing you from the account. You'd have done what they wanted you to do. And you've never liked the work."

"That's a terrible gauge for making business decisions." I caught his wrist. "Stepping down could be dangerous. The board members will be able to move as they please without you in the room."

"But I'll be scaling mudslides in those rooms forever. I'd still have Meyer on the inside, and funding-wise, I've got my off-book accounts." He turned his hand over, threading our fingers together. "It could work."

I rose from the bed. "I still have to go, figure out how to be off-boarded, sign NDAs—"

"That's what comm-mail is for."

"I thought you didn't know what that is. Seeing as you've never used it," I teased, relocating my clothes and shrugging back into my shirt. "I also have to get my comm scrubbed. It's like being in the army again, bomb in my wrist, day in and day out." I fumbled through the buttons. "Until then, send Ewing on a plane with more letters."

He hooked his arm around my stomach and dragged me back onto the bed. "I'm serious, Nick. We'll replace your comm first thing tomorrow. Leave the suits to me." His fingertips crawled over my chest, parting the folds of my shirt, and I thought he was invoking his miracles again, but his eyes were serious. "I just want you to have a choice for once."

Then he spoke about running away to somewhere gorgeous and quiet. That was far less serious, but for a short while, we were suspended in time and a dream, allowing ourselves to share a fantasy of a place where the things that had been broken here wouldn't follow us.

He unfastened my shirt buttons. "Have I earned your name yet?"

"You're still going on about that?"

"You have mine. I want yours. Fair trade."

I smiled. "You can have it if you're patient."

"I'm not," he assured me. He did not have a corpo's hands. His palms were rough, unmodded, as they moved from my chest, down my torso, and across the skin he'd etched through with his teeth. Each callus seemed to hold an untold story.

Just one more night, I thought selfishly. "If you won't let me leave, then let me sleep."

His laughter was bright with victory. "But why leave it for the morning? The moon keeps secrets, and the sun confesses them—first words you ever said to me, remember?"

322

I wrestled out of his arms, but when he pushed down my shoulders again, I relented.

"Give me something to tide me over." He threw his leg over my hips. "A hint."

He shifted on top of me. He was hard again, and I reached up to pull his neck down. "It means . . . 'clear,'" I replied. "Sometimes, 'peace.'"

His smile grew slowly at this, like a shadow stretched under shifting sunlight. I traced a finger along the smooth skin of his nape, where perhaps in another life, the diving mods would have been implanted just like mine. A matching set. He exhaled, lowering himself, our chests sliding together.

"They're a rotten crowd, James," I whispered into his lips. "You're worth the whole damn bunch put together."

His eyes were glazed, red with emotion. Perhaps he didn't believe me. Perhaps it wasn't even true. But I wanted him to know I meant it—that he was always most worthy as himself.

It didn't matter that everything would go up in flames all over again. Right then, he was infallible, banishing any final anguish I'd harbored for falling in love with him, for I'd never stood a chance. I was certain that Gatsby—James Gatz, as he became in my arms—resembled one of those strange creatures that could register colors imperceptible to human eyes.

I wanted to be that person James Gatz believed I was. I wanted to be all the colors he saw in me, to believe in his miracles. To hold onto his infinite faith in the smog-filled future.

[LOADING]

.

.

.

[PLAY]

"Dreams? I only want simple things. I want to build mods that make folks happy. I want my wife to have anything she wants. You're probably wondering how a woman like her fell in love with a fellow like me. . . . Well, she was a singer once, had big dreams for Broadway, but sacrificed a lot to marry me. I'm going to make it up to her by giving her a good life. Of course, that's not easy now. That's why I'd like to start my shop. The valley's all we can afford at the moment."

"Mr. Wilson."

"Yes?"

"You seem a good man. But you're in a—*niche* business. By the law's standards, that is. There'll be some risk to the owners you're renting from, and that's going to be reflected in the price. Not to mention the valley's a harsh place to live and work."

"Harsh?"

"Well, it changes a man, living in a place like that. A lot of our clients are residents there. We see the effect it has on good people."

"Oh, I'll be all right. I know I'm not the smartest or strongest or handsomest, but I strive to be guided by goodness at all times—even when things aren't looking up, you know. Even if things in life go awry. That's God's truth."

[STOP]

.

[ERROR—]

.

[ERROR: ACCOUNT NOT FOUND]

Thirty-Four

I N THE BLUE THRUM OF twilight, I woke to Ewing's hand rustling my shoulder, alone between cold sheets.

Alone in a new world.

I couldn't recount this day any better in the moment than I can now, after two years. What is there to say, except that I don't believe I've ever really left that bed? That death isn't just a fiery crash of pain or a dot of light in a tunnel, but the crisp nothingness where a warm body should be?

The night had kept its secrets, and the sun had stolen them away.

◇——◇——◇

On Wednesday, September 25, 2075, George Barrett Wilson entered the residence of Jay Gatsby, president of Gatsby Corp, at 4:38 a.m.

It was reported that Wilson flew a stolen Veluz from the valley to West Egg, armed with an assault rifle arm-mod, implanted just seventy-two hours before. The smog, which had pervaded the skies all month, had allowed him to slip through West Egg's police presence undetected. There was much confusion about how Wilson had been able to enter Gatsby's tower, however. The initial speculation was that he'd been working in tandem with a skilled netdiving team that'd commandeered the security system, or that he was at least cunning enough that Mr. Gatsby had somehow allowed him inside.

But according to Wilson, it was simply that he'd walked through the front door.

When he found Gatsby, around the tower's fortieth floor, he emptied a whole round into the man's chest before calling the police on himself.

Sitting in a pool of Gatsby's blood, Wilson was "cooperative" and "extremely polite" about his arrest. Why had he done it? Well, it was Mr. Gatsby who killed his wife and so many others, of course. It was Mr. Gatsby's drones that fell carelessly from the sky, tearing down God himself, and if there would be no justice, then at the very least, there ought to be retribution.

Did Mr. Gatsby struggle? No, said Wilson. At the time of his death, Mr. Gatsby was, in fact, submerged peacefully in a Happy Sleep.

◇——◇——◇

When Ewing concluded his recitation of the report, the police presence in West Egg had tripled, concentrated in the skies above the tower. Their sirens ebbed and flowed, tides of red light rising and rising through the windows.

There was no oxygen in the bedroom. A hard, violent pressure burgeoned in my throat, swallowed my lungs, a gush of acid.

He couldn't be gone, I thought, because I'd fallen asleep holding him.

Because, because, because—

"There was an urgent matter he wanted to attend to in his Happy Sleep lounge, sir," said Ewing. "I was ordered not to wake you." He paused. It was an odd thing to see an android hesitate—a small but devastating trick of technology that replicated the very human instinct of sympathy. It was only in that hesitation that this dark new world became incarnate. "I apologize, sir, but I must also inform you that you are needed in the dining room."

I can't remember how I stood up, but it must have happened eventually. My feet moved me out of the bedroom as the first tendrils of dawn stretched across the floor. Glancing down the windows, every club, shop, and bar across West Egg seemed to have leaked onto the street, making a howling scene before the tower doors. Furious flashes from a swarm of camera-bots went off from somewhere below, and gathered in the dining area was a pair of tired, mumbling suits who

shook my hand in tandem, sharing their comm-screens. Holo-badges—
police detectives.

I was told to give my account of the night. Two hours vanished in
a barrage of questions, corroborated shortly after by Ewing's cam-feed.
When they left, another woman came out of the elevator.

She introduced herself as an estate lawyer. "You're Mr. Carraway?"
I said I was.

She had a name, too, but as with all things from that day, I didn't
catch it. We sat at the dining table. She clasped her hands together
formally. I remember hating this formality the most, her unaffected
sternness.

He couldn't be dead, my mind whirred uselessly, because I was still
warm where he had touched me.

Because, because, because—

"I've been told you were a Gen Wealth diver. But beyond that?"
She considered my casual, rumpled clothes.

"What's this about?" I demanded.

It was a matter of Gatsby's assets, she explained, and threw the
paperwork up between us—ownership of the tower, his shares of
Gatsby Corp, access to all his bank accounts, and more.

I blinked at the holo-screens in shock. "Why—why are you ...
telling me all this? Doesn't he have a will? An inheritor?"

The lawyer regarded me, stunned. "Mr. Carraway," she said carefully.
"It's *you*."

◇——◇——◇

Fanfare splintered West Egg throughout the day, brought on by the
news of Gatsby's death. Some concerns that the tower would be targeted
again were shared among the officers, so in the afternoon, an NYPD
diver came by to reinforce the surveillance systems, patching a link
from the alarms to the nearest police station. Come evening, the streets
were cordoned off, and the officers, medics, and reporters finally left.

Ewing led me to a wing of the private suite that I had never seen
before. It was Gatsby's study, a small cave hidden down a narrow hall
behind the bedroom. In the corner, cutting elongated shadows across

the hardwood, a fireplace spit softly into the silence. I took a seat behind the rustic oak desk whereupon a lit holo-bar, displaying Gatsby's will, glowed brightly in the dark room.

Ewing requested my arm. I asked what for.

"To transfer the tower controls to you, sir."

A hot, needle-point pain prickled in my chest.

So he had left me with this hollow skyscraper—not a home anymore, just an undead memory, and I felt myself plunging unwillingly into its bowels. I stared at the crackling fireplace, inside of which I could still see the valley's crashed drones, and I was sure I would see them forever. The ghosts and sins and their dying embers.

Reluctantly, I offered Ewing my comm, and he pressed our wrists together. A series of screens flared up like a lit match.

"Ewing."

"Sir."

"The funeral. When is it?"

"It is for you to arrange and decide." That unsettling hesitation again. "Although the board has advised that if there is to be a funeral, that it be a private affair. As you know, the public opinion at this time is that Mr. Gatsby rather deserved—"

"Ewing."

"Sir."

My head spun. "*Why* did he do it?"

"Sir?"

"I told him ... I told him I disliked his gifts."

Now I was shackled to them—his riches and his burdens.

"I am not quite capable of speculation, Mr. Carraway, but I can think to tell you this," said Ewing. "Mr. Gatsby did not write a will until recently. I don't believe he ever thought you'd even know about it. Mr. Gatsby never thought much of death, you see."

Of course he hadn't. Anti-aging mods were getting cheaper on the market by the day, and aside from his own self-aggrandizement, the death of a billionaire was an event less common than calamitous tsunamis or raging blizzards.

"You're saying he put me down as his sole inheritor on a—whim?" I said, incredulous.

"Not a whim. A formality," explained Ewing. "I believe it was his good friend, Mr. Meyer, who warned Mr. Gatsby that if he didn't write a proper will, then should an unlikely event like death occur, the board would close in on his assets. That was the last thing Mr. Gatsby wanted. As you know, he had no family, so he arranged for Mr. Meyer to be his inheritor. That is, until he decided to list you instead, Mr. Carraway."

I dismissed Ewing and walked from the desk to the leather couch opposite the fireplace, sitting gingerly upon the cushions, unyielding as if they had never seen use. My eyes drew to a spot of color on my wrist, kissed less than a day ago into my skin—the marks on my body the last proof that he'd ever been alive.

Unlikely. The word reverberated like a gunshot. Gatsby's unlikely life, unlikely death, unlikely money. In the end, his miracles were made of the same stuff as his tragedies.

"You're a fool, James," I whispered into the empty room.

The fireplace before me streaked like watercolors. I shivered.

The tears fell and the pain surged and I was dragged into the tower's fragile pulse—his waning voice, a deathless song in the distance. . . .

Miracles are everywhere, if you just know where to look. . . .

Indeed, Gatsby had forced his own miracle upon me—his precipitous, infinite wealth—as if even from beyond the grave, he was determined to prove me wrong.

GENERATIONAL WEALTH INC. DATA BREACH
INVESTIGATION (CASE STATUS: OPEN)
TRANSCRIPT: ETTY ANAND (AGE: SEVENTY-ONE)
LOCATION: HEADQUARTERS, GATSBY CORPORATION
(NEW YORK CITY, NEW YORK, NEA)
DATE: JUNE 15, 2077

[LOADING]

.

.

.

[PLAY]

"The Gen Wealth gallows were yours to run, but when the breach was detected, it was far too late. Then you and your entire team quit. Interesting timing."

"Damn right, I quit! I had to protect my people from an impossible nightmare to solve. You think I haven't seen dens turn into *real* gallows from breaches like this? From the overtime and the punishments? I've seen it all. When you've unhooked half as many hanged bodies as I have in my life, you'd walk away too. You want someone to lock up? It won't be me."

"If you know something, Mrs. Anand, tell us. You'll be rewarded."

"You suits haven't gotten a single lead, have you? You don't know what you're up against."

"How do you mean?"

"I've been in this field a long time—back when diving was something you did in a dark basement with any junkie who was just as

331

crazy as you. Back when the dive could melt your brain through your ears. You forget the first divers in the world used to drive empires into the ground over their morning coffee."

"Mrs. Anand, it sounds awfully like you *do* know more than you're admitting to."

"What I know, Chairman, is that you're trying to catch a damn good diver. But the truth about all damn good divers? They can't drown."

[STOP]

[ERROR—]

[TRANSCRIPT DELETED]

Part IV

The Orgastic Future

Thirty-Five

BEFORE DAWN, I WALKED TO the nearest mod-doc. To call it a clinic would be charitable. It operated out of the cellar of a speakeasy, between wine racks and piles of vacuum-sealed synth-meat. I'd followed the twitching holo-signs through the dingy bar and down the stairs, as brooding patrons threw me dubious glances before returning to their whispered conversations.

"I'll pay double if you work fast," I told the young doc who was snoring behind a counter with a lukewarm beer in hand. She jerked awake with a snort. "Need a new comm. Full replacement."

Her neon-blue eyes peeled open, irritated, eyelids blinking vertically like the pages of a book. "Crew?" she sighed.

"Not local."

"Then either you're a corpo or a soldier on the run. Whatever it is, no one wants trouble right now." She finished her beer, shooing me away. "Big man in the tower got himself shot yesterday. Got what was coming, if you ask me, but downside is the whole Egg's crawling with PD. Emergencies only, yeah? Come back if you're dying."

She turned. I picked up her empty beer bottle, smashed it against the counter, then pressed the sharp point of a large glass shard into my comm-sensor. I gritted my teeth, smothering the pain, as a geyser of blood sprang from my wrist.

"*Hey!*" the woman exclaimed. "What the *fuck* is wrong with—"

"It's an emergency." I threw the shard aside. "You have five minutes to override it."

She stared at me in disgust, then with exasperation at the blood staining her concrete floors. "Double," she muttered. "Hurry up, then. Fucking suit."

My vision feathered, jolting my synapses into hot little sparks. "No suits here."

◇———◇———◇

I did not step outside for a week after. Though entry into West Egg opened again, the street remained blocked by police. Once or twice, I swore a stray car was flying closer to the tower than it should, but if Trimalchio had sent someone after me, I didn't know and wasn't sober enough to care.

Days later, I received an invitation to an event from Newtonia Orchid. The first Gatsby Corp Happy Sleep lounge in Manhattan was unveiling a beta-launch of their new memory diamonds, and it would be an honor if I attended, they wrote, as the data from my session at the studio had greatly aided this prototype. I went, compelled by some horrified curiosity, for Gatsby had thrown so much behind the project and I wanted to know what had enamored him so.

A large media presence swallowed the venue as I arrived. Orchid's demo had attracted news outlets across the globe. Not only had their team developed the most significant innovation of virtual entertainment, but the advancements made in their research would soon open doors to a stunning application the world still could not presently comprehend.

"Technological reincarnation," they announced.

Those were the words spoken aloud, but, of course, what everyone heard was "immortality." Together with scientists and doctors from Fay Medica, they were one step closer to preserving human conscious-ness past death and implanting it into advanced androids. The newest models of Klipspringers would thus be developed for their next phase of experiments.

I couldn't bear much more past that, so I left and began wandering the empty lounge rooms.

The fixation on helping the wealthy live forever, instead of helping everyone else live at all, poked some dormant violence within me anew.

The oversaturated fog of summer had long dissolved, and I'd awoken wholly from a deep, poisonous slumber, as if in looking back at my own memories, I might have been remembering someone else's life. I'd spent so much time judging these egotistical corpos while drinking their champagne, determined not to be overly frustrated with the cruel world as long as I never had to touch such cruelties with my bare hands.

But I'd touched it now. I'd groped all the sharp edges on my way here, to the top. I'd cut myself on so much brokenness, I could no longer pretend I wasn't bleeding.

An indescribable and ridiculous sequence of events had brought me to this mountain of riches, to this convention of immortality, and the ceiling of that madness finally caved in on me.

By this point, I'd been wandering around the lounge so long that for a moment I forgot where I was. I found myself in front of one of the premium rooms—spacious, done up in magenta-hued gauze, and alluringly dim. I sank tiredly into the L-shaped couch opposite the terminal and stared at the blinking green light, realizing it would have been the last thing Gatsby saw before he went under and never surfaced.

To die in his lounge, of all places, for something as "urgent" as those spec Sleeps.

A bad habit, he'd called it. One he hadn't quite shaken, in the end.

Suddenly, the door of the room slid open, revealing a gaunt-looking Tom. He stood there in the entrance with a parted mouth, tight brows, and my name on his lips. When he held out his hand, I stood up, attempting to move past him.

He blocked me with his broad body. "What's the matter, Nick? Do you object to shaking hands with me?" He was unshaven, the lines of his face more sunken than usual.

"Yes," I said. "You know what I think of you."

He stared at me with scorn, but the expression faded, as if it took an unsustainable amount of energy to stock his usual rancor and he couldn't manage it now. I could tell, despite the depth of his intoxication at the Plaza, that he hadn't forgotten what he'd hurled in my face that afternoon and what I'd said in return.

"You're crazy, Nick," he muttered. "Crazy as hell. . . ."

He didn't say this with much anger; more like it was a recent observation he'd made that he was still processing.

"What are you doing here?" I snapped.

He hesitated before moving slowly into the room. In front of the terminal, he lifted two headsets out of their cases and handed one to me. "Would you just—come in for a bit?"

I think it was the shock of his asking rather than demanding that made me intrigued enough to oblige.

He sat on the far side of the couch, and together, we dove.

The cold room softened with heat, and the water appeared first, in a glittering expanse. I waited for something spectacular to happen, a Happy Sleep star to emerge on the horizon, but it seemed this Sleep wasn't one of the sensational ones.

"It's Honolulu." Tom appeared beside me. "This beach doesn't exist anymore. Eroded a while ago. It was Myrtle's favorite. We used to sit here for hours together. She ... always liked to listen to me." The sadness in his eyes lifted for a moment as he flashed me a defensive look. "You think I didn't really love her. But I did."

I had never expressed that to him, or anything close to it, but something about him had tenderized. This was the only way he could speak honestly—inside of a Sleep, with our emotions dulled and surreal. The true world was a flash bomb against his insecurities, and with them so exposed, even he couldn't deny them anymore.

"She could be anyone you wanted her to be, at a moment's notice," I said. "If that's love to you, then so be it."

His lip ticked disapprovingly. "What is love to *you*, then, Nick? Pining quietly until anyone cares to bat their eyes in your direction? And when they don't, you resent them and feel sorry about it? I don't know what you did to Jordan, by the way, but she became a shadow around the house."

The beach looped endlessly as we walked, a carpet-soft length of sand. Looking out at the ocean again, a small white sailboat wobbled hazily along the horizon like a Monet, and there were birds soaring overhead, toward nonexistent destinations.

I thought about Jordan's last contemptuous glare. I'd cared for her and wanted her, and unquestionably she'd looked out for me, too, but our kisses were always a little bit like apologies.

That still didn't quell the tide of shame rising inside me, realizing I'd hurt her to that extent—someone who I knew couldn't be hurt all that easily.

"Didn't leave her room, skipped the last two games of her season, up and disappeared after. Don't know where in the devil she went. I didn't expect she'd leave like that. As long as Daisy was around." He kicked sand up with his heavy steps. "I should have noticed what was going on there sooner. Jordan came around often in Chicago too."

I remembered Jordan's careless driving, her careless lies. She'd made it sound like that carelessness had started and ended in their youth, but I wondered if she hadn't been truthful about that either.

"I never thought she'd flee before Daisy did," said Tom.

"Wait—what?"

He stopped walking. "Well, that's why I came," he muttered. "I was hoping you'd know where she went."

The breeze washed in and rattled us there on the shore. *"What?"* I repeated.

"Daisy's gone. Took the baby and rushed out in the middle of the night," said Tom blankly.

My mind raced, struggling to imagine Daisy alone with a child in that condition.

"Where?" I demanded.

Tom shook his head and moved toward the water. The shy tide came, licking our bare toes. As he turned his chin up at the fake, everlasting sun, I saw some pastoral stillness overcome him, and it struck me as a definitive defeat—one he had, in fact, been waiting for all along.

"She doesn't want to be found. I thought I ought to ask, at least," he murmured over the whispering winds. "But I know she's ... not coming back to me this time, Nick."

It was like aged grief, the way he spoke, as if Daisy had been gone for decades.

There was nothing left to say after that, and right before we resurfaced, there was a second where I looked over at him and noticed, in the Sleep, that he and I stood at about the same height. In all the years I'd known him, he'd always been several inches taller than me and took an inappropriate amount of pride in that.

Body-mods didn't register inside of Happy Sleeps, and a suspicion started to form in my mind. "How'd you get into that club?" I asked. "You know, the one where we ran into each other early in the summer. Unmodded folks aren't allowed entry."

The question caught him off guard. He erupted, at first, in his usual angry defense, before clenching his jaw and narrowing his eyes at the sparkling ocean.

"Height-mods," he confessed quietly. "Most athletes get them done before their college careers. I had them installed in my calves against my parents' permission when I was eighteen . . . when I thought perhaps I could . . ."

The warmth of the fabricated beach seeped away. I opened my eyes once more into the gauzy room. Tom, in his restless nature, must have moved around while he was under, for he'd ended up on the floor, lying flat on his back. He was slower to wake, and in this moment where his bleary gaze blinked up at the magenta ceiling, he looked quite hollow, and I understood why the shameless exuberance of Jay Gatsby had distressed him so.

I saw the flicker of that eighteen-year-old Tom Buchanan, smaller and leaner, and who—with a fraction more courage and a fraction less pride—might have left the comforts of his established name and dared to taste hardship.

But that dream was only a mirage in his rearview mirror, diminishing forever as he imagined what lay around the bend of the untaken path. Certainly, he knew it would have led him away from his East Egg mansion, away from the glamour of Daisy Fay, and instead toward a great unknown—possibly horrible, possibly wonderful.

Thirty-Six

THERE WERE PEOPLE FROM GATSBY Corp in and out of the tower all month—investors, real estate agents, gaggles of portfolio managers, and other superfluous corporate titles. They wanted me to sign off on things before I could make sense of them. Gatsby had a collection of villas along the Mediterranean that I had no use for, so they had to be put up for sale. There were several hundred investments to track under his name, reports on relevant market conditions, ventures to pursue and others to scrap. They spoke at me—through me. I retained not a single word, smoking through meals, sleeping for days at a time.

On a bone-chillingly cold Thursday, Meyer called. He informed me about a meeting with the board of directors, though I knew that it wasn't so much an invitation as it was a summons.

It was Halloween that day; I remember because it cast the whole afternoon into a comical surreality. At only five o'clock, West Egg's gaiety was in full swing. I learned that the neighborhood was somewhat of a Halloween destination, so herds of extravagant costumes roamed the streets, shrieking in stimulated laughter as the mod-docs lit up their signs with generous annual discounts.

A chauffeur came to pick me up an hour later and flew me to the city. At the headquarters, Meyer came out, clapping my arm in greeting—not quite a hug nor a handshake, just an awkward gesture of comfort. The autumn fog caressed the top of the ominous building, partly obscuring it. "I know you've a good head on your shoulders, dear boy. I also know your grief is raw, as is mine," he murmured as a row of attendants led us into the gleaming lobby. "I am an empathetic man," he added, "but not everyone in that boardroom is."

I couldn't tell what prompted him to say that. Perhaps it was that I failed to hide my distaste about being there, or even simpler, that I was wearing yesterday's clothes and hadn't showered.

We were brought to a private waiting area in a room behind the reception desk. Jade-green synth-vines curled out over the walls, with a holo-waterfall streaming down from a round skylight. I seated myself upon one of two gaudy pompadour-style sofas, and Meyer sat across from me. He sent the attendants away with an order of cigarettes and highballs, and when they returned, instructed them to wait outside.

"Jay left you everything. I'm sure you're starting to see what that means," said Meyer once we were alone. "It is a lot for one man, especially if you aren't prepared for it. I sympathize with what you must be feeling right now."

"I suppose you thought it would all be yours instead," I said, recalling what Ewing had told me about Gatsby's will.

Meyer took this as an accusation. He scooted forward on the sofa and released his full exasperation. "Mr. Carraway, *listen* to me. I told you, I only ever wanted to build a good life for myself and my wife, and now I'm trying to spare *you* from any unnecessary hardships."

His single organic eye blinked slowly at me; then he took an extended sip of his highball and lit a cigarette.

"The board doesn't like what Jay chose to do in the valley—all the money he's sunk into a place that won't reap any profits. They thought he went crazy, you know, when he revealed all the land he bought up for no ascertainable reason," he explained. "Now, I'm well aware you're not going to adore these people, but you *must* find it in yourself not to show it, and what's more, no one's expecting you to assume this responsibility at all."

The untouched highball before me conjured up a memory of my first outing with Gatsby in the club, how he'd said Meyer rejected the "corporate hustle." Right away, I'd seen in him the rare, enviable gift of being able to live life, not just survive it, and now he wanted me to embrace the same thing.

"You're asking me to step away," I said.

342

"Far away. You've come into a great fortune, just as I did. It's why I see myself in you. I see that you're faced with—with the question of what you 'should' do with your accidental situation, but the truth is, why, there's no such thing as right and wrong, but there *is* such a thing as being smart." He pinched his cigarette hard, knees bouncing. "Jay's given you a lifeboat. Now leave the dead to their dying."

There was almost a contempt in him, however thin, as if I'd misplaced my grief inside too much maudlin immaturity.

"You were his closest friend," I said. "So I know you'll want to come to his funeral once it's arranged."

Meyer sighed, glancing away, and I realized no matter what I said then, it wouldn't change the fact that the name "Jay Gatsby" was a curse. His death had not only salvaged the Fay Medica acquisition once again but lent Gatsby Corp a convenient off-loading of accountability about the fallen drones, which had solidified into the public consciousness as a national tragedy.

Even Meyer, who had called Gatsby a son, would choose not to grieve him like one.

"Let us learn to show our friendship for a man while he is alive and not after he is dead," he said solemnly. "After that, my own rule is to let everything alone."

I watched as his remorse receded into a vague expression—one of cold, inaccessible wisdom.

"That's a coward's answer," I said.

Meyer fell silent.

A knock came from the attendant outside. The board was ready to see us.

◇—◇—◇

The mood in the boardroom was jubilant. A hover-bot did slow laps around the table, holding various brandies and rums and an ice bucket. Amidst the chatter, I heard laughter over a Caribbean vacation, a trip out to the Martian industrial facilities, and a birthday party in New Oceania where an entire hover-district had been converted into a recreational bullet-golf course for the weekend. Someone was halfway through a story of how they'd managed to squash a protest over a worker's death in the Klipspringer factories, but the chatter dribbled away at my arrival.

I was offered the spot at the head of the long table. The pleasantries began, though they didn't last long. Some boring questions were asked about my upbringing and education, including one stupid inquiry from the chair about whether it was difficult for me to contract for American corporations.

I squinted. "What?"

"Well, it can't be easy," he said. "Seeing as your family business was a Veluz body shop. On top of that, I'm sure being at odds with your home country is—"

So that was the insufferable tenor of the conversation for about fifteen minutes.

My résumé illuminated the holo-bar in the center of the table. Directly beneath my name sat the line: "Place of Birth: St. Paul, Minnesota."

The chair, I learned, was a recent elect into the role—a Harvard graduate from an established clan in politics across both Americas. He couldn't have been more than five years older than me, and he'd come onto the board less than nine months ago.

"In any case, you've had quite the career," he offered. "Fun things on the horizon for you now, Mr. Carraway?"

I replied that I hadn't found my next contract yet.

"Why find another contract at all? I'd think a man like yourself has plenty for a lifelong vacation," he said.

"I like to keep busy."

He smiled slightly, and it transformed his face from ignorance to something more nauseating, prying, as if he were hoping to catch me in a hostile act. "Stepping into the shoes of Mr. Gatsby doesn't keep you busy enough?"

"Drinking in nice boardrooms once in a while is already closer to 'vacation' than work."

I spoke the words without a single thought, but even when those ten pairs of eyes moved between shock and scorn, including Meyer, I found I didn't regret it.

344

Glancing at the chair however, I saw plain triumph. He'd hoped for this reaction, had needed me to bend first so that he could speak his next statement with confidence: "I'd never thought Mr. Gatsby the type to break rules in his own house."

"Pardon me?"

"I can see why he was so taken by you. Even though you were his employee." The chair cocked a thin, pale eyebrow. "So taken, in fact, that he'd entrust you with his whole empire."

The blow was quick and decisive, for they'd never had any intention to accept me at this table in the first place. I was an intruder, allowed inside through a back door, and now they had to rid themselves of me quickly. Walking away, as Meyer had insisted I do, would be just what they wanted.

"I'm very uninteresting," I replied evenly. "I suppose Mr. Gatsby's decision says less about me and more about how limited his options were."

The chair waved the hover-bot toward him, poured himself a neat rum, and reached visibly for some professionalism. "All right, Mr. Carraway. Mr. Gatsby started making some ill-informed decisions this summer," he said. "We hope that, in inviting you here, we can show you why we ought to rethink the strategy of his passion projects."

The holo-screen rippled away from my résumé into a series of complicated charts. Rebuilding a whole district from the ground up, as Gatsby had intended, would cause them to leak money for at least the next half decade. The budget would be much better spent elsewhere—for instance, on several new marketing campaigns for Gen Wealth with a focus on acquiring new clientele.

The screen cycled again, this time into a wide map. I recognized it as the same one Mrs. Anand had shown me when I'd worked some shifts in counterintel—a complete overview of the Gen Wealth accounts across the Americas.

This was the "bright side" of the valley incident, said the chair. Now was a perfect opportunity for rebranding and expansion, perhaps into an international market soon. All they needed from me was to cancel the property purchases that Mr. Gatsby had put in motion and upsell the ones that had already been finalized.

I paused, studying the man's pressed suit and unblemished skin, the slope of his condescending gaze as it slid down a high, fake nose, then out at the rest of the table too. Their sleek, store-bought faces shone like gray marble under the glow of the holo-screen and the blinking green dots that, in this room, would never be people.

I stood up, leaving without a dismissal, and Meyer's sad, watchful eyes followed me out the door.

Thirty-Seven

U NDER THE SUGAR DUST OF November snow, I commenced the painstaking task of collating a guest list for Gatsby's funeral.

The names of roughly a thousand business associates were kept in the contact directory of his holo-bar, all of them attendees of his summer parties at one point, though most would be too fearful of a scandal to attend. The real effort thus began amidst his off-book acquaintances—his bootlegging contacts. Ewing provided me with a list. By the fiftieth name, about thirty had answered, and of those thirty, only ten had floundered through detached condolences, irritable platitudes, and not a few rude insistences that they didn't know Mr. Gatsby at all.

On the day of the funeral, Ewing and I went to the rooftop, where the dome was up to keep out the chill. A sad ring of candles had been lit before a holo-altar. I'd waited around the lobby for an extra hour in the hope that a guilty straggler might still wander to the doors. But no one came, and though a brief solemnity hung in the silence, it dissipated as quickly as it had formed, for in the absence of guests, eulogies, and the body of the dead man himself, the whole affair malfunctioned like a failed theater play. I was alone, with only an android and a colorless sky as holy witnesses.

I stayed on the roof as the evening deepened. Ewing brought up a cart of Riesling, and I downed it straight from the bottles. Flushed, I looked around and imagined the old revelers sprouting from the pool like flowers, the holo-plum trees shining, the crystal fountains alive once more.

With every sip, the visions became so strange that I was sure I must have passed out and not even noticed, for when I blinked, I saw Pammy across the terrace. She'd donned a black dress, a matching frock, and thick stockings. Little ribbons pinned her cinnamon hair into two perfect pigtails.

"Tito!" She skipped toward me. I lifted her into my arms, nearly gasping because the girl was real. "I have a new dress. Mama said it's for very special occasions."

"Nicky."

I turned. A dark cashmere figure materialized at the top of the staircase, swallowed in a fur scarf and large sunglasses. She glided down the steps, a painting come alive, and in her soft, storybook voice, Daisy Fay said, "You told me ... I could call you if I ever needed anything."

◇——◇——◇

Ewing relit the candles, laid out a plate of good synth-fruit for Pammy, and brought up the piano to entertain her with a spirited rendition of "Jazz History of the World."

Daisy and I sat before the altar. Gatsby's wavering face stared back at us—his Oxford portrait. I'd found the image saved on one of his holo-bars, the only portrait of him around. In it, he gave a sort of nervous half smile, and the set of his eyes strained self-consciously.

"I'm sorry to come without an invitation," said Daisy.

I didn't apologize for not reaching out in the first place. I'd written her off, for I knew that was what she did—turned her back on her own failures, sped away from them as if she could forever be the beautiful, carefree girl with a white roadster, setting fires and then forgetting about them.

"He'd be glad you came," I replied.

"But you're not."

Not even slightly. When she removed her sunglasses, she looked ill. It seemed she hadn't seen her mod-doc in a while. Heavy shadows sat beneath reddened eyes. I swore there were wrinkles in her forehead.

"Look, Nick. I got Pamela out of that damn East Egg mansion, didn't I?" A plea crackled in her throat. "I got us both out. I mean— doesn't that count for something?"

I was appalled that she was still chasing some cleansing of her character, so instinctual she couldn't resist.

"You didn't come just for Gatsby. Out with it," I said.

She unfurled her scarf, folding her hands unsteadily in her lap. "I've overheard some things. In certain Medica boardrooms." She gazed up at the dome—at the black November sky beyond. "Things I believe you'd like to know."

She pulled a square velvet box out of her purse. I realized it was a ring before she even lifted the lid, but upon closer inspection, I noticed the gemstone was in fact one of those curious crystalline beads Gatsby had shown me before at his studio.

"A memory diamond?" I lifted the ring out. "What's stored in it?"

"The first time Jay and I met in Louisville. I believe he made it about a year ago." She paused uncomfortably. "I suppose he thought it would be very sentimental, but the truth is, by the time he gave it to me, the face he made as I slipped it onto my finger—it's like when a person has walked into a room and forgotten why."

It was modestly designed, the band almost as thin as a string, and so unlike the ostentatious emerald that Tom had gifted her. I envisioned a younger, lovesick Gatsby crafting the piece with the dream of its being akin to a final consummation.

I reset the ring into the box. "What does this have to do with Medica?"

"The acquisition." She frowned. "It's disrupting the original purpose of why half our team began researching memory in the first place. To treat trauma, addiction, and cognitive decline, and to make it accessible."

I recalled Newtonia Orchid's recent launch event—all the money, new and old, in attendance.

"Technological reincarnation was always an eventual goal, but there are some scientists who think this launch is too fast, trying to plunder as many pockets as possible, promising immortality by the next decade," said Daisy. "The tech is farther out than that." She traded a grave stare with Gatsby's portrait on the holo-screen.

My breath caught. I'd been so stupid not to have considered it before. "He opted in too," I realized.

"Yes." Daisy sighed. "But it's not so simple."

I tensed. "What do you mean?"

"Perhaps they do reconstruct consciousnesses—someday. Perhaps all the memories are there, sequenced correctly, and the last thing a person remembers is their own death."

"Or *what*?"

"I've been told memories, in that state, can be altered, omitted, rearranged. It's a method they're hoping to perfect. Just a matter of trial and error," she said. "But the room for 'error' is ... rather large in the experimentation phase." She grimaced. "It's the risk of being an early adopter."

I ripped open my collar, choking and breathless. My head spun. The nausea I'd felt for three months straight blew through me again. "Then people can forget entire years of their life or—have memories that aren't even theirs? They could reincarnate as a whole new person?"

Daisy's rigid, sorry face was confirmation.

"Did he know?" I demanded.

"Not entirely. That's the cost of business. You say the word 'innovation,' and everyone loses their heads," she muttered. "It's what his board members advised him to do. They've all done the same for themselves. Got their own diamonds, staving off sickness and aging as long as they can. They own the tech. After death, they own the bodies and the memories that are extracted, and they'll earn royalties by selling all of that to Medica for their R & D. Jay knew there'd be risks, but has he ever been the type to care for them? Besides," she said grimly, "dead men can't complain."

We watched Ewing guide Pammy's fingers across the piano keys. As the melody came together, Pammy giggled, swinging her feet in delight.

"He mixed up loving me with wanting to rescue me." Daisy's eyes glimmered. "He wouldn't let it go. Now I ... I can't even return the favor. I can't save him back. Not alone. I don't know how to—" She rose up in a panicked haste, and the thin calmness she'd been wearing poorly over her mourning clothes fell away like a discarded shawl.

350

"I just don't *know* what I'm supposed to *do*, all right? But by God, I'm fucking trying here!"

She kicked her chair. It crashed into the bottom of the stairs. At the harsh sound, Pammy startled on the piano bench, then began to wail. Daisy turned, hobbling toward her daughter, kissing her hair and whispering apologies between her black ribbons.

"Mommy didn't mean it, darling." She wiped Pammy's face with the back of her hands. "I didn't mean it like Daddy."

When Pammy stopped crying, Daisy returned her to Ewing. Then she wandered back to the altar, trying to light a cigarette, but the flame wouldn't catch.

After some hesitation, I stood up, pulling my own lighter from my jacket and holding it out for her.

"I hear the drones in my sleep, Nick," she said hoarsely. "I ... see them on the backs of my eyelids and on the ceilings. In the sky itself." She opened and closed her hand into a fist repeatedly, but the shaking did not subside. "'Daisy Fay' used to be my horrific shadow, and now it's *him*. Him and a hundred voices—wailing ... begging."

The ash fell like snow from the end of her cigarette, resting between the wavering candles at the foot of Gatsby's ageless photo.

My mind reeled. I had a million questions, but I didn't know where to begin, and Daisy had a flight back to Kentucky soon. No one knew she'd flown out here.

On the landing pad, she unlocked her Veluz, and I set an exhausted Pammy into the back seat of the hover-car. "Tito. Your trick. You never showed me ..." Drowsily, she grasped my hand, drooling thinly onto her frock.

"You once said I ought to keep her," I reminded Daisy. "If you meant that, with even a bit of sincerity, then tell me now."

Daisy bristled. I could see she hadn't forgotten this, nor did she pretend to, and perhaps that was her last, if not minimal, redemption to me.

"You told her she had to be good for me." She stroked Pammy's cheek. "But it was always the other way around, wasn't it?"

One day, I imagined finding the girl grown—perhaps as tall as her father, wiser than her mother. Kinder, hopefully, than the both of them combined.

Before Daisy opened the driver's side, I stopped her, recalling Gatsby's ring box I'd pocketed earlier.

"Keep it," she said.

"What? No—"

"I sensed Jay and I were doomed before he ever did. He was always glancing elsewhere. I thought I was imagining it." She stared at me with a half measure of sympathy. "I shouldn't speak about this. It could get many people in trouble, but perhaps it'll make you understand." Her whole body trembled again, but not from the cold. "There's a schism brewing between the Medica scientists. A group of them have set up a new facility. One that'll handle these diamonds with the right care, time, and expertise. It's just a matter of *getting* the diamonds out of the hands of the Gatsby board. Not that it matters to you, but you're still . . . the only one I could trust."

Money was the only language Daisy had ever known. It was the world that had birthed her and formed her. It was the refuge she sought out time and time again. It broke things; it repaired them. . . .

And yet, on its own, for the first time in her life, it wasn't enough to escape into—to resurrect the dead, to wash the bloodstains from her shaking hands, or to quiet the haunting whispers in her mind. I saw that coming here, telling me all this, was the closest thing she could grasp in the shape of atonement.

"Also, could you—" she stuttered. "Why, if you happen to see Jordan, might you tell her . . ."

Whatever she hoped to say, I watched her confidence disintegrate immediately, moth-eaten under her own disgrace. I guessed that the two of them hadn't spoken since the Plaza, when Tom had laid us all bare in that stifling room.

Though no matter how good Jordan was at lying, love was inherently honest, a game in which the players could cheat only if they never spoke about the rules. Now that Tom had done just that, Daisy's reckoning had left her with no more cards to play, no more suitors to throw at Jordan like proxies—understudies to her own fear.

"I'd never let you near her again," I said. "But if *she* does, then you'll tell her yourself."

Daisy's tears did not fall that day, but they purged the stars in her eyes for good. She took a shuddering breath and disappeared like a myth into the autumn night.

◇——◇——◇

I retreated inside, opened one of Gatsby's untouched whiskey decanters, and drank a quarter before it slipped unceremoniously from my fingers and shattered across the marble. Stumbling to the bedroom, I cut my bare feet on the glass.

I'd adopted the habit of sleeping in the study, so it was my first time in the bedroom since the tower had been turned over to me. The pillows smelled faintly of him, the sheets still creased with the imprints of our bodies. I rolled onto my stomach, holding my breath until my lungs burned—until all I could feel was the phantom press of his hands, his mouth.

The ceiling did a series of pirouettes. Eventually I stood up, head throbbing, and teetered into the bath, where I threw up once or twice before deciding I couldn't stand to be in the private suite anymore.

I roamed around for hours, a shadow in a state of potent delirium, and there was suddenly a fresh mythology to the desolate tower.

I was moved by the same dignified awe that came with wandering the ruins of an old civilization, feeling the history of something lost, but at one time teeming with indescribable profundity. The Parthenon, the Colosseum, Pompeii . . . Gatsby's magical realm surely among them in the lore of the growing universe.

And I had been entwined with the core of this place too. With its master. I could tell you that I loved him even after the curtain fell, and I saw that he was no virtuoso, just a man. Or perhaps it was that I'd loved that shade of him most—the shimmer of James Gatz that he'd opened up to me like an invitation into a fading dream, and it was better and more beautiful than all the expensive invitations I'd received from him before.

In the swimming pool, I floated along in my funeral-black suit. The holo-cherubs on the ceiling twitched now and then, as if threatening to vanish so I would be wholly alone, laughing at me from their clouds.

The water was freezing against my hot skin. It washed over me like cyberspace. Weightless and cold, perhaps I'd never resurface.

I remember thinking that if I stayed in that pool forever, if I turned my head away from the cherubs, that I might see him floating beside me, with that promise of a smile, toward those paradises he dreamed up so fervently. Or else I could sink endlessly, and the turquoise tiles would open up into a new world and take me away.

My lungs clenched, and my eyes stung. The chlorine burned my throat. The thought of dying unspooled before me, as irresistible as any fantasy, and a darkness swelled in the distance, at the center of the topaz water, the edges of my vision dotting over like distant stars. . . .

And then, almost against my will, this image of death escaped me, melting away into my memory of the Gen Wealth map.

That constellation of accounts, of faceless dreams and pocket-sized hopes.

My body flew to the surface, as if plucked from the water by a spiritual hand, and then I was gasping for air, heavy and firmly within myself. An idea of pure insanity began to develop, stepping out from whatever shadowy corner of my mind I must have banished it to.

I hoisted myself out of the pool, pacing wildly up and down, unsure if I had emerged sober or even more intoxicated, but I knew what had to be done.

I brought up the contact list on my comm.

A pitchy voice burst through on the other end, and I knew my courting with death had reforged me into a state of ardent resolution.

I stood there—dripping wet, shivering, alive.

"Failing to weather the storm?" the voice greeted. "Or to what do I owe the pleasure, Mr. Nicholas Carraway?"

Thirty-Eight

T
HE HOLO-BAR ON THE POOLSIDE table chimed and lit up into an urgent sight.

It was the tired spokesperson of the ISC, staring out intently at the camera flash, as a hundred reporters yelled rapid questions in a hundred languages. The announcement unfurled across the bottom of the holo-screen:

"International Space Council to Announce Findings in Decoded Space Probe."

"Holy hell!" shrieked Owl Eyes over the comm. "Are you seeing this?"

There was a moment in which the planetary horror of that single headline settled into my bones, tossing me adrift. The probe—the flare that had signaled the start of the ruthless summer and then refused to go away.

"Meet me in the valley," I said. "We'll go over the plan."

When we hung up, I changed into dry clothes and went out onto the street. Others milled outside, too, congregated despite the late hour. Inside bars and shops, behind cloudy, darkened windows, strangers were bumping shoulders, and loaded glasses clinked together in crazed tribute. Farther down the block, outside the train station, a crowd had formed beneath the holo-screen of the main square, and I realized it was a funny thing, this alien mystery. Even funnier, I thought, was the human compulsion that had indeed carried me and everyone else here at the same time, as if to ensure that the end of the world would not be witnessed alone.

My thoughts meandered to Jordan, who had "up and disappeared," according to Tom, but who all summer had been there for me in a way that was more significant than friendship and more honest than lovers. We'd fumbled at the end, but we'd been accomplices up until that point.

I called her, waiting for the melodic ring of the comm to click, cut off, then morph into her shrewd, steely voice.

"Well, you beat me to it." The sound of her draped me like a forgotten comfort—the sharpness she refused to smooth down for anyone, and her greeting that was never a hello, but which embraced me, all at once, as both reprimand and forgiveness. "An occasion like the apocalypse calls for some company, don't you think?"

◇——◇——◇

The valley hadn't changed much since that fiery August evening, the debris still strewn about like fossilized remains, half-split drones hanging off the corners of crumbled buildings. But the starkest difference was, strangely, that the neighborhood seemed busier than ever.

The security androids that had previously patrolled the valley to deter any encampments had been crushed beneath the rubble, too, for there were now a few clusters of folks gathered around small bonfires, huddled together in quiet merriment.

"I didn't know if you'd still give a damn about me," I said as we ambled across the ruins. "I'm sorry I spoke to you that way before."

"East Egg brings out the worst in everyone. I'm no exception. I shouldn't have gone back into that house," she replied. "Anyhow, it was a new experience for me."

"What was?"

"You said a bad driver was only safe until she met another bad driver. Well, I met another bad driver, didn't I? I mean it was careless of me to make such a wrong guess." She bumped our arms together. "I had always wanted you to lose your obnoxious manners and speak how you truly feel." She laughed humorlessly. "But then, once you did so, to me, I felt dizzy for a while."

I was rather touched she was still willing to flash me this vulnerability, and it made me wonder how much she had tried being in love with me as I had with her. Perhaps we'd both made a concerted effort and both failed, but somehow, come out the other side more whole than before.

"I thought it was your secret pride," she added lightly, "being so disaffected by horrible things and horrible people."

"It used to be." I thought again of that skin-crawling boardroom, but I knew my mind had been made up even before then.

It began to snow, light and twinkling, and Jordan took my arm like she always would when we walked through Gatsby's spectral parties. Then her face hardened the way it did right before the timer started on a bullet-golf course. "You know, when Tom said my career was 'washed up,' I felt right then that I'll have to reclaim my legacy if it's the last thing I do," she declared.

We had walked all the way to George Wilson's abandoned shop. Across from it was Michaelis's place, where the doors were open. Music and light spilled out from inside, and we saw the ISC news conference up on the holo-bar, projecting widely across the wall.

Behind the bar, Michaelis fielded orders of frothing beer pitchers and bronze liquor shots to a crowd of dozens, and beside him, the child was seated on the countertop.

At about the same time, they noticed me through the windows.

Glancing between Jordan and me, they raised their arm, and I saw the light of their new comm, blinking beneath their wrist. They made a face—almost a smile, but too somber, too aged for a child.

I nodded, and they nodded back in quiet acknowledgment, before redirecting their attention to the holo-screen.

"I suppose I've resolved myself toward a certain legacy too," I said to Jordan. "Not as glamorous as yours, but no less reckless. In any case, you can't talk me out of it. In turn, I won't talk you out of your decision to push the limits of your body."

"Oh dear," she replied, bright with anticipation. "Now, how terribly are we enabling one another?"

Flakes of snow nestled delicately in her curls, just as a leather-clad figure emerged behind her—the troublesome flash of two shining oc-mods.

◇──◇──◇

Michaelis dragged three flimsy stools out from his storage closet and made room for us in the very back of the packed shop. A tray of sloshing beers was crowd-surfed toward us, landing at our table nearly half emptied.

"Two years?" exclaimed Owl Eyes. "You think it'll take that long?"

"You wanted a mentor. There's your first lesson—no slapdash moves. We do things my way," I said. "We don't go near the facility until we know what's in it. Blueprints, intel on the personnel, full scout of the VINEs. In the meantime, we focus on Gen Wealth."

"Gen Wealth?" demanded Jordan. "What *else* are you planning?"

"Hack some corpo bank accounts and start paying off some debts?" suggested Owl Eyes. "Very Rosenthal. Cause a big stir."

I shook my head. Plucking down a few accounts wouldn't change a thing. "We dig it out from the roots. I've seen their VINEs. They're fortified well for a siege, but not from the inside. We plant pyres, set them off at intervals. Give them time to panic before aiming for the head."

Owl Eyes shifted to the edge of her stool, her oc-mods swelling an inch out of their metal frames. "The head?"

"The board. I'll handle that part," I said. "You focus on programming the pyres. They need to be small but mighty, a big flame but without smoke, and with enough delay that when they burn, you've already surfaced. Think you can handle it?"

She grinned. "I know I can." In her dizzy elation, she jumped up for another round, skipping toward Michaelis's bar.

"A bad driver, too, that one," muttered Jordan.

I tapped my glass against hers. "Yes." Still, she'd kept her word, given a corpo a cut of her earnings instead of going to a mod-doc, saving her own skin with nothing but spite and resourcefulness. "The worst of us and I'll need it."

As Owl Eyes coerced Michaelis into serving her a tray of colorful shots, she nearly knocked over a tower of beer cans. An old man beside her with quick instincts steadied the base just in time. He threw her a lazy scolding, turning his head toward the holo-screen, and I saw the gnarled scar on his chin.

I got up, weaving through the maze of tables, and snagged a pitcher from Michaelis's bar.

"Mr. Chase, I'm glad to see you—here." *Not imprisoned*, I almost said. I could tell he didn't recognize me at first. I pointed to my oc-mod, the one he'd patched up. His eyes flashed. "Do you still have a practice nearby?"

"Why? So you can tip me off to the police again?" he said gruffly. "Figured that was you. Jay didn't keep friends. Then you come out of nowhere, looking as corpo as it gets, and my spot gets raided two days later?" He didn't wait for an answer. "Had a bad feeling, so I stayed away to see what would happen. I was right. Which *consultants* do you work for?"

"No one. Not anymore." I held up my wrist to show him the scar over my comm. It was about as wide as the one on his face. "I'd like your professional opinion on something. A hypothetical situation."

I refilled his glass. He lifted it to his mouth as the beer foam sailed to the rim. He said nothing, but I was heartened that he didn't dismiss me.

"Let's say there's a biotech company experimenting with memory transplantation," I said. "Let's say someone has caught wind of a schism, thinks the mutiny might be what's best for the good of the research. But that someone needs to crack the main facility in order to transfer some, well, key resources from one side to the other."

Chase scratched at his scraggly brow. "Mm-hmm."

I slid into the stool beside him. "Hypothetically—he has connections that might give him a peaceful way through the front door and can work out how to lock down the facility VINEs and comms, but he needs to handle the personnel on the inside. Discreetly, quickly."

"Hypothetically"—Chase chugged his beer in one breath—"I'd say he ought to consider silver-plated finger mods. Torches through the nerves quieter than any gunshot, cleaner than any blade. I'd also say it breaks no less than six prohibition laws, and it'll give him a nightmare at airport security forever."

"Nightmares are fine," I said. "Perhaps he's survived a couple already."

Chase wiped the foam from his lip. He poured himself another glass, and just as I thought he was going to shoo me away like a fly, he said, "If the world's not ending tonight, come by tomorrow. I have a place here in the valley."

I smiled, reached over the bar, grabbing a clean glass. Before Chase could fill it for me, I took the pitcher from him. "I'll serve myself. Never too late to start, you said."

He laughed, a smug and baritone laugh. We shared the pitcher in silence. The little shop was bursting to the door now, and when I squeezed my way between lively bodies and back to Jordan, she was picking quietly at a sugar stain on the table.

"Where did you get this intel? About Medica? Gatsby's diamond?" she asked, though it seemed she already knew the answer.

"An inside source."

She set her elbows on the table with a heavy sigh. "Well? How was she?"

I thought of Daisy's broken face, the tremor in her hands she might live with forever. "Lost." I hesitated. "She came to the funeral."

Jordan reached into her coat for a cigarette and steadied herself through a few slow drags. "She's only ever existed for others," she said—frustrated, in weak resistance of her own sadness. "Doesn't know who she is. Truth is, I don't know if I ever have either."

Shouts exploded at the table beside us. Bets were being placed about the press conference, what sort of announcement would be made. It seemed there was a tie between alien missiles and the whole space probe being a hoax.

"She wants to see you," I said. "There are things she's never told you, not because she doesn't want to, but because she's hardly told them to herself."

Jordan stared pensively out the window, as if seeing, one last time, an image of Daisy's everlasting performance. The final curtain call.

"If you really go through with this," she said, "you'll never work another contract. No matter how careful you are, someone will always be looking." Her gaze wavered with concern, rather like Meyer when he cautioned me to take Gatsby's gifts and flee. "I think you need to be sure he's worth all of this, Nick."

If there was still such a thing as an inner peace that could be salvaged, if it had ever existed at all, I knew it could only be reached far beyond Gatsby. There was no parachute in his money that could steer me to safety, and retrieving what remained of him was only a layover in an interminable journey ahead.

As long as there were people who could decide who lived forever, and people who stole the fruit of family trees before they could even grow, there would be more corpses like the ones beneath us, unpreserved and without diamonds.

"Maybe he's not," I murmured. "But the rest of us are."

Jordan took my hand in her lap with a resolute smile.

The news report interrupted us once more. Owl Eyes rushed to the front for a closer look at the holo-screen that had switched to a live feed of the grand Dutch exterior of the ISC headquarters. The director had just arrived, descending from her hover-car with an opaque, dignified expression. An entourage fanned around her as they climbed the steps together, carrying the secrets and futures of our civilization.

I began to tell Jordan that the probe had once been a nostalgic thing to me. Back when it was a glorious story from an old generation, and not an ominous symbol of the unknown, I'd viewed it with deep fondness. It made me feel closer to my father, who'd sworn so much fealty to what the probe had represented at the time of its launch—a unified planet's shout into the void.

"We don't look out at the cosmos with such romance anymore," said Jordan.

"No. But I think we all want to. If only the cosmos felt closer."

People used to look to the heavens to be alone with their thoughts. To be humbled by the great universe. But now, glancing out the window, the obnoxious ad-drones twirled and twirled over the looming silhouette of the Queensboro Bridge—guessing at our desires before we even knew them ourselves, screaming incessantly for our hollowing souls. Still, the only thing it had brought us closer to was death.

The beer was catching up to the whiskey. I was numb. My head pounded.

Jordan smiled, exhilaration in her eyes. "My aunt used to say that a headache is really just your past life trying to speak with you."

We laughed, watching a trail of hover-cars smear the sky, soaring fervently toward the cold city, and I imagined gazing at our neon fires through the refracted lens of one of these supposed parallel universes—of time travelers peering forward to see the world changed in a thousand different ways. Perhaps they'd return to their time and proclaim that humankind could fly, kiss whomever they want, replace any limb and organ, swimming inside pools of dreams.

But the Valley of Ashes, they'd say in the end, was still made of ashes.

On the screen, the ISC director entered the conference hall. Jordan and I recalled that first party at Gatsby's and how the probe used to be nothing more than a hot fragment of that arcane summer.

The memory settled between us like a warming stone, unobstructed by all the chaos that followed—the one and only time we'd enjoyed that mythical tower as wholly as Gatsby had wanted us to.

The director stopped before a microphone-bot, bobbing at her mouth, and a hush blanketed the crowd of reporters, and all of us in Michaelis's refuge.

"Thank you all for your patience," she began. *"I am greatly honored to stand here, on behalf of the International Space Council, to share with you what is undoubtedly one of the most stunning events of our species. . . ."*

It was midnight, and the enchanted hour was upon us, when the day folds over and transforms. In that final moment before our world changed forever, I believe I tasted that nectar of awestruck humility that must have held my father in place all those years ago and instilled in him his unshakable reverence for humanity's smallness.

"Some of you may remember that fifty years ago, at the launch of this probe, it was filled with a capsule of humanity's great history and culture. We could never imagine how far it would go, and moreover, could never have dreamed we'd see it again. Now, five decades later, it has returned to us with a message—a string of audio, encrypted by a means unseen before. The ISC, through a titanic effort, can at last confirm what we know has been the source of so much speculation over these many months: the technology is not of human origin." A light, prickling silence ensued. *"Before we say anything more, we do believe it is best heard for oneself."*

Then the decoded message, which had indeed traveled from afar to our insignificant planet, rang out across the world.

It began as a series of rapid, high-pitched scratches, incoherent for several beats, before finally it unveiled itself.

A tinny, familiar melody.

Jordan gasped. "Oh—" she whispered. "Oh, Nick! That's ..."

I laughed—at first, a disbelieving tremble of emotion, and then something like fizzling euphoria.

The shock of undefined terror, which had barreled us toward our worst fears, blew up like a shower of confetti, and in one exalted breath, the universe transposed itself into a new key, lifting us all into a state of extraordinary wonder—and into the promise of tomorrow.

That day, we knew our smallness.

We knew that when humanity screamed into the heavens, something had listened and answered.

For through the irregular tempo and foreign instruments, what we heard was no heralding of our extinction. It wasn't a missile, a war, a hoax.

It was, quite simply, a song.

A fresh rendition of "Jazz History of the World" from beyond our known galaxy.

Two Years Later

GENERATIONAL WEALTH INC. DATA BREACH
INVESTIGATION (CASE STATUS: OPEN)
TRANSCRIPT: NICHOLAS PAULO CARRAWAY (AGE: THIRTY-ONE)
LOCATION: HEADQUARTERS, GATSBY CORPORATION
(NEW YORK CITY, NEW YORK, NEA)
DATE: JUNE 22, 2077

[LOADING]

.   .

.

.

[PLAY]

"That'll be all."

"Chairman. A word alone with you, if that's all right."

"Make this quick, Carraway. Got several fires to put out before dinner. Big robbery at the Medica—"

"Speaking of fires, you'd know all about those."

"What—what the *hell* am I looking at?"

"Photographs of a half-burned construction site in the valley."

"And?"

"Come now, Chairman. After two years, your lack of tact is stunning."

"Quite the accusation! Some of us are able to separate our personal lives from our business strategy. I know you hardly have the correct education but—"

"You've hired a private security team to patrol the place like an armed militia. Caused fifteen resident deaths so far, and there'll be more if you don't call it off immediately."

"'Residents'? The word for them is 'trespassers.' They aren't paying a cent, and we own the entire land—thanks to Gatsby, I'll remind you. You see, Carraway, this is why you just aren't cut out for this boardroom. And really, *he* wasn't either. When you're at the helm of a ship, and you're taking on water, you have to do all you can to set things straight. To ensure you don't sink."

"Sounds awfully like you're calling these people excess cargo."

"They are. The fact is, people *do* bite the hand that feeds them."

"I'll only ask once more."

"Or else what? The security can't be removed. The valley ought to be kept in line, or it'll produce a hundred more insane criminals like George Wilson, and then we'll *all* be hunted down and blown open. You heard about yesterday? An armed robbery at the main Medica facility! Surveillance went down in a flash, and a diamond was stolen—"

"Yes. Impressive, those diamonds. Far from perfect, however. I've learned a great deal about them."

"And what would *that* be?"

"You don't know? That's unfortunate. Not all deaths are created equal, you see—that is, the kind that completely destroys the neural pathways of the brain. If that happens, well, apparently it becomes very hard to recreate the consciousness once the nervous system is so . . . damaged. Impossible, actually."

"What?"

"As it happens, I did see *your* diamond at the facility too. Yesterday. Didn't touch it. Figured there was no need."

"You—stop! What the hell have you *done*—"

"I did try asking politely, Mr. Chairman. I always do."

[STOP]

.

[ERROR—]

.

[TRANSCRIPT DELETED]

[VIDEO:] BREAKING NEWS—JORDAN BAKER, THIRTY, TO BOW OUT OF SEASON EARLY AFTER SETTING NEW BULLET-GOLF RECORD; ANNOUNCES OFFICIAL RETIREMENT.
DATE: JUNE 22, 2077

[LOADING]

.

.

.

[PLAY]

"It was a shocking and climactic development in the bullet-golf world when ten-time world champion, Jordan Baker, clocked in a career-high speed of 15.3 seconds. Not only did Miss Baker finish in first place and was on track for clinching playoff berth early in the season, the performance now sets the record for the fastest time in the history of the sport.

"The joy of this achievement was short-lived, however, when reports surfaced that Miss Baker had inexplicably returned to her training center in Brooklyn, and just this morning held a surprise press conference to officially announce her athletic retirement.

"Since her lackluster 2075 season, speculations about Miss Baker's retirement are far from new, but on the heels of a near-perfect season this year, the announcement has left fans and sporting professionals alike utterly blindsided. In her presser, Miss Baker went on to explain that the decision to step away from competition is not a sudden one, citing the realities of mod strain on aging bodies.

"Despite this bittersweet end to her career, there is certainly no denying that in her final, brilliant appearance, Jordan Baker has solidified her place as the foremost pioneer of her generation.

"What ventures she will pursue next, she has yet to confirm."

[STOP: END OF VIDEO]

Jordan's in a yellow sundress, lighting up the gray West Egg street, when I meet her outside the tower doors. She leans against her battered hover-car, pulling her sunglasses up to reveal one of those secretive smiles she reserves only for her best of moods. Retirement, and all its jaunty freedom, suits her.

"I just saw," I tell her as she kisses my cheek in greeting, "your announcement."

"Oh yes, I was the talk of the town for about half a day. And I would've *stayed* a number one story," she says, "if you hadn't gone and stolen the spotlight. You and the bird had fun, I see."

My comm blinks. I stop to read the messages.

> UNKNOWN: "Investigation into Gatsby Corp Chair's Death Continues—'No New Leads,' Says Police Chief."

> UNKNOWN: What a fucking headline.

> UNKNOWN: Back court's huddling. Next assignment.

"I'd never do such a thing on purpose," I assure her, flicking the messages away. "Steal your spotlight, that is."

She pretends to evaluate me. "At least you haven't lost that habit of apologizing."

I smile. "Not to you."

An appointment with a real estate agent had been set for later in the afternoon, and though Ewing had cleared the tower thoroughly a long time ago, there is one untouched area that remains. That I can't face alone.

Jordan nods, taking my arm through the tower's doors for the last time.

> UNKNOWN: Consider this a head start. Old times' sake.

I send a reply before blocking the contact.

Mag ingat ka.

◇——◇——◇

We ride the elevator up—to the graveyard of dreams, where that summer started and ended.

"Mr. Wilson gave a primetime interview from prison recently," says Jordan, brightening the opaque windows. The sunlight drips down the sky in golden hues. "He said even though God had fallen, he was still watching over him. That it could only be an almighty force that corrupted the Gen Wealth system, relieved him of his financial burdens, and the burdens of all the others."

I gaze at the apartment across the street, at the window that had once been my bedroom, imagining the shadow of my body on the other side—what Gatsby might have seen that night two years ago.

"Listen to me." Jordan sighs. "Before you know it, you're a reincarnated Rosenthal. Sit in any bar long enough, you'll hear people are already whispering about it. But I don't like the way *his* story ended—chased to the edges of the planet and killed."

"You said it yourself. You met another bad driver."

"I did," she says tiredly. I sense she's holding something back. After a long moment, she adds, "I know some minds can't be changed and some wallets can't be opened. I also know we promised not to talk each

372

other out of ... drastic actions." Her mouth sets in that stubborn determination. "But the Medica job only worked because you had the intel. If there's more you want to do, you need more people in high places you can trust. You can't burn bridges without building new ones."

I realize what she's offering and shake my head. "You've retired, Jordan. I could never ask you to—"

"Drive into hell with you?" She laughs, but I hear the resolve in her voice. "I lied in my presser, you know. My mods are all right."

"What?"

She cups my shoulders between her hands. "I've decided I'll follow this bad driver wherever he's stupid enough to take himself."

"Jordan ..."

Her eyes glisten, holding the sunlight. "I like small parties now. Don't you remember?" she murmurs, wrapping me in her arms.

I hold her tight, stunned and entirely grateful, our heartbeats racing in step. When we pull apart, I glance at the Happy Sleep terminal.

It's right where Gatsby left it. I can still envision him in the reclining chair, cleaned thoroughly of his demise, with the headset pinned over his eyes, completely at peace in his waning moments, unsuspecting of the horror that would follow.

Even in death, not a single flash of terror.

"I think he really wanted to keep her Sleeps," I tell Jordan. "He wasn't supposed to leave the suite that night. But he told Ewing he had to do something urgent."

Jordan waves a hand over the Sleep terminal, and the holo-screen lights up. She navigates to the session menu. "Urgent?"

"Those dreams with Daisy were his only prized possession." That familiar itch expands in my throat. "She was his last memory. I couldn't bring myself to get rid of them. I know I shouldn't have put it off so long." I fumble through my pockets for a cigarette, but the crushed pack is empty. "It just—it felt like I'd be killing him all over—"

"Nick ...," says Jordan. "Come look."

I don't know what to make of her expression, grave and unsteady. I move across the room. The terminal's light winks.

"This was the last one he was watching." She points to the holo-screen, where there is only a single session loaded. "This isn't one of

Daisy's, is it? The date is too recent. Recorded on the seventeenth of July, 2075?"

My test session. The afternoon I had gone to the studio with Gatsby.

I catch a glimpse of the title scrolling along the top bar of the holo-screen.

"Happy Birthday."

The ground tilts.

A small thing, he had called it. A final gift.

"That's odd," mutters Jordan. "It's addressed to someone too."

Her finger moves to a string of smaller glowing text beneath the session title.

My vision blurs. I grip the sides of the terminal, shaking, and Jordan's voice fades back into my ears. She rests a gentle hand on my back. "Nick ... what is it?"

You have mine. I want yours.

I fold over in the cold room.

"To Mr. N. Kalinaw."

It unravels, a ribbon of a dream, the path to my name as I had walked his. I imagine once again the warmth and pressure of him—of Gatsby or James Gatz, or some unassailable amalgamation of both. . . .

I'm noticing now—ever so earnest, a handful of pure light tossed like a stone over the midnight ocean; in it, the spark of a whole future, briefly glimpsed, perishing before it could form.

But it appears before me again, against all odds, in the terminal's green light, daring and hopeful and wondrously bright.

I'm noticing now.

◇—◇—◇

And I see, within this infinite space suspended above time itself, the comings and goings of the auspicious continent. I see the Indigenous peoples, and the Dutch sailors, the blue lawns and the summer cottages, the modest village giving way to the incandescent skyscrapers, and the lights of the roaring parties—old and new. I see the inevitability of you and me, across all our foretold existences, in the humble glow of your window facing mine. . . .

So the truth of the "great unknown" is this:

That humankind will forever seek to illuminate the things we do not know, and as we do, the unknown, year by year, recedes before us, commensurate with our expanding universe, and with all the questions civilization has yet to answer. . . .

But we cannot possibly answer them all.

For the edges of the world will always move; brilliant mysteries will beckon us anew, and we will follow. . . .

And it will be in that sliver of the unknown, ever shrinking but never fully closed, where we are borne ceaselessly forward into the orgastic future . . .

where I hope you find me again . . .

where I still await your invitation. . . .

Something in his leisurely movements and the secure position of his feet upon the lawn suggested that it was Mr. Gatsby himself, come out to determine what share was his of our local heavens.

—F. Scott Fitzgerald, *The Great Gatsby* (1925)

Author's Note

I'm often asked, "Why a cyberpunk retelling?" to which my simplest, and most honest, answer is, "Why not?"

Here is my longer answer.

When we study *The Great Gatsby* in an English classroom, we learn about the green light at the end of the dock and the tragic pursuit that sends Gatsby barreling—openhearted and soul bleeding—toward his demise. We observe him through a narrator who leaves us with many questions. We are left lamenting his fallen dreams. We describe the tale as "timeless." Perhaps because it's undetachable from our image of that exuberant Jazz Age and Fitzgerald's words simmer longingly off the page every time we return to Gatsby's doors.

It is my deep love for the original work that fueled this story, but it is fear that shaped the details. This fear is that of a bleak, profit-driven world that crushes real people under its foot and stomps forth, uncaring. And yet, I have been (since my own youthful introduction to Jay Gatsby in an English classroom) enamored with what Fitzgerald so deftly described as his character's "romantic readiness"—his mystical ability to believe that the future, no matter the impossibilities of the present, can still be filled with wonder.

I knew the title of this book had to salute its source material, but for three years, the manuscript remained nameless. Until one afternoon, on my countless rereads of *Gatsby*, when the phrase "local heavens" struck me as one of the most stunning bits of language Fitzgerald offered us. Both grand and intimate, it speaks to those cosmic connections that exist between people, their shared spaces and sense of purpose. Whether it is Nick and Gatsby sharing a lawn, Gatsby and

Daisy sharing a fantasy, or humans sharing the world with something beyond our galaxy, we are all of us searching for these places to belong.

As well, the following materials aided the writing of this book:

- The Scribner trade paperback edition of *The Great Gatsby* published in 2018, which includes an introduction from Jesmyn Ward, notes on the text from scholar James L. W. West III, and a foreword by F. Scott Fitzgerald's granddaughter Eleanor Lanahan. This is the edition I annotated, bent, and dog-eared while I wrote this retelling.
- The F. Scott Fitzgerald Papers dated 1897–1944, available online courtesy of Princeton University Library. Of particular interest to me in this collection were scans of the autograph manuscript. This provides a look into an earlier iteration of the novel, presented in Fitzgerald's own handwriting.
- Keath Fraser's "Another Reading of *The Great Gatsby*" (1979) and Edward Wasiolek's "The Sexual Drama of Nick and Gatsby" (1992) for its discussions on the book's themes of sexuality and the compellingly private shades of the most mysterious character of all, Nick Carraway.

There is often an air of sanctity when it comes to classics. A reimagining presents all sorts of challenges: *Is it "right" to change this? Is it "right" to keep this?* I asked myself this with every draft, and I still don't know the answer. What I do know is that a "timeless" story to me is one where the parts can be disassembled and used to craft something new—to open paths unexplored, proposing fresh questions that reflect the fears, insecurities, or desires of our evolving generations.

This is where I believe that leaving some of that sanctity behind is not only fun, but important. Everyone has their own relationship with Gatsby, so I could only attempt to make sense of my own.

To any remaining questions, I offer again Gatsby's answer: Why not?

Acknowledgments

Every book is its own miracle. Thank you to the people who made those miracles happen, who took a chance on a debut author and brought *Local Heavens* over the finish line.

To Kathryn Budig, who saw right to the heart of this book and whose fierce passion has meant more to me than I can put in words. They say phoenixes rise from the ash, and your love for *Local Heavens* resurrected it from the cold place I'd buried it in my heart. I'm honored to be part of the Inky Phoenix family. Thank you for giving this strange, indulgent story a chance at life.

To my agent, Laura Rennert, who championed this book first with compassion and expert guidance—thank you for believing in me and giving me the courage to take the story to greater heights.

On the US side, Bindery Books team—Meghan Harvey and Matt Kaye for building much-needed bridges in the industry and CJ Alberts for leading the marketing charge. The stunning US cover is owed to the incredible design and creative direction by Charlotte Strick, and artwork by Karan Singh, who took "Jazz Age cyberpunk" straight out of my dreams.

To my editor, Zhui Ning Chang, for helping push the story further and tightening the gaps. To Abi Pollokoff, for steering the ship and managing this entire project, and to everyone at Girl Friday Productions for polishing this book to a shine—to Alyssa Brillinger for the production support, Jane Steele for copyediting, Rachel Marek for designing the interior pages, and Brittany Dowdle and Valerie Paquin for reviewing everything with fresh eyes. Thank you as well to Brittani

Hilles at Lavender Public Relations, and everyone working behind the scenes to get the book into readers' hands.

On the UK side, my deepest gratitude to everyone at Zaffre and Bonnier Books UK for bringing this story to a whole new audience. To my wonderful editor, Kelly Smith, who acquired *Local Heavens* with so much passion and understanding. Thank you for embracing a far-fetched remix of an American classic and shepherding it across the world. Thank you as well to Tamara Douthwaite for the marketing support and to Jake Cook for illustrating the brilliant UK cover.

To my early readers and the talented writers I'm blessed to call my friends—Lynn D. Jung and Kelley Tai, who let me blow up the group chat every day as I navigate the perils of publishing, and to Rachel Lachmansingh, for all the café yap sessions and for loving even the roughest versions of Nick. Without your friendships to keep me afloat, I would have already drowned.

To Susan J. Morris, for the encouragement as I embarked on my debut journey. To Emily Xiang, for being the only person to read the first iteration of "cyberpunk Gatsby book" years before it became *Local Heavens*, and for her tireless support for my writing over the last decade.

To Camille Edwards, Hania, Ndidi Aguwa, Diamond Fore, Chloe T., and my entire online writing community—followers and fellow authors alike—who've offered so much motivation and kindness. You've all made writing less lonely.

To the editorial team at Augur Literary Society, who break genre barriers and lift up diverse Canadian speculative-fiction voices, and who first made space for my cyberpunk work. To Claire Tacon, my creative writing instructor, and the Winter 2019 ENGL336 workshop at the University of Waterloo—my very first critique group. I am a better writer because of you all. To Sal Catalano, my grade twelve AP English teacher, for putting *Gatsby* on the syllabus, and for making me love learning.

To Celine Lee, my best friend and other half, for always being there for me. To Pearl Leung, for being the big sister I never had. To Mom and Dad, for helping with the Tagalog translations, raising me as a book lover, and loving me unconditionally. When I said that getting published was "impossible," you prayed to Saint Rita—saint of impossible causes—and she answered.

To my kuya, Jeremy—the best parts of *Local Heavens* belong to you. Thanks for holding *Gatsby* up to a mirror with me, smashing it over and over, and helping me rearrange all the pieces. Your opinion will always matter most.

Countless more thank-yous to all my friends and extended family, from North America to the Philippines, for their enthusiasm and support.

To F. Scott Fitzgerald, for crafting a tale to outlive his Roaring Twenties (and ours).

To the queer community everywhere, who continue to love, resist, and inspire. To my younger self, for never giving up.

Bringing a book into the world is like diving into a long, scary Happy Sleep. To you, the reader—I thank you, most of all, for taking the plunge with me.

Thank You

This book would not have been possible without the support from the Inky Phoenix community, with a special thank-you to the Inky Inner Circle members:

Aniela Kuzon
Ann Levine
Brit Liegl
Deni Eksioglu
Emily Williams
Erin Tonda
Hollyn Cook Chapman
Jessica Limbach
Kitty Moffett
Kyleanne Hunter
Lindsay Warren
Marguerite White
Marion Kathryn Nielson
Mary Jane Goodman-Giddens
Shawna Hawes
Stephen Johnston
Sweet Lu
Tess Carver
Tiffany Curren
GrettyVB
Esh
maryfrances

Annie2023
Max
BookeBerg
olivia8397
NicciB
Brookelikesbooks
RaeBroderick

Do you want to lose yourself in a magical realm,
journey beyond the known universe or fall for a
charming rogue, all within the pages of a book?

Join

ZAFFRE DAWN

The home for all science fiction and fantasy readers

Be the first to hear about our new releases and access
exclusive, subscriber-only fan content including author
Q&As and interviews, competitions, events and so
much more . . .

Scan to sign up to
our newsletter:

Follow Zaffre Dawn
on social media:

@zaffrebooks

@bonnierbooksuk_

@zaffrebooks

WE RISE AT DAWN . . .